When the
ICE MELTS

CLIMBING HIGHER

When the Ice Melts

Where the Wings Rise

Why the Mountains Stand

When the ICE MELTS

ASHLYN McKAYLA OHM

Words from the Wilderness

© 2022 by Ashlyn McKayla Ohm

I don't know how the thaw came. All I know
Is that the solid ice on which I stood
Gave way beneath my hopes. The frigid fall
Left me begging breath. At first I sought
To gather all the wounding shards and thus
Rebuild my frozen world. But then I saw
The ice was just the crust; and underneath,
And vaster far, the patient deeps still stir.
All this time
The water yet was welling, cold, but clear;
I will not drown, but dive into its heart;
Beneath the ice, I seek the springs of soul.

CHAPTER 1

*A*ny minute now.

Addisyn gripped her thighs so hard she could feel the sweat from her palms, even through her tights. What was taking so long?

After the frosty temperature of the ice rink where she had performed, the backstage area felt warm, even stuffy. It wasn't enough, though, to keep her teeth from chattering, or goose bumps from crawling up and down her arms. The climate of her mind, not of the room, was responsible for those reactions.

Addisyn glanced at the benches that lined the area. Most were occupied by competitors just as nervous as she was. The blond, willowy skater currently in first place was biting her lip and clutching a teddy bear one of her fans had tossed onto the ice. Like that of nearly everyone else in the crowded room, her gaze was riveted to the giant screen that gave the skaters isolated in the green room access to footage of the event—other performances, commentary, and of course, final scores.

Although there were almost seven thousand people in the arena, stacked row upon row around the rink, no trace of the crowd's murmur penetrated the soundproof walls. Inside the little chamber, silence spread like a slow shadow—the silence of agonizing impatience that the chatter of the TV couldn't begin to break.

156.65. No need to repeat the numbers to herself again. They were tattooed on her brain, the digits of the score she'd received for what was certainly the most momentous performance of her life. A good score, sure—at the time she finished her performance, she'd led the field—but would it be good enough?

Since her program had been only halfway through the whole event, she'd undergone the torturous experience of watching other competitors and waiting each time in breathless suspense for their scores. Three of those scores had been incredible—meaning that she'd been displaced, over the course of the competition, to fourth place. The pewter medal position.

For a girl who considered any medal besides gold to be a consolation prize, that was hard to stomach. Addisyn took a deep breath. She had to remember that her placement, as galling as it was to her competitive soul, was excellent for a competition of this caliber.

Anyway, this was just a stepping stone, a link in the championship chain. Brian said she only needed to medal in this event—any color would do.

And now, she'd almost done it. The very last competitor had just finished her skate, and the judges were deliberating over her score. In a few minutes, Addisyn would either be clutching a pewter medal and cruising on a smooth highway toward her dream…or…

No. She couldn't acknowledge the alternative. Thinking about what was riding on this event made her heart rate triple. When she'd first started competing in the world of figure skating, she'd assumed that the hard part was over as soon as she struck her final pose, snapped on her skate guards, and made her way through the gaggle of reporters to the green room. She'd reasoned that sitting in that post-performance area, shaking hands with other competitors and waiting to hear the final scores, would be simple, even relaxing, compared to the rigors of competing. She'd quickly learned, however, that the most difficult moments—the ones that made souls soar or dreams crumble, the ones that could catapult skaters into glowing futures or toss them into the ditch—happened not on the ice, but afterwards.

In rooms just like this one.

Seeking a distraction, her eyes roamed over the plain, sparsely furnished area. A banner fluttering over the EXIT sign snagged her attention. LAKE PLACID OLYMPIC CENTER.

Her spirit tingled all over again at the sight. Lake Placid. Home of the

1932 and the 1980 Olympic Winter Games, now the host venue for the U.S. Eastern Sectional Figure Skating Championships.

And skating on the ice of a former Olympic rink was a good reminder: she wasn't stopping here. She was going on—on to the U.S. Nationals—on to the Olympic Games!

At least, she hoped she was. Her mind darkened with doubts as she recalled the many setbacks she'd faced—the injury that curtailed her last season, the frustrating weeks of recovery, her disappointing performance at Regionals only a month ago. Hurriedly she shoved the fears away. Why let yesterday's failures dampen her hopes today? That was then.

And this was Now—a glorious Now that would lead to an even more glorious future. If all went as planned…

Addisyn felt hands on her shoulders, adjusting her jacket collar, pulling it more securely around her neck. "Hey, baby. Don't be nervous."

She turned and tried to muster a smile for Brian. Despite his encouraging words, there was quite a bit of "nervous" written across the face of the man who'd been much more than her coach for the last three years. His hands stayed on her shoulders, soothing her. She allowed herself to lean into his supportive gesture, drawing from his strength.

"Did I do okay?" Her whisper sounded hoarse; the anticipation had turned her mouth to cotton. She'd already asked him the same question a dozen times since her performance, but she needed to hear his answer again.

"Better than okay. Great. Incredible. Undefeatable." A proud grin spread across Brian's handsome face. "I already told you, you'll medal. Promise."

He leaned toward her, clearly seeking a kiss, but she jerked away and turned her head. "Brian! Not now. Please." How could he even consider romance at a time like this, when her future dangled by a spiderweb and her emotions were stretched thin with tension?

"Okay, okay." Brian held up his hands in a defensive gesture and shot Addisyn a disgusted look. "Just trying to make you feel better, baby."

"This isn't a good time." Irritation snarled inside her soul, struggling for release, but she forced herself to keep her voice low. Fortunately none of the other contestants seemed to be paying attention to their conversation.

Brian's eyes snapped cold blue sparks. "Yeah, well, you never seem to think it's a good time anymore." He folded his arms and angled his body away from her—as if punishing her for her refusal.

Addisyn pretended not to notice—either his words or his body language. No way was she going to fight this battle with him again—not here, not now, and not in front of all her figure skating peers. Like a maddening insect at a picnic, her annoyance with Brian invaded her soul, begging to be noticed. After all, she'd already explained to him over and over that she wished he would focus less on the physical part of their relationship. Why wouldn't he listen?

Brian was intentionally ignoring the screen. Addisyn frowned and yanked her jacket sleeves down further over her hands. Fine. Later she'd have to try to calm him down, but right now, her impatience was consuming all her emotional resources. Let him sulk if he wanted to.

Wistfully she pictured them as they had been in the earlier days of their relationship, when every moment had been magic. What had happened to them, anyway?

Probably it was just the stress of the last two seasons, with the maelstrom of wins and losses and practices and disappointments. The strain was sure to fray any relationship. But after today—after the medal—things would be good again between them.

Right?

The screen was showing footage of the judges' table. Addisyn scrutinized the scene for some sign, some clue, but saw only nine distinguished-looking people studying their computer screens, faces expressionless.

The scene changed to slow-motion replays of the last performance, given by a girl named Sheila Harbor. Watching the highlights, Addisyn had to grudgingly admit—there was no question the girl was good. Sheila had skated to a lyrical interpretation of "Bring Him Home" from *Les Misérables* and worn a costume to match. Still, Addisyn couldn't help but feel that her own scarlet outfit and snappy routine to Avicii's "Wake Me Up" had held much more pizzazz. But of course, she wasn't on the judging panel.

And that panel could easily award the *Les Mis* girl a higher score than

156.65. Brian could say what he liked about the quality of Addisyn's performance, but she knew that when it came down to it, judges were unpredictable. They might rank a skater who'd fallen three times higher than one who'd flawlessly performed multiple clean landings. Brian swore that outward appearance—makeup, hairstyle, and overall attractiveness—influenced the scoring, but Addisyn always flinched at such an idea. Surely skating wasn't a mere beauty contest!

No, skating was about guts—real, raw guts. It was nothing less that had brought Addisyn this far. For a second, she pictured herself as she'd been at the beginning of her skating journey—a troubled kid growing up in New York City, skating at Rockefeller Center to blow off steam. She'd come all the way to who she was now…a talented, twenty-year-old figure skater looking to set the sport on fire after having trained professionally for only five years.

A miracle, Avery might have called it, with her constant tendency to see a divine hand in everything. Addisyn wrinkled her nose in skepticism. There'd been nothing miraculous about her journey. She'd climbed every step herself, with hard work, hard work, and more hard work.

Yet Avery had always insisted that the hardest work and the best-laid plans were worthless without God's blessing—as if people's lives had to be rubber-stamped by some sort of heavenly holiness patrol. The mere thought was enough to make Addisyn roll her eyes. Of course, Avery was wrong about most things—blinded by the confines of her religious views. All the same, Addisyn did wish Avery could see her now. She'd juggled competitions, received accolades, and salvaged her career even after the crushing defeat of her injury. And in a few seconds—fingers crossed—she'd stand on a podium wearing a pewter medal and celebrating a score that took her one step closer to the Olympics!

Yes, if Avery could peek into Addisyn's world for just a moment, she'd have to admit she'd been wrong. She'd have to swallow all those delusional ideas she'd had, all her warnings and gloomy prophecies. She'd claimed she was worried about her sister's "spiritual health," whatever that was supposed to mean.

This is the wrong road, Addisyn… For a minute, Avery's voice flickered in the back of Addisyn's mind.

A prickle of something almost like fear crept over Addisyn. The next instant she frowned and shifted in her seat. What was the matter with her? The words were meaningless—just more sanctimonious preaching from Avery. And wrong road or not, her course had led her here. To her biggest moment yet.

Anyway, why was she thinking about Avery? She shook her head, annoyed with herself. Her big sister was out of her life. And most of the time, Addisyn kept her out of her thoughts also.

"Here it comes, baby." Brian's words slipped over each other in his agitation. He wrapped his arm around her shoulders, their earlier spat apparently forgotten—or temporarily overlooked.

Sure enough, the echoing voice of the announcer was reverberating over the speaker system. A vacuum seemed to suck the air from Addisyn's lungs. She felt Brian's arm tighten. "Sheila Harbor has received in the free skate a score of"—impressive pause.

Addisyn leaned forward, tingles rushing up and down her legs. If she had subscribed to Avery's school of thought, this might have been the moment she said a prayer. The tension was a giant balloon, expanding, expanding, and preparing to burst any second.

"—156.68."

No.

Addisyn didn't hear what came next. She didn't see how Sheila Harbor reacted. It no longer mattered that there was a Sheila Harbor in the world as she slumped forward, face on her knees, collapsing under the weight of every fallen ambition, every plummeting hope.

All she could feel was the world dropping out from under her, crumbling, falling in pieces. All she could hear was the cracking and crashing of her dreams toppling, shattering into shards as hard and brittle as the ice itself.

She'd been balancing on a knife edge, a skate blade width between her and her goal. Now the tightrope walk was over.

And Avery had been right.

⋀　⋀　⋀

THREE MONTHS HADN'T lessened the pain.

Addisyn slumped in one of the ornate chairs in the main room of Brian's swanky apartment in New York's prestigious Upper East Side—her apartment, too, since she'd moved in with him over two years ago. Normally the opulent furnishings and the incredible view comforted her, but since Sectionals, nothing seemed able to soothe her heart.

Brushing her palms over the stiff taffeta weave of her fuchsia dress, she wished for the hundredth time that she could just snuggle in some comfortable pajamas and spend the bitterly cold night at home—curled up with a good book, maybe. Instead, Brian had insisted she accompany him to a Valentine's Day gala—some fancy get-together he'd snagged tickets for.

Irritation swelled inside Addisyn's soul. Surely Brian could see how depressed she was. Valentine's Day or no, did they have to go out tonight? She was in no mood for small talk, didn't want to force a glamorous façade—especially since she was more than a little miffed at the man. He'd always had an uptight personality, but over the last couple of months, he'd been extraordinarily cranky. Oh, she knew he was disappointed by her defeat at Sectionals, but really, shouldn't she have the most right to grieve? After all, it was her plans—her dreams—her whole life that had vanished in a nanosecond, like her breath on a freezing New York day. Brian's emotional investment wasn't nearly as high. Couldn't he shrug off his own frustration and try instead to help her through her pain?

Well, no use thinking that way. She was going, certainly. Brian could pitch a royal fit if he didn't get his way. Addisyn tried to shake off her pessimistic mood. Maybe the party could help them rekindle their bond. It was Valentine's Day, after all. And Brian always went big for this holiday. Last year he'd bought her a box of real Swiss chocolate truffles, a dozen long-stemmed red roses, and some fancy Parisian lingerie.

Addisyn glanced at the clock. What on earth was taking Brian so long to get ready tonight? She had been ready half an hour ago—mostly because wasting time agonizing over her appearance wasn't high on her priority list right now. She left her chair and strolled to the window, gazing out over the city.

Square towers and skyscrapers stretched as far as she could see, sprawling over the earth. If she looked down—down—down into the narrow slits between buildings, she could see the yellow smears of taxis, darting this way and that. And even from the height of the townhouse, she could hear the horns blaring and sirens wailing and the music from Times Square—an unnoticed backdrop for anyone living in the Big Apple.

Home to over eight million people. Did any of them feel as lost and lonely as she did on this frigid night? Did any of them feel as if the cold and sadness had soaked deeply into their soul, double-dying it in melancholy?

She returned to her tufted wingback chair and tucked one leg under her. The longer she thought about going to the party tonight, the more she felt as if her emotions just would not cooperate. How could she possibly keep everything together without falling apart?

And if she had a meltdown while at the party, it would undoubtedly embarrass Brian to death. He'd drilled into her the need for glamorous appearances and correct social behavior. She winced, remembering how mortifyingly frequent her faux pas had been when she'd first come under his tutelage. Avery, of course, had seen teaching her younger sister socialite manners to be about as useless as teaching her how to skydive.

In his career, image was important, Brian had often told her. It was the main reason he went to these parties—to project a good vibe, hobnob with connections who might be valuable later. And as his date, her behavior and appearance were a reflection on him.

Yes, the more she thought about it, the more it seemed best to skip the party altogether. Just as the conviction settled into her mind, Brian arrived in the doorway, tugging on his navy bowtie and whistling a catchy tune. His eyes gleamed when he saw her.

"Hey, baby." He sidled up to her and grinned. Wrapping his arms around her waist, he looked her up and down. "Wow. You sure look hot tonight. That color suits you, all right." Without waiting for a response, he leaned forward and kissed her on the neck, snuggling her into his chest.

"Thank you." His words didn't leave Addisyn glowing and giddy, the way they once would have. Why couldn't Brian compliment her every now and then on something besides her appearance? A feisty surge of irritation surprised her.

But she couldn't waste this opportunity. Now was the time to ask—

while he was in such a good mood and happy with her. Addisyn took a deep breath. *Here goes!* "Brian, could we—well—would you mind if I stayed home tonight?" Seeing his frown, she rushed her next words. "I mean, you could still go, of course. I wouldn't mind. I just—just don't want to go out right now."

With a grimace, Brian pulled his arms from around her waist and stuffed his hands in the pockets of his Calvin Klein suit. "Look, baby, I know you're still upset over the competition and all, but don't you think a night out might help you?" His voice changed, the way it always did when he was pleading with her—forsaking the annoyance and taking on a cajoling tone. "I don't want to go all by myself. No fun that way." He dropped a kiss on her forehead. "Anyway…" he reached for her hands, lacing his fingers through hers and tugging her closer to him. "It doesn't look right, us not going together. Makes people talk." His breath on her face smelled like mint. "Come on, baby, you know how people talk."

"But, Brian—" *Never mind.* Addisyn clamped her mouth shut. Any protest would only put him in a foul mood. "All right." She nodded meekly. "I'll go."

"That's my girl." A satisfied grin spread over Brian's face. "Ready?"

Without another word Addisyn took Brian's arm and prepared to follow him outside. Time to put her smile on and be Brian Felding's girl.

△△ △△ △△

THE ROOM WAS much too warm. Addisyn took a deep breath, trying to find fresh air somewhere that wasn't suffocatingly heavy with the aromas of cologne and champagne.

She glanced at the stylish mirrored clock on the wall. She'd been there for half an hour, with probably another two hours to go. The thought of spending another two minutes at the party, never mind two hours, made her feel as if she might scream.

She'd spent the time since she'd arrived gliding across the room attached to Brian's arm, mingling with the other distinguished guests. Like a parrot, she'd said every perfect thing to every perfect person and somehow said nothing at all. Now Brian had excused himself to look for a colleague, and she'd immediately sought refuge in the shadows created by the potted palm in the corner. Finally, a moment of relief from the mental exertion of maintaining her mask.

It was hard to believe now that there had ever been a time when she'd found these parties wonderful—the height of excitement and enjoyment. But she had, when Brian had first ushered her into his world. The glitz and splendor had been intoxicating to a girl who'd grown up poor on New York's Lower East Side. She had felt like a princess come home to the enchanted castle—introduced to a life she could have only dreamed of while she pinched pennies with Avery in a one-bedroom flat. She'd been impressed by Brian's affluent, successful friends, captivated by their luxurious surroundings, and thrilled with the rush and twinkle of social life.

Of course, she'd also been fascinated by Brian himself. Maybe it was the glitter and glamor of being in love that had made everything else so titillating—and maybe everything was fading now because her hypnosis with Brian was waning, a candle burning ever and ever dimmer.

Guilt over her recent irritation with Brian heated her cheeks. He loved her, that's what he said. He claimed she just had unrealistic expectations. Which could be true. After all, she couldn't explain why his caresses had begun to annoy her. And was it very kind or realistic of her to expect him to forgo his dinner plans just because she was upset? Maybe she was being too hard on him.

And Brian was such a wonderful guy, most of the time. Sure, he lost his temper some, but apart from that, he was impeccably charming. And he was as devoted to her career as she was. She reminded herself that she'd be nowhere if not for his patient tutelage and support.

Perhaps none of this was Brian's fault—just a natural reaction to the letdown of Sectionals. Given the stresses they'd both been under, it was no wonder their relationship was tense. For crying out loud, she'd probably been pretty hard to live with herself for the last few weeks.

Yes, that was all. Addisyn stepped out from behind the palm with a renewed determination to give her boyfriend the benefit of the doubt. She needed to find him and be with him. He was probably wondering where she was. Addisyn glanced around the room and finally spotted Brian talking to a few other men. She edged her way through the couples until she was close enough to hear their conversation.

"...one of the best in the field," Brian was saying. He nodded seriously at the other man. "Definitely, if you can get her case, take it."

"I'm just not sure about the opportunity cost." The man rubbed his chin. "I have a full caseload already, so..."

Brian never looked around. Addisyn waited a few moments and then turned away. They were engulfed in the business conversation, and evidently her disappearance wasn't bothering Brian in the least. Annoyed, she made her way through the room, weaving among the tables covered with dainty white tablecloths.

The weight of disappointment flattened her own defense of Brian's character like the flimsy barricade it was, powerless against the rush of strong emotions. Really, it had been downright inconsiderate of him to insist on going to this party tonight. Never giving her feelings any priority. Only focused on what he wanted. Addisyn was no expert on happy couples—goodness knew her mom and dad hadn't given her any role models—but still, even she figured that a good partnership required some give-and-take from both sides.

Instead, she was doing the giving, while Brian enjoyed the taking. Like tonight. She didn't want to be at this party. Certainly not. Yet here she was, plastered against the wall, waiting for her wonderful boyfriend to notice she wasn't around.

All of this was too much to try to ponder right now, when the room was full of chattering elegant people. Addisyn drifted over to the table of hors d'oeuvres, an elegant arrangement complete with effervescent puffs of red tulle and live flowers. An array of alcoholic beverages sat nearby, some already poured into glasses. Addisyn glanced at the labels—cabernet, bourbon, pinot noir, champagne. She didn't drink, except at dinners or parties like this one—Brian had always told her that waiting until twenty-one to drink was a senseless formality, as long as you didn't overdo it, but she still had reservations. Residual outdated morality from Avery, probably. But tonight she needed something to help her survive this ordeal. She selected a glass of the champagne and took a pungent sip as she glanced around the room.

Perfectly paired couples dotted the grey-veined marble floor, talking and laughing in the stringently choreographed dance of social etiquette. Occasionally a man's hearty voice or a woman's rippling titter would rise above the general murmur of conversation. In the far corner, a chamber quartet provided a soothing string number while a handful of couples danced slowly.

For a moment, Addisyn experienced a surge of insecurity, strong enough that she glanced down at herself, with the sinking fear that she had been so distracted by her emotional turmoil that she'd neglected some aspect of her personal appearance. No, on the outside, she looked impeccable—flawless makeup, beautifully tailored dress, glistening stiletto heels.

It was more about her heart than her body, a sudden weariness of this life of the rich and famous, a floundering feeling that she didn't belong. Like a tap on the shoulder from a voice inside her spirit. Deep inside, where a girl had once lived who was radically different from the Addisyn of today.

Stop it! Why was she having such troubled feelings tonight? What a rollercoaster her mind was! At a Valentine's party to boot. Addisyn sighed and took another sip from her glass.

"Miss Miles?" A voice sent her ramshackle thoughts scattering in all directions. Startled, Addisyn turned to see an older gentleman standing at her elbow. His neatly combed silver hair reminded her of an old silent film star, but the lines about his eyes seemed less than open. Immediately she donned her most charming smile—more out of habit than anything else. "Yes, sir?"

He held out his hand, and she quickly switched her glass of champagne to the other hand so she could daintily offer her fingertips. "I'm Martin Moorehouse, Marty Moorehouse, they call me. I heard you were looking for a new job, and I think I just might be able to offer you one." The man smiled in a pleasant, grandfatherly way. As though he expected her to be overjoyed by this news.

"Looking for a—I'm sorry?" Addisyn furrowed her brow. What was going on? Surely the man had confused her with someone else. "I—I must have misunderstood."

"Yes, forgive me for being unclear. I'm the general manager at the Showtime Dinner Theater here in town. Corner of Forty-sixth and Ninth.

We offer meals with entertainment—all kinds. Burlesque, drama, singing, all that. I'm looking to hire three or four talented skaters." Mr. Moorehouse waved his hand in the air, as if gesturing to his grand scheme. "You know, skating exhibitions during dinner. Guests'll love it." He studied the drink selection and chose a glass of bourbon. "Anyway, I thought you might be interested. My theater is top-notch."

Confusion squiggled through Addisyn's chest. What in the world had this man heard? The very thought of displaying her skating in that way—lumping her soul-fired performances in with burlesque and opera, selling her heart like a cheap commodity—nauseated her. "Mr. Moorehouse, I'm—" She caught her breath. Remembered to be polite. "Thank you very much for the offer, but I'm a competitive skater. On my way to the Olympics. Brian—Mr. Felding is my coach." She knew her smile was weak. "Perhaps you weren't aware."

Mr. Moorehouse's eyebrows rose in sharp peaks. "Well, yes, I was aware." He paused. "But Brian told me that competing hadn't worked out for you—that you weren't going to be able to make the Olympic team after all. Said you had a real bad loss at Sectionals and didn't have much hope of getting any further." He shook his head contemplatively. "No surprise there. Sectionals gets harder every year. Kids are skating younger and younger. Last statistic I heard, something like only five percent—"

"*Brian* told you I would want a job at your theater?" Addisyn felt as if she might laugh. Or maybe cry. Or maybe run across the room screaming and wallop Brian over the head with the champagne bottle.

"Well—" Mr. Moorehouse seemed much less confident now, apparently sensing tension between them even if he couldn't diagnose the cause. "He—he told me you needed a job, yes. We've known each other for years, him and me. We always help each other out like that." He sipped his bourbon, then shrugged. "Just think it over. I pay good wages. Solid benefits. And working for me, you can still skate, even if you can't compete." He clinked his glass to hers. "Cheers." And with that he was gone.

The room spun crazily around Addisyn. With shaking hands, she set her drink down before she dropped it. There had to be some mistake. There had to be. Brian was her coach. He was supposed to be encouraging her, training her, helping her fight to the top—not going behind her back like this!

Of course there was a mistake. Brian would never, ever do such a thing. But to make her heart beat normally again, she had to hear it from him—had to see the shock on his face when she told him what Marty Moorehouse had pitched to her. Addisyn felt alternately hot and cold as she threaded her way through the crowd, muttering "Excuse me" indiscriminately.

Brian was still rapt in business chatter with his associates. She tugged on his sleeve, oblivious to all but her angst. "Brian, I need to speak with you." Her teeth were chattering; she could barely get the words out.

He turned with a frown. "Baby, I'm busy right now."

Busy? No, she needed him now. The gaping hole in her heart was threatening to suck her into it. Only his reassurance could possibly ease this moment. "This is important."

He shot a smooth smile at his group. "Excuse me one moment."

The others cheerfully obliged, with one man cheekily cracking some joke about a lady being in charge of "her man." At any other time, Addisyn would have been indignant over the weak humor, but now nothing mattered except the truth. She all but dragged Brian to the edge of the room and launched in without preamble. "Why did Mr. Moorehouse come and offer me a job at his theater? He said that you told him that I—" Addisyn choked over the words—"That my career was ruined. And that I needed a job besides competing. What is that about?"

Brian's face flushed. He glanced around the room. "Moorehouse said that?"

"Yes." His obvious exasperation slowed her breathing and calmed her nerves. See, Brian hadn't really done such a low-down thing. Of course he hadn't. He'd explain to her that he was innocent, and then he'd find Moorehouse and give him a piece of his mind.

"Well, baby, I—" Brian ran his hand over his hair. "I mean, Moorehouse said he had this job opening. I thought it would be a good fit for you. You still get to skate, you know, and—" His words seemed to fizzle out. "I—I didn't really expect him to bring it up here…"

"So you told him that? You told him I wasn't going to be competing anymore?" Addisyn's stomach was cold inside.

Defensiveness glazed Brian's eyes. "Look, you know this—your career, your skating—it's just not going well. I mean—it's a sinking ship." He spread his hands helplessly. "I just thought this would give you the—"

"Never mind." Addisyn blinked back the stinging in her eyes and lifted her chin. She would not let Brian see the tidal wave of emotion that was drowning her soul. A sinking ship? Really? She was one of figure skating's fastest rising stars. Hardly a sinking ship. A few small losses couldn't stop her. "I'm leaving." She gripped her clutch in both hands. "I'm taking a cab home." She spun and began walking for the exit as fast as her stiletto heels would allow.

"Addisyn, wait!" Desperation rang in his voice, but she didn't look back.

She'd already heard enough from him. More than enough.

CHAPTER 2

A sinking ship. The words throbbed in Addisyn's ears as she paced the room, her footsteps leaving impressions in the thick Oriental rug. *A sinking ship.*

Was that really what she'd become? A failure so pathetic that even her coach—her boyfriend, for crying out loud—was trying to pawn her off as a cheap entertainment skater?

Her thoughts whirled, refusing to settle on any one idea for very long. She'd kicked off her uncomfortable heels as soon as she crossed the threshold—she'd only worn them because Brian liked them—but her mind was far too agitated for her to even consider changing the rest of her clothes. *Sinking ship?*

All the time she'd ridden the taxi home, she'd only felt fury, a bonfire in her chest that snapped with heat despite the cold night. But now, that burning anger was freezing into the ice of despair. What if Brian was right? What if her skating days were behind her?

Sure, she'd known her career was in trouble. She'd been uncertain of her next step. But until tonight, she'd always believed that a next step existed, always believed there was a way to climb out of the mess. And to hear the opposite—from Brian, of all people, the man who'd hugged her in the green room and cursed viciously at the nosy reporters as they left the arena—to hear that made it real. She, Addisyn Miles, was a failure at the age of twenty.

Just as Avery always said she would be.

Snatches of her sister's lectures tumbled around inside her head.

"You're making a big mistake, Addisyn…God won't bless your choices…"

God? Addisyn tossed her hands in the air, defeated. Okay, so she'd made mistakes. Done all the wrong things, apparently. And evidently God—like Avery—wouldn't accept anything less than perfection. Was He truly punishing her? Her mind slipped and slid in its frantic search for logic. Nonsense. Why blame a supernatural power for her demise? She didn't have to. The answers were as close as herself.

She drooped into a chair as the realization wrapped a cold, numbing pain around her heart. More out of compulsion than desire, she reached into her clutch bag and pulled out her iPhone. Woodenly she typed her name into Safari and stared at the list of articles, photos, and videos that rose to the screen.

She clicked on one of the links. "Addisyn Miles: A Greater Skater." This was an article from three years prior. There was a picture of Addisyn herself, seventeen years old but looking thirteen, grinning with a little-girl joy as she flourished her medal over her head. That had been a good year, when her career really began to soar. She'd made the regional championships.

And she'd met Brian.

The next article was from last season. Her eyes flicked over the words. "One of figure skating's fastest-rising stars, Addisyn Miles, has suffered an injury while practicing for…manager and coach Brian Felding has stated that Miles's injury, while not expected to have long-term effects, will still prevent further competition this season…"

Addisyn could still remember the frustration of that moment. Just two weeks shy of Regionals, she'd torn her meniscus practicing a jump sequence. The immediate pain had been nothing compared to the agony of facing defeat on the very doorstep of her dreams.

Just like this time.

Back to the search results. Another link, this one only three months old. This title felt like a punch to the gut. "Dreams Over for Addisyn Miles." A video from Sectionals.

"…in a performance that showcased her artistic flair," a female voice-over cut in. The footage shifted, and there was Addisyn herself, gliding over the Lake Placid ice. Addisyn kept her eyes glued to the image of herself, reliving every moment of that skate.

The woman's voice continued. "At twenty years of age, Miles was on a fast track to success in the field of figure skating. After her astounding performances last season were curtailed by injury, Miles had come from behind this season in a bid to reach the U.S. Championships.

"Miles's performance at the Upper Great Lakes Regional Championships was disappointing, with a final score significantly lower than her average pre-injury ratings. However, she advanced to Sectionals and was still considered a strong contender, especially given the fact that she remains one of the first American females to perform two quad jumps successfully in a non-Olympic routine…"

Yes. Those quads. The feat that had catapulted her into the spotlight two years before. Addisyn's legs ached just remembering the hours of practice she'd poured into the perfection of that movement. Yet another feat she hadn't been able to duplicate since the injury.

"—all eyes on her in this year's Sectionals. With the help of manager and coach Brian Felding, Miles had choreographed a snappy routine to Avicii's 'Wake Me Up.' Her performance was impressive, and Miles …"

It was so surreal, watching herself skate. Like the girl on the ice was someone else. In one sense, that was true. No longer was she the starry-eyed dreamer.

"…unfortunately, at the end of the day, Miles was three hundredths of a point behind her nearest competitor, Sheila Harbor. This has to be a disappointment since speculation had abounded that Miles, who did not begin training professionally until her teens, intended to try for the U.S. Olympic team. Her chances of appearing on Olympic ice have noticeably slimmed with this inability to advance to Nationals, and…"

Addisyn swiped the video closed, abruptly cutting off the sportscaster's bland tones.

Why hadn't she accepted this before, realized what all these defeats meant? They weren't just setbacks—they were endings. Endings to everything she had ever hoped to have and do in her life. Endings to her life itself. She moaned, a low cry wrung from her soul by the pain, an intense ache behind her heart that momentarily prevented her from getting a deep breath. A feverish sensation swept over her as she stared blindly at an abstract art painting on the other wall. Trying to block the cruelty of the moment, she closed her eyes.

And then she was jerking herself awake as a key clicked in the door. Had she dozed off? Rubbing the back of her neck, she realized the answer was yes. She glanced at the clock—ten forty-five. The key continued to rattle in the lock. She set her jaw. Brian hadn't hurried getting home, even knowing how upset she was.

When she felt his presence in the doorway behind her, she maintained her rigid position on the chair. She expected he'd try to apologize, maybe get a little defensive. Well, if he was feeling his way, he wouldn't get any help from her. This time she wasn't buying his excuses. Nothing he could offer would atone for what he'd done.

"I've never been so embarrassed."

The shock brought Addisyn out of her chair. Jumping to her feet, she spun to face Brian. She saw not guilt or sheepishness on his face, but—anger?

"What?" *He* was *embarrassed?* What about her?

"Pulling me out of conversation like that. Running out of the party. Catching a taxi home. Leaving me there to look like I'd gone stag." The cold sparks in Brian's eyes burned brighter with every phrase. He shrugged out of his expensive coat and tossed it with disgust on the back of the sofa, never taking his eyes from her face.

Addisyn's mind whirled. What was he saying? Had he forgotten she was mad at him? Did he care at all?

"Brian—I'm—" Suddenly she stopped. She'd meant to back down, apologize the way she normally did. But why bow to the blame? She hadn't done anything wrong. She straightened her shoulders and stared defiantly into his face. "I just left the party. It's no big deal."

Now he was the one to be shocked. "You don't see anything wrong with that?" His fury was like a tangible force, shoving her into a dark corner of the mind. "You didn't think about how awkward it would be for me?"

Addisyn wanted to remind him that he could have left when she did, but she decided not to. Getting to the bottom of whatever Brian had been thinking when he tried to get her a gig as an entertainer made any other disagreements seem petty. "Have you forgotten why I left?"

That dart pierced his façade slightly. "No." Some of his anger seemed to leave with his weary sigh. "Look, Addisyn, I can tell you're upset. I don't know why Marty brought that up at the party."

I can tell you're upset...as if it were surprising that she was, and he was extraordinarily perceptive for noticing. Addisyn gritted her teeth. "You don't know why he brought it up?" A hard laugh jerked from her throat. "*I* don't know why you ever mentioned the idea to him!"

His eyes narrowed again, signaling the end of his brief conciliatory moment. "I don't appreciate the way you've handled this." For the first time, his eyes looked too hardened. "I did you a favor, trying to get you a good job. It's steady income, and it's skating, and then if you decide you want to try competing, you can always—"

"*If* I decide?" Everything was swirling together, a weird distorted version of reality. "Brian, you know I'm competing! That's what I do!" Her voice echoed in the apartment. "Do you honestly think I would give up a shot at the Olympics for a cheap gig in some—some trashy theater?" She paused for a moment, then asked the question that truly mattered. "Do you think I *should?*"

Brian's lips tightened. When he spoke, exasperation scorched his tone. "Okay, baby, I know you won't want to believe this, but your career is in serious trouble." For the first time during their exchange, he glanced away, his eyes searching for a spot on the carpet. "Look, I wanted to break this to you more gently, but—" His voice trailed off as he rubbed the back of his neck.

"But what?" Addisyn wiped her sweaty palms against the sides of her dress. A hard lump plummeted into the pit of her stomach.

"I got a letter a few weeks ago. From Mitch Shapiro." Brian paused and finally lifted his gaze. "He's the financial director of the Rising Stars Foundation."

Rising Stars.

Addisyn's heartbeat was a sledgehammer, jarring her chest. No way could she have ever had the money to compete in a sport as expensive and uncertain as figure skating—not as a nearly homeless teen growing up in the New York City slums. But after her first few competitions, she'd been awarded one of the coveted Rising Stars scholarships, elite sponsorship packages for young skaters with great potential. Whatever could the letter have said…unless… She had to swallow before she could whisper the word on which her future hinged: "And?"

Brian pressed his lips together. As if even his stony soul was feeling some of the devastation of the moment. "You've lost your sponsorship. They—the organization has more worthy applicants."

"More—what?" Addisyn couldn't breathe, couldn't think, couldn't feel anything besides a huge void of blackness, spreading over her future.

"We should have seen this coming. They took a chance by renewing your sponsorship even after the injury. But—well, fourth place in Regionals was bad enough. Now you've failed to medal in Sectionals."

"So what?" A rising swell of anger blocked the pain. For now. "That doesn't mean anything! I just—"

Brian held up a hand to stop her. "It does mean something! It's your ticket to Nationals. And Nationals is your ticket to the Olympics!"

Addisyn lifted her chin. No way would she back down—even if she was starting to tremble. "I'll work extra hard. I'll ace Regionals and Sectionals next season and go on to Nationals. And I don't need sponsorship, not anymore, because you're coaching me. So, no big deal." She wouldn't let Brian know how cold and quivery her insides felt.

"You're not hearing me, Addisyn!" Brian's words were jagged with impatience. Two steps toward her, and he grabbed her shoulders, yanking her upward and forcing her to meet his gaze. "Look, this was your time to go to Nationals. Okay? Not next year, not the year after that. Make Nationals this season, keep the momentum going next year, and you would have been an easy nominee for Team USA." His words kept climbing a ladder of anger, a fury that billowed and rose like a storm surge. Without warning, he shook her once, a hard yank to reality. "The only way you'd be going to the Olympics now is to blow the top off Nationals next season, and you can't get there. And if you don't make that, you can't wait years to compete!"

"I'll wait as many years as I need to!" Who was this man? This monster, clutching her shoulders and screaming until his face was distorted? Addisyn's heart was galloping now, faster than the whirlwind in her mind, faster than the beat of the song she'd skated to. "This is my one and only dream! Don't you get that?" She didn't care now that she was yelling. "I'll wait my whole life if I have to for the chance to compete!"

"Shut up and listen to me!" Brian's voice thundered through the room. His thumbs seemed to be boring through her shoulders.
She'd seen him lose his cool before, but never like this. He was like a bad imitation of her dad. Old memories twisted with present pain to wrap panic around her soul. "Let go of me!" Anger and betrayal writhed within her—along with another emotion she'd never associated with Brian before—fear.

Brian released his grip and took a single step back. He swiped a hand hard across his mouth, apparently grappling desperately for control. When he spoke again, all emotion had drained from his voice, leaving it hard and sharp as ice. "Figure skaters are going to the Olympics these days at sixteen, seventeen years old. I mean, look at Tara Lipinski. She was training when she was six and already had an Olympic gold medal before she turned sixteen." He paused to let his words sink in. "Come on, Addisyn. You didn't start training until you were a teenager, and you've done a remarkable job in the time you've had, but, well, you're at a disadvantage. I thought at one time we could get past it, but"—his voice dwindled—"we can't."

Was Brian saying she would never be an Olympian? That her life's goal was out of reach—forever? No. No, he couldn't be. "What are you saying?" The words sounded breathy, as if she'd just finished a long workout.

"I'm saying you'll be twenty-one in two months. By the next Olympics, you'll be almost—"

"So now I'm too old on top of everything else." The zip and twang of fury was like a lightning strike to her soul. She'd never hated anyone more than she hated Brian at that moment.

He just shrugged. A cool, mechanical gesture. "Look, I get it. I'm disappointed too."

No, he didn't get it. Not at all. "This is my dream. I can't just give up!" The words were frantic, tumbling over each other.

The corner of Brian's mouth twisted cynically. "You can't medal, and you're broke. Maybe you need a new dream."

Addisyn suddenly laughed. Hysterically. Was this happening to her? Was she really standing here, close to midnight on Valentine's Day, trying to stop the man she'd considered her biggest fan and the love of her life from tossing her grandest dream in the garbage? "There *is* no Plan B, Brian. You're my coach! Of all people, you ought to know——"

"Yeah, I know." Brian broke in. His voice was loud again. "I know you failed at Sectionals!" He cursed, his tones rough and thick. "If you can't even get a pewter medal, you've got no business thinking about Nationals."

"Brian, I gave a wonderful performance! You said so yourself in the green room!"

"Yeah, well, what else was I supposed to tell you right then?" Brian huffed. "You were already a basket case. I thought you might just lose it on me. And let me remind you, you weren't as wonderful as four other people in front of you!"

Ow! Addisyn flinched at the thorn prick of his jab. Tears sprang to her eyes, but Brian merely sneered at her.

"And there were things in your performance." He glared at her, scorn curling his lip. "If I've told you once, I've told you a hundred times about under-rotating your jumps. But I'm sitting there that night, and what do I see?" He gave a bark of a laugh. "I see you out there, doing sloppy jumps like an amateur. And on the double Axel in the middle, you let too much time elapse between your landing and your triple toe." He rolled his eyes. "That's just the beginning. I could go on."

The words struck her mind like summertime hail on a car roof, but they weren't really hitting home. They couldn't, yet. Until tonight, Addisyn had been skating on a sheet of ice three feet thick. And suddenly, with no warning, that solid, reliable ice had turned to mush beneath her feet—and she was drowning, dragged under frigid waters, sliding into the depths of an unthinkable reality.

"You just can't make it." Brian's hissed condemnation seared her soul. "You've tried to play with the big boys. You're not good enough."

His words were more water filling her lungs. Black spots danced before Addisyn's eyes. She reached behind her, gripping the chair for support, digging her fingernails into its plush fabric. "I *am* good enough." She'd meant to yell the affirmation with power and courage, but instead, it barely trickled out.

"Face it, Addisyn." Brian's every word was coming straight from her darkest nightmare. "You're sweet, you're cute, but you're not good enough for this job. And anyway—I can't coach you anymore."

A blow to the gut couldn't have knocked the air from Addisyn more effectively. "Brian—what?"

"The money, baby." Brian rolled his eyes. As though she were stupid for not prioritizing the financial side of this. "Look, figure skating is a business. A very lucrative and also very expensive business."

"Brian, what are you saying?" A sob jerked from Addisyn without her permission.

Brian gave an elaborate sigh, as though he were reasoning with a stubborn child. "Don't you realize that Rising Stars has been paying my salary? Where do you think the money comes from for me to train you, manage your career, travel with you all over the country?"

Addisyn opened her mouth to speak, but no words were ready. She hadn't considered the monetary side of skating—not really. Beauty on the ice and perfection in competitions were her concerns, not dollars and cents. She'd known that the sponsorship was providing financial support, of course, but she'd trusted Brian with the details. Not for a gold medal would she admit now what she had always believed—that Brian had been doing everything for her because he wanted to.

Because he loved her.

So, for every moment he spent with her in a rink, every flight to a competition, every hotel room where they shared the night before a performance, his pockets were being padded with sponsorship dollars. And somehow the knowledge made her feel incomparably dirty and used, like the streetwalkers that roamed the Big Apple.

She'd drown for sure, any second now. She couldn't keep her chin above the water much longer as she floundered helplessly, grabbing at the seemingly solid ice that had splintered into wounding shards under her.

"I'm sorry, baby, but without Rising Stars, we're at the end of the road. It's just not a wise financial decision for me." Not a speck of remorse appeared in his eyes.

A wise financial decision? Really? "Brian!" A hysterical laugh snagged in Addisyn's throat. "A—a wise financial decision? I thought we were—we had—more than that!" Angrily she swiped at the tears trickling down her cheeks. "Is that all I am to you? Just a—a ticket to big money?"

"Oh, Addisyn, of course not." Brian huffed loudly, as though she were being completely ridiculous. "But you've got be reasonable. Take the job at the theater, and you still get to skate, or find another job, or something, but you're not going to the Olympics. Period."

Tears streamed down Addisyn's cheeks, dripped onto the satin dress. The pain dragged scarlet claws through her soul as Brian's words crashed inside her mind. Not going to the Olympics? "You promised to take me there! You said I was good enough—you said—"

"I did my best. It didn't work out. *You* didn't work out." Brian stretched his hands over his head and picked up his coat as casually as if they'd just had a perfectly nice chat. "It's late. I'm going to bed. You coming?"

On the heels of a conversation like the one they'd just had? Really? Addisyn laughed—a brittle, enraged laugh. "No."

His eyes narrowed. For a moment she thought he might erupt again, but he just shrugged. "Fine."

△△ △△ △△

ADDISYN TOSSED HER iPhone onto the couch with a sigh. Still no texts or calls from Brian—and checking her phone every hour wouldn't make them magically appear. She flopped onto the sofa beside her phone and stared around the apartment. Its emptiness made it feel unfamiliar.

Being by herself for three days had taught her how lonely she really was. Had she always been this isolated, even when Brian was there? Had his presence been a way to numb her loneliness, not cure it?

She'd spent the night of the party fuming in the living room. Sometime just before dawn, when the glow of the morning sun was rising out of the Atlantic to overpower the hectic lights of New York City, she'd fallen into an uneasy sleep right here on the couch. She'd dreamed about

Avery, of all things. Dreamed of Avery furious, scolding her, listing all the reasons Addisyn's choices had been wrong.

When she'd awakened later that morning, the silence of the apartment had seemed to shout at her. At first she'd just assumed Brian had already left for his swanky office on Thirty-seventh Street. But when she went into their bedroom and found some of his clothes and toiletries missing, she'd remembered—he'd told her earlier that week he had to leave on a business trip after Valentine's Day and would be gone for five days. He'd been headed to Buffalo and then Harrisburg to interview some potential clients. In the heat of the argument, she'd completely forgotten.

Now it had been three days, and the silence had only become louder with every hour Brian was gone. He still hadn't reached out to her once. No calls, no texts, no emails. His way of reminding her that he was still mad.

Addisyn had always accepted Brian's temper fits before. She had been so in love with him—infatuated by him—that she dismissed his anger. Now, with the clarity born of three days of silence, she could see that fear had played into her resigned attitude—the fear that Brian would turn away from her and banish her to a loneliness that would freeze her soul. She needed him too badly to find fault with his personality. Beggars couldn't be choosers—and when it came to his love, she was definitely a beggar.

Plus, he usually blamed her for his outbursts. She pushed his buttons, or she wasn't training hard enough, or she didn't understand how life worked in his upper-echelon world. And until now, she'd believed him, worn the saddle of guilt rather than be left behind.

But this? Screaming at her over leaving a party? Going behind her back to betray her dearest dreams? Even grabbing her in anger? The moment flashed in her memory like a scene from a horror movie. She could still feel the painful grip of his knuckles, still see the wild fever in his eyes. She'd never been afraid of him before, but when he'd shaken her like that, she'd thought he might lose control entirely.

Emotional discomfort was one thing, but she wasn't going to put up with physical violence. Wasn't that exactly why she and Avery had worked so hard to escape their dysfunctional family?

The phone vibrated in Addisyn's hand, startling her from her thoughts. In spite of herself, a surge of hope flooded her soul. Maybe it was Brian, calling to apologize.

Instead, an unknown number flashed across the screen. Addisyn sighed. Probably some hacker or salesman.

Her thoughts drifted back to Brian. Had he always been this way? Self-centered…narcissistic…ruthless…even violent. She shook her head. It didn't matter now. What mattered was the fact that she, Addisyn Miles, was alone. No true love…no chance…no dreams. Although she'd grown accustomed to the idea over the last few torturous days, the pain was still as incredible as anything she'd ever felt.

But she hadn't just been sitting alone in the apartment and listening to the silence. She'd made a plan—a crazy one, but a plan all the same.

Her phone chimed. The unknown number had left a voicemail. Well, might as well check it. A few quick flicks and a man's voice began speaking. "Uh, yes, this is Marty Moorehouse. I was just wondering if you'd had time to decide if you were interested in my offer. If so, please give me a call at this number to schedule your audition. I'm planning to open applications and begin the hiring process this week. Thank you."

Addisyn groaned. Thank goodness she hadn't answered the call. The thought of auditioning for a burlesque dinner theater when she'd just for all intents and purposes auditioned for the Olympic team made her feel sick.

"No, Mr. Moorehouse," she said aloud into the empty room, "I am *not* interested in your offer."

Nor was she interested in hanging around New York any longer. What was there for her now in the city? She was leery of Brian, her dreams were broken like delicate porcelain on a tile floor, and without Brian's help, she was basically homeless. She needed to get out. The very air in the city felt as if it were poisoning her.

Hence her new plan.

Addisyn rose and slowly headed to the rolltop desk in the corner. If she remembered right, what she was looking for was in the top left drawer, under the stack of skating documents. Her fingers felt unsteady as she shuffled through the papers. Where was it?

She paused for a moment. Thinking—remembering—wondering.

Her pulse was light and fluttering in her wrists. Once she did this, there would be no going back. Was she ready to take this big of a leap?

Maybe it would be better if she forgot about the whole thing. New York City was a pretty nice place, after all. Plenty to do—lots of opportunities. And Brian—well, maybe he would come around—maybe he would agree to coach her again—maybe—

She struggled for a moment, her mind teetering on a tightrope between two worlds. Suddenly her song from Sectionals came back to mind. Once again she was on the ice, skating her heart out. *Wake Me Up…*

She squared her jaw. Took a deep breath. No more maybes. No more excuses. No more mollycoddling Brian and passively accepting his bad behavior.

It was time to find that place where the part of her that lay still and dormant could wake up again. No matter how crazy the journey there seemed.

Resolutely she thrust her hand back into the drawer. And there, pushed far in the back, she felt it. The outline of a thin booklet, with a faux leather texture. Her breathing sounded loud in the quiet room. She grasped the object gently and pulled it out of the drawer, where the morning sun glittered on the gold letters emblazoned proudly on the cover.

For a moment she stared at the little object. So many hopes and dreams were crowded into it. At one time, she'd expected this treasure to take her around the world to compete for the Olympic Team. But now— now it would no longer help her pursue victory. Instead, it would be her ticket to escaping defeat.

Gently, she brushed her finger over those gold letters and studied them again.

PASSPORT.

CHAPTER 3

Maybe I'm not the same, but it sure is.

Addisyn stood for a moment at the mouth of the Whistler Village. The sight that met her eyes was identical to her memories. For all the difference she noticed, her last visit could have been two days ago, not two years.

The snowcapped mountains still sparkled in the sun, still ringed the town like a circle of heavenly guardians. The village was as picture-perfect and inviting as ever, nestled in the heart of the peaks like a priceless jewel. And overhead still arched the unfathomable crystal of the British Columbia sky.

Yes, this had been a good destination. Whistler had always had a special magic for her, but right now, it felt more inviting than ever. It was her sanctuary, where she could be safe from the ghosts that lurked in her past and the real, live threats in her present. Like Brian.

Addisyn shifted her backpack higher on her shoulder. She glanced ruefully at the overstuffed bag and realized that in a town this quaint and well-groomed, she probably looked like a homeless person. She was wearing her oldest jeans and several shirts, surmounted by a puffy parka. In addition to her backpack, she had two more small carry bags looped around her arms and neck, and she was dragging a pull-behind suitcase. The stressful flight hadn't helped her appearance any either.

Embarrassment crawled up her neck as she remembered how the driver had eyed her when she boarded the bus at the airport. He'd probably questioned if she had the money for her fare. If only these people knew. Maybe today she was a nobody, but a week ago, she'd been a rising star. She fingered the small wallet in her pocket.

She still had the cash to prove it.

She set her jaw defiantly. Brian controlled all the Rising Star funds, but amazingly, he hadn't confiscated the prize money she'd won at competition after competition. Enjoying Brian's deceptive generosity, she hadn't needed the money… until now.

The slanting rays of the sinking sun were spilling shadows from all the buildings, shadows that seemed to creep like relentless wraiths toward Addisyn as she stood on the hill. She shrugged her shoulders uneasily, as if the motion could erase the omen. Better to turn her mind to more practical matters. Speaking of shadows, what time was it, anyway? It had to be like seven at night, right? Addisyn twisted her wrist to see her watch. Nope, only 5:07. She rolled her eyes. Jet lag was the worst, and her flight from New York had rewound the clock three hours.

Sunset would be in less than half an hour. She needed to get busy finding a place to stay. Addisyn began walking again and tilted her head as she considered her options. As she recalled, there were some really nice hotels up by the golf course, with panoramic windows and private spas. But maybe she should look for something a little more modest. Sure, she had plenty of money, but that didn't mean she should waste it on useless luxury—especially since she didn't know where she would get more money, or when.

The thought of her tenuous situation doubled her doubts about what had seemed like a great plan. She'd been resolute as her flight raced sunset across America, but when she first stepped off the airplane in Vancouver, she'd felt a sudden lurch—as though an earthquake had tilted her world. The two-hour bus ride to Whistler had only given her worries more time to incubate.

Part of her argued that this wasn't practical, that nobody just left their entire life and took off to a small town in another country on the other side of the continent. But the other part of her insisted that it was her only option—her last chance to grab hold of the final vestiges of who she'd been, try to examine the shattered slivers of her life and decide what was salvageable and what was only fit for the garbage.

Stop! Addisyn shook her head roughly. She was too tired tonight, too frazzled by all that had been happening to think clearly. Who said she had to make plans tonight, or tomorrow, or even next week? She'd just spend some time here, try to feel what her next move should be. Try to gain a respite from those demons at her heels. Try to remember who she had been—before the spotlight.

A blast of cooler air snatched her attention back to her current situation. The shadows had stretched themselves across the valley, and the air was thick with dusk. She needed a hotel before she was stranded on the streets of a Canadian border town during a frigid night.

The irony brought a small, twisted smile to her lips. The week before, she'd been one of America's finest figure skating stars, leaping for the moon and tolerably certain of reaching it. She'd spent her days training in professional accommodations and her nights relaxing in one of the poshest townhouses in New York City. Now, she was a nobody, an abandoned young woman dressed like a tramp, beating the bushes for the cheapest hotel.

But she was also free.

Fingers clumsy from the cold, she pulled out her smartphone and began searching. In a few minutes, she found the Gold Aspen Lodge for $46 a night. That was probably the cheapest she'd find. She sighed and rubbed her exhausted eyes. It would almost be worth blowing her cash to get a room in a nicer place. This was probably some rat-trap motel, and Addisyn hated cheap motel rooms. They made her skin crawl—probably because they reminded her of those days of running from her father.

The Gold Aspen was several blocks away, and Addisyn had to pass through the pedestrianized Whistler Village to get there. As she shuffled along the sidewalks, she couldn't help but feel a release of some of her tension, at least for the moment. No one could have resisted the town's magic on a twilit winter evening. Artisanal stores exuded a warm glow from the windows, and their quaint construction made Addisyn feel as if she'd wandered into a Lincoln Log town. Tourists rushed here and there— confidential couples smiling in each other's eyes, gaggles of effervescent young girls swinging shopping bags and giggling, elderly pairs perched on benches, families pushing strollers and towing young children. It was all so idyllic that Addisyn could feel the tightness in her chest easing. She decided to fold up her problems and lay them to rest, at least for a moment. With the snow that still drifted on the mountains and scrunched beneath her favorite suede boots, the place was a perfect Christmas card scene.

After all, despite the oddness of her situation, it was rather exhilarating just to be alone—to be solely responsible for her own welfare. No pandering to Brian's snits, no enduring Avery's lectures, no dodging reporters and concocting training schedules. Like the heroine of an epic tale, she'd transported herself to another country, assuming another role, another life, and certainly another state of mind.

The Gold Aspen Lodge was surprisingly difficult to locate, but after what felt like miles of wandering and more than a few wrong turns, Addisyn noticed its sign swinging in the breeze. Finally. She was in the best shape of her life, but still, she felt completely exhausted. The last few days had drained her more than any competition ever could.

Within minutes, she was in Room 312. It was actually much nicer than she'd expected, with a big window overlooking the Village, a thick green carpet on the floor, and a few other plain but solid wood furnishings. The twin bed was draped with a red plaid quilt that made the room feel almost homelike. Which was good, because this was home, at least for a while.

Kicking off the boots, Addisyn flopped back on the bed and stared at an Africa-shaped stain on the ceiling. In the fire of her rashness, she'd had no reservations, no qualms. She'd thrown her things—most of them—into the bags she now carried. She'd left a perfunctory note for Brian on the back of the couch—of course, he wouldn't be home for another day or two. Her sense of betrayal and search for escape had swept her along in an unconquerable tide. She'd bristled with righteous anger until it was too late to change her mind.

Now she was starting to collapse emotionally. She could feel it. The exhaustion dragged at her body and spirit as doubts hissed at her. Was it really wise to just leave like that? Throw herself into a strange environment?

Addisyn closed her eyes, trapping the tears inside. Suddenly every atom of her being cried out for Brian. She wanted his arms around her, wanted his breath on her cheek, wanted to hear him whisper to her that she was his world, that what he'd done had been for love, not money. She wanted to wake up in his arms in their cozy townhouse and laugh with him about her crazy bad dream.

You're sweet, you're cute, but you're not good enough. Suddenly the words blazed hot and brilliant in Addisyn's mind. She clenched her jaw. No, this was not a bad dream. And no, she would not pine over Brian. The man she'd known had been a fake, a façade. The true Brian Felding was ruthless, selfish. Even—her mind flew to the vise of his hands on her shoulders— violent.

Brian aside, there were many other valid reasons to leave New York City. She'd seen how the media treated other "failed" athletes. The sight wasn't pretty. She wasn't going to stick around and let the tabloids, like rabid jackals, shred her into tiny bits. She'd seen a taste of that already…that video… "Dreams Over for Addisyn Miles." The words were still as sour as a sip of vinegar.

Come on, Addisyn. This was no way to start a new beginning! Addisyn sat up on the bed, crossing her legs and staring out the window. Even in the indigo February night, Whistler Mountain was still visible, the snow on its knobby slopes making it look almost otherworldly under a few perfect stars. Yes, there was no doubt Whistler was a special place—a very special place. She'd made the right choice.

Now if only her heart would agree.

Addisyn tried to lift the leadenness from her soul by humming a few bars of "Wake Me Up." No use. She lay back down and drew her knees to her chest—a position she'd found comforting ever since she was a small child, when she'd curl up like this to shelter her soul while her dad raged downstairs. She tried to focus on the mountain, tried to buoy her spirits. For the first time—maybe more so than when she'd held the world in her hands—there truly was nothing holding her back. She was free—free to do whatever she liked, to take as much time as possible figuring things out, to be gentle and kind to herself. But somehow the prospect was no longer invigorating—it now sounded frightening, lonely, even exhausting. And all that pounded in her mind was one phrase, over and over: *"Dreams over for Addisyn Miles…Dreams over for Addisyn Miles…Dreams over for Addisyn Miles…"*

Yes. The dream was over. And without her dreams—what was left?

That was what she'd come to Whistler to find out.

△△   △△   △△

THE SUNRISE WAS exquisite this morning—breathtaking colors, flung against the doorway of the heavens by the Maker of the universe.

It was the kind of sunrise Avery loved best, when tiny tufts of cloud caught and held the sunbeams, like fluffy lambs skipping through the sky. She drew a deep breath and leaned more securely against the railing of her porch—breathing in the glory, watching the wonder, cherishing these misty moments of elusive artistry before the less subtle beauty of full daylight was upon her.

El Shaddai, thank You for this glorious morning. Avery heard a whoosh of wings and glanced up to see a lovely Clark's nutcracker skimming over the treetops, the bird's smooth body a grey so delicate that it was more beautiful than any color. She shivered suddenly for no other reason than a jolt of joy, a burst of radiant love for this place and the God Who ruled it.

This is Your country, O El Shaddai. Thank You for the privilege of living in it. Thank You for making mountains, for forming the earth and calling it good. Thank You for the birds and the animals and the trees. All creation sings Your praise.

Every morning while she watched the sunrise, Avery prayed some version of this prayer. No matter how long she lived in Colorado, she'd never lose sight of the wonder that she was blessed enough to live here, among the mountains—or the joy that she was alive at all.

I praise You, El Shaddai. Marvelous are Your works. Avery focused on the dirt road that bumped in front of her cabin. *Lord, that way is Estes Park...it's full of people, some people who have spent their whole lives here...don't let familiarity blind them to the miracle this place is. Let them see Your fingerprints in it...let them come to know You through the things You have made, like Paul said in Romans 1...*

Since coming to Colorado, Avery had met some veterans of the area—people who were born in the mountains, grew up in the very shadow of the High Peaks, and were now raising children of their own. How they could live their lives with their heads down, ignoring the glory of the place in which they lived, was a mystery to Avery, but certainly some did. They became calloused to the beauty.

Avery knew she never would. The road to this place had been too agonizing for her to ever cease to revel in the contrast between these mountains, the temple of the Lord, and the hell she'd clawed her way out of.

For a moment, she could feel it again…that insidious darkness, creeping from behind, stretching greedy talons toward her soul. She shuddered and abruptly changed her position. No time for torturous reflections this morning. This moment belonged to El Shaddai and her.

El Shaddai. Of all God's titles throughout the Bible, this was the most precious to Avery. She remembered how excited she'd been as a new believer to study the attributes of her Master, how many hours she'd spent with a dilapidated Bible she had purchased for $1.75 at a Goodwill store. It had been the Names of God translation, and Avery had been awestruck to learn how many different titles were bestowed upon the Lord.

There was *El Elyon*, God Most High…*El Rapha*, God Who Heals…*El Roi*, God Who Sees…but the most beautiful was *El Shaddai.*

God of Strength. God of Power. God of Provision.

And best of all, God of the Mountains.

God of the Mountains. All around Avery, the soothing aroma of peace spiraled skyward. Behind her log cabin, pines pointed dark green fingers to the heavens…and the Lord of the heavens. Around her, rocky mountain crags stood immovable, rugged monuments to His faithfulness. In the sky, birds swooped and soared, secure in the care of the God Who counted the sparrows.

Was there anyone who could come here and not feel the power, the way that the land throbbed with God's very heartbeat? This was His country, after all. The native habitat of El Shaddai, the vigorous, the powerful God, not the anemic copy of Him that was locked up in sanctimonious church buildings.

Pure gratitude gently lapped at the edges of Avery's soul. She lifted her face to the heavens and closed her eyes, letting the sunlight bathe her countenance. *El Shaddai, I praise You. I love You, Jesus, my Lord. Holy Spirit, breathe into me.* She held out her arms. *Fill me full and overflowing. Help me walk in Your paths and follow Your ways. Grant me a clean heart before You, God of my salvation.*

Avery smiled and opened her eyes. All around her, the new day was unfolding. In New York City, each day had been another rut, another maddening rush and dash that sucked away her spirit and dwindled to soul-numbing nothingness. But here, every new day was an invitation—a bejeweled necklace to wear with grace, not a chain to struggle against.

The last edge of the sun cleared the horizon. The shade patches on the snow were clear-cut now, purple shadow puppets leaning toward her cabin. Avery shivered and turned to head inside. The late February air was bone-chilling, and even with the sun shining brightly, the temperature probably wouldn't rise much above freezing that day.

Sure enough, when Avery was ready to leave for work an hour later, the thermometer on the porch was huddled at twenty-four degrees. Tugging a ski hat over her head, she pushed her hair behind her ears. It still felt a little strange, having only shoulder-length hair. For most of her life, her hair had been long, but she'd had it cut right before coming to Estes Park. No sense in having to spend extra time grooming long hair that would only get in the way outside. Her sleek lob was much simpler—just like her life in the mountains.

"Mercy, you ready?" Avery glanced down at her black Labrador Retriever. The dog seemed to grin back, waving her tail so exuberantly that she knocked over Avery's pair of hiking boots. She enjoyed Avery's job working in Laz Jobe's outdoor shop as much as Avery herself did. And no wonder. Mercy spent the hours there in luxury—snoozing in the back room, sniffing new merchandise, occasionally munching the treats Laz gave her. Now she darted out the door ahead of Avery at a purposeful trot.

In the driveway, sun glinted brilliantly off Avery's truck—a 2001 Nissan Frontier, forest green, that looked like the automotive version of a tramp. The paint was peeling, the leather seats were cracking, and the gearshift made a terrifying grinding noise at times. Yet Avery was still proud of it. It was a good truck—solid, reliable, and trustworthy. Much more than she could say about the people who'd been in her life so far.

Mercy, accustomed to this routine, hopped into the passenger seat and nestled down. Avery slid the key into the ignition and the truck coughed and rattled to life, backing out of the driveway with only a few jerks along the way. Then began the twenty-minute commute to work.

Yes, this truck was a good old truck. It had carried her, after all, on the most important journey of her life—eighteen hundred miles from her tiny apartment in New York City all the way to her new home in Estes Park, Colorado.

Avery's breath stalled in her throat. She swallowed hard, remembering the horrible year she'd gone through after—well, after Brian had stolen her sister. Just when she'd thought she couldn't bear things any longer, just when she'd feared the darkness would swallow her soul completely…El Shaddai had made a way. She'd bought a flimsy road map, loaded her sparse possessions, and taken off, driving into the sunset, until she came to Estes Park. When she arrived, she could tell she was home by the feel—the way the sun made her smile, the song of joy her heart sang in the mountains, the fact that she understood what the wind was saying in the pine trees. This was where she was supposed to be.

She'd always wanted to live in the mountains, after all. Always yearned for wilderness, for a place where she could gaze forever and not see power lines and interstate highways and the insolent neon of gas station signs. Growing up in an elegant suburban house outside Syracuse, where her father's psychiatric practice was based, had taught her early on how wearisome and unnatural that kind of life felt—a life of deadly safety, totally disconnected from the natural cycles of the earth—seasons and moon phases and rainfall and sunshine. And the years she'd lived in New York City had been—

Avery shuddered. No sense going back to the past. Hadn't she promised herself she would only look ahead, only give praise for each sunrise and thanks for each sunset? The eight months she'd spent in Estes Park were healing her, she could tell—soothing the scars. She wouldn't undo all the good that had been done so far by ruminating on the difficult and incurable past.

She leaned over and rubbed Mercy's head. "Ready for work?"

As Avery made the final turn onto Marys Lake Road and marveled at the jewels of morning sun twinkling on the water, she decided the appropriate response right now wasn't fear, or guilt, or regret.

The proper—the holy—response was gratitude.

THERE WAS A bright light on Addisyn's face. A single, intense beam, like a spotlight. She was at a competition, the most important one of her life. But as she stood alone on the ice, she couldn't remember a single step of her routine.

From the front row of the audience, Brian scowled at her, ugly anger twisting his features. Addisyn wanted to run from the rink, but then she found her feet couldn't move. She was stuck to the ice—unable to escape the accusing finger of that bright light, laughing at her failure.

As Addisyn's eyes flew open, she shot to a sitting position on the bed, panting with the emotion of the image. Glancing wildly around the room, she squinted against the glare of the sunshine streaming in the window.

Her heartrate began to settle as she shook her head, trying to detangle reality from dream. She wasn't glued to the ice—she was safely in Whistler. And there was no unfriendly spotlight, just the bright sunshine on her face.

Wow, had she really been so tired that she'd fallen asleep in her clothes? Evidently. She rubbed her scratchy eyes, then massaged the back of her neck. Her hair was a tangled mess, and her face felt greasy from the all-night makeup exposure. Great. What a way to start this excursion off.

Well, a hot shower and some fresh clothes would rejuvenate her. Yet as Addisyn finished dressing thirty minutes later and shook the excess water droplets from her hair, she realized her soul still felt flat and heavy. She paused in front of the mirror and peered at her eyes. They looked uncertain—lonely—scared. Defeated.

Losing had that effect on her.

With a frown, she turned from the mirror and paced aimlessly across the floor. She felt as dizzy as if she'd just wrong-footed a combination spin. What was she doing here? The reality of her isolation struck her with the force of a freight train. She was alone in British Columbia for an indefinite period of time with a limitless number of unspecified options. What could be more bewildering?

Hysterical laughter suddenly bubbled upwards. "Well. Here I am." Her announcement echoed in the empty room. The giggles continued—born out of sheer nervousness. The air around her seemed as ominous as the silence before applause.

Pull yourself together! First things first—she was starving. What if she went and had breakfast in one of those cute coffee shops? Well, why not? Whistler was a tourist town, and right now, that's all she was—just a tourist on a somewhat unconventional vacation.

No need to bother with her usual long makeup routine. Addisyn grabbed her purse from the nightstand and wriggled her feet into the suede boots from yesterday. They might not have been designed for snow, but they were the warmest footwear she had. Plus, they always gave her confidence.

And she needed plenty of that.

△△   △△   △△

Love You A Latte. Addisyn smiled at the clever wordplay over the door of the little coffee shop. She stepped beneath the pink-and-white awnings and peered through the glass door. Well, why not get breakfast here?

A bell over the door tinkled as she entered, the delicious fragrance of coffee and spices welcoming her. The wood floor was a deep brown, and the sun splashed through the windows onto the Corian countertop. One young woman with frizzy blonde hair darted about, preparing some elaborate concoction for a tall guy leaning on the counter. Addisyn slid him a cursory glance. She could just see that he was wearing a heavy nylon coat, jeans, and a beanie over shoulder-length black hair.

"Here you are, sir. One Cuban latte." With a bright smile, the barista handed the cup to the man and turned to Addisyn. "Yes, ma'am?"

"I'd like a glazed donut please. Chocolate." Addisyn grinned inwardly. Glazed chocolate donuts were taboo for future Olympians. She was definitely going to enjoy this breakfast. "And—" Well, she'd never drunk coffee before, but wasn't the whole point of this trip about disassociating from her past life? "I'd like a cup of coffee."

"Yes, ma'am." The young girl gestured to a blackboard scrawled with an overwhelmingly abundant list of choices, most of which were unfamiliar to Addisyn. "What kind?"

"Uh…" Addisyn stared at the board, scanning the list of names. What was the difference between a mocha and a latte? How did you pronounce either one? "Uh…I want…an espresso." The words sounded lame even to her.

The girl smiled, a bit patronizingly. "Well, actually all our coffee is espresso. It's a brewing style."

Addisyn felt heat squirming up her cheeks. Here she'd been in Whistler for less than twelve hours, and she was already embarrassing herself. "Um…I guess you can tell I don't know much about coffee." She gave a weak laugh.

"If I may suggest, get the Cuban. Cuban latte, demerara sugar, tiny splash of vanilla. It'll be the best thing that ever happened to you."

Startled at the voice behind her, Addisyn spun around to see the guy in the nylon coat. His close-cropped dark beard parted, and he smiled disarmingly. "Trust me on that."

Addisyn couldn't find words to reply. Her eyes were tracing the man's face, studying his features. It wasn't his good looks that had caught her attention; it was his familiarity. *Where have I seen him before?*

"The Cuban?"

"Yes, ma'am." The guy had a reassuring way of speaking, steady and smooth and at ease. He held up his cup. "Promise you. It's the best ever. I drink one every morning before work."

"That he does." The barista smiled at him, clearly appreciating his handsome appearance.

"Okay, then." Addisyn cleared her throat. "I'll take the, uh, Cuban latte." She turned back to the guy. "Thanks for the hint."

"No problem."

Surely he would leave now, but instead, he took a sip from his coffee and smiled at her again. Almost as if he were waiting for her to say something else.

"Do you live here in Whistler?" She hoped the question didn't seem impolite. Maybe she'd seen him on her first visit, though it seemed unlikely she would remember a chance encounter this long.

"Yep. I've lived here all my life." He leaned on the counter casually and glanced out the window at the morning sunshine with pride in his gaze. "It's a great place."

Maybe he just had one of those universal faces. Not really, though. His eyes were especially striking, anything but ordinary. She'd thought they were green, but in the sunlight from the window, they looked almost blue.

"Ever been to Whistler before?"

A common question, but somehow, this guy had a way of making the dullest platitudes seem interesting. Or maybe it was just him that Addisyn found interesting. She narrowed her eyes. "Wait, now how do you know I'm not from around here?"

"No accent." The man winked at her.

"Caught." She smiled lightly. "I'm from America. Just visiting." She turned her attention to the barista as she claimed her order and fumbled in her pocket for some dollars, but she could still feel him watching her.

"America, nice."

"Yeah." If only she could mumble a magic spell and have a locker of witty banter at her command. This guy probably thought she was a half-witted dud. Not, of course, that it mattered. At all.

She took a sip of the coffee and smiled. The rich, nutty flavor seemed to sparkle in her insides. "Good coffee. Thanks for the tip."

The morning sun reflected in his eyes as he smiled at her. He had a very attractive smile, slow, unhurried. And he tipped his head to one side while he did it. Addisyn couldn't help but admire the effect.

He offered his hand. "I'm Darius Payne."

"Nice to meet you—uh—Mr. Payne." How old was he, anyway? He looked fairly young, but he seemed to carry a certain seriousness— melancholy, maybe—that didn't match his years.

"Oh, call me Darius." His beard parted in another dazzling smile. "And you are?"

Why couldn't she think today? "Addisyn. Addisyn Miles." She panicked for a moment. Had she just blown her anonymity? Should she have given a fake name? The next instant she chided herself for her unreasonableness. Really, how could some guy in another country have heard of her? He probably knew nothing about figure skating and cared even less.

"Well, Addisyn, the pleasure is all mine." He stepped back, folded his arms. "Are you staying in Whistler long?"

"I'm—I'm not sure yet." Could she sound any more pathetic?

He nodded politely. "I hope to see you around again while you're here." He backed toward the door, but his gaze never left her face. "I have to get to work. Bye."

"See ya." Addisyn waved, trying to seem casual. Watching the guy stride purposefully out the door and toward his car, she scrambled through her memory, searching for his face. There was some kind of mystery about him. She could just feel it. Good grief, now she sounded like her sister, with her crazy intuition. But still…

"Where in America do you live?" The barista's question snapped Addisyn back to reality.

"Um…New York City." Addisyn took a sip of her coffee to avoid answering anything more. Why did she feel more like an escapee from justice than a famous figure skater? The fact that she'd even considered going by a pseudonym made her feel six inches high.

"Cool." The girl grabbed a rag from the cabinet behind her and began swiping the counter. Suddenly her elbow caught a stack of Styrofoam cups, which tumbled to the ground.

"Here, I'll help you!" Addisyn bent and began gathering the cups. "Are these trash now?"

"Yeah, unfortunately." The girl knelt to help her. Between the two of them, they quickly collected the mess.

"I'm super clumsy." The girl dumped the cups in the trash can and brushed her palms together with an embarrassed air. "Happens all the time."

"Don't worry about it." Addisyn felt a little sorry for the barista. "Say, are you the only one working here?"

"Yeah, we're shorthanded at the moment. My aunt owns this place, and she used to work here some, but she's visiting some friends in Toronto for the summer. And there was a guy named Jeffrey that worked here, but he ended up moving to Ottawa to work for his cousin's business." The girl's eyes brightened. "Hey, are you looking for a job? We need someone!"

"I—" The words caught in Addisyn's throat. Of course she wasn't looking for a job. Or was she? At some point she would have to have a source of income, but she didn't even know if she were staying in Whistler long-term, and—she forced her brain to let go. These days, her thoughts were like a skein of yarn that had been dropped and become unwound—tangled and sinuous and never-ending. She lifted her cup to take another sip of coffee.

"I sure do miss Jeffrey." Fortunately the girl seemed to have dismissed the job offer. "Not just because of the help, but because he was sorta cute. You know, in a way." She giggled. "Not like Darius though. You know, I think you caught his eye for sure." The girl jerked her chin toward the door where Darius had just left and winked coyly at Addisyn.

Somehow the coffee burned down Addisyn's airway instead of her throat. She coughed violently. "I—*what?*"

"Caught his eye." The girl sounded matter-of-factly confident. She grinned smugly and turned to wipe up a spill on the counter. "Believe me, Darius Payne does not look at many girls that way." She shrugged a shoulder. "He's kind of moody. Stand-offish, if you know what I mean."

"He seemed friendly." The words were out before Addisyn could explain to herself why she felt the need to defend him.

"I guess. He's just different. Dreamy, though." The girl batted her eyelashes.

Addisyn frowned. For some reason, the girl's comments were seriously annoying her. "He said he comes in every morning before work." It wasn't so much an observation as a distraction.

"Uh-huh. Guess where he works?" Without waiting for a response, the girl answered her own question. "At iClimb Whistler."

"What?" This girl was speaking a different language.

"iClimb Whistler. The climbing center." When she saw Addisyn's confusion still didn't disappear, she added, "He takes groups climbing up Whistler Mountain. Every day."

"Wow." Addisyn looked out the window at the mountain with awe. She couldn't imagine climbing it once, let alone several times a week. "That's impressive."

"Sure is." The bell over the door chimed merrily, and the girl called a welcome to a young woman in a cream-colored cardigan. She smiled at Addisyn. "Enjoy your stay in Whistler. And hey, don't forget about the job!"

As Addisyn stepped out of the shop into the cold air, she couldn't help looking down the street for the man, even though she knew he was long gone. Oh, she wasn't swayed by the flirty girl's idle comments. It was just a weird feeling she couldn't shake—Darius Payne wasn't a stranger.

Somehow, somewhere, she'd seen him before.

CHAPTER 4

After having lived an exceptionally crazy and chaotic life, Addisyn had expected to appreciate downtime more.

For seven days, she'd had nothing—*nothing*—to do.

Seven days of Nothing. No PR interviews, no gym workouts, no date nights with Brian. Not even a phone call—she'd turned her phone off after her first night in Whistler and hadn't restarted it all week.

She should have felt relaxed, rejuvenated. But instead she felt unanchored and purposeless, like a small boat turned loose from its moorings and left to drift on an enormous sea. The freedom had become mere blankness.

Addisyn stepped aside to let a group of tourists hurry by. She was wandering about the Whistler Village—a daily habit that had become a necessity. Roaming around, looking at the people, the shops, the mountains.

Looking anywhere, in fact, except inside herself.

She'd hoped she would begin to heal in such a peaceful place, begin to feel the cracks in her soul shrinking. Instead, she felt lost, strangely bewildered, uncertain of…well, everything.

Perhaps it was finally time to do the one thing she'd been putting off.

Fifteen minutes later, Addisyn slowly made her way across the herringbone-patterned sidewalk. Black lampposts gave the area a Dickens look. She stopped to examine one of the colorful banners hinged to the posts. WHISTLER, it proclaimed in large block letters, the swathes of azure blue and lavender purple blending harmoniously.

And there, directly in front of her, was the sight that had haunted her night and day for four years. The sight that was at once her greatest love and her most fiendish fear. The sight she had once dreamed of tattooing on her arm, along with a year and a location.

A larger-than-life silver statue of the five Olympic rings, mounted at the entrance to the Whistler Olympic Village. Home of the 2010 Winter Games.

Everything else blurred into the background, the rings overshadowing her entire being. Addisyn didn't allow herself to turn away. She needed this time to let the image sink into her. To acknowledge her broken dream and then let it float gently away.

Her eyes traveled beyond the rings and lingered on the beautiful facilities of the Whistler Athletes' Center. It boasted a gorgeous eighty-room lodge and many smaller buildings—gymnasiums, arenas, weight rooms, swimming pools. And it all existed for one purpose: to help train exceptional athletes.

Addisyn had been one of those exceptional athletes. Because of the Rising Star endorsement, she and Brian had been able to attend the Next Wave conference in this very center. It was six weeks of intensive training, where expert coaches provided assistance to promising young athletes of all nationalities. Addisyn's training partner at the conference had been from Czechoslovakia, and she'd met skaters from many other countries— several Canadians, of course, along with Russians, Japanese, Lithuanians, Argentinians. Many of them, having started their training earlier than Addisyn, had easily qualified to be Olympians, starring in the next Winter Games.

The experience had been one of her life's high points. Memories, at once beautifully delicious and intensely painful, rushed through the floodgates of her mind. She could still identify the window of the room that had been hers, still recall the name of her favorite coach, still envision the path she'd walked to the rink each day to train.

She began walking closer, slowly drawing nearer to the mecca of Olympic training. *I should be there now. Getting ready for…*

"Excuse me!" She hadn't even noticed the golf cart that had pulled up beside her. A burly fellow in overalls peered at her.

"Yes?"

"I'm sorry, ma'am, but you'll have to turn around. Just athletes allowed here." The man gave her a quick, apologetic smile and pointed to a sign she'd missed: ONLY AUTHORIZED PERSONNEL BEYOND THIS POINT.

"I…" The words shrank and stuck. What was the use? The man was right. She had no business being here.

She wasn't an athlete anymore.

She swallowed the burning in her throat and forced a glassy smile. "Yes, sir. I'm sorry, I didn't notice the sign." Then she turned and walked away from her dream.

She wasn't authorized. Leave that to the likes of Sheila Harbor.

Unbidden, tears crawled down her cheeks. Angrily she swiped at them with the back of her hand. How could things change so quickly?

She ducked her head and hurried back to the entrance. Enough exploring for one day. She'd head for the gym and hit the weight equipment—the second component of her highly simplified new life, the second anesthetic she used to numb the emptiness she felt.

At the rings, she paused one more time. This was important, she knew—a path to acceptance. If only it didn't have to hurt like crazy.

People walked by, laughing and chatting. A lean guy with a chiseled face zipped by on an upscale bicycle with handlebars curved like rams' horns. A tall young woman with blonde hair posed with a dark-haired man for a selfie in front of the rings. But Addisyn felt as though she'd been removed to a deeper world, a world beyond the meager influence of such trivialities. Mechanically, she took a step forward, then another. The rings seemed to draw her in the way that a tantalizing flower might entice a hummingbird. Only the flower was, and always had been, just out of reach.

She stepped onto the little platform almost reverently. Very slowly, in the time it took a lone scrap of cloud to brush against the sun, she placed her hand along the side of the sculpture.

She didn't know what she was expecting—something more, maybe, than just the painfully cold metal, the unchanging silver curve. For a moment she breathed in, breathed out, waited. For what?

"This was all I ever wanted." The whisper shivered in the air. Leaning her forehead against the rings, she struggled to not cry. To not lose hope. To not writhe in the scorching flames of abandoned dreams. "All I wanted."

"Excuse me, would you mind taking our picture?" Addisyn snapped her head up to see the blonde girl holding out an iPhone uncertainly.

"Oh!" She quickly took the phone, made a feeble smile. Hopefully the girl would think her eyes were watering from the wind and cold rather than from sharp-edged emotion.

She snapped a couple shots, the guy's arms wrapped around the young woman's waist while both of them beamed with excitement.

"Thanks! These are good." The girl seemed impressed. "Do you live around here?"

"Just visiting." Addisyn smiled politely.

"Us too. Actually, this is our honeymoon." A sparkle danced within the girl's eyes.

"That's wonderful." As raw as Addisyn's heart was, she couldn't hold back a slight smile. The two seemed so energetic, so happy together. "Congratulations."

"Hey, Catherine!" The man had wandered to a display sign at the other end of the platform. "Come check this out!"

"Thanks again!" The girl waved to Addisyn and started to walk away, then suddenly turned. "Wait, do you want your picture in front of the rings?"

Addisyn stared once again at their endless circles. Those rings. Strong and proud and unflinching. She'd attempted to enter that circle, but it was charmed, a magic place where she could not go. She cleared her throat. "That's okay. Thanks."

She didn't need a picture. Those rings were emblazoned on her heart more indelibly than she could have ever tattooed them on her arms.

△△　△△　△△

WINTER HAD BEEN relentless, but now spring was gradually peering around the corners, dropping little hints of its presence. By the last week in March, the temperatures were warmer, but the fabled Pacific Northwest rain had also come to visit and didn't seem to realize it had overstayed its welcome.

Addisyn attempted to shake some of the raindrops from her hair as she entered the gym—or rather, as she blew through the front door in a curtain of precipitation. She'd naively assumed an umbrella would protect her during her walk from the hotel. Big mistake. Apparently Canadian rain fell parallel with the ground.

The gym was the other half of her life—the half not spent wandering through Whistler. A girl accustomed to practically living in the gym couldn't be expected to quit exercising cold turkey. So even though Addisyn had often moaned about sore muscles and tough workouts in her past life, she was now voluntarily putting herself through equally grueling routines most days. What a joke her mind was.

Elliptical first. Addisyn gripped the handles and began pumping her legs—faster, fiercer. She bumped up the incline factor on the display and churned even harder, until she could feel sweat trickling down her back under her purple tank top. Her thighs burned with the exertion, but she gritted her teeth and kept pumping.

Exercise was the one thing that was easy. Not easy as in effortless— her legs were now shaking with the intensity—but easy as in—controllable, maybe. Simple. Predictable.

Walking endless loops through Whistler, staring at the Olympic rings, and lying on her bed in the Gold Aspen were the activities in which her mind ran faster than her body, trying to desperately understand what in the world was going on. Scrambling to unravel the tangled threads of her life, to figure out what had brought her here and what she needed to do to fix it and where she needed to go next. She vacillated between crying and enjoying the scenery, between wanting to forget she'd ever lived anywhere else to craving the next flight back to NYC. She could almost feel the mental groove that the repetitious thoughts had worn in her brain. And instead of resolving itself, the uncertainty was becoming more and more intense—as though, in the back of her mind, a yawning black chasm of question marks was slowly spreading, threatening to engulf her soul altogether.

But in exercise, her feet could outpace her mind. Exercise was comforting, familiar. Exercise required no complex decisions, no analysis of consequences. Just pump the iron, keep the tempo, don't forget to breathe. Exercise numbed the mental pain, gave her mind a chance to quit floundering in all the craziness and just rest while her body did the work for a change.

She hadn't stopped by the little coffee shop anymore, although she'd considered doing so a few times. Occasionally she found herself wondering if they were still hiring and if she should apply. It might give her a purpose, some order to her life, if nothing else. But she couldn't promise permanence. Was it fair to take a job when her life was such a bundle of loose ends?

Enough with the mental gymnastics. Addisyn forced her fears to shut down and pushed herself through an intense workout for the next hour and a half, combining cardio and strength training and using nearly every machine in the gym. By the time she finished, her body was aching and sweat was making salty tracks down her face, but her outlook was much more cheerful. Well, maybe *cheerful* was the wrong word. Hopeful, perhaps. After all, she was a fighter. She'd figure something out. And realistically, she had to admit that the weather might be influencing her dreary mood. She hadn't seen the sun now for four days straight. Before coming to Whistler, she'd usually thought of Seattle as the target for persistent rainstorms, but now she realized the rest of the Pacific Northwest was apparently plagued by them also.

Thoughts of the rain reminded her of her miserable walk to the gym and useless umbrella. Addisyn grimaced. She wasn't going back to the hotel on foot—no way. She didn't feel like facing the downpour, especially since darkness was rapidly approaching. Plus, her workout had left her feeling limp and exhausted. What about calling an Uber? She fished her phone out of her bag and opened the app, pressing the button for the nearest driver.

She peered out the window into the greyness of the early evening. The rain made a rhythmic gurgling sound in the street drains. Already street lights were beginning to flicker to life against the darkening blue sky.

"Hello, hello!"

Addisyn knew that voice. She turned quickly to see the guy from the coffee shop. Darius.

"Hey." She felt her cheeks turning even pinker than the exercise had left them. Almost without thinking she brushed back her hair. Why did she have to see him when she looked like a mess? Her embarrassment was eased somewhat when she realized that he'd obviously been working out too. He wore black shorts and a black long-sleeved shirt made from some kind of slick, quick-dry material. His hair, which she now noticed was not black but instead dark brown, was pulled back into a short ponytail.

"You called for an Uber." He grinned, holding up his phone, then gave a mock bow. "Your coach awaits, m'lady."

"Wait, you're an Uber driver?" Addisyn laughed. "I had no idea—the girl at the coffee shop said you worked at a climbing center—" *Shut up,* she ordered herself. The last thing she needed was for this guy to think she'd been covertly inquiring about him.

Darius paused to wipe his face with a towel slung over his shoulder. "Yup, I work at iClimb Whistler, but I drive for Uber in the afternoons and evenings. Whenever I'm off work." He shrugged one shoulder. "Pretty painless way to earn a few bucks. Ready to go?"

"Sure thing." Addisyn followed Darius through the doorway. She appreciated the fact that he held the door for her to exit. Once outside, he opened an umbrella—bigger than hers—and held it over them both. "I'm parked right over there."

Together they hurried to a maroon Chevy Traverse, where Darius once again opened the passenger door for her, then ran to the driver's seat. In less than a minute, they were on their way back to the Gold Aspen.

The car was quiet except for the *shh-tikk* of the windshield wipers. "Care for some music?" Darius asked, breaking the silence. "I always let my passengers pick the station." He gestured to the radio.

"No, I'm good. Thanks." Addisyn didn't understand why she felt so awkward around Darius. She straightened the hem of her workout top, wishing she looked more presentable.

"I'm a little sweaty." She laughed self-consciously. "Hope I don't ruin your seats."

"Nah, don't worry about it. As you can probably tell, I've been working out myself. Hope my deodorant's doing its job." Darius laughed, and Addisyn joined in. Really, it seemed impossible to feel uncomfortable around him. He had such a nice way about him—slow and easy, like his smile.

"You work out a lot?" His lean frame attested to that, but she needed a conversation starter.

"Most days." He came to a halt at a red light, the wipers flashing frantically as the downpour intensified. "Actually, I usually go to Cardio City, across town, but they were closed today because of a major water leak, so I came here." His smile sparkled in the dim interior of the car as he gazed at her. "I sure am glad I did."

Addisyn dropped her eyes to her lap, but she couldn't keep from smiling all the same. Darius seemed so kind.

The light switched to green, and Darius accelerated, tires sloshing in the water. "So, Miss Addisyn, how are you enjoying Whistler?"

"Very much." It was true. Love for the city was growing in her daily, even in the midst of her perplexities.

"So you're from America." Darius cocked his head. "What brings you to Whistler?"

Addisyn hesitated. She wasn't ready to tell the whole truth—not yet. The story of shame and regret and crazy uncertainty was still too raw. She fumbled for some excuse, some impersonal reply that wouldn't give him a window to her within.

But for some reason, the words slipped out before she could catch them, fence them in behind walls of perfection. "I came here…looking for answers."

Instantly she regretted her comment. But when she glanced apprehensively at him, he was slowly nodding, as if he could understand totally. He kept his eyes on the road. "And have you found them?"

"Them?"

"The answers."

Addisyn looked out her window. The streetlights were in full bloom now, radiant in the dark but illuminating nothing. The headlights caught a green road sign that said **WHISTLER OLYMPIC VILLAGE →**

"No." She sighed. "Do—do you think I'm crazy?"

"Crazy? No way. Everybody needs answers at some time." Oh, his voice was so gentle. His eyes met hers for a second, and they shone with a compassion she didn't expect. "Lots of question marks floating around in this big old world, huh?"

She thought of Brian and skating and Avery and dreams and wishes and sorrows. "Yes." She waited for her voice to steady before she spoke again. "Are there—do you think there are answers? Out there somewhere?"

"I do." The resolve in Darius's voice was a rock, a fortress. "I believe in answers. I mean—at least—"

His words suddenly broke off, and Addisyn peered quizzically at him. Even though the car interior was mostly dark, lit only by the light off the street, she could see a pained expression in his eyes for a moment. He bit his lip silently, as if wincing at the ache from an old wound.

They were turning onto the street that led to the hotel, Addisyn noticed with surprise—and a little bit of regret. Darius pulled up to the breezeway outside the Gold Aspen. "Here we are."

"Thanks." She'd already paid for her ride through the app, but now she pulled out a tip and laid it quietly on the console, then grabbed her umbrella and opened the door before Darius could offer.

"Addisyn?"

"Yes?" She stopped, the door handle in her hand, rain chattering on her umbrella.

"Keep believing in your answers. Just ask the right questions and wait for the responses. They'll come."

Addisyn drew a long, deep breath—the first one in many days. Answers were coming. She believed it. "Okay." When was the last time anyone had been this kind? This compassionate? "Thank you."

"You have a good night." He smiled and gave her a little wave.

After Addisyn ate her dinner in the hotel dining room and took a warm shower, she sat cross-legged on her bed, finger-combing her wet hair and thinking about the evening. When she remembered Darius's face and the caring in his voice, she felt a wonderful sense of peace and comfort. He was such a kind man—strong but gentle. How sensitively he had held her soul tonight.

Yet something about him still perplexed her. She had seen him before. She was so sure of it. And why had he looked so sad when he spoke about answers?

Something told her Darius Payne hadn't received his answers yet.

Addisyn rose and went to her window. The rain was lighter now. Instead of roaring in a bleak monsoon, it now pattered gently like a warm harbinger of spring.

A surge of resolve and hope filled her soul. Addisyn would be patient. She would wait for her answers. But in the meantime, she would take control of her life, her choices. She would make a direction for herself. Right now—that direction was *here*.

△△   △△   △△

DARIUS GLANCED AT his console as he drove. Oh, there was a nice tip from Addisyn. He chuckled slightly. For a moment he'd forgotten that they were an Uber driver and a fare; they'd seemed more like friends out for a drive.

It had to have been their conversation. He shook his head, remembering the haunted look on her face. She needed something—something for which she was hunting desperately.

His mouth crooked in cynicism. Sure, he was the man to be dispensing life advice, all right. Why had he even said something like that, about searching for answers? He was in no way the wise sage or the skilled self-help coach. The mess he'd made of his past disqualified him from helping others find their path. Good grief, he was far from certain of his own.

He didn't expect magical solutions for himself. No, he'd blown those chances a long time ago—broken his soul when he still did have choices, and joy, and freedom. Before those things had indefinably vanished. But— well, for Addisyn it should be different. He wanted to believe it would happen for her, wanted to believe that a girl like her would get a square deal.

A girl who seemed far too good to be true.

Knock it off, Payne. He silently chided himself as he drove. But the part of his heart that tugged him toward Addisyn—what a pretty name, like a melody of music—was surprisingly persistent. That first glance in the coffee shop had absolutely taken his breath away. He'd never forget how sweet she looked, leaning on the counter, hair spilling over her shoulder like a waterfall. The way she tipped her head to one side, both shy and slightly sassy.

Quickly he shook his head, as if to send the thoughts scattering. *Come on, Payne. Get real, man.* Of course Addisyn was a nice girl, but thinking of her in that way would only lead to trouble. For heaven's sake, she might already be married. Or have a serious boyfriend. Good grief, he'd seen her only twice in his life. He knew practically nothing about her.

And that didn't even take into account the darker reasons, the reasons he couldn't get involved with her. He was washed up, damaged goods. He'd been born only twenty-three years ago, but he'd been through hellacious lifetimes of anguish since then. He had to face facts—he wasn't good enough for any girl.

Darius took a deep breath. A weight of sadness settled over him, as dark and foggy as the night. No, it was no use thinking of Addisyn, no use at all. Just an exercise in heartbreak—and he certainly didn't need more of that.

As he parked in his driveway and stepped out of the car, he noticed the rain had almost stopped. In fact, a few stars were just peeking out over Whistler Mountain.

He gazed at their bright pinpoints for a moment. The stars, the mountains—at one time, these had reminded him of his greatest answer.

Jesus.

But that was years ago. Lots of water under the bridge. God was— well, God and Darius didn't speak that often anymore.

But Darius still believed that somewhere in the crazy universe, answers truly existed. And if they did exist—as firmly and unwaveringly as he had once, in a brighter time, believed—then they would surely find their way to this girl.

A girl who was sweet—beautiful—captivating—whose eyes, even on this dark and soggy night, had held the promise of summer.

CHAPTER 5

Spring was a healing time of year. A time for growing, for rejoicing, for releasing the darkness and bitterness of whatever winter the soul had experienced.

Of course, today didn't look much like spring—never mind that the calendar heralded it as the vernal equinox. Avery put down the book she was reading and strolled to the large glass window of her log cabin. What little sunlight she'd seen today had been weak and diluted, and the weather was still cold enough to burn the inside of her nose when she stepped outside. March and April were the snowiest months in Estes Park, or so Laz had said.

With the landscape as sullen and forbidding as it had been on this day, Avery hadn't found her usual afternoon hike too inviting. Instead, she'd spent the last few hours doing chores around the cabin—housework, cleaning, laundry—and then curled up in cozy flannel clothing.

She peered across the snowy fields, watching the place where the High Peaks sprinted to the sky, their summits brooding within purple fog. From her cabin window, she could see forever.

To eternity.

It was still hard to believe that all of this—the cabin, the land, the incredible view—was, for all intents and purposes, the gift of a man who had hated her.

Whenever she remembered her father, it made her want to crawl into a hole and never come out, like a little kid still scared of the dark. An involuntary shudder darted over her as she pictured him in her mind—his deeply lined face, with iron-gray eyes that matched his hair. Ulysses Miles had been a venerated psychiatrist, a respected name in therapy and counseling circles. His extensive research had provided untold contributions to the field of mental health. In public circles, he was wealthy, distinguished, influential, and charming.

At home he was a monster.

Avery racked her mind, as she had so frequently over the years, for one instance, no matter how trifling, when her father had expressed any form of affection. When he had shown, for just one second, that he cared about someone besides himself.

The mental search always ended the same way: she couldn't remember a time. Because there hadn't been one.

The wind was intensifying even as the daylight faded. Avery watched gray clouds scud across the silver sky.

Chance—the god her father worshipped. He was a satirical atheist, a man who delighted in using his glittering intellect to make a mockery of faith. So virulent was his belief that he hadn't allowed God's Name to be spoken in his home.

But looking back now, Avery realized that she'd always known her father was dead wrong. She'd always believed in some sort of higher power—a divine Spirit that surrounded her, even in her bleakest moments. When a friend led her to Christ during her high school years, it wasn't an introduction—it was a homecoming. As if she'd finally put a name to a face she'd always known. And faith had empowered her—shown her just how heinous her father's conduct really was, shown her what love was supposed to be and how strong and mighty the heart of God was for her.

And created an unbridgeable tear between her and her father.

After her parents split and she and Addisyn were left with him, the darkness that had always filled their home became even denser—even though she hadn't believed that possible. That's when she'd made the biggest decision of her life. When she'd trusted the word of El Shaddai and thrown her destiny—and Addisyn's—into His loving hands.

Avery knew deep in her soul that it had all been worth it. She wouldn't change a thing about the four years she and Addisyn had lived alone in New York City. All the cheap motels, all the meals of ramen noodles, all the dead-end jobs, all the stress of keeping Addisyn in high school in New York. All the pent-up exhaustion she'd experienced, trying to be an adult at seventeen, living in a place that rubbed her soul backwards with its noise and stench and unrepentant ugliness. It had all been for her sister—so no price had been too great.

No, what Avery regretted came later. When her sister met Brian Felding. When she fell in love with the lure of his glitzy but artificial world.

And then the real regrets began, piling up faster than the clouds boiling over the mountains. First there had been her own uncertainty about how to handle the situation. She'd been so inexperienced, still broken herself and unprepared to deal with such a calamity. More than anything, she'd been terrified. And like a frightened animal caught in a trap, she'd panicked, fighting back with blind ferocity. She'd tried to force Addisyn to stay with her, to make the right choices—and in so doing, she'd burned the bridge between them entirely.

And now, she'd been completely shut out by her sister. The sister who had been her world. The sister for whom she'd lived in hell for four years— the sister for whom she'd do it all again tomorrow—the sister for whom she'd cried and bled and sweated, who now had forgotten her altogether. The day Addisyn left their apartment to move in with Brian had confirmed that. And if there had been any doubt, that had been erased the next day— when Avery tried to call her only to find her number had been disconnected.

That still ached and burned inside her heart. Avery pressed her palm gently against the glass, feeling its cold slickness. Outside, a violent gust of wind slapped the side of the house with chilling fury.

Avery had stayed in New York for over two years after that. Her life had been nothing more than mechanical—just a robotic performance of her daily routines because she had no other option. Even now, her throat tightened when she remembered how unspeakably nightmarish the time had been. There wasn't a word for the kind of pain that she'd experienced, a pain that tore and gnawed at her heart and soul.

Then the letters from the attorney had come. How the man had traced her, she had no idea. But he had news. Ulysses Miles had passed away from a brain aneurism. He'd named her his sole heir—leaving her the astounding inheritance that she'd later used to purchase her cabin and land.

The thought still made Avery shake her head. Why would her father be that generous in death when he'd been so brutal in life? Finally she'd decided it didn't matter. It was all a gift, not from her earthly father, but from El Shaddai—the Giver of all blessings.

Even then, she'd hesitated about leaving the city—silly doubts, caused by the even sillier hope that Addisyn would come to her senses and head home. She'd finally decided to leave her new address with a woman who worked at their old apartment complex. If Addisyn ever tried to track her, Maggie would be able to help her.

But apparently Addisyn had never given Avery a second thought.

Another mighty gust of wind, as if it were the weather blowing all these memories in. The log timbers of the house creaked, but they held firm. Avery shuddered slightly and wrapped her arms tightly around herself. It was time to stop. Time to reject this useless circling over old ground. Hadn't she promised herself she wouldn't rehash her mistakes with Addisyn? There was no point to it, after all. What was done…was done.

A shaft of sunlight suddenly cracked a cloud, spreading its warmth along the gray earth. Something about the contrast—the eternal hope of the sunshine pouring from the black clouds—created a release in her spirit.

Yes, her life had known dark valleys. But now it was bathed in light. The only important thing to remember was that she'd escaped that pain. She'd followed her spirit west and found a place of peace on the rugged crests of the Rockies. And now, she could never be hurt again by all that she had left behind.

Including her sister.

△△ △△ △△

SPRING IN WHISTLER arrived leisurely, but surely. The rains came more frequently, drowning the old snow. Soon flowers began peeking from behind grassy hedges. Instead of a watery warmth from a faraway gray sky, the sun was now larger than life, beaming with promise and potential.

Addisyn couldn't believe the changes in the landscape. It was a far cry from that dreary night at the gym, when Darius had driven her home.

"Hand me a spoon, will ya?" Her coworker's voice broke into her daydreaming.

"Sure." Addisyn grabbed a spoon from the metal jar on the back counter.

Taking the job at Love You A Latte had been one of her best decisions so far. She'd been working there for almost a month and found herself enjoying it far more than she'd thought possible. Something about creating the specialty drinks seemed like an artistry, reminding her almost of the poetry of skating. She liked the cheerful atmosphere, the delicious aromas, and even Chelsea—though she could be annoying at times.

"I think we're set." Chelsea swept the area with an expert glance. "I'm gonna open up."

"Sounds good to me." Addisyn resisted the urge to roll her eyes. Chelsea made a big production each morning of opening the shop at seven thirty on the dot—as though there were lines of customers outside, holding their breath in anticipation. As usual, Chelsea strode purposefully to the glass doors and flicked on the pink-and-teal neon OPEN sign with a flourish, then unlocked the doors. "We are officially open for business!" she cried, as if it were the most exciting event of the day.

Addisyn just shrugged and lifted the lid of the big icemaker. So far, so good. Yesterday it had begun spasmodically freezing up. Chelsea would be making a trip to Vancouver on Thursday to buy its replacement, but until then, this one had to be guarded.

Chelsea sauntered back behind the counter. "How's the ice machine?"

"Still working." Addisyn slammed the door shut and looked around the shop, watching the way the sun splashed honey-colored squares on the wood floor. The first customers would arrive soon.

Including Darius.

Looking for something to do, she began idly straightening the contents of the counter. Chelsea slumped against one of the barstools and pulled out her phone. Probably scrolling through Facebook. It hadn't taken Addisyn any time to learn that Chelsea was a social media fiend.

"Addisyn, are you on Facebook?"

Addisyn's heart gave a wild leap and then took off running. "Uh…not really."

Why had she never thought about that? Never considered that anyone who found her on social media would know every detail of her past?

She hadn't posted anything since the night of Sectionals, but her old content dealt almost exclusively with the two things she now wanted to conceal the most—Brian and skating. If Chelsea—of all people—found out…

"Not really?" Chelsea giggled. "Either you're on Facebook or you're not, right?"

"Right…well…what I meant was, I have an account, but I don't post anything." The statement was true. She made a mental note to deactivate her account as soon as she was off work.

"Oh." Chelsea's tone had lost interest. She sighed and—to Addisyn's great relief—laid her phone down. "No fun." She made a pouty face. "What's the use of having Facebook if you don't do anything with it?"

The danger was far from over. Addisyn hated the feeling. Would she always have to keep looking over her shoulder? She stopped herself. No sense peering too far ahead. "I had to get it…for work."

"Really?" Chelsea looked at her with renewed curiosity. "What kind of work did you do in the States? I don't think you ever told me."

By a saving grace, Addisyn noticed the container of straws was empty except for three or four. "Hey, do we have more straws?"

"Yes! In the back room. I meant to grab a new box before we left last night. Be right back." Chelsea scurried away, the conversation apparently dropped.

Addisyn allowed herself to sag limply against the counter. What a close call. But relief that she'd escaped detection was overpowered by the dread the event had raised—the dose of reality it had rudely forced in her face.

Did she think she could hide forever? Never divulge who she was, where she had come from? People didn't just vanish and start new lives these days. Too many paper trails—government records, IDs, websites. And of course, social media. There was no way to just blot out twenty years of life simply by changing location. The truth about Addisyn was as close as Chelsea's sleek pink iPhone.

With a clang, the bells over the door sang out the arrival of a customer. Addisyn looked up quickly, ignoring the way the fringes of her heart were fluttering. Their first customer each day, without fail, was the same.

Darius Payne, on his way to work and in need of a Cuban latte.

"Good morning." His shadow crept over the counter, and his lopsided smile tipped his face. "How you doing?"

"All right." Addisyn smiled brightly back at him. "Cuban?"

"You know it." He leaned leisurely against the counter and gazed into her eyes.

It wasn't his words, or even his tone, that made Addisyn's breath catch and her world tilt slightly. It was the look in his eyes—a look she couldn't quite figure out.

"I'll—I'll get the coffee." She spun to the opposite counter, placing her back to him, jerking against the invisible lines that seemed to be drawing them together. Good grief, what was the matter with her?

She could feel his gaze on her as she deftly prepared his favorite beverage, but with a task to occupy her hands, her breathing slowed.

"You've turned into quite the barista."

Darius's tone was as light and teasing as normal. Whatever had been dangerously deep in his eyes a moment before had vanished.

Addisyn let out her breath. It was still a bit shaky. "Yes…I guess I have." She popped a plastic lid over the top of the drink and skewered it with a straw. She turned and slid the drink toward Darius, finally daring to meet his gaze again. "There you go."

"Thank you kindly." Darius took a sip and smiled. "Perfection." He paused. "You've come a long way since the day you didn't even know what coffee was."

"You could say that again." Addisyn chuckled slightly, relieved the dangerous undertow she had felt was gone. "Glad you like your drink." She expected him to back away, say something about being late for work, but instead he leaned across the counter toward her.

"Enjoying working here?"

"For the most part. It's a pretty stress-free job. Not like—" Addisyn clamped her lips shut. She had almost said *like skating*. How long would it take for her to fully process the reality that everyone around her had only read the last paragraph of her story, not the last chapter or even the last few pages? She dropped her gaze and brushed invisible crumbs off the countertop into her hand. "It's—it's nice."

"That's good." He took another sip of his Cuban, then set his drink down and cocked his head. "And have you found what you were looking for yet?"

Addisyn blinked, caught off guard. "Found—what?"

Movement caught her eye. Chelsea was bustling around the end of the counter, carrying a cardboard box. "Got the straws. I do need to order some more, though. This is the last. Do you think we should keep getting plastic? I mean, I can kinda get behind the whole paper-straw—" Her rambling broke off as she caught sight of Darius. "Why, hello there, Mr. Payne!"

"Found what, Darius?" Addisyn's voice was barely above a whisper, but she needed his answer, before Chelsea could arrive and shatter the moment.

His green-blue eyes bored straight into hers. "Your answers."

Answers.

What she'd come to Whistler to find. What she'd told him, on that long-ago rainy night, she needed so desperately.

Like a touch on the arm when she didn't know anyone was around, the question startled her—and challenged her. Had she become so preoccupied with hiding her questions that she'd forgotten her need to find answers?

She still didn't know where her life was headed or how to do more than just maneuver through each day. She was still treading water, marking time. On the flip side, she'd been in Whistler for almost two months. Her thoughts of Brian were more blurry, more distant. And she'd landed her first job outside of skating. Addisyn took a deep breath— somehow, a cleansing breath. "I think so. Some of them."

His smile was as gentle as a spring sky. "Good."

Then Chelsea was there, pushing up next to Addisyn. "Good to see you this morning, Darius." Admiration dripped from her tone. "Want me to make you a nice Cuban?"

"Thanks, but Addisyn's already taken care of me." He lifted his cup as proof, then backed away from the counter. "See you later." His words could have been for both of them, but his eyes were fastened on Addisyn alone. As he reached the door, he turned one last time and mouthed the words *Keep looking!*

Addisyn felt a flurry of hope in her spirit. She returned his grin and watched as he strolled across the sidewalk to his waiting vehicle.

Answers—hard to find, harder to hang onto. Yet as Addisyn watched the maroon Chevy drive down the street, swerving to miss a pothole full of brownish snow melt, she had two very distinct ideas.

The first was bewilderment at the fact that somehow, for some reason, Darius Payne seemed like an answer all by himself. The way he made her feel special and listened to and—and—*safe* was incredible. He was a rare kind of man.

She snapped her thoughts away from Darius to acknowledge the other emotion. One that had been so badly beaten down inside her that its wings had been broken, and for a while, it had lain as still as death. But now, deep inside her, Addisyn felt the stirring of wings—the faintest flutter—of something that she hadn't greeted for many dark days.

Hope.

CHAPTER 6

Addisyn gritted her teeth as the bike clanked annoyingly, grinding through its gears while she pedaled. What a cantankerous contraption.

Once again she berated herself for the impulse buy. She'd been on her way home from work the afternoon before—walking, as usual—when she passed the Wheel Power Bicycle Shop, a tidy corner establishment right in the middle of the Whistler Village. With the late April sun melting the remains of the snow and the sky beginning to soften into a particularly beautiful shade of blue, Addisyn had suddenly envisioned herself gleefully biking to and from work each day. She could even use a bike to check out some of the cool local sites, which she was ready to explore now that winter was over. And, after the rigorously athletic lifestyle she'd once led, even her grueling gym workouts weren't satiating her need to move. Biking would help take the edge off—especially in a community as outdoorsy and athletic as Whistler.

Yes, it had sure *seemed* like a good idea.

She gripped the handlebars more tightly and swerved to miss a pothole. The steering was looser than she expected, and she nearly pitched off the curb. Addisyn released a slow, even breath, determined not to lose her cool. When she'd returned earlier this morning to purchase the bike and plunked down the price of $89.99, the proprietor of the shop had assured her that it rode "like a dream."

A nightmare? she asked herself wryly.

Well, it was what she could expect from a bike that cost less than a good pair of tennis shoes. The coffee shop was fewer than three blocks away now. She maneuvered around the corner—narrowly missing the street sign. Too late, she remembered the final hill. She leaned forward over the handlebars, determined to churn upwards, and tried to downshift. Not early enough. In a cacophony of snappings and rattlings, the chain slipped loose.

Momentum was too much, and with an impact that felt as if it were flattening her ribcage, Addisyn landed on the pavement. Her hands flew out to catch her even as she slid across the asphalt. The bike flopped over in its own ungraceful way—partially beside her and partially on top of her.

Addisyn sucked in a ragged breath and fought the tears pooling in her eyes. She was no stranger to falling. She did it all the time on the ice—had even broken her shoulder blade once in a devastating fall out of a triple Lutz. But this—this was different. She wasn't used to falling on asphalt, wasn't used to the rough surface scraping her palms.

And maybe she was also tired of falling with no one to help her stand back up.

She was vaguely aware of a car pulling close to the curb. As she struggled to raise her head, the tingles on the back of her neck told her who was there before he said a word.

Oh no.

"You all right?"

Darius. That compassionate tenor voice with a hint of West Coast accent could only be him.

Addisyn couldn't even meet his eyes. "Uh…sure. Yeah."

As if she had intended to recline here on a public thoroughfare, underneath a clunker bike.

Awkwardly she began the attempt to rise, but the bike pinned her down. Shame seared her cheeks. She had to be the world-record holder for Most Unattractive-acting Female.

Darius swung himself out of his car door, his gaze riveted on her. "Are you hurt?" He reached back inside the car to switch on his hazard lights, then closed the few feet between them.

"Uh…" Before she could say anything, he had grabbed her shoulders and untangled her from the bike, gently helping her to her feet. He held onto her shoulders even after she was upright and leaned back to look in her face. "Okay?"

She shrugged, determined to laugh it off. "Sure, I guess. I just—well…" She brushed her stinging palms against her leggings. "It's been a while since I've taken that hard of a fall."

"Hey, falls are never easy." His tone was warm and caring—like a sympathetic hug. He released her shoulders and bent to straighten her bike. "Looks like your chain slipped."

She groaned. "Don't even bring that up! I bought that contraption for a good ninety bucks today." Her grin eased the pain of the accident.

He laughed. "Looks like you got your money's worth."

She assumed a façade of mock dignity. "Hey, now I never said I was good at negotiating. I'm not a business guru."

"No, you're a barista. And a super one at that." His words were muffled as he bent over her tire. "Are you on your way to work?"

"Yes." Addisyn sighed and flicked an embedded bit of gravel off her palm. "I'll probably be late now."

"Don't worry about that. I'll give you a lift. Get you there in no time." Darius was tinkering with the chain, his fingers crawling nimbly along its links. "You know what, your chain actually broke."

She groaned. "No. You're kidding."

"Wish I were." He sat back on his heels and winced apologetically at her. "You won't be riding this till we get it fixed."

"Ugh." Addisyn groaned. She'd wasted her money, she was late for work, Darius had seen her lying on the pavement like a wet washrag, and now her bike was smashed on its maiden voyage. Could anything else go wrong? "I know nothing about fixing a bike."

"In that case—" He stood and pulled the bike up beside him. "I'll fix it."

Her jaw went slack. "You can?"

"Sure. I have plenty of tools at my house." He squinted overhead at the bright British Columbia sun. "In addition, I happen to be off work today, so I also have the time."

"But your day off…" Addisyn hesitated. "You really want to spend that fixing my bike?"

"Sure. I like tinkering around with things." He winked. "Guess I never outgrew my childhood love of Legos." The impish look in his eyes made Addisyn laugh despite her misgivings.

"Well…okay. That would be great." She couldn't help but notice how the sun glinted off his rich brown hair.

"Tell you what." Darius paused and brushed his lip with his thumb. Almost as if he were nervous. Then he plunged ahead. "How bout I pick you up after work today and take you to my house? We can have dinner, and you can get your bike. I should easily have it fixed by then."

Addisyn's heart surged upward in her chest, almost choking her. Darius was inviting her to his house? What did that mean? A thousand questions swirled in her mind, but somehow the one that mattered least was the one that slipped out before she could stop it. "You can cook?"

Darius must have read the skepticism in her eyes. He threw back his head and laughed. "Sure I can cook! What, you think I'm only good for climbing mountains and whatnot?"

"Well, a man of your physique seems more at home in the woods than standing over a stove." She didn't try to hide the playfulness sparkling in her eyes.

Darius cocked his head in attempted seriousness. "Hey, it takes a real man to survive in a kitchen."

Addisyn couldn't help but laugh again.

"What time do you get off work?"

"Four thirty. Maybe four forty-five." The shop technically closed at four o'clock, but on the days Addisyn worked the afternoon shift, she usually stayed late to help Chelsea close.

"Great. I'll come to the coffee shop around three forty-five. I don't mind waiting till you're ready to leave. Then we'll head to my place for dinner and a bike transfer. Deal?"

What could she say? Addisyn twisted the bike helmet in her hands. This guy was unlike any other man she'd ever met—and just one look in his eyes was enough to unravel all her excuses.

"Deal."

◬ ◬ ◬

TELL ME THIS is not my life!

Brian clenched his jaw until his whole face hurt. In an explosion of raw frustration, he hurled his cell phone across his office. It landed with a dull thud, cushioned by the luxury rug.

He gripped the arms of his desk chair, seething. Red specks danced before his eyes.

He'd been so confident. No, more than that—absolutely positive. Positive that very soon, Addisyn would break down and confess the simple truth: she needed him. Emotionally and professionally, she was doomed without him. And that gave him a trump card that couldn't be outmatched.

So this morning, when he'd seen, at long last, a missed call from her, he'd been delighted. Not surprised, exactly—he'd always known the girl couldn't resist him—but still delighted.

But this…

How dare she leave him a voicemail like that? Coolly and curtly telling him to get himself out of her life. That's what it amounted to, anyway—because she was "not certain of her career direction."

Brian gritted his teeth and thumped his fist on his desk. Not certain of her career direction. What a joke. *Baby,* I'm *certain of your career direction. Without me, it can only be down.*

Suddenly even the opulence of his fourteenth-floor office in the New York Figure Skaters' Agency felt stifling. The mass of papers on his desk were a vicious whirlpool, sucking him down. He muttered a curse under his breath and snatched his coat from the stand near the door. If he didn't get some fresher air, the walls would cave in on him.

Ten minutes later he was sitting on a bench right outside Central Park. Odd, but even with his intimate knowledge of posh restaurants and upscale business centers, this humble bench had always been one of his favorite spots in the city.

At this corner, with the urban grace of Central Park behind him and the ritzy glitz of Fifth Avenue ahead of him, Brian had always felt powerful, invincible even. As though he were so close to the throbbing heart of the world's greatest city that he could absorb some of its boldness and magnetism into his own soul. A horse-drawn carriage filled with chattering tourists rumbled past, the horse's head wearily bobbing in time with its steps. The afternoon sun blazed from the sleek metallic sides of the skyscrapers. A gaggle of mustard-colored cabs jockeyed for dibs on the pedestrians thronging the curb.

He loved this world, loved its crazy chaos. What's more, he was sure Addisyn loved it too. And she loved him. And she loved skating. The combination would irresistibly draw her back to the Big Apple like a triple lodestone.

Right?

Brian sighed and massaged his temples with his fingertips. If only he could be so sure. But after this morning's voicemail…

For the first time, he forced himself to stare head-on at the question that was constantly intruding itself, the question that was becoming impossible to ignore. What if Addisyn wasn't planning to come back? Ever? What if she disappeared permanently in the hollow vastness of the world?

The panic of the thought was drowned in a surge of anger at himself. This was a joke, right? He couldn't have really been this stupid. Couldn't have actually let his golden girl get away.

Sure, she wasn't as good as she thought she was, and she was nowhere near Olympic caliber, but really, who cared? Even if she would never glide across the world's biggest stage, she could still compete in smaller events— events where artistry was more important than technical perfection. And artistry she definitely had in spades. Each lonely night, when he once again watched that video of her performance at Sectionals, the truth stuck an accusing finger in his face. He'd been out of his mind to insist she had no future on the rink. He was always annoyed when sensational reporters used vague, sentimental terms like *magic* and *elegance* to describe skaters, but he had to admit those words fit Addisyn perfectly. Her skating was magic.

And it wasn't just her skating.

"I want to skate more than anything." For a moment that sweet voice sang so vividly in his memory that he was almost sure she was there again, right on the bench next to him. Where they'd sat when she'd told him those very words.

He remembered how innocent she'd looked, how wide and trusting her gaze had been. He closed his eyes, basking in the memory, tracing the faultless perfection of her face.

She'd cocked one knee on the bench, hugging it to her chest. "Skating has always been my thing. It's helped me through some—stuff." For the first time her lids had dropped, her expression mournful.

Brian had itched to put his arms around her, kiss away the shadows. But he'd told himself to take it slow. Thanks to her holy-roller older sister, a religious prude, the girl had been more naïve than he would have believed possible of someone who'd grown up in the tawdriness of New York. He forced himself to focus on her words instead of her beauty. "Stuff?"

Addisyn had sighed. "My sister's great. I love her to death, don't get me wrong. But...she doesn't understand how important skating is to me." She'd turned troubled eyes to him. "She wasn't even at my last competition. Said she had to work or something." She shrugged. "She just doesn't care."

"The world is full of people who don't understand. The bigger your dream, the louder your critics." Brian's lofty answer had been a spur-of-the-moment inspiration that impressed even him.

"That's right. That's exactly right." Addisyn had gazed at him admiringly, as if he were some kind of erudite philosopher. The truth was the words had just popped into his brain out of thin air, probably something he'd heard in some superhero movie. "And I'm finding that out with Avery. She's such a Nazi. Definitely not my biggest fan at all."

He couldn't wait any longer. He was ready to open the door for Addisyn, teach her things she'd never imagined. "No...she's not. But it doesn't matter." He'd struggled to keep his focus enough to just say the next few words. "Cause you've found your biggest fan."

"Who?" The question had been a whisper.

Brian had leaned forward and carefully, carefully, brushed her cheeks with his fingertips. "Me." It was like stroking a butterfly. "I'll always be your biggest fan, Addisyn Miles."

Her eyes had widened, and she hadn't pulled away. Slowly, as if it were the closing scene of a romantic movie, Brian pressed his lips to hers. The moment had been perfection. Then he'd pulled back and stared at Addisyn. "Your biggest fan." He ran a finger across her brow. "You're gonna go to the top, Addisyn."

Her face wore an expression he'd never seen there before. Cautiously, yet as naturally as the changing tides, she'd leaned toward him. "The very top." She settled her hands on his shoulders. "And you'll go with me." This time she'd initiated the kiss.

Just the lingering perfume of that three-year-old memory made Brian ready to go through any hell for one thing only—to get her back. To have Addisyn as his own, to feel her hands in his. To see her sitting beside him on that very bench where he'd introduced her to a whole new world. To watch her wake up in the mornings and sweep her across ballroom floors. He opened his eyes, shaking off the reverie, but the vision still wavered before him.

Magic.

If Addisyn wasn't magic, nothing was. A surge of emotion rose in Brian, so powerful that it shocked even him. Yes, he needed Addisyn professionally—she could be the lucky horseshoe of his career.

But on a deeper level, he needed *her*—not just her abilities. He craved her desperately. He wanted to see her smile at him more than he wanted his next breath.

Focus, he told himself. He'd use his go-to attributes—ruthless determination, business acumen, and a dash of plain old luck—and he'd make good on his mistake. He needed something, some peace offering to use to woo her back to New York. And right now, he couldn't think of anything more convincing to use than her own dearest dream. If he could guarantee her another chance at greatness, surely that would be too big a carrot to turn down.

But how? Okay, maybe his delivery had been crude, but not everything he'd told Addisyn had been inaccurate. As talented as she was, she still was a relative newbie to the world of ice. She wouldn't have the technical foundation to make it to the Olympics the traditional route, through Regionals and Sectionals and ultimately Nationals. And although Brian realized he'd put his foot firmly in his mouth when he'd made the comment about her age, the general truth still remained. Building her technical base to the point where she could breeze through Nationals would take time she didn't have. She couldn't afford to wait much longer if she wanted her Olympic chance. Not with the skating world being flooded with fierce competitors barely past puberty.

He chewed his lip in concentration. He just needed to find Addisyn's niche, he told himself. Some arena where she could use the full extent of her artistry but where her technical deficiencies wouldn't derail her entirely.

Possibilities zigzagged through his mind like runaway cats, and though many he instantly dismissed, a few of them began gradually unfolding into feasible plans. He pulled out his cell phone and flicked through his voluminous roster of contacts, looking for a name he hadn't needed in a while. Yeah, he was still in there—Ed Bourns. The business title line under his name—Brian often used those, having so many connections it was hard to keep them all separate—read "Team Unlimited Agent."

Team Unlimited. Brian suddenly smiled. This could be just the ticket he needed to get Addisyn back to him—for good. At any rate, he thought as he tapped the number and waited for it to ring, he had to try.

Because she was magic…and he couldn't live without her.

△△　△△　△△

SILENCE WAS NOT one of Darius's favorite things, so whenever he was alone in his house, he turned on some nice instrumental background music. Usually something modern yet old-fashioned at the same time. This afternoon he opted for a volume of Brooklyn Duo's top tracks. The soft strains of mingled piano and cello wafted through the empty rooms— rooms that were otherwise shrouded in too much silence and harboring the ghosts of too many memories.

It was because of all that silence that Darius didn't spend much time at home. Either he was at the climbing center, or at the gym, or enjoying an open-air concert downtown. In his spare time, he clicked on his app for Uber and cruised around Whistler ferrying tourists—as he'd planned to do this afternoon, on his day off. No problem. He'd rather fix Addisyn's bike.

He grabbed a roll of paper towels, a wrench, and a can of chain lubricant from the garage, then headed into his mudroom, where he'd parked Addisyn's bike. He squatted by the wheel and began carefully threading a new chain around the sprocket; he'd picked it up at the bike shop on the way home.

He examined the raw-boned bicycle ruefully. It was clear she hadn't purchased the best machine on the market. Well, but who knew how much money she had.

Who knew anything about her, really.

The question he couldn't entirely shake returned, buzzing annoyingly around his mind. It was a simple question but one that he had no idea how to answer.

Why was he fixing a bike for a girl he didn't even really know?

The haunting melody of one of his favorite songs began playing—"Hallelujah." He hummed along softly as he greased the new chain methodically, unhurriedly. The music seemed to envelope him, carrying his mind on a journey toward a more peaceful place.

He thought about the lyrics as he continued working. The song had always been his anthem—beautiful yet sad, singing about loss and passion and how dangerous love could be. Yeah, he knew that, all right.

There was no explanation for why a vision of Addisyn suddenly appeared in his mind. He saw her as she'd stood on the street, helmet in her hands, the sun making copper flecks dance in her silky hair. The memory snagged his breath, and the chain seemed to knot itself in his hands.

He didn't know how it had happened, but his heart didn't belong to him anymore.

It was in the hands of a girl with the sweetest soul he'd ever seen.

He took a deep breath and twisted the sprocket. Looked like her back brakes were loose too. He swiped his hands on a wad of paper towels and reached for the wrench. He might as well fix those while he was at it.

He wanted this bike to move as gracefully as she did.

C'mon, Payne. All that "love-at-first-sight" business was for the real men. The guys who could actually charm women. The guys who were everything he was not.

What had happened to him? He could usually stay in control of his heart. Keep his soul locked away. What was going on?

Darius rested his hand on the main frame of the bike. A quiet frustration, its edge dulled from years of bumping around in his heart, pushed itself to the forefront of his thoughts. He was scarred and world-weary, guilty and ashamed. He had nothing to offer any woman, certainly not a golden-hearted soul like Addisyn. He would have stood barefoot on an Arctic iceberg if he could have erased his shame, but a redo wasn't possible for him. And the sordid truth remained, leering at him mercilessly.

If Addisyn truly knew his story, she wouldn't be able to get away from him fast enough.

As he worked, it occurred to him that maybe that was part of the problem. She didn't know his story. In fact, she knew nothing about him, except that he was an Uber driver who liked Cuban lattes and hit the gym regularly. And that wasn't fair. He needed to let her know who he really was—at least enough to give her an idea of his poor track record. As far as the deep wounds were concerned, there was no need to even go there.

Just the bare facts would be enough to turn her away.

$$\triangle\triangle \quad \triangle\triangle \quad \triangle\triangle$$

THE CONVERSATION WAS making Addisyn want to scream or climb the walls of the coffee shop. Or maybe both.

If the explanations such a move would have required wouldn't have been so embarrassing, she would have asked Darius to drop her off a block away from the coffee shop. As it was, though, he pulled right up front—even hopping out to open her door like the gentleman he was. Then he followed her inside for his daily Cuban.

The whole time, Addisyn could feel Chelsea's questions, like tiny invisible barbs just beneath the surface. Sure enough, as soon as the door swung shut on Darius's heels, the girl's excitement began spouting.

"Oohhh…so you came with Darius this morning?" Chelsea winked conspiratorially.

Addisyn still couldn't explain the irritation that had swept over her at those words. Really, it was none of Chelsea's business. *Who made her the hall monitor?* "I was biking to work and had a wreck. He happened to see it, picked me up, and gave me a lift. That's all there is to it."

"Mm-hmmm." Chelsea bobbed her head sagely. Like some wise old palm reader. "Mm-hmmm. So you say."

Addisyn could hear the frustration in her own voice. "He's an Uber driver, Chelsea, in case you forgot. Giving people rides is part of his job description, not a come-on."

Chelsea didn't respond for a moment. When she did, she had veered off on a completely different tack. "I saw him open the door for you. He's so chivalrous." She leaned over the counter and batted her eyelashes. "Like a knight from King Arthur's court."

"Yeah, he's nice." Addisyn tried her best to infuse a sense of finality into the words.

Fortunately, customers had begun arriving about that time, and the place had been hopping ever since. Chelsea had been too busy to push the matter further—although she'd still managed to insert sly comments here and there. Now, at three o'clock in the afternoon, the stream was just starting to slow down.

And Chelsea's tormenting was just picking up.

"You said you were coming to work on a bike?" Curiosity gleamed in the girl's innocent-looking eyes. "Didn't know you had a bike."

"I bought it this morning." Addisyn sighed. "Too bad it's already out of commission."

"Yeah." Chelsea nodded sympathetically. "Are you taking it back to the shop? Or can you fix it yourself?"

Addisyn took a deep breath. "Actually, Darius offered to fix it for me this afternoon." She avoided Chelsea's eyes.

The girl squealed as if someone had just presented her with a bouquet of long-stemmed roses. "What?!" She clapped her hands to her face and danced around behind the bar ecstatically. "See, he likes you! He totally likes you!"

Addisyn could feel the heat surging through her face. For a second the fiendish desire to douse Chelsea in a wave of boiling hot coffee flitted through her brain. "Chelsea, stop! He's just a nice guy, okay?"

Chelsea just giggled, not at all cowed. "Sure…he's a nice guy. A nice guy who likes you." Coyly she batted her eyelashes. "Lucky you…catching Darius Payne."

Addisyn was weary. A humiliating bicycle crash, a whole day of Chelsea's unsolicited matchmaking, and some unaccountable butterflies in her stomach over tonight's plans were all taking their toll on her. "I have not *caught* Darius Payne," she repeated, emphasizing Chelsea's word. "He's just being friendly. Now, that's all I want to hear." She tried for the older-sister tone she'd learned from Avery.

"Aw, you're no fun." Chelsea stuck her bottom lip out in a pretend pout and slouched against the counter, arms folded like a petulant child. "You should be elated right now. I mean…you definitely aren't the first girl to try to catch Darius Payne's eye."

Addisyn just shrugged. She was tired of constantly declaring the platonic nature of their relationship. Maybe if she seemed uninterested, Chelsea would lose interest as well. "Makes sense. He's a pretty attractive guy."

"Well, *that*, of course." Chelsea rolled her eyes, as if completely exasperated with Addisyn's surface understanding of the situation. "But certainly his star power doesn't hurt either."

What? Addisyn stared at her coworker. For the first time all day, the annoying girl had her undivided attention. "His star power?"

Chelsea looked equally puzzled. "You mean…you don't know what he did?"

Addisyn shook her head, confused. "I know he works at iClimb and he drives for Uber…"

"But you don't know what he did *before* that?" Chelsea's eyes were enormous.

"No…" Addisyn had to remind herself to breathe. Something told her that for once, Chelsea was about to say something important.

Chelsea drew in a long breath. As if she weren't even sure where to begin. "Well…you might know him as Andrew Payne. Does that ring a bell?"

Andrew Payne? Like lightning, the realization sizzled in Addisyn's mind. *NO! It couldn't be!* She grabbed Chelsea's arm sharply. "Chelsea! Do you mean to tell me—is he—"

Chelsea was nodding vigorously, a knowing smile spreading across her face. "Yep! Andrew is his middle name."

The shock had created a vacuum in Addisyn's lungs. She let go of Chelsea's arm and stepped back, then crossed her arms and studied the floor. Darius was Andrew Payne? No wonder he had looked so familiar to her!

Her heart was galloping now, running away with the new knowledge, but her inside felt almost hollow, as if the unbelief had left her a shell. She looked hesitantly back up at Chelsea, who was grinning like a Cheshire cat. "Really?"

Chelsea just laughed and shook her head. "Yes, really!" She lightly bumped Addisyn's shoulder with her fist. "And you've served him coffee every morning!"

CHAPTER 7

Darius stole a sideways glance at Addisyn as he pulled up in front of his trim yellow abode. "Well." He cleared his throat. "Here we are."

He watched her expression register surprise and delight as she gazed at the house. "You have a lovely home."

Not as lovely as you are, girl, he wanted to whisper. It was no use telling himself to be careful, to take it slow, to watch his step. He might as well shout the same advice to a man caught in a whitewater river—because he was caught up and borne along by a current of emotions too strong for him to fight.

Every glance from her eyes was like another hook in his soul, pulling him closer to her. Did she feel it too? Or was she entirely unconscious of the power she had over him?

"This was my parents' house." Darius hopped out of the car and ran around to open her door. As if he were a real gentleman. What a joke.

She stepped out slowly, her beautiful eyes still absorbing the surroundings. "So do your parents live with you now?"

"No." That answer would never get easier for him. Darius jammed his hands in the back pockets of his khaki pants as he strolled up the walk beside her. "They—they passed away. It's been five years ago now. Car crash."

Concern for him widened Addisyn's eyes. "Oh. I'm so sorry."

"Me too." Tears pricked his eyes. He still couldn't think of his parents without tears. His two best friends, gone in a single moment. He pushed the door open and stood aside so Addisyn could enter.

"So you inherited their house?"

"Yup. Lived here ever since." He darted ahead of her, flipping on light switches, finding a piano radio station on Pandora.

He sneaked another look at her as she stood in the center of the living room. She'd seemed quieter than normal on the drive here—almost distant. Even now, he could feel the space of her reserve. What could be wrong? He cleared his throat and absentmindedly smoothed his hair. He'd pulled it back into a short ponytail for this evening, with the help of a lot of hair gel.

"Well." He rubbed his hands together and gave his best "host" smile. Maybe Addisyn was just nervous. He could relate. "As you can probably smell, dinner is ready."

He marched to the kitchen and opened the oven door. A wave of steamy fragrance issued out. Addisyn wandered after him to the kitchen and grinned. "Sure smells good. Maybe you really can cook."

He returned the grin. "I'm good at it. See here?" He proudly produced the pan. "Baked salmon and roasted vegetables. Then after dinner we have some of my famous two-ingredient cookies."

"Two ingredients?" She cocked her head charmingly.

He winked and glanced elaborately around, as if checking for eavesdroppers. "It's a secret. They're just oatmeal and banana."

"Wow!" Her laugh was like a string of bells. "You know more about finding your way around a kitchen than I expected." Her gaze focused as she studied his face, peering deep into his soul.

He could feel the red staining his face. "Yeah, a little." His hands wobbled as he placed the salmon on a cooling rack.

This girl had a lasso on his heart, and she was pulling it tighter with her every breath. And he noticed something even stranger.

He didn't mind.

◣◣ ◣◣ ◣◣

ADDISYN WATCHED DARIUS with new eyes as he loaded two plates with generous portions of salmon and vegetables, along with a side salad. That lean yet muscular build—those unusual eyes—how could she not have remembered?

She waited as he pulled out a chair for her and then sat down himself. He was quite the gentleman, she had to admit.

He picked up a fork and smiled awkwardly at her. Maybe he sensed she had something she wanted to say.

"Darius," she began.

"Yeah?" He was giving her his full attention.

She took a sip of water. Why was it so hard to get right to this? "You have a secret you didn't mention to me."

Darius put down his fork and stared at her.

She braced herself with a deep breath. *Here goes!* She matched his gaze. "You, Darius Andrew Payne, are a world-renowned ice skater, Canadian national champion—and a two-time Olympian."

Shadows pooled in Darius's eyes. Time seemed to hold its breath. He bowed his head for a long moment, the lamplight running up and down the smooth curve of his hair.

"Is that true?" Addisyn could feel her hands quivering.

Slowly Darius raised his head. His eyes glistened.

"Yes."

His voice was the softest whisper of a breeze through the forest.

"Yes, it's true."

Addisyn's body sagged with the release of the moment's tension. She let out a long breath. For a moment she simply stared at him, absorbing the full impact of his statement. Wondering how to possibly carry forward.

Darius was the first to break the quiet. "How—how did you know?" He kept his eyes fastened on Addisyn's face, probably trying to gauge her reaction.

She shrugged. "From the first day I saw you, I knew there was something familiar about you. Today, Chelsea mentioned that you also went by Andrew Payne." The truth still felt surreal, as if the room was tilting a little to one side. "I remember seeing you compete on TV at the Vancouver Olympics."

What she didn't mention was that Darius had been her hero. For both nights of the Vancouver Olympics figure skating, she'd been on her knees in front of the television, watching him perform—a flawless athlete, the darling of the figure skating world. As a romantic preteen, she'd been enthralled—both with the sport and with the cute fifteen-year-old.

"Yeah." Darius leaned back in his chair, an odd mixture of joy and pain filling his eyes. "I was so excited. Representing Canada. Right here in my hometown."

His tone was somber, even melancholy. Addisyn stared at him. He seemed more like an ex-con admitting to a capital crime than an amazing athlete revealing himself as an Olympian. Why?

She swallowed hard and asked the only next question she could think of—a bit lame, perhaps, but necessary. "Why—didn't you tell me?"

For the first time Darius looked slightly annoyed. "Why would I?" Then he sighed. "I'm sorry. I don't mean to snap at you. It's not your fault."

"What's not my fault?"

"That you found out." Darius stood up and walked a few steps away from the table, then turned and paced back.

"Found out?" Addisyn was even more bewildered. "Darius, this is amazing that you're an Olympian. It's not something you should want to hide."

He sighed. "It's—complicated."

Complicated? If Addisyn had made it to the U.S. Championships, she would have been over the moon. And if she'd competed in the Olympics, she'd have shouted the news from the rooftops. What could Darius possibly mean? Why had he wanted to bury his greatest accomplishment?

△△ △△ △△

"HOW MUCH OF the story have you heard?" Darius knew his tone sounded borderline desperate, but he couldn't help it. Inside he wanted to cry or yell or maybe throw something. Good grief, would the ghosts never stop chasing him? Ever?

"Most of it, I guess. Chelsea filled me in." Addisyn looked caught, as if she couldn't figure out what she'd done wrong.

He couldn't blame her. His reaction must seem completely irrational to her. "So…what did infallible Chelsea tell you about my life?" He knew his grin looked fake.

Addisyn quirked a brow at him. "You grew up in Whistler, but your parents homeschooled you and took you all over the world to train at the best locations, starting when you were six years old. You competed here in the Vancouver Olympics." After that, she hadn't followed his career, but Chelsea's gossipy tongue had revealed the next details to her. "You changed your focus to short-track skating and went to Sochi for the next Olympics. In Sochi you won the bronze medal in the thousand meters, but then in the five hundred meters—your signature event—you fell and were sidelined by injury. But—" her voice became softer—"your greatest years were here in Whistler—and this is where you won your gold medal."

Darius's face felt hot and throbbing, as if he'd been slapped by something. Well, he had. His past. Sighing, he relinquished any hope of concealing his story. Quietly, unceremoniously, he slipped off his loose jacket and turned his arms palm-up. He watched Addisyn, gauging her reaction to the two matching tattoos on the insides of his lower arms. Each one featured the Olympic rings with the location written underneath: Sochi on his left arm, Vancouver on his right.

"Wow." Addisyn looked up at him with huge eyes. Respect shone in her face.

Darius shrugged and yanked his jacket back on, hiding the tattoos again. He hated the way she was looking at him now, the way people always looked at him. That starry-eyed stare of pure awe at his greatness. If only they knew the truth.

"Yeah…well…" He had nothing to say, really. He didn't want to talk about the Olympics, and he couldn't change the topic now.

Addisyn shook her head. "I can't believe you didn't tell me."

Darius narrowed his eyes. "Sorry." The word sounded more curt than he intended.

"Well, no, it's just…" her voice trailed off. "I just thought you would have told me because—"

"Because why?" The frustration built in Darius like steam exploding from a kettle. "Because it was the crowning moment of my life? Because I'm this incredible athlete? The hero?" A sarcastic laugh jerked from his throat. "I'm none of those things."

"I'm—I'm sorry." Addisyn shrank back.

Now he felt even worse. Did he have to act like even more of a loser than he'd already proven himself to be? In front of Addisyn? "It's fine." He sighed and ran his hands over his face. "Just—it's over. In the past." If only it would stay there. "It was a lifetime ago."

Addisyn was still staring at him, as if searching for clues to a mystery. "Why aren't you skating now?"

He sucked in a quick breath, steeling himself against the pain of the memory. "Because of the fall. In Sochi." No need to delve into the details. "Another skater's blade sliced my leg." He absently rubbed his knee. Remembering. "Broke my wrist too."

"Ouch."

"Yeah. The worst was my back. I fractured one of my vertebrae, which ended up doing some nerve damage." He shrugged. "So, no ice now. I have to avoid high-impact sports. No lifting anything heavy, no sudden twisting or jarring." He gave a half-smile. "Kinda rules out ninety percent of what's done on the ice."

"Yeah, I know." Addisyn blinked suddenly. "I mean, I've seen it—on TV."

Darius absently nodded, distracted with the fragments of his past swirling about in his brain.

"What's it like—winning a gold medal?" Addisyn's question was timid, soft.

Darius paused, gazing over her head. What words could describe that experience? A smile, exquisite in its rarity, gently thawed his face. His gaze found hers. "Incredible." He shook his head and sighed, partly with joy, partly with pain.

The memory of that moment in Vancouver when he'd stood on a podium, hand over heart, with the weight of his gold medal around his neck, would never lose its magic. He could feel the tautness in his soul lessen. "It's like—like flying over the moon. Like finding the greatest treasure on earth—inside yourself."

"I bet." Addisyn's eyes held longing and wonder. She cleared her throat. "Which did you like better, figure skating or short track?"

"Figure skating." The answer came as easily as his own name. He smiled a little sadly at Addisyn. "Did you know my grandpa was a figure skater too?"

"No!" She grinned. "That's cool."

"Very cool. His name was Darius Payne too. In fact, that's why I competed under my middle name. I didn't want people getting us mixed up." He didn't know if he was sharing this because he wanted to tell her or because he wanted to postpone relating his story as long as possible.

"So you're his namesake." Addisyn smiled. "I bet he was super proud of you."

"He was." Darius blinked back tears at the memory of his loyal grandpa—his mentor, his role model, his hero. "He almost made it to the Olympics himself, but he got injured and missed his chance. I think he kind of relived things through me." He paused. "His story was my introduction to figure skating—and to the whole idea of being an Olympian."

When Darius first started skating at age six, it had been under his grandfather's tutelage. By then the man had been off the ice for years, but he'd still watch from the edges of the rink, making suggestions and telling tales of his own competitions. And standing on the ice, listening to his grandfather's stories, Darius had known where his path would lead. He'd come home from the rink the first day, dumped his skates in the corner, and marched to the living room where his dad was reading a magazine.

"How'd your day at the rink go? Grampy help you a lot?" His dad was tall and muscular with a blond crew cut, the typical athlete.

"Yup." Darius hopped onto the couch beside his dad and looked the big man solemnly in the eyes. "Daddy, I'm going to be the bestest figure skater ever and I'm going to go to the Olympics!"

His dad had laughed, but he'd stuck out his hand seriously to shake Darius's. "Deal, son."

That conviction had been with Darius night and day. It had warmed him on the coldest nights, comforted him in the scariest times. Most of all, it had given him a sense of purpose—as if he were poised atop a breaking wave of destiny. He wasn't just anybody. He was a figure skater—a figure skater who was going to the Olympics.

"And you did!" Addisyn's eyes were shining, her whole attention absorbed by the drama of his story.

"Yup." Darius pictured himself, a teenager with dreams bigger than the Canadian Rockies. "With my dad training me."

"Really?"

"Yeah. He was a professional figure skating coach. He and my mom both worked at the Centre." Looking back now, Darius sometimes wondered if he'd been pushed into the path, if his dad hadn't tilted the scales a little too heavily in favor of his son becoming an Olympian. But he couldn't blame his parents. It was in his blood, his DNA. And he had wanted it, after all, had yearned for it as much as they ever could.

"Was it neat having your dad coach you?" Addisyn frowned. "I mean, I would think it would be, but there had to be some awkward parts too."

"Yeah...definitely." Darius paused. "Like, when your dad is your coach, you never get away from the rink. Not really. You train all day and take your trainer home with you at night. And—I think the pressure is worse." He could see by Addisyn's nod that she understood. "Because, you know, it's your parents, training you, and you want to do well—not just for you, but for them too."

These days, he wished his dad had understood that, had sometimes taken off his coach hat and just been a dad. Had reminded his son that he was his son before he was his racehorse. But the pressure to perform had always been there.

"Like, when I was fifteen..."

That was the year that Darius took the world of Canadian figure skating by storm. His life had become a lightning rod, crackling with the possibilities, in the weeks leading up to the national championship in London, Ontario. His dad had watched his meals relentlessly. Monitored his workouts. Reminded him to soak his legs in Epsom salts every night. They'd worked straight through the holidays because his dad's meticulous training plan had to be followed so that Darius's form would peak the middle of January—competition time. He could even remember having a workout—a shorter one, but a workout nonetheless—on Christmas Day.

Looking back now, it was a wonder to him that he had made it to Nationals at all, that the huge top-heavy load of expectations hadn't flattened him under its own weight. Right before he'd gone on the ice, his dad had gripped him by the shoulders and stared him straight in the eye. "Go out there and win." His dad had been breathing hard, eyes like chips of ice, face cut from iron. There was no mistaking the passion in his voice. "This is the moment you were born for. Everything hinges on now."

Addisyn let out a low whistle. "Some pressure." She took a sip from her glass of water, but her eyes never left Darius's face.

Darius sighed. "That was just the beginning. But I delivered." He clenched his jaw tightly. "I always delivered."

He had gone out on that ice and done his level best. He'd choreographed his own routine, a beautiful, lyrical number set, of course, to an instrumental rendition of "Hallelujah." His moves were soaring, exalted. His whole being had flowed with the beauty and grace of the song. It had been the performance of his life.

And he had won.

The exhilaration he had felt had shot fire through his veins. He'd skimmed off the ice, screaming with pure joy. His dad and granddad were both waiting at the edge of the rink—and Darius saw something he'd never seen before. His granddad was crying.

"It was like a dream come true for him." Darius pressed his fingertips together. "His grandson, following in his footsteps." He looked up at Addisyn, his own eyes now moist. "That was my qualifier for the Olympics."

He rose and crossed to a small desk. He'd never wanted to see this again, but he was too far into the story to turn back. Might as well go all the way. Using just the tips of his fingers—as if his past might somehow burn him—he carried the eight-by-ten photograph back to the table.

It was too hard to look at Addisyn, after all he'd said, so he studied the picture instead—studied it with the eyes of the stranger to the moment that he now was. A young boy was standing on an ice rink in black pants and a blue sequined V-neck top. His fists were raised to the skies, and the expression on his face was one of complete victory and raw joy.

Darius exhaled. It was him—a million years ago. Shorter hair curled about his forehead and brushed the tops of his ears. His smooth chin framed an enormous smile. If only there were still some part of that dreaming boy alive in him—in him, a beaten-up, broken-down, old-souled man.

"You look pretty happy." Addisyn's words were gentle, almost whispered.

"Yeah. Yeah, I was." Darius sighed.

Was.

That had been the high point—the Vancouver Olympics. He'd surpassed himself, skating in his hometown area with an amazingly supportive audience. Overnight he'd become Canada's sweetheart—the precocious golden boy who was skating in the Olympics at the age of fifteen, the youngest age allowed for a figure skater.

The excitement and dream of it had filled him with unspeakable joy. He'd been flying high, on top of the world. When all was said and done, he'd come back to Whistler with a gold medal—and an unquenchable thirst for more Olympics.

"So what happened?" Addisyn was staring at him, eyes enormous, lips slightly parted. Clearly she was hanging on his every word.

"Oh…" Darius sighed, waving his hand disgustedly in the air, trying to shoo away the memories. So far, telling the story had been simple, effortless, like floating in a hot air balloon. But now the balloon was collapsing, and he was ready to be done. Before he crash-landed into the hard ground of reality. "I—I switched to short track instead."

"But why?" Addisyn's voice was soft. "When you loved figure skating so much—why did you leave it?"

He gritted his teeth. That was the question, wasn't it? The question that never died. He rose abruptly and walked to the window. In the dusk, the profile of Whistler was still visible against a sky of deepening indigo.

Even with his back to her, he could feel her watching him, waiting, for the answer that never came. Not even to him. The choking bitterness of the past rose like bile in his throat—the same mocking malignancy of mistakes and heartaches and a life forever marred.

All because of that one question.

He turned and faced her—her impossibly gorgeous eyes, her hair that shimmered in the light. She looked like all that was good and right and true in life. All the things he wasn't.

Darius tightened his jaw. No way was he going to tell her. Ever. No way in all the world.

"My coach wanted me to switch." He sat back down at the table. He couldn't decide if he was more relieved or disappointed that—for now—

the deep pain would stay hidden.

Mr. Fobb had contacted Darius's father after the Vancouver Olympics and offered to train Darius. It had been a dream opportunity. Chuck Fobb had been training figure skaters for forty years—working with some of Canada's brightest stars. He'd been a gruff old goat, not one given to much emotion—or tact. He had his opinions—and his clients always knew exactly what they were. "You're too fancy, boy," he'd huffed almost from the beginning, wilting Darius's intricate choreography.

He had another complaint too. Darius remembered the day he'd been skating practice laps just to warm up. An exhilaration had overtaken him, and he'd fairly flown around the ice. When he glided to a halt in front of his coach, hands on hips, he noticed something shiny in the man's hand. A stopwatch.

"Boy," he demanded gruffly, "do you realize what you just did?"

"What?" Darius had no idea what the old guy was talking about.

The coach had coughed and flashed the stopwatch in front of Darius as if he were accusing the teenager of a crime. "Boy, you're wastin' your time dancin' around on this ice. You're too fast for this." His eyes had traveled expertly over Darius's lean form, his sinewy legs, his long arms. "You've got speed to burn. Should've been a short track guy."

"And so you finally took his advice." Addisyn tipped her head to the side.

"Yes." Darius sighed. There was more to the story—much more—but it didn't need to be rehashed. "And I've always wished I hadn't. I loved figure skating—it was everything to me." He paused. This was the realization that had been quick to come and slow to leave—the truth that had haunted him for the past four years. Ever since Sochi. "I should have never given it up."

That was an understatement.

△△ △△ △△

ADDISYN SAT QUIETLY, staring at her plate. She couldn't process all of this—all the triumph and yet the despair of Darius's story. Her pulse was throbbing with empathy. For a moment she'd had a desperate urge to tell him everything—how she had tried to climb that sacred ladder herself, how she knew all about the cruel twists the game could take.

At the last minute she told herself to hold back. Sharing that would require that she also mention Brian. And she wasn't ready to go there—not yet.

But she did have one request. Anybody would have wondered the same, and with her dreams, it was impossible not to ask. "Can I—do you mind if—I mean—would you show me your medal?"

A smile, slow and gentle, spread across Darius's face. "Sure."

He left the room and came back a few minutes later with a shoebox in his hand. Setting it on the table, he pulled off the lid.

Leaning forward, Addisyn saw it was full of skating memorabilia—a pair of tacky old skate guards, some brochures and photographs, a few crumbling dried roses.

Darius reached under the layers of memories and pulled out a box. He opened it carefully—reverently.

Addisyn pulled in a breath so sudden it was almost a gasp. The dim lighting shimmered along the finely tempered edges of the metal, which was fashioned in a uniquely curved pattern. On the flat surface was an almost holographic design, elusive and intricate, emblazoned with the Olympic rings.

"Here." Slowly, Darius lifted the medallion from its cushioned nest. It was bigger than she'd expected—as wide as his palm. "Wanna hold it?"

"Do you mean it?" Addisyn couldn't believe his offer.

"Sure." The bittersweetness in Darius's tone and eyes was unmistakable.

Addisyn struggled to keep her hands from shaking. She couldn't drop such a precious thing. It felt heavy in her hands, with the solidity of true value. The gold was duller than she expected—a regal matte finish, not the shiny flashiness of cheap wealth. She held the medal by the blue silk ribbon, allowing the gold to spin freely. "What's the language on the back?" she asked.

"French." Darius kept his eyes on her, his chin in his palm. "The name and number of the games are written on the back in French and English, since Canada's bilingual."

"It's amazing," Addisyn whispered. She gave the medal one last look, then returned it to Darius. Suddenly she giggled nervously, overcome by the evening's impact. "I'm sorry, that's just so cool for me—getting to hold an Olympic medal—"

Darius smiled in return. "It's pretty cool, all right." He gazed at it one last time—lovingly, almost. Then he sighed and replaced it in the box. "You know, one day when I was a little kid, I asked my grandpa if he had bad dreams about not getting to go to the Olympics."

"What'd he say?"

Darius paused. "He said no. That he'd had a wonderful life and he didn't regret a thing. He told me a medal was just—metal." He smiled—a little sadly. "At the time I was horrified. Growing up on Olympic lore like I did, that seemed next door to blasphemy. But now…well, I can kind of see what he meant."

Darius grabbed the shoebox and hurried out of the room with it. Addisyn sat at the table, still considering his story.

Amazing. Darius had climbed to the top. He'd been where she longed to go. He'd glided across that ice dyed with the sacred Olympic rings. He'd stood on a world stage and won the accolades and affection of all. And yet here he was, obviously beaten. Somehow, Addisyn suspected there was more pain beneath the waves of his story, a pain he couldn't mention.

For the first time, Addisyn began to wonder. What was it really like at the top, anyway? What was up there that she so desperately wanted? If she decided to pursue her dream, what was she really chasing?

And more importantly, once someone stood on the mountaintop—where did they go from there?

CHAPTER 8

"**Y**es, yes, Ed, I totally understand."

Brian rested his elbow on the arm of his chair and pressed the phone even closer to his ear. With his free hand, he drummed impatiently on his desk. He gritted his teeth and mentally cursed himself. *Brian, if you'd just kept your mouth shut and thought outside the box a little, none of this would be happening right now.*

What was Ed saying? "Brian, if she can't make high enough scores in the traditional route, the fact is that she simply might not be the best choice for the next group of Team Unlimited athletes. I'm sorry, but I have a responsibility to my superiors. You understand. I'm on a short chain, and the decision isn't always mine, and for every athlete that gets to be a part of Team Unlimited, there are ten more that may be just as deserving but don't—"

"But, Ed, I don't think you hear what I'm saying to you." Brian fought to control his voice. *Don't panic.* "Miss Miles is a truly exceptional athlete, one of the best in her field. She is a—" Brian searched for the psychological combination of words and found it—"a rising star, full of promise and potential. She didn't even begin skating professionally until her late teens, yet she's still been able to achieve incredible milestones. She's one of the first American women to land two quads in a non-Olympic competition, she bounced back from a terrible injury, and she placed fifth in the Eastern Sectional conference of the U.S. Figure Skating Championships. In fact, she missed the pewter medal by only three hundredths of a—"

"I know all of that, Brian. You don't have to read me her resume. I keep abreast of events in the figure skating world, you know, and I am well aware of the fact that Miss Miles is a very gifted and exceptional young—"

"But I don't understand what else you think you have to know!" Brian's irritation frayed the edges of his control until his voice was only a couple of decibels below shouting. He stood abruptly and paced around his office to try to release the excess tension. *Get a grip, man.* It wouldn't do to irritate Ed at this point. He forced himself to lock his frustration away and bring his voice under control again. "I don't understand what more I could do to convince you to accept Miss Miles as a member of Team Unlimited. I mean, what else do you need?"

Ed gave a long sigh. "Brian, I need to see her. In person, on ice. I need to see a solid routine with pizzazz and talent. Miss Miles has to prove to me that she's a future Olympian."

Well, there it was. This was what he had been afraid of. Brian strolled to the window and glanced out at the city, thirty-four stories down, a tangled mess of cars and people and lights and buildings. Somewhere in the wilderness of the world, Addisyn was floating. He just didn't know where.

"I would think her record would prove that." No way would he even consider admitting to Ed that the future Olympian had flown the coop. "She has worked her rear off to get to where she is today. I mean, Eastern is not an easy division, yet she—"

"Look, I know all the numbers, okay?" The rising annoyance in Ed's voice shot Brian's excuses dead in their tracks. "I understand she gave a strong performance at Sectionals and that she's willing to work hard and that she's up to her ears in passion for the sport. I get all that. It's not enough. I hear that all the time from managers. I need to see her, not just her numbers."

"But why—"

Again, Ed cut him off. "Brian, the Olympics are about more than numbers. They're about people—real, individual people with stories and passion and determination." His voice was undeniably sincere, no longer agitated. "I don't want to know the stats on your girl; I want to see her passion. And I want to see how her passion translates on ice."

Brian could feel his throat tightening. What nonsense. Ed was sounding like one of those maudlin reporters—passion and magic and whatnot. "Ed, you've seen her on ice. You said you were there at Sectionals."

"Yes, I saw her. But I need to see her again and evaluate her by Olympic standards. By Team Unlimited standards. I need to look at her performance from a more critical viewpoint."

"Can't you watch a recording of her performance? It was really—"

"I could, yes. But I'm not going to do that for two reasons. First of all, I want to meet her. You know, shake hands, get to know her story. Secondly, I think it's only fair to give the athletes the chance to really develop a routine that puts their best foot forward. When they audition for me, it's more like an exhibition skate, if you will; I obviously want to see technical prowess, but I don't require them to follow all the choreography guidelines that Sectionals and Nationals impose. I want them to show me their heart. So I don't think it would be fair for me to judge Miss Miles's fitness for Team Unlimited based upon her performance at any other competition, even Sectionals." Ed's voice was becoming increasingly aggravated again. "Listen, Brian, we're talking Team Unlimited here, okay? This isn't a call I can make lightly. There's a significant amount of sponsorship and promotion involved, not to mention financial support."

"I know, I know." Oh, how well he did.

"So, can I see her?"

What could he say? This was a take-it-or-leave-it deal. Either throw all the cards on the table, or fold his hand and walk away. Jump for the chance, or chicken out. Brian clenched his jaw. Chicken out? Never. He could do this. He was used to taking risks.

"Brian? Are you still there?"

"Yes, absolutely." Brian lowered himself into his desk chair and prepared to take the plunge. A leap of faith, he might have called it, if he were a religious man. "Okay, you got it. It will put a lot of stress on Miss Miles's—uh—training schedule—competition planning—and so forth…but…yeah, you can see her." He glanced at the calendar on his desk. Good grief, it was still on May, four days into June. He pinned it to his desk with his elbow and used his other hand to rip off the defunct page.

"When do you need to see her by?"

"Let me check my calendar." There was a brief pause. "Tell you what…I'm already going to be in Chicago the first weekend in August to scout the competition for the National Showcase. I can come a couple of days early. How about we meet…uh…Wednesday, August first?"

August first? Brian couldn't believe it was happening this fast. "Uh…I didn't think Team Unlimited auditions began until mid-August, right?"

"Yeah, I'm doing you a favor. Look, maybe I shouldn't say anything, but the athletes that audition first have the best chance of being picked. Sure, maybe it's not fair, but it's just life. You know that."

Of course he did. Brian was no stranger to the rules of the game. "Well—thanks, man. I appreciate this. You won't be disappointed in Miss Miles, I can assure you of that." *If I can find her.*

"I'm sure I won't. I look forward to meeting her in person. I must admit, on paper, she sounds exactly like the kind of person we're looking for."

Looking for. Brian thought he might choke on the irony. *Where is she?* "She is. Totally. See you on the first, then."

They exchanged a few more pleasantries before saying goodbye, but Brian couldn't concentrate. After he hung up, he rested his head in his hands and stared at his calendar.

August 1. And today was June 4. Addisyn would require at least three weeks to help him choreograph a smashing program and learn it down pat. Three weeks? Anger bubbled through him. No, he'd make her do it in two, by gosh. This was her fault, anyway. Some nerve of her, taking off like that.

Okay, so even if she learned the routine in two weeks, there was still transportation to consider. He'd have to fly her to Chicago from wherever she was now. His eyes narrowed as his mind scrambled through the calculations. Basically, he had about six weeks to find Addisyn.

What should he do? Where should he even start? Calling wasn't an option. He'd tried over and over, only to have his calls sent straight to voicemail. Either she'd turned off her phone permanently…or she'd blocked his number. The last possibility wasn't one he was ready to consider.

He thought for a moment, then pulled out his iPhone and tapped

Facebook. She'd never been good about posting regularly, but maybe—

Her account was gone!

His breath caught. He flicked madly through the list of results, but the truth was obvious—her account had disappeared.

Just like her.

He sighed. She must have deleted or deactivated it. No help there.

His mind skipped madly through all possibilities. Should he phone the police? Hire a private investigator? No solution was too expensive or far-fetched—not in view of what the payoff would be.

Slowly an idea began dawning in Brian's mind. It was a radical option, yeah. But this was a ridiculously huge opportunity for both of them. Why not try it?

After all, he told himself as he closed his Facebook app and pulled up Google Maps, desperate times called for desperate measures. He snickered a bit. Sure, the phrase was overworked, trite even. But as he typed "Hudson Apartments" into his Google Maps search bar, the hackneyed old aphorism had never seemed so apropos.

Because for the first time ever, Brian Felding was truly desperate.

△△ △△ △△

DARIUS WISHED THE sun weren't shining today.

It wasn't that he was normally a fan of rain. He had more than his fill, living in the notoriously soggy Pacific Northwest. Usually he would have welcomed a sunshiny day, especially in June, with summer taking its first steps.

The light made him squint as he flipped on his blinker and turned left at the intersection. He frowned, yanking his visor down.

No, Darius wasn't opposed to sunshine in general. But it was too bright, too annoyingly hopeful, for his mood today. He glanced down at his own attire—somber maroon shirt, black pants. Even his usual beanie was black today.

The donut-shaped green of Spruce Park flashed by on his righthand side, followed by the Whistler Waldorf School. He was on his way out of town, driving into the countryside where things were freer, cleaner.

He glanced around at the mountains. Blackcomb, Brandywine, Mt. Weart, The Spearhead—he knew all their names as if they were old friends. It was comforting at a time like this, the familiarity he had with this place.

On this day, five years ago, his parents had passed away in a car wreck. Nobody's fault, really—his dad had apparently swerved to avoid a deer crossing the road and lost control. The car had been found upside down in the ditch, slammed against a tree. The investigator had assured Darius that they'd more than likely died quickly and painlessly, and at least they had died in a beautiful place. Darius had always been thankful for that. They'd been exploring one of the winding mountain roads, out for a late-afternoon wildlife watching expedition. Spending time together, the two of them. Sharing their love.

If he was being purely unselfish, Darius had to be grateful that his parents had gone to the next world together. They had loved each other deeply, and he couldn't imagine one being taken and the other left. They'd died in the way they would have chosen—together.

At times like this, he wondered if he would ever have someone to love, the way his dad had loved his mom. At one time, it had seemed possible—but a lot of things had seemed possible then.

His mind drifted to Addisyn. What a girl she was. Charming, fun, but gentle, too—not loud and giggly like the young women who sometimes came to the climbing center. Their incessant chatter made Darius's ears ring. But Addisyn only said what was worth saying, in a way that was kind and thoughtful.

The tightness in his soul eased as he pictured her flawless face. Absentmindedly he rubbed one hand over his beard. He couldn't quite put his finger on why he liked her so much. Maybe it was the way she seemed to dance effortlessly through life, with a view only for the bright parts. Maybe it was the way she balanced on the line between utterly sweet and a little playful. He grinned. He guessed that she had a bit of a temper—and he found that quite charming, actually.

For a second, he dreamed of actually walking up to her and asking her out on a real-life date. Somewhere romantic, somewhere out of the ordinary. No "dinner and a movie" for him. He'd decided that early on—from the time he was an introverted teenager. Funny, he'd been Canada's sweetheart, with no lack of attention from young female fans, yet he'd never had the courage to ask a girl out. And now, he was anything but the put-together paragon of a man who could do so in good conscience.

Shame clogged his soul. If only he could. If only he could envision a future without the dark cloud of guilt that clung to his spirit. He smacked his palm on the steering wheel, suddenly frustrated. Addisyn thought he was a hero. What could be further from the truth? And how could he look her in the eye and tell her about the other side of himself—the side without the roses and trophies? He couldn't—that was all.

Enough. Darius exhaled. Today was a day set apart to honor the past, not wallow in the misery of the present. Every year, he took off work and spent this day quietly remembering his parents—and his grandfather. Since his parents were buried in the cemetery of the little church Grampy had pastored, it felt right to include his grandfather in his remembrances on that day. He visited their graves and spent his time in reflection. The first year, he'd also included prayer. Just not anymore.

He pulled into the spacious dirt parking lot and turned off the motor. He'd arrived—Somerset Christian Church, at the margin of the mountains. He studied the church he'd known as well as his own house for his growing-up years. It looked the same, really—a squat tan brick building with a white steeple, now a bit greyish with wear. There were a few more cracks in the sidewalk where the roots of the pointy evergreens had tunneled under the concrete, and a letter missing from the sign out front, but other than that, the place was ageless. Even down to the vile lime green paint in the youth activities room, probably.

He took his time getting out of the car. No need to rush the moment, to skip over the memory. His hands in his pockets, he strolled across the gravel, breathing the cleaner air. Somerset Christian was nestled in the pines, at the edge of civilization. Past the cleared area that marked the boundaries of the church property, mountains rolled their enormous shoulders. The road that had brought him to this place lost its way shortly thereafter in the thickness of nowhere.

Darius tilted his head back to watch a brown-headed crow—a common British Columbia bird—slice its way through the sky. Besides the birds, the church was deserted at ten o'clock on a Thursday morning. Here, a man was alone—alone with his thoughts and alone with his Maker. Both of those made Darius squirm.

He gently lifted the latch on the iron fence around the cemetery—built as tall as he was to prevent mule deer from entering—and made his way through the rows of gravestones. The cemetery was well-maintained, but some of the older stones were wearing away. He paused in front of one whose name he could no longer decipher. All that was legible was something about "our beloved father" and the date of death—either 1952 or 1956, he couldn't be sure. A wave of shadows fogged his soul. When he'd been dead over sixty years, would people still visit his grave? For that matter, would anyone remember him at all?

And what would they say if they did? *Darius Andrew Payne, failed Olympian. Wasted his potential. Died alone and lonely.*

The thoughts made Darius feel hopeless—like an animal that had been caught in a trap and finally ceased struggling. He winced at the lump in his throat as he crouched beside the gravestone and gently brushed the dead leaves from its surface. "Whoever you are—I remember," he whispered.

Then he made his way to the two simple granite monuments, near the western fence. Side by side, they waited for him. Unhurriedly he crossed to them and carefully sat down on the grass. Facing the stones.

He knew the inscriptions by heart, but he read them again anyway. **CYNTHIA EMILY PAYNE. AUSTIN ZACHARY PAYNE.**

He'd kept the memorial text pretty simple, and it matched more or less. **DEVOTED HUSBAND AND FATHER. LOVING WIFE AND MOTHER.** And underneath, the verse—**WELL DONE, THOU GOOD AND FAITHFUL SERVANT; ENTER THOU INTO THE JOY OF THY LORD.**

A soft breeze stirred the pine needles, rattling them slightly. Darius pulled off his beanie deliberately, almost reverently. He could feel the sun on his hair—too sunny for early June.

He stared at the stones. For a moment, he pictured his mom and dad standing there, instead of the twin monuments. Shame whispered in his ear. After the way he'd failed them, the sorry shell of himself he'd turned out to be, they'd probably be no more excited to see him than the grim stone slabs were.

"I'm sorry, Dad—Mom," he murmured. Tears prickled his eyes. Mercifully, his parents had died before his final horrible mistake, but they'd lived to see him trade figure skating—his true passion—for short track. They had always supported him, even in short track, but he knew they'd been more than a little disappointed by his choice.

"I wish I could undo it all. Really I do." Tears were streaming down his face. Darius didn't mind. He rarely cried anymore—it was unmanly. But on this day, he allowed all the hurt to leak out. Trouble was, no matter how many tears he cried, the pain never seemed to fully drain.

"If I could, I'd have another gold medal for you right now." A sob caught in his throat. Oh, for one more chance. "But I don't—and I'm not—" Suddenly the hopelessness crushed his soul, and he dropped his face into his hands.

The pain wracked his ribs, tore at his soul. He swiped one arm across his face and kept weeping. How long would he do it? How many anniversaries would pass before he could come here and celebrate their lives instead of mourning their loss?

In his heart, he knew he wasn't simply crying for their deaths. He was crying for his own—the death of the man he'd been—the death of his soul and his heart and his dreams. He was crying for the death of his hope and his joy and his love for God. All that had been good and true and pure about Darius Payne had died, and when he mourned for his parents, he felt not only grief, but guilt.

Guilt—that he'd ever quit figure skating at all. Guilt—that he hadn't medaled in his last Olympics, in Sochi. Guilt—that his parents would be devastated if they could see the choices he'd made. Guilt—that he'd drifted so far from the faith his family had embraced.

After a few more minutes, Darius wiped his eyes. He was done crying. What good did it do anyway? No amount of tears could give him back all that he had lost. He tucked his knees close to his chest and rested his chin on them, exhausted from the grief.

The place was utterly quiet. Utterly peaceful. A few yards away, a bee buzzed fumblingly among the tiny electric-blue forget-me-nots. Darius's mind wandered slowly back through the portrait gallery of his memory.

Things his parents had done—said—felt. Incidents in his childhood—mindless little things that hadn't seemed important.

Now that his memories were all he had, he wished there were more normal ones, more times of just being a kid and hanging out with his parents. Instead, most of his reminiscences were set against the backdrop of the electric air of a competition or the sweaty sternness of a training rink. Looking back, he couldn't remember when skating hadn't been number one—especially to his dad.

Darius had loved his dad like crazy, and he knew his dad had loved him. But now he regretted the tension that had sometimes existed in their relationship—the agitation caused by the stress of clawing their way to the top together, the way his dad had spent more time being a coach than a father. The ice had been so important to his dad. Darius had always wondered—and wished now he had asked—why his dad hadn't gone to the Olympics after his grandpa's attempt. It seemed as though it would have been a natural choice. In any case, however, coaching Darius had to have been exhilarating for his dad—a trainer with the assignment of his life. To propel his only son—his only child—to glory.

So yes, his dad had pushed him. Pushed him harder, sometimes, than the boy had wanted to go. Now he could appreciate his dad's efforts, could sympathize if not totally agree with the reasonings that had produced them.

And even when his and his dad's personalities had clashed, when both of them wanted the same thing but couldn't agree on how to get it, they'd loved each other. He'd wanted so badly to fulfill his parents' expectations for him. They'd been his larger-than-life heroes. He'd focused his entire career on making them proud. In fact, his life had been so bound in theirs that after the accident, he hadn't been sure that he wasn't dead as well.

A car passed, driving unhurriedly down the dusty road. Darius kept his eyes fixed on the dust, rising and rising, spreading ever thinner in the sunshine. He thought back to the dark, dull days after the accident. He couldn't bring himself to face the truth, couldn't handle that much pain that fast. Empty and broken, he'd spent his days driving aimlessly through the mountains, crying some, raging some—hurting all the time.

After the glory of figure skating, short track had been dry and boring. No artistry, no beauty, at all. Darius had worked at it, rigidly, mechanically.

But he didn't love it. Couldn't love it. Fourteen months before Sochi, he'd told his parents he wanted to put the ice behind him. He'd officially retired—hadn't gone to championships that January.

But the ice didn't give him up so easily. After four months away, that spring had found him longing for the ice—even dreaming of it. And when his parents were gone, that was the last straw.

He hadn't had anything left, so he forgot about retirement. Went back to the ice instead—even overcoming his disdain of short track. It was all he had. He'd flung himself into his skating with an obsession that was insane. He'd worked morning, noon, evening at the track. Sometimes he'd leave his parents' empty house at one or two in the morning, head to the track for a three-hour workout.

If he stopped training, he would start thinking. So he never stopped training.

No one else had worked half as hard. The next year, he'd been in Sochi, a member of the Canadian Olympic team. He'd been nervous— too nervous. And those late-night workouts, the obsession with which he'd pursued his goal, hadn't helped him after all. Instead, he'd arrived in Sochi grieving, frazzled, and definitely overtrained. Just one mistake in a long list of errors he'd made.

He squeezed his eyes shut, blocking off the flow of memories. The ones from Sochi were among his worst. No need to relive them. He'd left Russia with one pathetic bronze medal, a broken body—and a crucified spirit.

He sighed and gazed at the stones again. "I love you so much," he whispered, blinking back the tears. "Thank you for always standing by me—always believing in me. I know I've disappointed you."

He continued like that for about ten minutes, talking quietly to his parents. He wasn't sure if the dead could hear, if they knew what people on his side of eternity did and said and thought. But he hoped his parents still kept an eye on him—although he cringed to picture them watching him make so many disastrous choices.

He glanced up into the sunlight. Although he could see a cloud bank boiling over the far western horizon, the sky above him was completely clear. He scrutinized the crystal blueness. Somewhere on the other side of that was Heaven, where his parents were. That's what Grampy had taught in church—and what he'd believed, back when he believed anything.

His parents hadn't been very vocal in their faith, but he knew they were both Christians. No doubt they were with God now, resting in His presence. Darius's soul was another matter. He shuddered, wondering where he would go when he died.

Tears filled his eyes again. He wished he could pray. Wished there were some magic words to say that would erase the pain and shame of the past decade and leave him a starry-eyed teenager again—with the world before him and nothing but joy and love to remember.

He looked over his shoulder at the little church. That had been a part of his life, too. A grounding force that held him stable and secure. He'd believed the Bible. Trusted in God. An upright Christian kid.

Now he idly picked at the grass and wondered—what did he believe?

It wasn't a question he often asked himself, but he knew the answer. He'd have to say he still believed the Bible. Still believed in God Almighty, Who judged mankind according to His laws of morality. Still believed in Jesus, hanging on a cross, dying because of man's sins. Still believed in doing the right thing, in living life by God's laws and receiving God's blessings.

He just didn't believe any longer that it applied to him. No, God— the Holy One—was looking for strong, serious, clean-hearted men. Men who could point to their lives with no apologies, no shame. Men who stood by their actions and wisely stewarded the time they'd been given. Men who lived right and had no skeletons in their closets. Men like his grandfather had been.

Men unlike the horribly broken, tattered man Darius had become. He was left with a dreary quantity of life before him and nothing to live for. As a few clouds drifted across the smooth blueness and began to dim the sunlight, Darius bent his head onto his knees. He was nothing more than a man who'd wrecked his every chance. And a man who was left with the appalling truth—God would want nothing to do with him now.

CHAPTER 9

"So this is the trail system." Addisyn seemed to be suitably impressed. She brought her bike to a halt on a damp knoll carpeted in pine needles. Taking a deep breath, she gazed at the scene.

"Yep, this is it." Darius still couldn't believe she had asked to go bike riding with him. A twinge of uneasiness flicked at him. Hopefully she was up to the challenge. Mountain biking wasn't for the faint of heart, especially on Whistler's world-class Zappa trails.

But Addisyn had looked so eager when he'd come in for his coffee this morning. "My bike has been working great ever since you fixed it," she'd informed him with a big grin. "Since it's been three days, I've decided its probation is over."

Darius had laughed. "So I actually fixed it, huh?"

"You did." Addisyn had hesitated before blurting out her next question. "Want to see for yourself?"

"Huh?"

"Go bike riding with me." She'd pointed at him with mock sternness. "You own a bike. I saw it in your mudroom, so no excuses."

Darius had plenty of excuses. Like the fact that he was damaged goods. Or the fact that his mind was screaming at him to stay far away from Addisyn before his heart could be sucked farther into the whirlpool of emotion.

But all those excuses vanished like steam from a latte at the prospect of being near Addisyn for an afternoon. So as soon as he'd left work, he'd picked her up and brought her to the Zappa Trails, intending to take her to Lost Lake.

"This is the most beautiful place." Addisyn scanned the horizon, turning her face to the sun.

Darius too was enjoying the view, but he thought the prettiest part of the scenery was Addisyn herself. Perched on her bike with her silky hair pouring from under her helmet and a dreamy smile on her face. He was glad to see that smile. He had the idea there had been too much pain in her life thus far. Maybe this outing could bring just a little light to her life.

Certainly the loveliness of their surroundings would have whispered tranquility to any uneasy soul, and Addisyn couldn't seem to drag her eyes from the view. Which was fine, because Darius couldn't drag his eyes from her.

She was perfect. No, way better than perfect. She was everything he'd ever dreamed of in a woman—or would have dreamed of, had he known such a woman existed.

Which was why she could never be his. He clenched his jaw. Sure, she knew his story now. But she didn't know the whole story. If she did, she'd take off on that bike and never look back.

"So?" He suddenly realized Addisyn was watching him, those big brown eyes glittering with excitement. "How bout these trails?"

He forced himself to lighten up. "Absolutely. Right this way."

As he pedaled toward the trailhead for the Zappa Bike Trails, he reminded himself once more. There was no way he could ever approach Addisyn as more than a friend. She wasn't—what was it the guys always used to say?—*on his level.* She deserved the very best life could offer her, not some broken-down ruin like him. A guy who'd shipwrecked his life and made all the wrong choices.

If he had any speck of chivalry and decency left in him, the only thing for him to do was to stop thinking of her in that way. Stop losing his breath every time she glanced at him. Stop searching for ways to make her laugh, words that could bring her sparkling smile to her flawless face.

Stop losing every chunk of his weather-beaten heart to her.

"Darius, thanks for bringing me here. I can't wait to see the lake!"

He chanced a glance back over his shoulder. There she was, pedaling after him, eyes bright, cheeks the color of the first blush of sunrise over the mountains.

It was no use telling himself to be rational. His heart had gone tone deaf to his mind. In that instant, the realization hit Darius with more force than he'd ever felt in a fall on the ice.

He was in love with Addisyn Miles.

⋀ ⋀ ⋀

"EVER BEEN MOUNTAIN biking?" Darius's question floated back to Addisyn on the warm breeze.

"Um…no." She giggled, a little nervously. "It's not that much different from biking on a road, right?"

"Like the difference between walking and ice skating." Darius grinned at her over his shoulder.

"Great." Addisyn laughed, but Darius didn't join in. As they coasted to a halt at the trailhead, she studied him, somewhat concerned. Was he okay? He looked—worried, perhaps? No, maybe *preoccupied* was a better word. Distracted.

"Here's the trailhead." Darius sounded surprisingly out of breath, considering the fact that they had simply coasted across the parking lot toward the trail system. "Um…" he ran his hand over his face, seemingly trying to gather his thoughts. "The trails all connect, so you can make any length and any sort of ride you want, but the most popular is a six-mile loop." He looked directly at her for the first time. "Does that work for you?"

She shrugged. "Sure. Lead the way."

"Okay, then." Darius flashed his warm grin at her, and she felt herself relaxing. Maybe she'd just imagined his absentmindedness. And even if she hadn't, it likely had nothing to do with her.

"Then let's go!" He pointed forward in a dramatic fashion, and they headed down a narrow trail, about three feet wide.

Addisyn felt the increased resistance immediately in her legs. The trail was solid pea gravel, not paved. "Are all the trails gravel?" she asked.

"No, there's also rock, dirt, and roots." Darius's voice held a teasing lilt. "What, you're already tired?"

"Not on your life!" Addisyn was enjoying this way too much. She watched Darius's strong profile ahead of her, admired the way he masterfully guided the handlebars over obstacles.

A trail sign flashed by. "'Peaches en Regalia'? What kind of name is that?"

Darius laughed. "Ever heard of Frank Zappa?"

The shadows of the pine trees dappled the trail in sunlight. "No…"

"He was a rock singer. This whole network is called the Zappa Trails in his honor. Each trail is named for one of his songs."

"Cool." It was the kind of hipster creativity Addisyn had come to expect from the restless young town. "Are you a fan?"

"Not really. I'm more of a Coldplay kind of guy. U2. And a little bit of eighties hits." Darius paused at an intersection. "Here we go. This is the Dinah Moe Humm trail." They proceeded straight, without turning. "Although my dad used to play Frank Zappa before workouts."

"Really?"

"Oh yeah. My dad was a power song fanatic. Frank Zappa, Skillet, Eric Clapton, AC/DC. Heard it all."

Addisyn squinted at the incredibly blue sky. "Guess your dad liked rock."

"Yeah, he thought it inspired his athletes, or something. You know, fast beat, energy, all that." Darius brought his bike to a halt with a swoosh of gravel and waited for Addisyn to catch up. "But I disagree. Rock is a little too—" he gazed at the trail, searching for the words—"too rough for me."

"I understand." Actually Addisyn couldn't imagine Darius jamming to screaming guitars and staccato drum riffs. He seemed far too gentle to enjoy that. "So your dad liked rock, but you don't."

"One of many differences between us." Darius fumbled in a belt bag around his waist and drew out a pair of sunglasses. Once they were in place, the blue and orange mirror lenses prevented Addisyn from seeing his eyes. "It's not always like father, like son."

"I hear you there." Addisyn clamped her lips shut to avoid blabbing details about her childhood. Really, why spill her guts to a guy like Darius? A gold-medal Olympian, no less.

"My dad and I were close, though." Darius pushed off again, and Addisyn followed him. The flickering shadows of the pine trees dappled them in scintillating sunlight, like the sparkles from a disco ball. "I wish—" his voice trailed off, and he was quiet for a moment. "I wish I could have gotten one last medal. For my parents."

Once again, Addisyn was struck with the irony. Darius had climbed the mountain, the mountain she'd obsessed over for years. Yet if his reports could be believed, the summit wasn't as she had always fantasized. Here he was, a gold medalist, and yet he wasn't happy.

She wanted to make him feel better, scrape the sadness from his tone. "But you got bronze, you said." Immediately she felt dumb for the comment. To a guy as competitive as Darius, bronze wasn't good enough. She understood that mentality.

"Yeah." Darius's voice held no hint of acceptance. "But that was in the thousand meters. My signature event was the five hundred meters." He frowned, turning his head away. "I was pretty nervous that day. If I hadn't been—" He broke off sharply. "Well, no use crying over spilled milk. What's done is done."

His tone sounded almost angry, bitter maybe. Addisyn cringed. She could identify with his pain, but she couldn't let him know it. "I guess we all have goals we don't reach," she said tentatively, carefully phrasing her answer.

"Guess so." But the heaviness didn't leave Darius, and they biked for another few minutes in silence.

"How bout you, Addisyn?" he asked suddenly. "What are your dreams?" His teeth flashed in a grin—obviously he was trying to kick his bad mood. "Trying to make your family proud?"

"Hardly. My family isn't on my radar screen anymore."

Immediately Addisyn wished she could rewind the moment and retract her blunt, although truthful, statement. Why had she said such a thing? Yet Darius didn't appear rebuffed. Instead, he just shrugged sympathetically. "I'm sorry. I guess no family's perfect."

"Mine wasn't even close." An acrid wave rose in Addisyn's throat as she recalled the traumatic events of her past. "My father was—" She hesitated. All her life she'd used delicate terms. Terms like *troubled* or *angry* or even *dysfunctional.* But suddenly she had a feverish desire to tell it like it was. "My father was a monster."

Darius was silent, but he turned his upper body toward her as they rode, apparently waiting for her to go on.

"He was very abusive. He hated us all, I think. My mom and me and—" Another pause. Another demon chasing her. "And my sister."

"You have a sister?"

Why had she even mentioned this? "Yes. She's four years older than me." Addisyn gripped her handlebars a little more tightly. "We don't talk anymore."

"Oh." The air felt awkward. Finally Darius spoke, a bit lamely. "That's too bad."

"Yes." Addisyn let out a deep breath. Suddenly the sun seemed less bright, the sky a darker blue. Or maybe it was her mood that was turning bluer. "I wish things were different."

"I'm sure. That's rough." Darius was giving her space, allowing her thoughts to unwind. They continued onto Disco Boy Trail. The terrain became a bit bumpier, with roots wiggling across the path.

"What did your dad do for a living?" Darius's question broke the silence. Glancing at him, Addisyn realized that he genuinely cared, that he wasn't asking to be polite or to make small talk but because he wanted a look inside her world.

"He was a research psychiatrist." Addisyn felt the familiar churning in her gut begin—the same kind of nausea that swept over her whenever she considered her past. Which was as infrequently as possible. "Some kind of elite in his field. He'd go to his conferences and rotary club meetings and community functions, and everybody thought we were the perfect little family. 'Oh look,' everybody would say. 'There goes Dr. Miles with his sweet little wife and his cute daughters.'" The irony almost choked her.

"But he wasn't really like that." Darius's words weren't a question.

"No." Addisyn could still feel the frustration of those days, watching her father smile and shake hands with friends while she wore a long-sleeved shirt to cover the bruises on her arms. "He would scream and yell at us all. Horrible things. All the time. And he could get physical too, sometimes."

She could see how this roused all of Darius's protective nature. "He hurt you?"

Addisyn gave a wry smile. "Bruises and black eyes, from time to time.

Nothing serious, as my mother would say."

"Your mother said that?"

Addisyn shrugged. "Perfect doormat. She never defended us. Instead, she was always making excuses for him. He was tired or he was stressed or we were being difficult."

Darius frowned. "There's never an excuse for a man to bully a woman. Ever."

Addisyn took a moment to sneak an admiring glance at him. The respect he showed others was just one of the things she appreciated about him.

"I'm sorry." Suddenly the moment felt uncomfortable. Why was she telling him all this? Maybe because he made her feel completely accepted, as if nothing she said would shock or rebuff him. The security was something she'd never experienced from anyone—not her father, not Brian, and certainly not Avery.

"Hey, don't be. Always good to get stuff off your chest." Darius coasted for a moment, standing on his pedals. "So—how did you get away? From your dad?"

Addisyn paused. This was the most bizarre part of the story—and the part she was least willing to share. But she couldn't turn back now. "Well—it happened when I had just turned fourteen. Thanks to Avery."

"Avery?"

"My sister."

The words seemed to hang in the air. The veil between the life Addisyn led now and the life she had once called hers was fluttering in the wind of too many memories. "Avery...she saved me." The words came slowly. "She took me away with her."

Darius's front wheel swerved sharply. "What? Just like that?"

"Yeah...just like that." Addisyn's mind flew back to that night, the night that everything had changed. "She took me away from our father. Drove us to New York City." She leaned into a sharp turn, shifting her body weight. "In fact, she raised me from that point on."

"Wow. That was pretty brave of your sister." Darius ramped off a root, but Addisyn could tell he was listening intently.

"Yes." She checked the name of the next trail as they came to an intersection. Torture Never Stops. How true. "In many ways, things were worse for her than they had been before. She wasn't a big fan of the city. And she had to work a lot." Addisyn tossed a lopsided grin toward Darius. "Also, believe it or not, I wasn't always the easiest kid to raise."

"Now I would have never guessed that." Darius's laugh mingled with her own. His face grew serious again. "Your sister sounds like a great person. I mean, I'm sure that was super hard for her. But seeing the kind of person you are today—" he seemed to study her as they rode. "Whatever things are like between you, I know she's got to be proud."

Proud.

Shame squished Addisyn's soul. She couldn't tell him that of all the emotions she might evoke in her older sister, pride was most definitely not one of them.

△△ △△ △△

"THAT'S A PRETTY amazing story." Darius wasn't going to push Addisyn. If she didn't want to tell him something, he wasn't going to drag it out of her. But there was one piece of the puzzle that made no sense at all. "So…even after all you two went through together…you don't talk?"

Addisyn took a deep breath, then let it out. "It's—complicated."

Instantly he regretted the question. The last thing he wanted was to trespass on the private property of her memories. "I'm sorry. I don't mean to pry."

"Oh, no, it's not that." Addisyn lifted her shoulders in a small shrug. "Basically, we just—we just have different philosophies of life. I made my choices, and she—well, she didn't understand some of them. And that was that." A twinge of pain had crept into her voice. "End of discussion."

Her words were calm, even matter-of-fact, but something told Darius the discussion was sending shock waves through her heart.

Clearly this wound had never healed, and he ached for her. He thought back to his disagreements with his dad. If only there had been someone to tell him the truths he'd learned too late. How fragile people were—how quickly chances could spread their wings and fly away in a cloak of regret.

"Well…it's none of my business, I know." He paused, holding each word to the light and examining it before he spoke. "But…your sister must love you a lot. Even if you two disagree on some things."

"She doesn't love me. Not anymore." The speed of Addisyn's answer didn't match her apathetic demeanor. She glanced away, watching a brown-headed crow beat its way across the sky. "Maybe she never loved me at all."

"I'm sure she did. And still does." Darius knew it wasn't his place to interfere in this private dispute, but something urged him to continue. "And I don't want to sound preachy. But one day, maybe, try to talk to her again. You know, call her up, try to work stuff out."

Addisyn made a wry face. "Yeah, I don't think she wants to talk to me."

"I bet she does."

The flicker of curiosity in Addisyn's eyes showed that she was listening a lot harder than she pretended to be. "How—how can you be sure?"

How? "Because that's how love is." This he was sure of. He turned to face her, hoping the truth would somehow sink into her heart. "Love doesn't care if it's been hurt. Or if things are messy. Love just keeps reaching out."

"Hmm." Noncommittal at best, but at least she hadn't shot him down. "Never thought of it that way." Her eyes were pensive, staring ahead, not down the Zappa Trails but into a past he'd never experienced—memories she couldn't shake and a sister she wouldn't face.

Darius studied her, giving her a chance to listen to her thoughts. He'd never have guessed she'd been through so much trauma. Leaving her home—such that it was—as a young teenager…well, that had to have been hard. Crazy hard. For a moment he felt a twinge of uncertainty. Did he truly know Addisyn Miles? What if there was a lot more she wasn't sharing? She could have a whole other life back where she came from, in America. Even a boyfriend—though surely she would've mentioned such a thing by now. She didn't seem like the flirty type.

It certainly wasn't wise to lose his heart to any girl. But to a girl he knew nothing about? Darius was suddenly aware of the many blanks in her biography. He didn't know her vocation, her passions, her favorite food, or the name of her high school best friend. Even her reason for coming to Whistler remained a mystery. What if he was enchanted by an imaginary friend—and he didn't know Addisyn Miles at all?

"Oh! Darius, look at that!"

Addisyn screeched to a halt on her bike, bits of gravel flying up all around her. She pulled her helmet off, letting her shiny hair fly free in the sunlight as she gazed at the view before them.

Lost Lake was nestled in the center of the trees, a jewel in the woods. Under the glitter of the snowy peaks, the unruffled cerulean of the water sparkled in the sun, as if extravagantly bestrewn with diamonds. Pine trees fringed the shore, their fragrance floating in the air like a blessing.

Addisyn smiled at him, her grin brighter than the sun streaks on the water. "It's gorgeous!" Enthusiastically she jabbed her kickstand into the dirt and ran down to the water's edge.

"Darius, look at this! Is it a badger dam? I mean beaver, aren't beavers the ones that build the stick houses in lakes? Can you hear me?"

Suddenly Darius's soul felt light again. He grinned as he parked his bike. "I hear ya, girl," he called.

Because he did. He heard her—not just her story, but her soul. And as he ambled down to the lake, he was sure of one thing. He didn't need to know her whole past.

Because he knew her—the real Addisyn Miles, deep and true and beautiful.

△△ △△ △△

SHE COULDN'T GET the picture out of her head.

Addisyn sighed and flopped onto her bed. Ever since the bike ride, the same scene had been burning in her mind. A cameo from old times. She'd tried everything to ignore it, brush it aside, but it kept intruding.

Maybe the only way to make it go away, back to the shadowy depths of her memory, was to acknowledge it.

She closed her eyes. The picture was immediately before her, a technicolor window into her past. She was a grinning seven-year-old, soaring on the swings at the local park, her hair flying back in the wind.

And behind her was Avery. Pushing her.

Helping her fly faster and higher than she could ever have alone.

Their mom had snapped the photo one day—a rare moment of sanity, of normalcy, of a happy childhood. Avery had always treasured the picture. She'd even taken it with them to New York City. At the time Addisyn left, it had perched in a cheap white photo frame on the coffee table. Of course, Avery had probably thrown it in the garbage by now.

The happy-go-lucky scene was the polar opposite of their home life.

Addisyn opened her eyes and thought again of what she'd told Darius. A half hour of conversation on a rutted bike trail would never begin to unlock her history. She had given him the rough sketch, but only she knew the thousands of details that filled in the terrifying illustration.

Like the time she was ten years old and had the mumps. She'd known her father would be angry. He always threw a fit when any of them were sick. So when she heard his car in the driveway, she'd hidden under her desk upstairs.

The icy splash of the memory doused her consciousness as if it had only happened yesterday. She could still feel the agonizing fear—cramped in the too-tight space under the desk, her neck swollen and throbbing, her head aching with fever. Sure enough, as soon as her father had come in the door and heard the news from her mom, he'd started screaming. Avery had been at the library, doing research for a school project, so there was no one to distract him. He'd finished by coming to Addisyn's bedroom and cursing her up one side and down the other.

Actually, she'd been grateful. Grateful that he'd only tossed filthy derogatives at her instead of unleashing his fists.

She hadn't considered all this in years. After she'd left her father in the rearview mirror, there had been no need to look back. But tonight, she couldn't get her childhood out of her mind.

And Avery—Avery who had staked everything she'd ever had or hoped for in order to rescue her sister.

Addisyn could remember that night—the night her chains cracked. She'd been in her room, curled up on her side on her bed, hoping she could somehow escape the hurricane that raged around her. By that time, her parents had split, and her mother had disappeared from their lives.

Her father was downstairs, swearing at Avery. When she began to hear crashes and thumps, Addisyn had burrowed under her pillow to try to block her sister's screams.

She must have dozed off, because the feel of a light touch on her arm in the pitch-black room jerked her back to reality. The fright almost caused her to let out a banshee wail, but Avery's voice stopped her. "Ads! It's me."

"Avery." Addisyn had pulled herself to alertness in a hurry, sitting up on the quilt and flicking on her bedside lamp. Somehow she could tell that something serious was about to happen. "Are you okay?"

"Don't worry about me." The corner of Avery's mouth was swollen, the skin was discolored around one eye, and red marks stretched their ugly fingers up the side of her neck. But her expression was strong. Full of a resolve that was chiseled from granite. Ready to do and be and give anything. "I'm fine. But I'm done letting that man hurt us."

As if they could flip a magic switch and end the abuse. If only. Addisyn had shrugged, helpless. "What can we do?"

"We're leaving."

"What?" Addisyn had been shocked, but her sister's expression hadn't changed.

"I mean it. I'm taking you and we're leaving."

Avery had been seventeen—serious, studious, but far too young for the weight she'd had to carry. She'd graduated from high school only a week before, and she'd had her own vehicle for six months. Sitting on the foot of Addisyn's bed, she'd discussed her plan with her younger sister far into the night.

Nothing in all her life had filled Addisyn with so much hope. For the first time, they had a way out. The dark and horrible things were going to be gone.

Two weeks later, they had carried out their plan to the letter. At one o'clock in the morning, they'd climbed out Avery's bedroom window into the oak tree and slithered down its familiar trunk. Then they'd run a quarter of a mile down the road to the vacant lot where Avery had parked her car that afternoon. She'd told her father it was in the shop getting a flat fixed. Even that simple lie had wrenched at her sister's overactive conscience.

It didn't bother Addisyn. She was happy to escape, even happier to be part of a grand adventure. She'd often scoffed at Avery's anxiety—her terror that their father would somehow track them down.

"I'll be eighteen soon, and then he can't make me go back with him," she'd told Addisyn on more than one occasion, "but I can't bear it if he takes you back."

Addisyn had felt her sister's concern to be quite needless. Why would their father look for them? He hated them.

Now, Addisyn realized that Avery's fears were well-grounded. But of course, her sister had always been the wise, cautious one—planning ahead and solving problems before they even arose. She'd taken them from their home in Syracuse all the way to a place she was sure would screen them from discovery—New York City.

When they'd driven across the Brooklyn Bridge to Manhattan, it was like a whole other world. Addisyn could remember feeling so excited, a teenager standing on the verge of the great tidal wave of the world. The city had seemed so fascinating to her.

Not to Avery. Addisyn couldn't forget the trapped look in her sister's eyes, the way she'd cringed when horns honked and looked at the tall buildings like an animal staring at the bars of a cage. But with characteristic resolve, she'd found an apartment and worked day and night, paying the bills and keeping Addisyn in school.

Addisyn could see her sister coming home exhausted, maybe ten o'clock at night, hair in a messy ponytail and still smelling like cooking oil from her job serving at Burger King. During the day, Avery had worked at a law firm as a secretary, filing, answering the phone, and typing briefs and affidavits. In between times she clipped coupons, walked instead of riding the metro, and—Addisyn realized it now—often went hungry so her little sister could eat.

All the memories were making her feel disoriented, unsafe. Addisyn rolled onto her stomach and gazed out the window, watching the last rays of sun squint off the snowpack at the summit of Whistler Mountain. She took a few steadying breaths. She was safe now. All of her past was just that—past. The fact that her conversation with Darius had sent her mind down outdated trails was no reason to panic.

Every bit of that was true. So why did she still feel caught off guard? And why were her thoughts of Avery so persistent tonight?

Addisyn didn't often think of her sister. Yet tonight she was being bombarded by memories—and one glaring truth. Why had she never realized this before?

Your sister sounds like a great person. Darius's words rattled around in her soul.

A great person.

He was right.

The story she'd told him had been part of the fabric of her being, as close as her own name. The memories she was replaying now were just as familiar. Yet somehow, she felt as if she were viewing the whole situation with new eyes. Maybe it was being in Whistler, removed from the setting of the events. Maybe it was just being the narrator for once, listening to herself tell the story of her life.

That was pretty brave of your sister.

Addisyn felt a sudden surge of exasperation with herself. At fourteen years old, had she really been so self-centered, so naïve, so unobservant, that she'd thought their new life was simply a gateway to a big playground? Meanwhile, Avery had shouldered the entire load—juggling menial jobs in a place that terrified her, all while doubling as two parents to an emotional teenager.

The picture on the swings flickered in Addisyn's mind again. What a perfect image of the two of them. Avery had always been the cheerleader behind Addisyn—giving her strength—sending her flying high. Shame trickled through Addisyn's spirit. She'd never even told Avery how much she appreciated what she'd done—because until tonight, she'd taken it for granted. The idea made her feel slightly sick. Was she still that thoughtless that it took a random comment from a guy she barely knew to make her realize the magnitude of what Avery had done for her?

Her mind wandered to what Darius had said next. He'd urged her to try to make things right with Avery. Now there was where he was wrong. These days, the sisters agreed on basically nothing. And despite Addisyn's new perspective, the memory of Avery's endless lectures and unsolicited advice still made her groan.

Besides, what would she tell her sister? How everything with Brian had gone south? How her skating career was in ashes? How Avery had been right? Addisyn stiffened. No, she wasn't about to admit defeat to anyone, and she certainly wouldn't give Avery a chance to gloat.

The world was rapidly turning to dusk. Soft pastels washed across the sky. Addisyn glanced at her watch. Had she really just spent over an hour musing about Avery? How stupid of her. Especially when Avery probably never gave her a second thought.

But Darius had a point. Addisyn nodded to herself. One day, she needed to contact Avery again. Someday when she was successful, established, happy. When there'd be nothing for Avery to pick on her about.

Yes, she'd talk to her sister—someday.

CHAPTER 10

Darkness had never been Avery's favorite thing.

In fact, she downright hated it, whether it was the starless curtain of night…or the shadows she sometimes saw in people's souls.

So no matter how busy she was or how far she traveled during the day, she always made it a point to be safely in her cabin before sunset. With Mercy by her side, she usually lit a fire in the fireplace, cooked something nice for dinner, and spent the evening reading, journaling, or just daydreaming.

And most of the time that was enough—but not tonight.

Tonight things felt wrong—as if a mysterious enemy lurked right outside the door of the cabin, watching Avery with hungry eyes, yearning to devour her new life.

This wasn't Avery's first experience with these feelings. At such times, she could actually sense the tension in the spiritual realms, as if she stood before a window to a world where angels and demons waged war for the souls of mankind. Even before she knew that a God existed, she'd had the "knowings," as she called them. Once she met El Shaddai, she understood the experiences for what they were—moments of a special knowledge not unlike prophecy.

At such times, there was nothing to do except pray, remain calm, and listen to see what the Lord would say. And write poetry—a way to release the pent-up emotion and settle the turbulence. Avery glanced down at her paper, where two lines were scribbled:

I thought I was safe, but behold the fight
Mutters around me in the depth of the night

I thought I was safe.

Avery curled her legs under her in the comfy chair. She glanced at Mercy, relieved to see that the dog was snoozing soundly in front of the fire. If there was any physical threat—an intruder, a wild animal—Mercy would know before she did. No, the danger tonight was the more insidious kind—spiritual darkness.

Just leave me in peace! I don't want to see

What rhymed with see? Tree…free…be…me. Me.

What's taking place in worlds far from me

Avery put her pencil down and rubbed her eyes. That was true. She hadn't asked for the ability, hadn't asked to be able to peer into people's souls as she often could. And she certainly had never asked for the loneliness that accompanied such a power—the feelings of isolation that had dogged her throughout her entire life, as though part of her soul still belonged in those spiritual realms and was unable to speak the language of this world.

She rotated her shoulders, rose from her chair, and crossed the room toward the big windows, trying to peer into the darkness outside. Instead, an oddly irrelevant image drifted into her mind.

Addisyn's face.

Avery closed her eyes quickly, as if to stifle the pain of the memory. Her sister had been just one of the casualties of her mysterious gift.

What had she done wrong? As always on the rare occasions when she allowed herself to think of Addisyn, tears burned behind Avery's eyelids. They'd been best friends, their bond only strengthened by their shared pain. But slowly, gradually, the light that had always glowed in Addisyn's soul became shadowed, concealed, stealthily suffocated by something much more sinister.

Avery had always been afraid of the dark, but that year, Addisyn had started running from the light.

Avery had tried to explain to her sister what she was seeing, but really, she couldn't blame Addisyn for not understanding. It was difficult to put the knowings into words, especially when she herself often didn't fully grasp their meaning. And of course, by that point, Addisyn hadn't even wanted to understand—especially when Avery brought up the subject of Brian.

If ever Avery had received warning messages about a person, Brian was it. There was so much raw evil in his soul that it leaked through his eyes, even during his most charming moments. Avery had been nothing less than panic-stricken when he'd come into her sister's life. And in her zeal to protect Addisyn, she'd gripped the situation with both fists.

And by doing so, she'd only driven her sister farther away.

Avery was tired of the thoughts. Every one was an old visitor, a familiar enemy sliding along a well-worn path. She could almost feel the furrow in her mind, etched from so many similar times of replaying the whole event. But since she'd come to the mountains, she'd been able to push the pain deep inside. Why was it insistently surfacing tonight?

The unease tickled up and down her spine. A board creaked in her kitchen, and she jerked as if she'd been zapped with an electric current. *Relax, Avery. It's all okay.* Purposefully she marched to the light switch on the opposite wall, flicked it on.

Sometimes she needed more light to help her fight the darkness.

With determination in every stride, she moved methodically through her house, flipping every switch she saw. Good thing her house was at least a mile from any neighbors. Anyone passing by would think the crazy hobo girl had finally lost her mind, with her house blazing like a Christmas tree.

The only response was prayer. It had always been. Avery hugged herself and lowered her head. *El Shaddai…something is happening, and I don't know what…but I pray that you will be glorified, no matter what. Bind the forces of the enemy and bring Your truth to victory.* Avery paused, instinctively clenching her fingers into fists. *O Lord…show me who to pray for…*

Her head jerked up. Had she really heard Addisyn's voice? Calling her…just as she always had…that same lilt in her high, sweet voice.

Sweat crawled slowly down Avery's back. Why was Addisyn so on her heart tonight?

Avery sighed and returned to her chair. Slowly, uncertainly, she pulled open the drawer of her desk and reached into the back corner until she felt something—something square and flat. Her breath caught as she drew the object into the light.

It was a white photo frame—the corners chipped now—with a single photo inside. Avery, eleven years old, pushing Addisyn on the swings at the local park. The afternoon light had made the picture almost glow.

Avery hadn't displayed the photograph since Addisyn left. It was simply too painful…just another form of torture. Yet amazingly, as she gazed at it now, she felt the same peace the image had always evoked in her.

Maybe it was time. Carefully, Avery propped the photo on the corner of her desk. The action, simple as it was, seemed to ease something in her spirit. Pulling out a new sheet of paper, she nibbled on her eraser for a moment before scribbling down some lines. She didn't understand the situation with her mind. But the words she wrote poured straight from her heart.

> Sister, I love you, I hope you still know
> I'm so very sorry that I let you go.
> One day, perhaps, if wishes come true
> El Shaddai will lead me to you.
> I know my opinions caused many a fight,
> But I wanted you always to walk in the light.
> Now wherever you are, in lands far or near,
> If ever you call me, you know I'll be here.
> Sister, I love you, I hope you still see
> You always have been so precious to me.

△△　△△　△△

THE TRAFFIC ON Elkhorn Avenue had usually been rather sparse during the snow-crusted months of spring. But now, the first week in June, the snow had retreated to the very highest peaks, and the tourists were descending on the town in droves. It was just past seven o'clock in the morning, and already people were strolling the sidewalks, browsing the gift shops, and playing Frisbee in Bond Park.

Avery was relieved to leave the congestion of the downtown area behind as she turned onto St. Vrain Avenue. She enjoyed this daily commute to work, delighted in the colorful street names—Elkhorn and St. Vrain, Pine Knoll and Axminister, Moraine and Pawnee. After the turmoil of last night, the familiarity of the drive was soothing.

In the crisp morning air, with the early sunlight trickling down the crevices of the High Peaks and birds raising their trills of praise from the arms of the pines, Avery could almost pretend that darkness was nonexistent.

"Almost there." She reached over to pat Mercy. "Hey, do you think we could roll the window up now? It's getting kind of cool in here."

Mercy obligingly pulled her head back into the car. They were going faster now anyway, too fast for a dog to hang out the window.

Just past the blue sheen of Marys Lake, where the mountains began to stake their claim against the city of Estes Park, was an A-frame structure—silvered shake shingles in a protective V over a simple wood base. Avery pulled into the parking lot, her tires growling in the gravel. In the window was a decal: LIVE BIGGER OUTDOOR SUPPLY.

As soon as she stepped on the creaking front steps and opened the door, Avery was greeted with an assortment of wilderness products. Taxidermied ducks hung from the ceiling, spinning lazily. Display racks of everything from clothing to bait lures to compasses dotted the wood floor. A galvanized pail by the front door was loaded with hand-carved walking sticks.

"Come right on in, Miz Avery!" bellowed a cheerful voice from the back of the store. "And do I see your sidekick with you today?"

Mercy immediately hurried toward the voice. Dodging a display rack of wool hiking socks and sidestepping a shelf of Estes Park T-shirts, Avery followed suit. "Hey, Laz!" She shook her head in mock frustration. "No matter how I try, I can never beat you here."

Laz Jobe cocked a shaggy brow at her. "Comes of livin' behind the store, girl. And of havin' no life."

Today Laz's hair, the color of a squirrel's fur, was mostly hidden under a green bandana. His deep-set blue eyes peered kindly at Avery from the concentric wrinkles that surrounded each one. "So, girl, how's the traffic in town?"

Avery groaned. "Terrible! Is it like this every summer?"

"'Fraid so." Laz had turned away to paw through a canister on the shelf behind him. "Hmm…Mercy, still remember how to shake hands?" When she saw the dog biscuit in his calloused palm, Mercy quickly offered her paw. "Good girl!" Laz tossed her the treat, which she snatched adroitly from the air. Then he wiped his hands on his jeans and turned back to Avery as though there had been no break in the conversation. "Yeah, gets worse every summer. More and more people comin' to the mountains."

Avery quirked the corner of her mouth. "Is that a good thing?"

Laz smoothed his reddish beard, now beginning to whiten. "Wal-l-l…depends on who you ask. The city council appreciates the business. Personally, I could do without them city slickers, messin' around, gettin' lost, knowin' no more of wildness and mountain country than that kayak on the wall." He jerked toward it with his chin, then winked at her. "Course, them bears in the High Country always enjoy a fresh supply of rookies to snack on."

Avery laughed. Laz was a bit rough, all right, and he could be as blunt and straight-shooting as one of his guns. But he was generous to a fault and had a heart as true as the steel blade of one of the knives in that glass case. Avery wasn't sure what she would have done during parts of the last winter if it hadn't been for Laz.

"How do you like the extra…excitement?" Laz folded up the newspaper he'd been reading.

Avery took a deep breath. "Not a lot. It seems like an invasion, like— like all these people are ruining the wilderness." She shuddered. "I came to Estes to escape people."

Laz's smile was sympathetic. "I know the feeling, girl. I had a special assignment for you today, but if you'd rather hide out here at the store, I can handle it myself."

"Anything you need." Laz had always treated Avery with the indulgent kindness of an uncle, and right now, he was the only friend she had. She'd help him any way she could, even if she had to face a mob of thoughtless tourists to do it.

"I've always had a booth at the farmer's market, in Bond Park. Now that you're here, one of us can man the booth, and the other can stay at the store. I was gonna send you to town, but you pick." Laz's eyes twinkled.

"A farmer's market?" Avery's attention was hooked now. She hadn't known Estes had such a thing.

"Yep. Eight o'clock to one o'clock on Thursdays from June through September."

Avery cocked her head. "But if it's a farmer's market, isn't it eggs and vegetables and such?" Laz was full of surprises, but she'd never noticed that he had any agricultural leanings.

"Naw, not entirely." Laz heaved a large cardboard box onto the counter. "There's plenty of arts and crafts there, too. You know, handmade goods an' such." He ducked his head almost sheepishly as he opened the box. "I carve these in the winter to sell durin' the summer. Helps keep me busy."

Avery pulled back the flap of the box and caught her breath. Inside were rows upon rows of carved wooden spoons. Many had decorative handles, etched with intricate bears or mountain skylines or kingly bull elk. "Oh, Laz! They're so beautiful!"

Laz's leathery skin turned a shade darker than normal. "Pshaw…ain't nothin.'" His tone was gruff, but the light in his eyes showed how much he enjoyed her reaction. Abruptly he changed the subject. "So, yes or no? You gotta be set up in half an hour, if you're goin.' I'll go along to help you get the booth standin' and then come back to the store."

Avery took one last look at the lovingly made spoons and closed the box. "Absolutely." She grinned. "I'll be a spoon saleswoman for the day."

"Perfect." Laz scooped up the box in his bulging arms and marched for the door.

The girl who'd clung to routine as her safety net in New York City now thrived on new experiences and adventures. Avery smiled and closed her eyes for just a second, relishing what her life had become, then hurried after Laz. She loved every minute of living here.

And for a moment—just a moment—the sharp-tongued fear from last night seemed far away. Maybe she'd been imagining things, anyway.

△△ △△ △△

I CAN'T BELIEVE I'm actually in this little Podunk town. Brian Felding looked about in distaste as he stepped out of the car he'd rented at the Denver airport. Ugh.

He didn't know where she was, but she had to be here somewhere. At least, that's what the talkative woman at the Hudson Apartments in New York City had told him. He began walking briskly up whatever road he was on—he guessed the main drag of this one-horse town, judging from the amount of traffic and tacky tourist shops. He stumbled over an uneven place in the sidewalk and cursed softly.

Nothing less than his current objective could have cajoled him into this trip.

He chuckled wryly as he eyed the establishments he was passing. About as far from New York City as possible. He rolled his eyes. Whatever was Avery thinking, hiding out here? Was it some sort of penance or something? She was always the weirdly religious type. Maybe she was doing atonement, or whatever people like her called it.

It didn't matter. In a town this size, he was bound to find her. She was Addisyn's only blood connection—she was bound to know where her sister was. Maybe, if he was lucky, Addisyn was staying with her. He let the thought dangle in his mind for a moment before dismissing it. No, after the rift that had arisen between the two, it would be a miracle if they were on the same side of the Continental Divide, let alone in the same household. Still, Avery no doubt could give him valuable clues.

Brian paused on a street corner and stepped aside to let a family with three chattering children pass him. There were certainly a lot of tourists here. *Guess there are more crazies in the world than just Avery.*

The family turned and crossed an expansive green area to his right—probably a park or something. For the first time, Brian noticed orderly rows of white tents lining the edges of the park. The hum of people mingled with the twangy rhythm of country music. What was this?

Curious, Brian stepped onto the brick walkway that formed the perimeter of the park. A large sign met his eyes—ESTES VALLEY FARMERS' MARKET.

Farmers' market, good grief. He really was in the boonies. Brian couldn't hide his sneer. Following the crowd, he wandered from tent to tent. What a pathetic sight. In one booth, a man was selling birdhouses carved out of gourds, and in another, a group of women were in raptures over some fresh tomatoes. Seriously, this was their idea of entertainment?

Well, interesting. It showed him just how pathetic a town he was in. He frowned at a tent where a man was hawking turquoise jewelry and turned to leave.

Wait! A jolt of excitement jerked through him. Right there, in the tent next to the jewelry man—was that Avery?

No, surely not…

Hastily Brian shouldered his way through the crowd until he was screened by a stand of hanging plants. With caution, he peered around the corner. The girl in the booth smiled confidently, seeming relaxed and open as she chatted with customers. Gee, it looked like her, but he'd never known her to be that at ease. He squinted. Had she cut her hair?

A sudden idea struck him. He fished in the breast pocket of his jacket and found a pair of sunglasses. Trying to banish cartoon spy images from his mind, he donned the shades and strolled casually in the direction of her booth, until he was at the next tent but one from hers. Here, an older man was selling farm fresh cheeses and eggs. Brian pretended to study the selection while tuning his senses to the girl who might be Avery.

Cheerfully she handed a young woman her shopping bag and waved goodbye, then turned to answer a question from a couple examining her wares. Mentally Brian compared her with the image of Avery he held in his mind—a serious, fiercely loyal woman with an eerie ability to see straight through him. He grimaced. He had always hated that creepy sixth sense of hers, and he didn't relish confronting her again, especially after their last nasty scene. For a crazy moment he wondered if he should shelve the whole idea.

But without Avery, he might never find Addisyn.

"You have a good day!" The voice was straight from his memories—a zap of reality. The couple called pleasantries back, but Brian couldn't drag his eyes from the girl's face. That was definitely Avery—her voice, albeit much warmer and friendlier than he'd ever heard it to be.

Yes! He could barely suppress a victorious grin. He'd found her.

What now? Perhaps the obvious response would be to walk up and make his presence known, but the thought was less than appealing. For a moment the truth laughed in his face—Brian, the man who could fast-talk his way out of any situation and stare down any foe, was scared of Avery.

And what those clear hazel eyes of hers could see.

In the next instant a tidal wave of anger swept his soul. Of course he wasn't scared of her! It just—it just wasn't a good time. Who knew what kind of reaction he'd get? The opinion of the good townsfolk didn't trouble him, but he didn't exactly want a public brouhaha either.

As he turned his gaze back toward her booth, he noticed the wording on the front of it for the first time. LIVE BIGGER OUTDOOR SUPPLY.

"Can I help you, sir?" The farmer's polite tone held a hint of uncertainty, and Brian suddenly realized he'd been standing in front of the same display of cheese for several minutes.

"Uh…no. Thanks anyway." He gave a sheepish chuckle and backed out of the booth. Then thought of something. "Actually, what time is the farmer's market over today?"

"One o'clock." The man seemed to study him. Probably trying to figure out what planet he'd come from.

One o'clock. Perfect. Brian cast one last glance over his shoulder at Avery, then turned and strode purposefully out of the park.

Never mind the strange feeling of intimidation that had come over him back there. This was best anyway—this plan that was beginning to develop. And wasn't that great luck, stumbling upon her so easily? Had he been a religious freak like Avery, he might have even considered it a sign from above.

A sign that, as always, Brian Felding would come out on top.

CHAPTER 11

Going to the farmer's market had been the perfect decision. Avery couldn't remember the last time she'd had that much fun.

"Laz, thanks for letting me go to the market," she called as she unlocked the door, pushing it open and pocketing her keys. "Best news is I sold almost two boxes of spoons."

Only silence greeted her. Avery frowned and peered around the store uncertainly. The farmer's market had closed at one o'clock, and she'd packed up and driven back to the store as quickly as possible. It was barely one forty-five now. Where was Laz?

"Laz?" Avery crossed the store and peered into the stock room. It was dark, and when she flipped the light switch, nothing but the normal hodgepodge of boxes, files, and cleaning supplies met her eyes.

As Avery returned to the front of the store, she suddenly noticed a scrap of paper on the counter.

Miss Avery, I'm leaving for lunch. Be back around 2:30.

Avery gave a sigh of relief. "Laz is okay," she reported to Mercy. "He just went to lunch."

With no customers, it seemed like a prime opportunity to check inventory and complete some order forms. Laz had no patience for such chores and was always more than happy to hand those details over to Avery. She had been in the back room for almost half an hour and was engrossed in the task when the bells above the door jangled sharply.

Laz, back from lunch already? Avery glanced at her watch. Only ten after two. He was early. The normalcy of the moment was shattered by a string of explosive barks from Mercy.

"Mercy!" Avery hurried to the outer room and felt her soul turn to ice.

Brian Felding, blond hair combed immaculately to one side, arms folded and eyes narrowed, was standing in the shop.

Avery's heart gave a mighty upheaval in her chest. No. Was this a dream? Some kind of crazy joke? Brian was in New York.

Mercy growled and bounced toward him on stiff legs, the fur along her spine bristling protectively.

"Whoa, hang on!" Brian held out his hands as if to ward her off and glared at Avery. "Get this brute away from me!"

Typical Brian. Avery could feel her hands beginning to tremble. "Mercy, come here." She hurried forward and grabbed the dog's collar. Mercy never displayed aggression toward anyone, but Avery could hardly blame her for her reaction this time.

Now for Brian. "Get out of this store." Avery struggled to maintain control of her voice. Every demon she thought she'd outrun seemed to have billowed in behind Brian, chattering and mocking her.

Brian straightened his jacket, seeming to regain his confidence now that Mercy was restrained. "Well, hello, Avery." He sneered at her. "You have quite the bodyguard there."

Avery's ears were humming gently. She swallowed hard and gulped another breath of precious oxygen. Somehow it seemed terribly wrong that Brian was in Estes Park, that he had invaded her private sanctuary. "I asked you to get out of the store." She would not let this bully see how frightened she was, would not let him know that a sickening dread was wrapping its tentacles around her heart.

"Heard." Brian casually leaned against the door, arms folded, legs crossed at the ankle. "Come on, Avery." He flashed her his most charming smile. "Aren't you a little glad to see an old friend?"

"We are not friends and you know it."

The charming smile now looked a little forced. Brian opened his arms to the sides, tipping his head. "Hey, now. No need to get testy."

Mercy snarled and lunged forward again, almost pulling Avery down with her. "Mercy!" The last thing she needed was for Brian to report her dog as a vicious animal. She released Mercy's collar and pointed to the storage room. Hopefully the dog would obey. "Get in the back room." To her relief, Mercy slunk into the storage room obediently, although reluctantly.

As Avery closed the door on the dog and faced Brian again, something that was still alive at the back of her frozen mind began praying hard. *El Shaddai...the Strong One...* Avery's gaze darted over Brian's powerful frame, shuddered at the smoldering hatred in his eyes. She suddenly felt lightheaded with panic. Sucking in a breath, she winced as her heart bounded painfully within her chest. *I need Brian away from me, Lord...* She felt so powerless—alone in a tiny store, far from town, without cell service. If Brian became violent...

Do not fear, My daughter. You have authority.

Were the words truly from El Shaddai? Or was it just a useless grapple for control on the part of her mind? Avery wasn't sure, but suddenly she felt calm again. Air filled her lungs, and her mind stopped whirling. She walked toward Brian with firm, even steps. She could do this.

"Brian," she began in a steady tone, "I want you out of my store. But if you have any good reason for being here, state it quickly and leave, or I am calling the police." He didn't have to know that she had no cell service.

Brian gave an exasperated sigh. "Okay, okay." He raised his hands in mock defeat. "I need to know—" his eyes narrowed at her, gauging her reaction—"where Addisyn is."

Where Addisyn is? Avery felt a wave of heat crash over her face. The pain made her eyes smart. He couldn't have possibly said anything that would have shocked and distressed her more.

Yet hadn't she expected this? Hadn't she known something was wrong—last night?

But Brian should know her sister's whereabouts better than anyone. "Brian, I have no idea." She paused. "I haven't spoken to her since she left with you."

"Do you expect me to believe that?" Brian sneered at her. "You two are sisters, and thicker than thieves."

We were until you came! Avery wanted to scream at him. Instead, she swallowed, her painfully dry throat constricting. "I don't know where she is." She stared into his eyes. "Have you ever known me to lie, Brian?"

He quirked his mouth and shrugged, a gesture she interpreted as conceding.

"The more important matter," she continued, hoping she sounded in control, "is how you found me."

He smirked, as if he were James Bond himself, hot on a clue. "I just went to the Hudson Apartments and asked for you." He rubbed the bridge of his nose. "To be honest, I didn't know you'd moved…here." The store seemed to shrink under his scornful gaze. "Anyway, a very kind lady named Maggie told me you had moved to Estes Park, Colorado, and that you had told her to relay that information to anyone who asked. The rest was easy. I flew into Denver, rented a car. Got in this morning and was walking down the road and what do you know…I see your little face behind a booth at some gypsy market. Next thing you know, I'm looking this place up on Google Maps. And here I am." He gave an exaggerated bow.

Avery still felt the urgency to get Brian away from her. Out of the store, out of Estes Park, out of Colorado, even. But overriding all other concerns was a whirlpool of fear about Addisyn. She couldn't forfeit this opportunity—maybe her only opportunity—to find out more details.

"Brian, how do you not know where Addisyn is?"

For the first time in their exchange, Brian looked slightly uncomfortable. Maybe even guilty.

"We had a disagreement." He cleared his throat, obviously refraining from saying more. "She, uh, left the city."

Avery's heart throbbed even faster—if that were possible. Questions sang in the air around her. Could Addisyn have finally realized the truth about Brian? But where was she now? And most of all, was she okay?

"So she broke up with you?"

Brian grimaced. "Like I said. We had a disagreement." He waved his hand in the air. "I was a jerk. Forget it." A pause. "I want to apologize to her, but…I have to find her first."

"She's not here. I figured she was still hanging off your arm." Avery didn't bother to sanitize her words of their scorn.

Brian's face flushed. "Oohhh. I was waiting for that." His eyes laughed into her stony ones. "Never thought I was good enough for your sis, heh?"

His eyes. Brian's words faded to meaninglessness as Avery met his gaze and probed his soul. What was really driving Brian? She didn't trust his platitudes. Apologize to Addisyn—or anyone? Him? Never.

What was she seeing?

Darkness behind his eyes. Shadows in his soul. Death wrapping around his face—slowly constricting, like gray smoke. Avery took a step forward. "I don't know exactly what you're doing." Her voice was firm. Authoritative. No longer was she the weak one, cowering in fear. She had all the power of El Shaddai behind her. "But you are just using my sister as a—a pawn in some bigger game you're playing." The shock in Brian's eyes told her she was on the right track. "Let me tell you this right now: You leave my sister alone. I hope by the granite peaks of the High Country you never find her. Even if I never see her again either, I'd rather she disappear from off the face of the earth than fall into your clutches. Now get out!"

Brian's suave demeanor was gone. "You're crazy." The anger twisted his usually handsome features. "You always were crazy!" A single laugh coughed from his throat. "Look at you now, living in the boondocks and working in some shoddy backwoods joint."

Avery's skin tingled with fury. "How I live and what I do is of no concern to you."

"Your sister was lucky to escape from you." Brian's voice was raspy with hate. He clenched his fists and took a step toward her.

She held up her hand, palm facing him. "Don't you even think about it, Brian!"

For a single terrifying moment, he locked eyes with her, his breath hard and fast. Then he grimaced and backed toward the door. "You religious nut." A few slurred derogatives stumbled from between his lips. "I should have known your sister would turn out to be as stubborn as you are." He yanked the door open and glared at her. No more was he Brian the charmer. Instead he was Brian the explosively angry man, the man who couldn't bear to be crossed. His eyes narrowed to slits as he spat the words. "I *will* find your sister." He cursed. "If it's the last thing I do!"

The door slammed, and in a moment a car motor roared to life, tires screeching on the pavement. Avery stood stunned as the growl of the motor faded. Then she crumpled to the floor in a rush of tears.

Waves of shaking ripped through her body as she lay like a broken doll on the hardwood floor. The sobs overlapped, the panic squeezing her soul.

Black spots whirled before her eyes. She wavered, felt her head falling forward. She fought frantically for a deep breath.

"Avery!" She couldn't answer the faraway shout. A dull roaring echoed in her ears.

"Avery!" This time the voice was closer.

She had been underwater, but she was rising through the waves…and then she surfaced, and snatched a great gasp of air. Someone was supporting her head and shoulders as she slumped on the floor. The face was blurry but gradually cleared.

"L-Laz!" she managed.

"Avery, girl, what the *devil* is going on here?" Laz's tone sounded angry, but Avery could see the concern in his eyes. He shook his head in disbelief. "Good Lord, girl, I leave you alone for an hour, and I come back from lunch to see some punk flyin' out of the parkin' lot and then I gets up here and finds you pretty darn well passed out."

The mention of Brian was enough to summon the sobs again. "I— I—" Her lungs were stretched too full, as though her chest might burst.

"Avery!" Laz's voice sent vibrations through the rafters. He gave her a single hard shake. "Pull yerself together and tell me what's goin' on." His eyes frantically scanned her body. "Are you hurt?"

Avery sucked in her first full breath. She gently pushed away from Laz and pressed her fingers to her eyes. *Great.* She hadn't meant to break down like this, certainly not in front of anyone else. And she didn't want to unveil the details necessary to explain why Brian's presence had been enough to rip open all her old scars.

Maybe she could give the general version. "I'm just upset."

Laz made an exasperated sound in his throat. "Good Lord, Avery, I got eyes. I can see that!"

She hesitated, teetering on the verge of all she couldn't reveal. "It's the man who was here."

"He hurt you? Steal anything?" Every muscle in Laz's face was taut.

"No, no." Avery gingerly stood up. Amazing how an episode lasting less than ten minutes could make every bone hurt. She felt more exhausted than she did after a long day's hike.

"He's—someone I knew. From New York." She paused. "We weren't, uh, on good terms. He managed to find me here, and he wanted some information from me. I did not give it to him, and he left." She made a "the-end" motion with her hands.

Laz was still kneeling on the floor, staring up at her. Clearly this was far too much to process.

"You used to live in New York? Like, New York City?"

More questions. Wonderful. "Yes. Didn't I tell you that?"

"You told me you was from back east."

Avery smiled nervously. "Well, New York is back east."

"I don't see you as a city gal."

"Because I'm not."

"But you lived in the Big Apple?" Confusion marked his every word. "It don't get any more big-city than that, girl."

Avery walked behind the counter and straightened a few papers. She noticed her hands were still trembling. Her fingertips felt icy cold. "It was a—a matter of circumstance. There was a specific reason I lived in New York. I left after—I left as soon as I could."

Laz shook his head, obviously still bewildered. "And this guy—just what kind of dope was he tryin' to get from you?"

Avery hesitated. She respected Laz, even trusted him—well, as much as she ever trusted anyone. He'd stood by her side during these last few months. But did she trust him that much? With the dark secrets of her past?

"He was looking for a mutual friend. He lost track of their whereabouts and wanted my help. I don't know where they are either, so I had nothing to tell him."

Laz still had questions. She could tell. She grabbed the door handle to the stock room and intercepted his next statement.

"If you don't mind, I'd rather not discuss this anymore." Her hands had stopped shaking and just felt a little weak. She opened the door, and

Mercy hurtled out. "We have a store to run."

◬   ◬   ◬

IT WAS ANOTHER typical afternoon at iClimb Whistler. Terry Morris absentmindedly took another bite of his deli sandwich while scrolling through his email. There was a lot involved in running this business, most of which he hadn't considered when he'd bought it from the previous owner six years ago. Seemed there wasn't even time enough these days to enjoy a bite to eat away from the laptop.

He had a full inbox today, as always, but at least most of the messages were positive. A+ reports from employees, community announcements, and the occasional mail-order sale notification. He'd just hit "send" on a reply to a notice of an upcoming fundraiser when he heard a light tapping on his open door.

"Yes?" He peered upward to see one of his employees standing awkwardly on the threshold.

"May I come in?"

"Certainly." One of Terry's policies was to always make time for employees. After all, they were the most important part of his business. He pushed back from his desk and gestured to a vacant chair.

"So what can I do for you?"

He studied the dark-haired young man across from him. One of his best employees—a quiet, studious young man named Darius Payne. In the three years since Darius had come to work at iClimb, Terry had come to consider him the most diligent and responsible employee at the center.

An alarming thought struck him with such force he leaned forward. "You're not thinking of quitting, are you?"

Darius grinned bashfully. "Oh no, sir. Nothing like that. It's actually not about work at all, but you've told us before we can talk to you about anything." He glanced questioningly at Terry.

"Absolutely! I'm always available to you guys." All the same, Darius had never taken advantage of the offer before, and Terry couldn't imagine what had driven him to do so today.

"You see—there's this girl—" Darius fumbled but pushed through the embarrassment. "I wanted to take her somewhere kind of special, but not with a group." He gulped a deep breath.

Ah, a girl. Terry smiled encouragingly. His heart went out to the kid, whose face was now the color of a Mother's Day carnation.

"I was wondering—" Darius forced his next words out seemingly in one breath. "Could I bring her here tomorrow afternoon when the center's closed and take her up Whistler? I'd be super careful and if I need to pay for her to come, I—"

"Whoa, hold on." Terry smiled and winked at the young man. "I think that can be arranged. And don't worry about paying for her to come! I'd say you're entitled to a special date with a girl after all you've done for this company."

"Oh, thank you, sir!" Darius seemed unbelievably relieved.

"Of course." Terry held up a finger. "Just one thing—be careful! Since this won't be during business hours, it will be your job to make sure everything goes safely."

"Right." Darius nodded vigorously. "We'll be really careful, and I'll take good care of the equipment, I promise."

Long after Darius thanked him again and left the office, Terry kept thinking about the young man.

Darius was an utterly dependable worker, thorough and careful with the safety of the iClimb participants. Yet he had always seemed sad—as though something painful lurked under his calm exterior. Terry wasn't prone to psychoanalyzing his employees, but Darius's reserve and strength had caught his attention early in the young man's career.

Darius had certainly never mentioned a girl either. Terry thoughtfully glanced at the ceiling and smiled. Whoever the young lady was, she must be pretty special to have struck Darius's fancy. And Terry could only hope that she would carry the power to erase some of Darius's gloom and open a brighter future for him.

⩍⩍ ⩍⩍ ⩍⩍

IT HAD BEEN months—years—since Darius had felt this good.

He rolled his windows down on the drive home and basked in the summer sunshine. He couldn't keep the grin off his face.

He was going to actually take a girl out! And not just any girl. The prettiest girl this side of the Arctic Circle.

If she said yes, of course. But Darius was somehow sure she would. She had to, right? It was like a book. The girl always said yes…eventually.

Sure, there hadn't been much fairytale in his life the last few years. But today…today he could almost see his way around the pain and guilt, the guilt that pressed on him like a heavy two-ton load of bricks. Today it almost felt as if the darkness was lifting, as if there might be a way to go on and to be okay. Finally.

It had to be Addisyn. The girl made him feel more alive than he'd ever been. On the ice or off it. No thrill of competition, no tang of victory, had ever been more meaningful than her smile. Somehow, when he was with her, he was healing. It was that simple.

Feeling generous, he paused on Main Street, letting three cars pull out of a driveway ahead of him. Well, why not? His eyes fell on the radio. Time for music. He twisted the dial.

He allowed his Uber passengers to select their preferred station, so he never knew what might come out of the speakers. Today he laughed when he heard it. It was so perfect—a cheesy oldies station playing Journey's "Don't Stop Believin'."

He wasn't much of a singer, but on this afternoon, he belted out the chorus.

CHAPTER 12

"**H**ey, pretty girl."

Addisyn knew the voice—of course. It was the same one that lurked around the corners of her mind, weaving itself through her subconscious. The warm, gentle tenor she was somehow constantly expecting—or was it hoping?—to hear.

She tossed a mischievous smile over her shoulder. "Hello, sir." She cocked her head to one side, allowing the morning sunshine to spill over her face. "You looking for a latte?"

Darius grinned, taking the easy teasing in stride. "Something much better." He leaned lazily against the counter, watching her as she poured steamed milk into the urn.

"Something better? Only thing better than a latte is a mocha." Something—probably the heat from the milk—was making her cheeks flush.

"Maybe." His West Coast accent was truly adorable. "But it seems I ain't seen mocha you lately."

"Darius!" She couldn't help laughing at the awkward wordplay.

"C'mon, girl, you know we need to hang out." He stretched his forearms on the counter.

"Well, yeah, I guess so." She accidentally clinked a glass milk jar against the side of the urn. Why was she always so clumsy around Darius?

"What time you get off work today?" He rested his chin in his palm, watching her make his coffee.

Addisyn concentrated incredibly hard on grinding the beans. "One thirty."

"Great." His leisurely grin sprawled across his face like a splash of sunshine. "I'll be at your hotel door to pick you up at two thirty."

Addisyn narrowed her eyes. "Wait, where are we going?" She slipped a cardboard sleeve on Darius's cup and slid it across the counter to him.

"Ah, now that's for me to know and you to find out. Just—wear warm clothes. And good shoes."

"Good shoes?" Addisyn wrinkled her forehead.

"Well, good from a guy's point of view. Hiking boots, or something."

"Okay…" Addisyn would have preferred more details, but from the teasing glint in her friend's eyes, she wasn't going to get any. "All right." She held up her hands in mock surrender. "I'll see you at two thirty."

"Good deal." He remained standing at the counter, as though hesitant to leave. Addisyn found herself slowing down too. She paused to look at him, at the angles of his face, the way he tipped his head slightly to one side. He was so…

"Uh…" He gave a nervous chuckle. "Uh, Miss Barista, I need a lid…"

Good grief! She'd given him a Cuban in a travel cup with no lid. Addisyn could feel the pink staining her cheeks. There was that absent-mindedness around him again. She was determined not to analyze her reaction. "Sorry." She nabbed a paper-wrapped straw from a nearby container and handed it to him, being careful not to brush his fingertips with her own.

"Thank you much. See ya." He raised the mocha slightly as if in salute, then headed for the exit.

As the door closed behind him, Chelsea wandered up to the counter and sighed dramatically. "Good-lookin' and sweet-talkin'. Girlfriend, you've got yourself one dreamboat guy."

The comment was as irritating as a scratchy wool sweater. Addisyn gritted her teeth. "He's not my guy!" She swiped her cleaning rag into the stack of foam cups so hard that they tumbled to the floor. Great.

Chelsea just raised her eyebrows and bent to help tidy the mess—the most recent instance of Addisyn's fumbling whenever Darius was mentioned. "Says you."

Five minutes later the shop was restored to order, Chelsea was happily waiting tables, and Addisyn was busy creating an iced tea for a young girl. As she clattered ice cubes into the plastic cup, she thought about Chelsea's remarks.

Addisyn wasn't stupid—not naïve like Avery. In fact, she flattered herself that she was fairly self-aware. And right now, her self-awareness was reminding her that no matter how attractive Darius could be at times, he wasn't her brand of Prince Charming. His long hair and plaid flannel shirts contrasted with everything Brian represented—glittering wealth and aggressive confidence and perfect poise. A wry grin twisted the corner of her mouth, and she glanced at Chelsea, scribbling something on her notepad. Now if Brian walked into the shop and swept her off her feet, that nosy girl would have something to talk about for days.

No, she decided as she snapped a lid on the woman's drink, making sure the string of the tea bag dangled on the outside of the cup, Darius was not her boyfriend. Nor did she feel in the least inclined to swoon over him romantically as Chelsea did. But she was still drawn to him—mostly because she genuinely enjoyed his company. She remembered the heart-pounding passion that Brian had evoked in her younger self. He'd collided with her world and shattered it all to pieces. She experienced none of those sensations with Darius. But he was funny and kind and held her soul with gentle hands. Why couldn't that be enough?

"Excuse me, ma'am?" Addisyn glanced back toward her customer, who had apparently just tasted her tea. She took another tiny sip, and her mouth puckered almost unconsciously. "Did you—put sugar in this?"

If I don't stop thinking about Darius, Addisyn admonished herself as she apologized to the young woman, *I'm going to get myself fired!*

⚠ ⚠ ⚠

"OKAY." DARIUS RUBBED his hands together in anticipation. "Here we are!"

Addisyn blinked, squinting in the bright sun. She fished for her sunglasses in the pocket of her jacket. Once her shades were in place, she gasped with amazement. "Oh, Darius! How beautiful!"

Ahead of her was the grandest mountain she had ever seen. Whistler

Mountain, larger than life, sharper than the most impressive IMAX movie. The craggy giant looked impossibly close, its indigo shadows sprawling against the sky.

"Yeah, my current place of employment." Darius was grinning, clearly enjoying her reaction. "Whistler Mountain."

Addisyn was still trying to register the significance of this moment. "You mean—we're going up Whistler Mountain?"

"Absolutely!" Darius beamed like a kid on Christmas.

Addisyn heard the hollow uncertainty of her laugh. "Well, but—I mean, don't I need a little training or something?"

"Not a bit of it!" Darius seemed completely at ease. "You forget I'm a certified instructor and guide." He winked. "And the Via Ferrata is really quite safe. It's a pretty easy climb. Some of it is just hiking and doesn't involve actual rock climbing at all."

That sounded better. Addisyn fell into step beside Darius as the two of them headed toward the cluster of buildings at the foot of the peak. "What did you call it? V something?"

"Via Ferrata." Darius nodded. "It's Italian for 'The Iron Way.'"

Addisyn tipped her head to one side. "Let me guess, because you need a will of iron to make it to the top?"

This time Darius laughed out loud. "Relax, will you? I'm not trying to kill you!" He glanced at her, and she couldn't read the expression in his squinted eyes. "Trust me, the last thing I want is for something to happen to you.

"The Via Ferrata," he continued, thankfully sparing her the need to answer him, "is a series of iron rungs in the rock face. So, for part of the climb, you're basically ascending an inclined ladder.

"We'll take that ski lift—" he pointed at thin, precarious-looking cables sagging under the weight of two flimsy-seeming gondolas—"hike a short section, and then use the iron rungs to climb the last part of the rock face. But don't worry"—he had to have seen the look on Addisyn's face. "We'll be using ropes and carabiners, so you'll be as safe as if you were at home on a big feather mattress." He tossed a teasing grin at Addisyn as he held the door open for her to enter the climbing center.

Taking in the wood-paneled building filled with outdoor gear,

Addisyn asked, "Ropes and what?"

Darius plucked a metal loop from a nearby display case and held it out to her. "Carabiners." He showed her how one side of the metal oval hinged inward, like a miniature gate. "These clip the ropes onto your belt. They're super strong, so the rope won't come unattached even if you fall."

Addisyn wasn't completely convinced. "The rope could still break…"

Darius's smile was pure patience. "Each piece of equipment we use here is inspected after every tour by qualified safety experts, so not likely. We'll be wearing helmets too." He slung a condescending arm around Addisyn's shoulders. "Come on, girl. I climb this mountain at least twice every day, and I'm still alive! Of course—" his grin turned wickedly teasing—"if you're scared—"

Addisyn had always been a sucker for dares, and the emphasis Darius put on the word *scared* would have convinced her to walk into a den of lions. "Of course not!" She pulled away from his arm a bit sharply and shoved him playfully. "Scared? How dare you. Lead the way!"

No, she decided as she trailed after Darius toward what he called the "outfitting room," she wasn't scared. Apprehensive? Yes. Nervous? Maybe a little. But somehow it seemed impossible to be flat-out scared with his protective presence nearby. And after all, this would be a new adventure. One that might turn out, as the others had, to be ridiculously fun.

⛰ ⛰ ⛰

DARIUS PEERED APPREHENSIVELY over his shoulder as he plowed through the always-treacherous boulder field on the slopes of Whistler. Good grief, he'd taken Addisyn for a mountain bike ride, and now a rock climb. The idea that had seemed so brilliant was beginning to wilt in the light of day. Didn't girls like going to malls and cutesy little boutiques and stuff like that? Addisyn was going to think he was some kind of livin'-on-the-edge adrenaline junkie. Then again, she might think he was the rugged outdoorsman, at home wrangling bears and eating raw meat and building tents out of his own socks.

He was a far cry from either of these scenarios. He simply liked being outside, breathing the crystalline air and daring his body to perform.

Somehow, the mountains rejuvenated his tattered soul, made him feel closer to something—the divine, the transcendent, the God he knew was still there, just mighty far away.

Our Lord is the God of the mountains!

The words seemed to burst into Darius's mind. He blinked, startled. He hadn't thought of the phrase in years, though he'd heard it many times from the pulpit of his granddad's church. The man had never gone to seminary, never been able to inscribe a bunch of letters after his name, and never captained a megachurch or worn a flashy three-piece suit. But he had the most spiritually-minded disposition Darius had ever seen. His sermons had the power to breathe grace on hurting hearts.

Darius should know. He'd sat through hundreds of them.

As part of his training, his parents had taken him to elite centers all over the world. But every time he was home in Whistler on a Sunday, he was with his granddad in church. Even in high school, when his eyes had wandered more to that cute blonde from his youth group than his granddad's impassioned gestures, he'd still occupied a corner of a pew every time the doors were open. Back then, he would have nodded to his granddad's sentiment. *Yes, God is the God of the mountains. And yes, He is my Lord.*

But now…

Well, he and God just—just didn't see eye-to-eye anymore.

Shame burrowed through his chest, as it did every time he thought of the Deity. Or of his granddad. How he'd failed them both.

He sneaked another glance over his shoulder. He was shocked to see Addisyn actually smiling. Actually looking pleased to be there. She caught his eyes and gave him an exuberant thumbs-up, a joyful smile stretching across her pink cheeks.

"This was an awesome idea, Darius!" Her words were made choppy by her panting, but she wasn't nearly as out of breath as Darius had expected. He could remember a lady on a trip last year who he had been sure would burst a lung.

"Glad you like it." He couldn't stop it—the little swoop upwards his spirit made every time he so much as glanced at the girl. He couldn't see her eyes behind the reflective goggles, but somehow he knew just how bright and sparkling they'd be.

He shook his head, frowning at his digression. Addisyn didn't suspect his feelings for her—hopefully—nor did she view him in that way at all. Nor would he want her to. He could never be the man she needed—the hero she deserved. Falling in love would only devastate them both.

It was good he was the only one affected. He'd rather break his heart than hers.

At the beginning of the rock face he stopped, waiting for Addisyn to catch up. Leaning back against the mountain, he gazed out over the town. The incredible birds-eye view was one of his favorite parts of the job. He could even pick out the greyish hulk of the training center.

Addisyn took the last few laborious steps to come beside him. Wow, she hadn't been far behind at all. She really had to be in excellent physical shape.

Darius took her upper arm to keep her from slipping. Even that platonic contact shot a jolt of electricity through his hand. *Man, I am a mess!*

△△　△△　△△

"NOW, WE'RE GOING to climb this rock face." Darius gestured upward at a seemingly vertical slab of stone.

"Sure. Okay." Addisyn nodded, trying not to totally embarrass herself by breathing as loudly as she would have preferred. Actually she felt like lying down and throwing up. They'd already ridden a gondola, hiked over a boulder field, and climbed two steel ladders. Yet this, according to Darius, was the *easy* part. He probably thought she was the world's biggest wimp. She swallowed a gasp that was just coming and tried to take a deep breath.

But that one question had to be asked. "And it's totally safe, right?"

Darius grinned. "Totally." He held up a carabiner. "As long as you have these little guys."

Bending forward, he carefully clipped one of the carabiners to Addisyn's special climbing belt. Dangling from it was a short piece of red-and-black silky rope, about half an inch thick and eighteen inches long. It had two carabiners clipped to the free end.

Addisyn fingered the cord. "What is this stuff?" It sure didn't seem strong enough to hold her. She would have been happy to have a rope the thickness of her leg.

"Paracord." Darius expertly clipped a similar rope to his own belt. "It might look flimsy, but it's supposed to support four thousand pounds if need be." He grinned mischievously at her. "And I'm pretty sure you don't weigh that much."

Addisyn shook her head and joined his laughter. "Yeah, I won't overload it, I promise."

"This is it." Darius smiled, gazing upward. "The Iron Way."

As far up as Addisyn could see, U-shaped metal rungs jutted stiffly from the cliff face. "We walk on those?"

"Yup." Darius nodded. "Just like climbing a ladder."

Not quite. Addisyn quickly focused on the ground to forestall an attack of vertigo.

Darius pointed to a metal cable running beside the rungs and anchored to the rock at intervals with rebar supports. "See that cable? That's what your carabiners connect to."

Stepping onto the first rung, Darius showed her how to clip both carabiners to the cable and slide them along as she climbed. "Then, when you get to a joint where the new section of cable begins, just do this." He unhooked one carabiner and clipped it to the new section of cable, then followed suit with the second one. "The important thing to remember is that you are always connected to the cable with one or both carabiners. Okay?"

The longer Addisyn watched, the more dangerous—if not downright deadly—this seemed. Why was this even legal? Avery would be in her glory up here, but Addisyn would be much more comfortable in a place where she might not die if she stepped a half inch in the wrong direction. She was absolutely regretting this whole excursion. And absolutely not going to confess that to Darius. "Okey-dokey." The attempt to sound chipper just sounded pitiful instead. "Here we go."

Taking a deep breath, she grabbed the first rung and fumbled with her carabiners.

And took her first step onto the Iron Way.

I CAN'T BELIEVE he does this every day. Addisyn glanced ahead of her to the lean, muscular frame of Darius with increased respect.

She reached above her head and clutched the next iron rung. How many had there been thus far? She'd lost count. Even through her special gloves with the sticky gripping palms, she could feel the cold from the metal.

Actually, the whole environment seemed to be getting cooler. She heaved herself onto the next rung and paused for a second, looking over her shoulder. Gray clouds were boiling ominously through the sky. As for the town—when Addisyn glanced into the valley, her stomach seemed to wad up and rise into her throat. She shut her eyes quickly and turned back to the rock wall.

She pulled herself up and worked one foot and then the other onto the next rung. The rungs were pretty close to the rock. She had to turn her feet slightly sideways to have enough room for them, which didn't help with her confidence. And why did the rungs have to be that skinny and that round? Large, flat steps would have been much better.

An elevator would have been best.

Pull, step, step. Pull, step, step. Try to breathe. Watch Darius ahead of her, moving methodically up the mountainside. Addisyn came to a joint and wearily leaned into the rock. She moved her carabiners to the new section of cable one at a time, just as Darius had shown her. Her gloves and chilly fingers made the chore awkward. How tall was this mountain, anyway?

"Darius?"

He paused and glanced back down at her. "Yep?"

"Are those clouds okay?" Addisyn didn't want to take her hands off the metal to point.

He glanced at the horizon, then pulled his goggles up to check again. A moment of quiet swept the mountain as the sun drifted behind one of the clouds.

"I'm not sure." His voice sounded uncertain. "Um…right up here is a rock ledge. Let's stop there and check the sky again."

When she reached the ledge, Darius was squatted there, smiling at her. "Just sit here for a moment and breathe." His voice was gentle. "You've done great."

Warmth swelled inside Addisyn's chest at his praise. "Thanks." Even that short word came out in a gasp. "I—can't breathe."

The corner of Darius's mouth tipped up sympathetically. "That's the altitude. Air is thinner up here. Be careful you don't get altitude sickness."

Altitude sickness? Whatever it was, Addisyn was sure she would get it. Or maybe she already had it. "What—is—that?"

"Comes when the body has a hard time adjusting to the thinner air." Darius shifted his weight slightly. "Watch for symptoms. Nausea, dizziness, confusion. Things like that. Breathing deeply will help." He pulled a water bottle from his backpack. "As will drinking plenty of good ol' H2O."

Addisyn reached for her water bottle as well. The water was cold—too cold. Or maybe it was she who was too cold. "Darius, it's colder."

"Partly the higher elevation, partly the cloud cover." He pushed his helmet back and eased to a precarious standing position to examine the horizon.

Addisyn followed his gaze. It was easier to look out when she was sitting down. "The sky looks bad."

"I know." Darius frowned. "I think we'll be okay, though. Right up here is a big level area where afternoon groups stop for lunch. The views are 360. We can check the clouds again there." He snapped his carabiners to the cable and forged upward again.

Wait for me! Addisyn thrust her bottle into her backpack and struggled to hoist the bag onto her shoulders. Why had she taken it off, anyway? She fumbled with the straps. Darius continued plowing ahead, unaware of her plight.

There, all set. She tried to climb quickly, but her legs felt more and more like lead weights. Something brushed the tip of her nose. Another something splatted on the back of her glove. And another one—on the rock in front of her.

Raindrops.

"Darius?" He didn't turn around, clearly unable to hear her gasping call. If only she didn't have to keep moving those darn carabiners, she could probably catch up with him. That slowed her down every few seconds, her cold fingers fumbling with the ornery catches. She looked around. This part was still a tough climb, but it was much less steep, with none of the sheer precipices they had encountered originally. What if she quit hooking herself to the cable? It wasn't like she was going to fall; she had the hang of this now. And it would save her a lot of time.

Yes, it would be okay. Carabiners dangling limply from her belt, she grabbed the next rung with renewed energy. Now she could hurry up there and be right behind Darius again.

DID IT HAVE to rain today? Darius shook his head in amazement. The stray raindrops had been joined by others, and already he could feel himself getting soggy. Call it karma, kismet, luck—whatever you called it, his was bad. The frustration made him feel like crying as he continued climbing.

His grip on the rungs momentarily tightened as a gust of wind whipped by. There had been no chance of rain today, but—"The mountains make their own weather," Terry always quipped. Apparently they were doing just that. Didn't anything ever go right for him?

He'd thought it would be a lovely day, a new experience that Addisyn would relish. They'd climb the mountain together, then relax at the top, basking in the warm sunshine while snapping photos and eating the PB&J's he'd brought. Maybe she'd lean her head on his shoulder and tell him what a great day she'd had.

Now it was cold, it was raining, and thanks to the low-hanging clouds, the views were as impressive as a smoggy city street. Darius swiped the back of his glove against his mouth. This wasn't fun even for him, and he'd known few bad days on this mountain. It must be pure misery for Addisyn. To top it all off, when he'd searched for his water, he'd found the sandwiches, slid to the bottom of his backpack—flat as a piece of paper.

The last thing he wanted was to turn around, especially since they weren't that far from the summit. However, a storm on Whistler was no joke. The rungs became slick in the rain, and since they were above the treeline, any lightning would be deadly. He would probably have risked it if he'd been alone, but no way could he take the chance of endangering Addisyn.

He stopped and turned. "Addisyn?"

"Uh?" Her voice floated up the mountainside. His heart melted as he watched her, clinging to the iron rungs, struggling up the rock—for him. What an idiot he'd been to put her through this.

Amazingly, she managed a smile. "I'm hurrying, don't worry!"

"That's not—" Darius started to say, but his sentence broke into a cry that wrenched at his lungs.

Addisyn's foot was slipping, the boot sliding backwards off the wet metal. She screamed and grabbed at the rungs above her, frantically grappling for balance.

It seemed to take no time and all time, a millisecond and forever. Darius could feel one slow heartbeat, as if time had frozen.

Thank goodness for the carabiners. This was when they did their job.

And then Addisyn was sliding down the rock, half rolling, half skidding. Her arms flailed wildly at the slick rock face as she screamed again in panic. Finally she landed on a narrow ledge a hundred feet off the trail.

For a moment Darius felt numb, frozen to the rock where he stood. His eyes were fastened to the back of her bright pink jacket. A cold sickness twisted his stomach.

"Addisyn!" Nothing. And more nothing.

"Addisyn!" The word sounded more like a howl than any word from a man.

There was no time to waste. He grabbed the rungs and began his way down—far faster than he had ever known he could go.

△△ △△ △△

AIR. SHE NEEDED air. Addisyn gasped, her vision fading in and out. Something blurry was preventing her from seeing.

Gradually her mind cleared. She had fallen. She had unhooked those stupid carabiners and she had fallen. Was she dead?

She reached frantically for her eyes. Why couldn't she see? Her fingers found her goggles, ripping them off.

Relief washed over her soul. That was better. The goggles had been foggy with humidity. She blinked against the pelting rain.

Groggily she rolled onto her side and tried to get up—then froze.

She was lying on a tiny rock ledge—a heartbeat away from a sharp drop-off. One wrong move now, and she'd plummet over the edge. She squeezed her eyes shut as sweat prickled all over her body.

What was that? It was Darius, bellowing her name in a tone of panic so desperate she almost didn't recognize his voice. *"Addisyn!"*

"Darius!" Her own voice was ragged, stretched thin and tearing from the fear. "Help me!"

"I'm coming! Lie still!"

Addisyn closed her eyes. The rain was loud on the plastic helmet. If only it weren't so cold. And if only she had left those silly carabiners hooked to the cable.

Her teeth were chattering. She kept her eyes closed and tried to relax, tried not to envision that gaping hole right behind her, waiting to engulf her. Unbidden, an image of her sister floated through her mind. *Avery…*

"Addisyn!" Thank goodness, it was Darius. His hands were on her shoulders. Addisyn looked up and was shocked to see that he had left the rungs and clambered directly across the rock face. How far had she fallen anyway? And how was Darius managing to keep his balance on the slick rocks?

"Are you okay?" His words rose above the gush of the rain.

"Y-yes." Addisyn tried to be stoic, but suddenly the panic, the cold, and the exhaustion were all too much. Tears mingled with the rain on her cheeks.

Darius must have noticed, because the expression in his eyes gentled. He had also removed his goggles, Addisyn noticed. "Here."

Slowly, expertly, he grabbed her shoulders and pulled her back from the edge. "Now get on my back."

"What?" Addisyn was trying not to start crying as hysterically as she wanted to.

"Get on my back!" Awkwardly, he crouched on the rock slope while Addisyn scrambled onto his broad shoulders. "Okay, now hang on."

Addisyn almost lost her grip when he straightened and began working his way across the rock—back toward the rungs. She wrapped her arms tightly around his neck and gripped his sides with her knees, hardly daring to breathe as he inched his way along the incline. He was using the tiniest foot- and handholds that made the rungs look like a smooth stairway by comparison. Addisyn burrowed her head into the back of his shoulders and berated herself again for ever ignoring Darius's warning about the carabiners. What if he fell now? They would both die, thanks to nothing more than her carelessness.

When Darius's foot slipped off a wet ledge with a squeaking sound and he barely caught himself, Addisyn decided to close her eyes the rest of the way. So it was a relief when she heard Darius say, as if from a long way away—"Okay. We're okay."

She opened her eyes. Yes, there they were, in a large flat area—apparently the one Darius had mentioned earlier. He knelt and gently helped her off his back.

"Th-thank you." Addisyn's legs were shuddering uncontrollably. She sank onto the ground and stared at Darius as he plopped down beside her, rain beading up on his beard and dripping off the brim of his helmet. He ran one arm across his shiny wet face.

"That was close." His shaky grin showed how much he'd felt the tension.

Addisyn just nodded. "Darius, I'm sorry." She swallowed hard and focused on the ground. "I took the carabiners off because it was wasting time moving them at each joint. I wanted to catch up with you."

"Aww…" Darius pulled one knee up and rested his elbow on it. "Girl, why didn't you just yell for me? I would've waited."

Addisyn hung her head. Somehow she wanted to cry now more than ever. "I tried. I don't think you could hear me. Anyway—I didn't want you to think I was a wimp."

"Are you kidding?" Darius's voice was like melted kindness. "You did great today."

"Really?" She sniffled, the rain still pouring down her face.

"Absolutely."

He smiled again, and she felt her heart flutter. She was still too cold, too shaken. She had a sudden desire to lean into him, to let him hold her and ease the fear. This was ridiculous. Why was she feeling this way? Around Darius, of all people.

"Want a sandwich?" Darius was holding out some squished mess in a Ziploc bag. Addisyn took it slowly and rather suspiciously.

"A what?" She couldn't stifle the giggles. Hysterical, that's what she was.

"A sandwich." He grinned sheepishly. "A PB&J I brought for you to eat on the top of the mountain."

Addisyn couldn't help it now. She burst into laughter, giggling until tears crept to the corners of her eyes. "It looks like it's been run over."

He shook his head and laughed. "This sure isn't what I had planned!"

Addisyn opened the bag, pulled out the squashy mess and took a big bite. "Delicious." She looked over at Darius and they both burst into laughter again.

He sighed and looked out into the thick clouds. Rain dripped off the end of his nose. "I'm sorry, Addisyn. This whole day has been ruined."

"No!" Why would he say that? "I've had fun."

He rolled his eyes. "Climbing a rock wall, freezing to death, getting soaked, and almost dying? That's not fun for anybody."

"Hey!" Addisyn pushed him playfully. "I'm serious. It was fun." She hesitated before bringing out her next words. "It was fun—being with you."

He gazed toward her again as she huddled cross-legged on the rock, clutching her slimy sandwich. For a long moment, their eyes held. As if they were speaking a language that needed no words.

Addisyn pressed a hand on the rock to steady herself. What was this weird feeling? It was like a magnetic pull drawing her closer to this man, so kind and gentle and caring. Her face turned toward him like a flower seeking the sun.

"You feel all right?" His question sounded breathy.

"Maybe—I'm getting altitude sickness." The words would barely form.

"Then we need to go down." But he made no move to get up.

"No." The response came from the part of her that only wanted to sit here on this rain-soaked rock with Darius for the rest of her life.

IN A WORLD of dross, she was a diamond, sparkling and genuine. Even with rain-drenched hair, shoulders hunched for warmth, and a nasty old sandwich in her hand, she was by far the most beautiful girl Darius had ever seen. And the beauty that irradiated her soul was even more rare.

He sucked in a quick breath. Never mind what he told himself. Never mind what he had always believed. Recklessly he shoved the memories of his failures and foibles deep into the cracks in his heart. In this moment, he was free to love again.

Hands trembling with the feelings he couldn't stuff into his soul any longer, he reached toward her and stroked her shoulder. She didn't pull away. With a movement as gentle as a falling leaf lighting on the forest floor, his arm was around her. With a sigh as soft as a butterfly's wing, she was leaning into him.

His arm tightened protectively. He held her there, inches from him, while the whole world spiraled around them and them alone. She was his perfect dream.

He could see the amazement in her eyes, the wonder that this had happened, that two friends had suddenly somehow in an instant of time become one person.

"Darius…" Her voice was the barest whisper.

"Shh." The disbelief on her face mirrored his own. "It's—okay."

Carefully she closed her eyes, her eyelashes lying softly on her cheeks. In an instant their lips were together. It was the kiss that Darius had waited for all his life—the kind of kiss that welded souls together, inseparable for eternity. When he pulled back, he had forgotten the rain, the clouds, everything.

"Addisyn." He gazed at her. For an instant, his soul, so long dead and denied, quivered with life and hope and faith.

Then it all crashed back in. And with it rushed the riptide of a blind panic. What was he doing? Hadn't he sworn not to let his emotions get involved? Why was he sitting on the edge of Whistler Mountain intentionally breaking his heart?

Get a grip! A wave of guilt crashed over his soul. Pure, black, suffocating guilt. Darius's stomach tightened into a knot. What had he just done? He jerked away, pulling back the few inches the narrow ledge allowed.

"Darius?" Addisyn was staring at him.

He couldn't listen to anything except the anxiety screaming inside his head. "I'm sorry."

"Darius…it's okay." Addisyn looked unsure, as though she sensed the darkness that had enshrouded his soul, but her words rang with sincerity. "If we feel that way about each other, then—"

"No." His teeth were chattering. He caught his breath around the lump in his throat. "No way."

It was like watching a flower die, like seeing a dream be crushed. The light fled from Addisyn's face. "What?"

She recoiled as if he'd slapped her. And in a way, he had.

"I'm sorry." It was all he could say. Anything else, and the explanations he couldn't hint at would be unearthed. He edged farther away, tears slipping down his cheeks, his lips. The hungry hound of shame was chasing him down.

And then the pain began. An exploding pain that wrenched at his soul and made it impossible to take a deep breath. A pain that transported him directly back to the darkest moment of his life—slamming into the wall of that Olympic ice rink. Except the pain was even more intense than it had been then. And now, he realized, that was no longer the worst moment of his life.

This was.

△△　△△　△△

ADDISYN COULDN'T BEGIN to understand what was going on. She'd endured a rollercoaster of emotions today, but she could never have foreseen this conclusion to the ride. She stared in confusion as Darius hastily grabbed his backpack.

"Darius, wait!" What had happened to completely alter his demeanor? His whole personality seemed to have flipped.

"I'm not that guy, Addisyn, that's all!" She'd never seen, never imagined, calm, collected Darius so upset. Angrily he flung his goggles into his backpack and fought with the obstinate zipper.

"What guy?" Nothing he was saying was making sense.

"The guy you think I am." Darius's voice was high, thin, as if his emotions might make it suddenly snap like a stretched rubber band. "The big hero all decorated with Olympic gold."

Olympic gold. And right on cue, there was that desperate look on his face again, the hunted expression of a trapped animal.

Tears were rolling down his cheeks, or maybe it was only the rain. "Just leave me alone." The words sounded more pitiful than angry.

Leave him alone? As though she had initiated the kiss. Anger surged within her, fighting to make sense of the moment. "Wait!" She was furious now, ready to slap him, kick him, send him rolling down the mountainside the way she had done. "You can't just—just kiss me and then run off!" The bile of betrayal rose in her spirit. She couldn't decide who made her angrier—Darius for the way he was acting now, or herself for being that vulnerable anyway.

How could the flower of their perfect moment have borne such bitter seeds?

CHAPTER 13

Slowly, the sun crept toward the waiting profiles of the mountains. In a moment of flame, it perched upon their roughened shoulders, bronzing their crevices even as dusk began filtering into the valley below.

The rain had ended—but the storm in Addisyn's soul was just beginning.

Addisyn leaned against her hotel window. As beautiful as the sunset was, it wasn't the focus of her attention. Instead, she was unable to drag her eyes from the craggy giant—Whistler Mountain. King of the high peaks. She stared at it until the outline blurred. It was hard to believe she had climbed its slopes—almost to the top.

Still harder to believe was the fact that she had sat on those slopes and kissed Darius Payne.

With a groan, she ran her hands over her hair and leaned her elbows on the windowsill. The whole afternoon was one big question mark that bounced erratically around her brain. Why had she experienced such strange feelings about Darius? Why had she pretended, for half a second, that she was free to lay aside her past, her secrets, and kiss him the way her heart had told her to?

And the biggest question mark of all—why had he turned away?

It was a question she'd pondered all evening. All during the awkward descent of the mountain, then the tense drive back to her hotel. Right before he dropped her off, Darius had taken her hand and gazed deep into her eyes. His face had held none of the love and desire from earlier—just a quiet brokenness. "I'm sorry."

Addisyn had nodded and hastily withdrawn her hand, opening her door herself and scrambling out of the car before her emotions could break free of the barriers she'd erected. She'd worked to wiggle her words past the knot in her throat. "Yeah, me too. It's okay."

And as she'd paused there, clinging to the car door, their eyes locked in an uncertain dance, she'd realized one horrible truth: they'd come to the end of the story. Darius could apologize. She could accept. They could chalk the moment up to adrenaline or temporary insanity or the emotional high that followed Addisyn's rescue.

But they could never rewind the tape, never go back to a time before. Darius wouldn't come into the coffee shop and joke with her while the light splashed across his face. She wouldn't playfully shove him and eat his squished sandwiches.

All of that was over. Forever.

Addisyn had given Darius the tiniest wave and slammed the car door. She'd felt his eyes on her all the way to her hotel door, but she never looked back. She didn't cry, either. She wasn't crying now.

What was there to cry about? No matter what his kiss and eyes had said, his words and subsequent actions screamed a painful message. Loud and clear.

I'm not that guy…the big hero all decorated with Olympic gold. Addisyn had replayed Darius's words a thousand times, but she still couldn't make sense of the statement. What did that mean?

Darius had already explained that his back injury wouldn't let him return to the ice. Did the accident still torment him that badly? But what bearing could it possibly have on their relationship?

Addisyn looked out the window again. The horizon was splashed with a gorgeous palette of pastels, the colors swimming before her eyes in a dazzling swirl. She shook her head, exhausted from all her worry. She'd focused a microscope on every detail of their afternoon, searching for clues. Clues that might explain what had happened or at least help her come to grips with reality.

But really, there was no reason to keep looking. No matter what hints she could find or explanations she could contrive, the bottom line was the same.

Darius didn't want her.

And why would he? She was far from worthy. Heat crawled up her spine and over her face as she remembered the past three years—the chapter of her life she'd give anything to undo.

Brian. At the time, she'd been flattered to have merited the attentions of a sophisticated, successful Olympic coach, a real-life Prince Charming. Even after coming to Whistler, she'd fantasized about him rushing after her, pictured him standing contrite before her and begging her to come home with him. Now the thought of his touches and kisses muddied her soul with revulsion.

When Brian had asked her to move in with him, she'd come up with plenty of solid explanations to counter the cautions of her niggling conscience. They were in love and always would be. One day they'd undoubtedly get married. Their choices wouldn't hurt anyone else.

Avery, however, hadn't bought any of those excuses. She'd insisted her sister's decision went against everything God had planned—the way He'd intended relationships to work—and relentlessly preached that conviction.

Addisyn could still picture Avery during one of those conversations, still hear her words. "Addisyn, please listen. You know, you won't be with Brian forever."

Addisyn winced now to remember how she'd huffed and rolled her eyes. "My prophet sister strikes again," she'd snapped.

Avery's eyes had filled with tears, and she'd bitten her bottom lip in silent pain. After a few seconds, she'd spoken again. This time, her words rang with an authority that went far beyond her big-sister tone. An authority that had pierced Addisyn's soul—that even now, years later, she remembered.

"One day, you'll break free of Brian. And you'll meet a man that you could truly love. But you'll have a lot of shame that will stand between the two of you like a wall."

The sunset was dead, washed-out smears of color on a blackening sky. Addisyn buried her face on her folded arms. What had she been thinking? And how could she have so misunderstood her sister all these years?

The tears glistening in Avery's eyes hadn't been tears of petulance or irritation or even rage. They'd been gut-honest tears of love and pain. Avery hadn't cried because she felt disregarded or because she wanted to have the last word or even because Addisyn had turned on her so viciously.

Avery had cried because she had known—somehow, someway—that a day would come when Addisyn would sit in a cold hotel room and cry over the biggest mistake of her life.

Avery had been right all along.

And the supposed harmless fun Addisyn and Brian had shared had mushroomed into a giant whirlpool of darkness. A whirlpool that had stolen her sister, soured her dreams, and robbed her of the joy of discovering love with the kind of man she hadn't even known existed.

Because the reason Darius could never love her was plain. And as Addisyn watched the lights of Whistler wink to life in the afterglow of the sunset, and as she replayed Darius's eyes darkening as he scooted away from her on the rock, she felt like that scared, lonely little girl again, looking for love but finding it nowhere.

It didn't really matter what was happening with Darius. What mattered was what had already happened with her. She was a girl with no future. A homeless drifter, floating through Whistler. A girl who was cheapened and dirtied by the attentions of a man who'd overawed her younger self.

And now the tears could come.

THE DOOR SLAMMED into the wall with such force that the cabinets rattled and a framed photo of Whistler Mountain crashed to the floor. Darius didn't care. He hurled his backpack into the corner, banged the door shut, and leaned his forehead against the distressed wood.

Why, why, why did he think this was a good idea? Mentally he berated himself. He couldn't believe that he'd let his emotions take the reins, couldn't believe that he'd actually been so vulnerable with Addisyn. Couldn't believe—especially couldn't believe—that he'd kissed her.

She'd hate him now, he knew. In a way, he'd violated her—kissing her like that when he knew full well he could never hold her heart. It was nothing short of theft.

He pounded his fist against the door. A moan of desperation throbbed from his innermost soul. He'd never hated anyone or anything more than he loathed himself now.

On the one hand, he'd give anything to undo the moment on the rock, kissing her as if all of life was a fresh and exciting adventure ahead of him. Confusing her about his intentions, entangling both of them in feelings that he could never allow himself to pursue.

Yet, at the same time, deep in his heart, was a certainty that he would give anything to repeat that moment all the rest of his life. That no one had ever made him feel that way, and that in those moments on Whistler, he'd never been more alive.

Selfish.

He pushed away from the door and wandered through the rooms where he'd grown up. Gradually the current of his thoughts began to settle from a raging river to the usual slow ooze of defeat. His heart felt numb, as if, after years of hard knocks, it had finally been bludgeoned beyond what it could take.

He hadn't intended for things to go this far. He hadn't wanted to see her vulnerable, ready for his love, and then slap her away. If only he hadn't endeared himself to her—hadn't hung around the coffee shop so much, hadn't shared his story, hadn't taken her on outings. Good grief, no wonder the girl was confused. If only he'd never walked into her life at all.

If only.

The two words that defined his life. Anger seared through him— anger at himself. What had he done? Actually, what *hadn't* he done? The pain of his past was ripping the old wounds wide open.

He rubbed his hands over his head. It was as if a giant morbid swamp inhabited his brain, its murky waters teeming with *if onlys*. Regret and guilt and shame.

Until Addisyn came, he'd been—okay. Not great, certainly, but able to survive. But now she had awakened his heart. She had roused him from the sleepwalking routine of the last few years—brought him back to life.

And it was a life he couldn't face. Because of his biggest mistake. The one that haunted his dreams and dogged his steps.

The one that was the reason he would never, ever, put a girl like Addisyn through the agony of living life chained to a failure like him.

Yes, Darius had a lot of *if onlys*. But by far his biggest one was this: If only he hadn't made that one mistake—the mistake that had ruined his life.

The one he'd never told anyone—and never would.

$$\triangle \quad \triangle \quad \triangle$$

BRIAN SIGHED AS he washed his hands, rinsing the heavily perfumed restroom soap from his palms. He glanced at his reflection in the men's room mirror, brushing his still-damp fingers through his styled hair.

As he headed for the door, he swept the room with a cursory glance. Another overused public restroom in another crowded airport. *Another airport.*

Back in the terminal, he slumped into a seat, his chin in his hand. Idly he watched the flight numbers flickering on the neon screen, the crowds flowing through the concourse, the wailing toddler who wanted his mother to buy him Goldfish crackers from the vending machine. He was sick of it all, sick of burning up his frequent flyer miles seeking Addisyn all across the country. With no success whatsoever.

Rage burned through his veins when he thought about Avery. He didn't believe for one minute that she was totally ignorant of Addisyn's whereabouts. Okay, maybe she didn't know exactly where her younger sister was hiding out, but she had to at least have some idea. Surely she could have narrowed his search field to a specific state or even just an area of the country. After all, hadn't she always been some sort of psychic or something? A sneer twisted the corner of his mouth. *Guess her powers aren't working too well now.*

Once again, he pictured Avery standing there inside the two-bit little cabin. He shook his head in disbelief. What in the world had possessed her to give up a life in New York City, capital of the world, and take a demeaning job working at some pathetic outdoor shop in a one-horse Colorado town? Had to be some kind of religious thing. Penance or something. Or maybe she thought she was some sort of missionary.

Uneasily he chewed his nail as a disturbing thought poked at him. What if Addisyn had done something similar? Escaped to small-town Americana, taken her place in suburbia? Panic engulfed him at the thought. If she had done that, he'd never find her.

In his mind's eye, he envisioned Addisyn living in some dumpy little town, working some menial job like a hotel maid or a restaurant server. The image forced the terror from his mind. There was no way Addisyn would make such a move. She enjoyed the lights and action of the big city far too much. She wouldn't trade the glitz and glamour, of that he was sure.

And he was even more sure of one other thing—she wouldn't give up on her dream of being an Olympian.

That's why he had narrowed his search field to cities with Olympic training facilities.

Brian stretched out his long legs and loosened his tie slightly. Fully half an hour before his flight would be called. Might as well relax some. He thought with satisfaction about the fine wines served on these flights. He was looking forward to a nice glass or two of pinot noir—none of that cheap chardonnay stuff. He deserved a little pampering after all he'd been through.

Mentally he checked his prior locations off in his mind. Of course Lake Placid, an easy distance from NYC, had been his first stop. He'd also tried St. Louis and Atlanta. His method was fairly straightforward. With his credentials and reputation, no one found it odd that Brian was visiting Olympic training centers. To the managers, he simply explained that he was looking for the best area for his athlete, Addisyn Miles. Sometimes this statement elicited blank stares, sometimes gasps of excitement—"Oh, that kid who almost medaled in Sectionals! I saw her performance. It was—" Not yet had it brought him any shred of confirmation that she was at a particular place or had ever been there.

He'd flown to Los Angeles day before yesterday and checked the Olympic center within the city as well as rented a cantankerous Honda Accord to drive to the training complex in Squaw Valley. The only reward had been an hour and a half of battling hellacious California traffic. Now he was at LAX, waiting for his flight to Salt Lake City, another Olympic mecca.

He'd really expected Addisyn to be in LA. For some reason he kept having the hunch that she was on the West Coast somewhere. Brian wasn't usually one to put much stock in instinct, but he was desperate for any help he could get.

She wouldn't have left the country, would she? Brian sighed. Maybe he should try some international destinations. He couldn't think of a lot of great choices offhand, but he did know for a fact that Montreal had an excellent figure skating presence. He should know; he'd almost taken Addisyn there three years ago for training before she'd landed the Rising Star sponsorship and been eligible to train in Whistler. It had worked out for the best, anyway, because the center in Whistler was much more—

Whistler! It hit him like a thunderbolt—so abruptly that he shot upright in the chair, gripping the arms and looking about him wildly.

How had it taken him so long? He remembered Addisyn's love for the place, her excitement over the beautiful landscape, her adoration of the local vibe.

And her near-idolatry of the state-of-the-art arena.

She had trained there for six weeks—one of the highlights of her career. Of course she would be there now!

"LAX TO SALT LAKE CITY...DELTA AIRLINES DL TEN TWENTY-FOUR...NOW BOARDING..." The intercom blared the news.

Impatiently Brian grabbed his luggage set and leaped to his feet. Then he began shoving his way through the mass of people headed toward security.

So his flight was ten minutes early. Well, he was going to miss it.

With purpose he marched toward the ticket kiosks. He wasn't going to Salt Lake City. No, he was going to buy tickets for what he was sure would be his final destination.

He was going to Whistler.

△△   △△   △△

DON'T MOVE.

Addisyn leaned her head against the stack of cardboard boxes in the back room of Love You A Latte, trying to breathe lightly for two reasons. First, she didn't want to inhale all the dust that was probably back here. Secondly, she wanted to hear what was about to unfold.

She hadn't seen Darius in a week. No texts from him, no random encounters on the streets of Whistler, no Cubans on his way to work. But now, today, right on schedule, the maroon Chevy Traverse had pulled up outside.

Even now, Addisyn's emotions darted all over her soul like runaway rabbits. The thought of seeing Darius had been completely unexpected, and in a moment of panic, she'd hustled into the back room before he could open the door. Until she could get a firm handle on her heart, it was too dangerous to see him again.

The bells jangled over the door. "Uh…hey." Darius's voice. "Uh…is Addisyn working today?"

So he hadn't just come for a Cuban. Addisyn's heart tumbled over in her chest. Maybe she should—

No. She couldn't.

"Well. So it's you, Mr. Payne. You certainly haven't been around in a while." Addisyn could envision the smirk on Chelsea's face.

"I've been busy." No surprise that his answer sounded curt. "Addisyn here?"

Chelsea cleared her throat. "You don't see her, do you?"

"No."

Awkward silence signaled a stalemate.

"Is she—is she working tomorrow?"

Addisyn squeezed her eyes shut. With every passing second, the struggle intensified—the struggle to stay in the back room when every word from Darius still made her spirit quiver. She clenched her fists and forced herself to stay put.

"I'm sorry, sir." Chelsea's answer dripped with triumphant self-righteousness. "We're not allowed to divulge employees' work schedules."

Addisyn rolled her eyes. What a lame excuse.

"Umm…okay." Darius seemed to be grasping for another way to ask his questions. Chelsea had hedged him in well, though. His next words echoed with defeat. "Thanks anyway. See ya."

"Good afternoon, Mr. Payne." Chelsea's tone would have brought a boiling espresso back to room temperature. In a moment, Addisyn heard the jangling of the bells on the glass door again.

He was gone.

Immediately Chelsea came bustling into the dark closet. "It's safe. You can come out now."

Addisyn sighed and pushed past Chelsea into the outer part of the shop. The sudden light made her blink. "I was not hiding, Chelsea. I just didn't want to see him right then."

"Well, and small wonder! You poor girl." Chelsea was brimming over with righteous indignation. "Creeping around here like that, looking for you! The nerve of him!" She pursed her lips tartly.

"It's fine, really." Addisyn attacked a stain on the counter, rubbing it with a soapy paper towel a little harder than it required. But Chelsea wasn't done.

"I mean, what kind of guy *does* that?" She lowered her voice to a husky hiss, as if discussing some heinous crime. "Leads a girl along, *kisses her*, and then tells her to get away from him?"

"That's not what he said." Addisyn was sick of reliving the whole incident. It already loomed over her mind like a constant specter, begging to be noticed. She even had nightmares about it. Could she not have just a little respite here at work?

Chelsea waved her hand impatiently. "Close enough! Well, I fooled him. I got rid of him in record time."

Addisyn ducked her head to hide a cynical smile. If Darius had any sense at all, he had to have known she was in the building somewhere. Chelsea had been anything but discreet. *Who made her my bodyguard, anyway?*

"When you told me he did that, I just thought—"

Addisyn did not waste any more concentration on what Chelsea had thought. She bitterly regretted telling the girl any part of the story at all. She hadn't planned to mention the incident to anyone, but when she arrived at work the next morning with eyes swollen from crying, Chelsea had insisted on hearing everything. It had taken her two hours of nagging, but Addisyn had finally given in. Chelsea had been so flabbergasted that she had rehashed the episode a thousand times.

Actually, Addisyn had to admit, it was more the presence of Chelsea than of Darius that had caused her to dart into the back room when she'd seen the car drive up and Darius leap out of the driver's seat like a man charging into the ring. Whatever he had to say—apology, explanation, formal break-up line—she didn't want to hear it with Chelsea standing right there gaping.

And part of her just didn't want to take any more pain. Didn't want to hear his false promises or—even worse—his polite apologies. Didn't want to gaze into those dreamy eyes again and feel her heart break open just a little more irreparably with each word he said.

How could this have happened? How had her feelings wrapped around a guy so unlike everything she had always thought she wanted? Who knew now. The important thing was that they had. And he didn't feel the same way. Had she scared him with her kiss? More than likely she'd scared him with her flaws. A former Olympian deserved better, any day.

"—never would have believed it!" Chelsea's tirade hadn't slowed down. "If I were you, I'd never talk to him again! Or—" she added after a moment's thought—"I'd punish him a good while first."

Fortunately, a customer came up just then, and Addisyn hurried past Chelsea with more urgency than was really required. "Yes sir, how may I help you today?" She beamed her biggest smile at the elderly man.

And tried to forget the image of Darius, dejected, leaving the coffee shop.

⩓ ⩓ ⩓

YES! ADRENALINE WAS shooting through Brian's veins. He couldn't refrain from giving one small, celebratory fist pump as he strode purposefully from the terminal, dragging his luggage behind him.

He looked back with distaste into the bowl-shaped room, filled with so many people that just the noise of their movements made the place sound like a hive of bees. Was this the sixth or seventh terminal he'd visited on his quest for Addisyn? No matter. It was the last. He was sure of that. He had a strong supposition. He might even call it a hunch—something like those creepy sixth-sense feelings that Addisyn's weird older sister often had.

Hunch, premonition, whatever—he knew he'd find Addisyn in Whistler. He remembered taking her there a couple of years earlier for training. Upon their arrival, she'd come out through these same glass doors, squealing like a sugar-fed toddler with excitement. Everything had been new and overwhelmingly exciting to her.

The last night of their stay, they'd been relaxing on the private balcony of their suite in the lodging for the athletes, enjoying Perrier and lime. She'd put her glass down and stared out over the mountains for a long moment. When she looked back at him, her eyes had that wide, soft look he found so enticing. "Oh, Brian," she'd sighed, "I wish we could stay here forever, you and me."

He'd leaned over to her, kissing her cheek. "One day," he murmured soothingly, his mouth near her ear, "we will." He had wrapped her in his arms. "After you go win all those gold medals."

She'd laughed slightly and settled deeper into his embrace.

The memory reminded Brian exactly why he'd made this trip. Yes, he needed Addisyn for his career. Yes, he had to satisfy Ed's overly curious mind. Yes, she could be just the star he was looking for.

But that by itself wouldn't have sent him through the fifty states, and across international borders, to retrieve her. She had never been just a source of income to him.

She had been his girl. And everything in him craved her. Why couldn't she see that she belonged with him? With her beauty and his charm, they made an ideal pair.

He'd never seen a prettier girl in his whole life. Features, voice, figure—everything about her was just what he wanted. Brian's grip on his luggage tightened. Yeah, she was perfect, for sure. And she wouldn't escape him. Not this time.

Not ever again.

⛰ ⛰ ⛰

IT WAS ONE of her favorite hikes.

Avery paused, drinking in the vista before her. She loved this moment in the trail especially, when the stony path burst from the tree line and arrived in the midst of the kind of incredible beauty that could only have come from the hands of El Shaddai. The High Peaks were seemingly only a heartbeat away. Their stone-strewed slopes arced high over Avery's head, patches of snow still clinging to the shadowed sides.

Avery took a long breath, enjoying the crackle of the cool, dry air in her lungs. Stretching her hands over her head, taking time to relax in the peace of the high country, she squinted into the late afternoon sun. There was Hallett, one famous peak with a sheer side and a squared-off top. Across from it, she could see the back of its less dramatic neighbor, graced with the uninspiring name of Flattop Mountain for reasons that were evident from its profile. And in the valley between them—the little rounded bowl—was the milky mass of Tyndall Glacier.

Avery pushed her hair behind her ear contemplatively as she pondered the glacier. It nestled there in its own glacially-carved valley—technically known as a "cirque" and looking like a small scoop out of the ridge. One of the last surviving members of the hundreds of glaciers that had once covered this area, carving the mountains from a granite as immovable as victory.

That was always fascinating to Avery. She gazed across the valley, trying to picture it buried beneath a creaking, groaning, and ever-expanding layer of ice. Had the land been undiscovered then, or had it been filled with people, people who were displaced by the rigors of the Ice Age? If so, had they realized the beauty that would one day rise from the pain of the process?

"Excuse me, would you take our picture?" Avery blinked from her reverie and turned to face the voice. A young woman stood behind her with a man—probably her husband. Awe of the landscape glowed on their faces.

"Sure!" Avery used the woman's iPhone to snap several shots of the two posing in front of the backdrop. Certainly the scenery was breathtaking—much better than the canned backdrops she'd seen on some people's vacation photos.

This was better if for no other reason than that it was real.

"Thank you so much!" The woman appeared delighted with the

photos. She turned her phone screen toward her companion. "Look, Rob!"

The man grinned at Avery. "Thanks a lot! Want us to return the favor?"

"Thanks, but no need. I actually live around here." Her soul would always give a leap of joy every time she said those words.

"Really? That must be cool." The woman pulled a pair of sunglasses over her eyes and held her phone at arm's length to take some more photos of the panorama.

For a moment, the vision of the hell Avery had escaped danced side-by-side in her mind with the mountains in front of her. "Yes. Better than cool."

She gazed again at Hallett's sharp-cut sides. She didn't need a photo to remind her of the mountains.

They were etched within her heart.

The couple hurried onward, and Avery resumed her climb. She could hike briskly if occasion required, but today she simply wanted to move at a leisurely pace and take time to bask in the beauty around her. Take time to commune with El Shaddai, here in a place that bore overflowing evidence of His majesty. She needed to speak with him about something very specific today.

The trail for a time ran parallel with the mountains, separated by the fathomless Glacier Gorge in which a river rushed and chattered. Avery knew most of the water in that river was snowmelt, leftover winter flowing down from the High Peaks.

She couldn't wait to arrive at her destination—The Loch. In her opinion, the lake that filled the valley like a bowl of blessing was one of the most gorgeous in the park—probably because it was one of the most pristine. She'd heard that Sky Pond, another mile beyond The Loch, was even more stunning. One day she'd have to hike up and check those rumors out for herself.

As always, her breath caught in her throat when The Loch opened before her, a sheet of glittering crystals beneath a cerulean sky. Ringed by craggy peaks, the lake twinkled in the late afternoon sun. The rays of light slanted lazily across the ridges, turning them a muted dove gray.

Avery shrugged out of her backpack and brushed a hand over her hair. She made her way to her favorite spot at The Loch—a twisted ponderosa pine growing from an especially rocky area. Seating herself on the warm rock, she gazed up at the gnarly tree. How did it manage to survive here, in the midst of the rocks?

"Would you be happier somewhere else?" she asked the tree softly. "Somewhere with more room for your roots?" She stretched her legs out comfortably and leaned back on her elbows, surveying the tranquility of The Loch. "But this view has to atone for much, am I right?"

A sudden fluttering overhead caught her attention. She looked up just in time to see a Clark's nutcracker alight in the branches of the lone tree, chattering enthusiastically. Avery smiled in sheer delight. She loved seeing those birds, the size of small crows, their smooth bodies a soft pearl gray. In a moment the bird flew off in a great fanfare of flapping, flashing its black-and-white wing bars as it soared toward the dark green bristles of the trees across the lake.

Besides the occasional bird song, the murmur of the aspen leaves in the wind, and the gentle lap of the water on the rocky shore, there was no noise at all. It was just how Avery loved it—quiet, gentle, solitary.

Safe.

That feeling of absolute safety was what she craved today. She wasn't accustomed to feeling fear in the mountains. But the last few days, she'd been haunted by an apprehension she couldn't shake. The feeling of spiritual trouble—the meeting with Brian—the memories of Addisyn. It was as if all her buried past was reawakening—and the thought terrified her.

For all that she had suffered, all that she had sacrificed, all that she had left behind—she had received her reward. This was the place where her own spirit became as clear and pure as the wind that made the aspens dance. Where there were no limitations—no fears—no pains. Her sanctuary, to which she had crawled, wounded from the world's mauling hands, and found healing and wholeness in the loving embrace of the Lord. The pangs of modern life had clawed and howled at her when she was in New York City, but now, in the country of El Shaddai, she was beyond their jurisdiction.

At least, she hoped she was.

But what if she was wrong? What if she wasn't really bulletproof? What if the darkness of her past could somehow find a way to scale the mountains, invade her soul once more? Avery felt her spirit sicken at the thought. No matter what, she would never allow that kind of pain to drag her into its clutches again.

For a moment, she could see herself, a broken woman standing on the iron steps of a cheap city apartment, screaming in sorrow as Brian drove away with her sister and decimated her world. She shuddered and pressed her palms to the warm rock, reassuring herself. *Relax, Avery. It's okay. You're all right now.*

How much easier, and safer, her life would be if she didn't have the thread of prophecy that ran through her soul. After all, she had never asked for the gift—if it was a gift—of knowing things. Given a choice, she wouldn't have the ability to feel the current of the spiritual realms. She wouldn't know—as she did now—that somewhere, someone was calling for help.

And she could think of no one whose desperate cries would be laid on her spirit except Addisyn.

Avery closed her eyes and tipped her head back, savoring the glow of the sun on her face. *O El Shaddai…I honor You, I worship You, I love You!* All her prayers began this way, no matter what else she said to Him. She could never praise Him enough, her Mighty God Who had brought her out of such horrendous darkness. It was a miracle she was even able to know His Name, let alone to live with Him in such a place. *I pour out my praise on You, O Glorious One.*

She settled deep down into her spirit and sat quietly for a time, bathing her soul in His Presence. Always before she had experienced nothing but peace here. Now her spirit felt an insistent prodding of anxiety. Avery could feel herself begin to sweat. She scooted closer to the tree—out of the direct sun.

El Shaddai, it's too much. I don't want to feel anymore. Avery swallowed hard. *Take this gift from me, please. I have been through so much pain, so much loneliness. Please, just let me live here in the mountains and be safe.* Tears seeped quietly from beneath her closed lids. *I can't help anyone anyway.* Her sister's face floated to her mind—a ghost she couldn't outrun. *Addisyn proved that.*

The sense of urgency only grew stronger.

Are you hiding?

It wasn't an audible voice or a spectacular sign, just a quiet question that appeared in her mind. Avery felt the breath leave her lungs. She drew her knees to her chest and dropped her head onto them, allowing her hair to screen her face.

Hiding. Hadn't that been what she did all along? She'd buried the horrific wounds of her childhood, rebuilt her soul, run away to the mountains, escaped the deadliness of New York City. But could she ever break the invisible bond that bound her spirit forever with that of her sister—whether she liked it or not?

Her heartbeat felt hard and uneven. She had done her best to scrub Addisyn's name completely from the pages of her life. For the most part, she had succeeded. But at what cost? Guilt burdened her soul. Hadn't she just acted out of fear—selfish, self-protective fear?

She hadn't even prayed for her sister since she came to Estes Park, trying to put as much distance between them as possible, to break that spiritual cord. Oh, why couldn't she just enjoy The Loch and live her life in the mountains and forget about her younger sister?

Because El Shaddai was asking her to fight.

Once again, Addisyn's face filled Avery's mind. This time, she didn't force the image away but instead allowed her soul to fill with memories of Addisyn—her wild, sparkling younger sister, impetuous, courageous, dazzling. Her sister who didn't love El Shaddai.

Maybe because Avery had let her go.

Her heart, shredded so many times, trembled at the thought of opening again. But she knew without question that this was her mission. Addisyn needed someone to be praying for her, begging El Shaddai to draw her to Himself, to keep her safe from the enemy's schemes. Without any further hesitation Avery bowed her head. She was ready to meet with El Shaddai, here on the verge of the crystalline splendor of The Loch, and accept His charge.

O El Shaddai…forgive me. I was so busy telling my sister what to do that I forgot to tell her how much I loved her. How much You love her. I let my fear speak to her, not my love. I told her the right things, but I said them in the wrong way. And then, after she *hurt me so badly, I was so busy keeping my heart safe that I locked it away.*

Avery wiped her cheeks with the back of her hand. This was a holy moment, and even in the midst of her uncertainty, her spirit was stirring. She continued praying, crying out to the Lord, seeking His face. Doing battle for her sister.

Finally, she opened her eyes and looked around. The shadows were seeping farther down the hillsides. It was time to go—but she had just one last request.

And, O El Shaddai…one day…please give me the chance to tell her how sorry I am.

Carefully, she began picking her way down the trail—the section nearest The Loch was muddy from the recent rains. When she made it back to a drier area, she noticed two very amazing things. First of all, she found that instead of growing heavier, the burden was actually lifting. In fact, she felt stronger now—resolute and courageous and able to fight for her sister.

And the second thing was this—a sense of growing excitement, bubbling from deep within her like a secret spring.

Because her intense desire to pray for her sister, her decision to stand in the gap for her spiritual safety, could only mean one thing.

El Shaddai wasn't finished with Addisyn yet.

CHAPTER 14

Another day at the climbing center. Terry dropped his coat over the back of his office chair and punched the power button on his computer. He glanced at the clock over his door. 7:32. Good.

Employees weren't required to clock in until eight o'clock, but Terry liked to arrive early to respond to emails, organize his to-do list, and generally collect the loose ends of his thoughts before the rush of the day. Today he had a lot of collecting to do.

Sinking into his desk chair, he pulled open a deep-bellied file drawer and removed a fat manila folder. Employee attendance rosters. Sure, most places probably had online records for that these days, but Terry was old-school. Every week he printed a new chart and marked any absentee employees. The folder held probably five years' worth, all neatly notated with the week, month, and year for easy location. Organization was paramount to Terry.

Unless there was a real problem or a serious trend, Terry rarely had to address issues of attendance with an employee. If they missed a day here or there, he let it slide, as long as they gave him advance notice and were doing a good job in other respects. He'd never been a stickler for counting up sick days or haggling over minor faults. But today, he had some checking to do in this overstuffed folder.

Beginning with the pages from three years ago, he worked his way through the file, sheet by sheet. Ten minutes later, he laid the folder down on his desk and leaned back in his chair. His suspicions were correct. Now, what should he do about it?

Idly he spun his swivel chair to face the window. The view of Whistler Mountain from his office was the best anywhere—which only made sense, considering his profession. Today the mountains looked especially inviting—alluring, glimmering in the early morning sun.

Terry propped his feet on the low, spacious windowsill and continued to gaze at the panorama, as if he might see an answer to his dilemma scribbled on the sky. With a sudden irritated gesture, he loosened his tie. Just minutes into his workday, and already the thing felt like a noose around his neck. Sometimes he wondered why he'd been so keen to get this position, wished he could go back to the old days of just climbing the mountain and not worrying about the business end of things. There were certainly a lot of problems that came with the big chair—and not just problems of budgets and schedules, either. Real problems, about the hearts of employees.

Like this. Terry laced his fingers behind his head and glanced back over his shoulder at the file.

Just as he'd suspected, Darius Payne had not missed one day of work in three years of working for the company—except for two days back in his first year when, according to Terry's meticulous notes, he'd been diagnosed with the flu. But this week, he'd been absent for a whole day. Hadn't even called beforehand, either.

It wasn't the missed day or the lack of notice that bothered Terry. Sure, it had forced him and the other employees to scramble a bit, but it wasn't that big of a deal. It was the fact that it came from Darius.

Unquestionably, the kid was one of the best employees Terry had ever had. Probably *the* best. He was hard-working, respectful, and diligent. Unlike most people of his generation that Terry had dealt with, he actually seemed to have a sense of responsibility, to be concerned with doing the right thing. Qualities that Terry valued highly.

So why would honest, reliable Darius Payne play hooky for a day?

Terry shook his head as he remembered Darius's response to the incident. He'd voluntarily come by his boss's office the very next morning. "I'm sorry I wasn't here yesterday." His jaw had been set, eyes focused on the floor as if he were resigned to whatever punishment came. "I should have called and let you know ahead of time. It was very irresponsible of me, and I apologize."

Terry had just shrugged. "Let's forget it this time. Just call me or shoot me a text next time, okay?"

Darius had nodded. "I will." When Darius had glanced up, Terry had noticed that his eyes were red-rimmed. And he looked utterly exhausted. Terry's annoyance had melted into concern. "Darius, is everything okay?"

"Yes, sir." Darius's face had immediately smoothed into something more presentable. Or tried to. "I just—something came up yesterday." He bit his lip. "Something unexpected."

Remembering the encounter, the same uncertainty and worry that Terry had felt then shivered through his chest again. He wished he'd questioned Darius further, but the young guy had just turned and headed into the breakroom. No further comment.

Something unexpected. Terry let the words roll around in his head. Taken by themselves, they could mean anything. But coupled with Darius's expression—the silent agony of a man who'd lost all hope—they seemed ominous.

Terry leaned forward in his chair and tried to think like Dick Tracy, the eponymous hero of his favorite comic strip when he was a boy. He racked his mind for any clues that might explain Darius's behavior.

He flattered himself he knew the young man fairly well. He'd hired him at a time when Darius's life was just emerging from a long, dark tunnel—the loss of his parents, his career-ending injuries at his second Olympics. Climbing Whistler over and over had been cathartic for Darius, helping him release some of the darkness and helplessness he felt.

Darius had always been a rather quiet and subdued type, never really mingling with the others for coffee breaks and pretty silent when they were all swapping stories of The Most Annoying Customers Ever. In truth, the kid seemed a bit melancholy always, but Terry figured he'd never really recovered from his parents' deaths—at least not yet.

He squinted, leapfrogging from possibility to possibility in his brain. Surely Darius would have explained if he'd had car trouble or some other circumstances beyond his control. Had he gone to the doctor maybe, gotten some bad news? Darius had always been incredibly lean and fit, but some diseases couldn't be staved off by a healthy lifestyle.

Was he tired of working at the climbing center, needing a change? He certainly always seemed to enjoy the job, though. And really, wouldn't he have just given notice if that were the case?

Or what about that girl? Terry suddenly realized he'd never followed up about that. He'd been excited to see Darius interested in someone—finally. He'd meant to ask the next day how their date went. How could he have forgotten?

From the looks of Darius, though, it wasn't something pleasant that had kept him away for a day. He had looked like a man trapped in a hollow nightmare.

Lord, what should I do? What is wrong with Darius? Terry sighed and rubbed his eyes. Maybe he was being too analytical, looking for a deep, dark secret where none existed. To be frank, had the problem ended that day, he probably would have dismissed the whole incident from his mind. But this secret misery—whatever it was—still had Darius in its power.

Oh, he hadn't missed any more work, and his performance was top-notch, as always. But his heart was gone. His eyes were dull, heavy. He showed up, did his job, and left—like a ghost. Something was gnawing at him from the inside out.

Terry sighed. That was it. He couldn't let this situation keep dragging on. Darius had had a week to figure this out on his own—and it didn't appear that he was making any progress. Terry had to talk to him. He frowned as another concern struck him. Was Darius emotionally stable enough to be taking people up the mountain? This was a challenging job, not a routine treadmill that could be occupied mindlessly by someone preoccupied with personal problems.

Terry cared deeply for his employees, always had. He'd eaten lunch with them, worn the cheesy Santa hats at the office parties each Christmas, and gently reprimanded them when they made the wrong choices—not just at work, but in life. Most importantly, though, he prayed for them constantly. Each one was special—like a member of his own family. And he didn't believe that any one of them was at the climbing center by accident. God arranged everything.

So now, he did exactly what he always did. He bowed his head and began to pray—that God would somehow use him to restore the light to Darius's eyes.

Before it was too late.

$$\triangle \quad \triangle \quad \triangle$$

BRIAN SETTLED COMFORTABLY into the cushioned chair. Aisle seat, just what he wanted. That way he could get in and out fast. Window seats didn't interest him. He wasn't here for sightseeing. Anyway, in this case, he'd seen it all before. Just boring mountains and rivers and wilderness, all the way between Vancouver and Whistler.

He'd decided on the way here that he was done with rental cars too. The Buick LaCrosse he'd been saddled with during his trip to Squaw Valley and back had only confirmed his impressions. The beat-up old thing had reeked of cigarette smoke and body odor, with Cheetos crunched under the seats. The cheap perfume some genius had sprayed all over the inside   probably in a futile attempt to mask the foul odors—hadn't helped a bit.

No, this time he was traveling in comfort and safety, making the two-hour trip from Vancouver International Airport to Whistler via the prestigious Pacific Coach Line. He remembered Whistler as being a pretty trendy city crawling with millennials, pro athletes, and tree-huggers. In a place like that, he'd definitely be able to get around via Uber.

Pulling out his iPhone, he quickly made a few swipes and presto—he was connected to the free WiFi in the coach. He leaned back a bit further and touched his lime-green phone app.

His Bluetooth was positioned in his ear, as usual. He scrolled through his voicemails. There was a missed call from Ed.

"Hello Brian, this is Ed. I just wanted to check with you and confirm our appointment to see Miss—uh—Mills perform in Chicago on August first. If your plans have changed, please let me know. I look forward to hopefully working with you. Thanks."

August first. It was coming fast. And couldn't Ed have gotten Addisyn's name right at least? Brian rolled his eyes and swiped to another message—one he'd played so many times over the last several months that he knew it by heart.

"Brian, this is Addisyn. I—uh—am not certain of my career direction at present and may decide not to pursue figure skating as my profession. Should I wish to speak with you in the future, I will call you. In the meantime, please do not attempt to contact me. I'm sorry to have to do this, but your behavior leaves me with no choice." There was a pause here. "Goodbye."

Brian ripped his Bluetooth out of his ear in exasperation. That had truly been his moment of idiocy. Good grief, he'd had the girl right there— and he'd lost her, all because he couldn't keep his temper.

He rolled the back of his head uneasily against the headrest. For the first time it occurred to him that this might not be as simple as just locating Addisyn. What if she flatly refused to come with him?

But as the bus wound its way along the rocky coast of the Pacific, Brian's confidence grew. By the time he hopped briskly out of the bus at the terminal and saw the familiar Whistler banners on the light posts, he was one hundred percent convinced he would find Addisyn. And she would come with him. And she would skate her heart out, as she always did.

He was sure for one simple reason.

Addisyn might not be in love with him. But she would be always in love with skating. And right now, the two of them were synonymous.

△△　△△　△△

DARIUS HATED RAINY summer days. Something about how the grey fog soaked the air, blotting out the trees and mountains and shrinking the world to the size of a single dirty puddle. Pacific Northwest humidity was nothing to joke about. He stood on his parents' doorstep and gazed grimly into the dreary wetness.

Every now and then a car zoomed by, windshield wipers wagging, water spraying in arcs from the tires. Clearly, though, traffic was much lighter than normal.

Well, he wouldn't be taking anyone up Whistler Mountain today. Inclement weather notwithstanding, the climbing center was always closed

180

on Mondays. That meant it was time to switch roles and don his other cap as an Uber driver. Rainy days usually meant more business for him in that line of work. Today, there should be people downtown wanting a ride home, maybe a drive through the area. And he'd be there.

Washed-up Darius Payne, once Canada's golden boy. Now a cut-rate Uber driver on a rainy afternoon.

He locked the door of the house, remembering to give the handle an extra tug to make sure it was shut securely. Strange, after all this time, he still thought of it as his parents' house, not his. As if they might yet return to claim it.

What would have happened if his parents had lived? He would have been retired from the ice rink, maybe going to college. He'd have spent his free time with the people who loved and believed in him the most. And he would never have fallen so far.

Both on that slick short track…and the night before. The night that had changed everything.

Darius grabbed a cheap black umbrella from the corner of the porch. It didn't open till the third try. He huffed in frustration as he ducked his head and raced to his car. The water vapor was so thick in the air that he felt as if he were drowning. Maybe he was.

He couldn't force the thoughts from his mind anymore. Ever since the day on Whistler with Addisyn, the darkness that had always lurked just underneath the surface had risen like a suffocating smog, threatening to destroy him. Guilt had beaten a well-worn path in his brain, one that his thoughts could easily find and follow.

He punched his app to clock in and then decided to head downtown. More from force of habit than conscious thought, he glanced at the wallet-sized photo taped to the dashboard, right below the radio display.

A selfie of Addisyn and him, that day on their bikes.

He quickly looked away. The pain was more than his fractured soul could stand right now.

He maneuvered slowly along the wet streets to the downtown district, pulled into a roadside parking space, and turned off the car. The rain was even heavier now. Sordid water gurgled down storm drains, carrying bits of trash and old leaves with it. The gray clouds were so thick that some neon signs were already beginning to light up.

Darius checked his app to make sure he was displayed on the map, then leaned back into the seat to wait. The rain on the roof was comforting white noise. It reminded him of being a kid. With a second-story bedroom, he'd always loved the rhythm of rain on the roof when he was studying or sleeping.

He closed his eyes and folded his arms across his chest. Again he wondered what would have been different if his parents had lived. Probably he would be a decent guy, with a nice, sweet girl by his side. A girl like Addisyn.

He didn't have to try to remember her face, her voice, the smell of her hair. Every tiny detail about her was locked into a secret treasure chest of his heart forever. Everything from the way she tipped her head to one side when she was teasing him, to the shimmer when the light hit her hair, to the soft pink she painted her fingernails. And most importantly, the way she lived her life. Just by walking into a room she seemed to be bearing a gift to the people there. As if she walked in a charmed world of innocence and enthusiasm.

Sure, Darius figured she'd had some tough licks. Sometimes, he'd see a hint of pain, of wistfulness, maybe even of regret creep into her face. Especially when she was quiet, thinking. He couldn't help but wonder what her life had been before she'd come to Whistler. He mentally reviewed what he knew of her past. He knew she was from America, that she'd survived a dysfunctional family, but that was all.

She, on the other hand, probably thought she knew his whole story. Well, the image of him she'd constructed based on the facts he'd given her was faulty. Maybe that was because he'd neglected to share one very important fact with her.

Darius opened his eyes and reached for the bottled water sitting in his cupholder. He took a few sips and scanned the murky sidewalks. Not many people were out and about today. The few small clumps of shoppers were usually traveling from store to store under the protection of the awnings or dashing with umbrellas to cars parallel-parked next to the sidewalk. He sighed and leaned back again. Nothing was working out lately.

Especially not in the two weeks since he'd seen Addisyn. He was finally past the stage of obsessively checking his phone, as if she might text. More times than he could count, he'd been on the point of calling her. But what could he say, short of confessing what he really was? And then watching her walk away.

Because that was exactly what she'd do. He knew it for one very good reason. After he'd left Love You A Latte, after her coworker had all but thrown him out the door, he'd peeked back in the window.

Addisyn had been behind the counter, smiling happily and making a nice cup of coffee for an older guy. She'd just been—hiding, he guessed.

The realization had felt like a fist in his stomach, but could he blame her? Given his behavior, she was probably hopelessly confused. She had no way of knowing all the wonderful ways she made him feel. And she certainly wouldn't understand that the reason he had checked out of her life wasn't because he didn't love her.

It was because he loved her too much to bring his baggage into her heart.

Well— Darius straightened up and peered out the window again. If possible, the foot traffic was even thinner now than before.

A sudden unaccustomed anger snarled in his soul. That was it. He was done just moping here on the edge of the sidewalk. He turned the key and brought the Traverse to life. Maybe he couldn't undo the past and heal his heart, but at least he could be successful as an Uber driver. Time to head for the bus depot. He always found passengers there.

A few minutes brought him to the terminal for the Pacific Coach line. The buses ran between Vancouver International Airport and Whistler, dumping a fresh batch of tourists every time they made the trip. Darius pulled up near the canopied waiting area and idled. He didn't even bother to turn off the car.

Perfect timing. Here came a big red-and-blue bus now, its mud flap splashed. The shiny giant roared to a halt and exhaled exhaust.

Bleep. Sure enough! A rider request. Darius instantly tapped "accept" and inched closer to the bus.

A tall, well-built guy came striding toward him, face contorted with impatience and disgust. He was dragging a black luggage set and was encased in a gigantic London Fog.

He yanked open the back door of the car, cramming his luggage inside. Then he scrambled into the passenger seat with a huff.

Great. Darius especially disliked grouchy passengers. *C'mon, man, how hard would it be for you to smile?* Still, he could try to break the ice. "Nasty weather today."

"Yes, it's horrible." The man snapped out the sentence as if the weather were Darius's fault. Pulling down the sun visor, he inspected himself carefully in the mirror on the back of the flap, lightly brushing his fingertips over his expensive blond haircut.

"Where to?" Darius kept his tone light. He prided himself on his professionalism. Even if this guy already rubbed him the wrong way, he wasn't going to let it show.

"Uh, can you recommend a good hotel in town?" The man looked at him for the first time. Darius studied his face. Handsome, sure, even with a few days' growth of stubble that proved he'd been traveling for a while. But his eyes looked—hardened, somehow. Darius shifted uneasily. He was getting bad vibes off this dude.

"Well." He scratched his head and thought. He had a feeling this guy's definition of good hotel was different from his own. Probably Mr. Hotshot meant the ritziest place possible. "There's the Canadian Queen about fifteen minutes from here. It's considered the most luxurious place in Whistler."

"Perfect. Take me there." The man checked the time on his shiny Rolex and pulled his seat belt on.

You're welcome. Darius couldn't wait to get this bossy passenger out of his car, but in the meantime, he needed to fill the silence. "So what brings you to Whistler?"

The man darted another glare at him out of those close-set eyes. "Business." An awkward moment slipped by before he firmly said, "It's personal."

Darius nodded. "Right." Inwardly he was writhing at his wretched luck. He'd braved the rain and waited all day for a passenger. Now he had this Grinch who was only traveling eight and a half miles. So basically he'd sacrificed his entire afternoon to make less than twenty dollars. *Swell.*

The guy gave himself one last glance-over in the mirror, stroking his chin as if he couldn't wait for a shave. Then he flipped the visor back up and pulled open the glovebox, inspecting it as suspiciously as if he expected to find a lethal weapon therein. Darius knew if he said anything at all, he would probably say too much. So he clamped his mouth shut and kept driving.

They had made it almost five miles when Darius heard the guy make a strange noise, something between a gasp and a shout. "Hunh!"

What now? Darius glanced over to see the man pointing at the picture of Addisyn. "That your girlfriend?"

"Oh…" Darius felt the heat rising in his face. He bit his bottom lip and reached to pull the photo off the dashboard, but the guy's hand was there first. The dude ripped the photo off and held it in the light from the window, studying it intently.

Darius felt his soul shrink within him. He didn't want anyone ogling at Addisyn, let alone this stranger who was scrutinizing the photo as if the fate of the nation hung on it.

"It's—well, it's just a photo of a friend of mine and me. We were on a bike ride and took a selfie." He could have sounded casual if his voice had remained steady. He reached out to take the photo from the guy, but the stranger ignored his outstretched hand.

"Interesting." The man looked up and grinned—the kind of grin Satan might give right before he carried out some diabolical plan. "Very interesting."

Darius said nothing. Partly because he couldn't think of anything nice to say. Partly because he was so done with this guy. A jerk like this didn't deserve the luxury of conversation. *Professional. Be professional.*

"What I find most amazing," said the man in a contemplative tone, "is not that you have obvious feelings for Addisyn Miles, but that she is willing to even look at you. That's really strange."

Darius almost drove off the road. "Wha—"

"Allow me to introduce myself." The man's eyes gleamed with sinister enjoyment. He placed a hand on his chest with a flourish. "Brian Felding, figure skating trainer—and personal coach to Addisyn Miles."

"Coach? Like—" None of this was adding up.

"Olympic coach." Brian gave a brief nod. "Miss Miles is on her way to the bigs. She placed fifth in the U.S. Eastern Sectionals last year."

"She's a figure skater?" This was some kind of surreal dream.

"Oh, so she never told you?" The gleam in the man's eyes said he was enjoying this for all he was worth. "Yes, she's a figure skater, and a very talented one at that. Unfortunately, she did not receive the score at Sectionals that would have qualified her for Nationals." Brian shook his head sadly. "A pity too. But she'll make her comeback."

"Her—comeback?" Darius's heart was beating hard and rough in his chest.

Brian puffed out his chest. "She has a personal exhibition skate at the Rayard Arena in Chicago. A week from Wednesday. And believe me, she'll come out on top." There was that sinister grin again. "I've seen some good skaters, but this chick is the best." He tapped his finger on Addisyn's face in the photo.

Darius couldn't process this. Any of this. Addisyn, a brilliant figure skater? Near Olympian? Why had she never mentioned this, this beautiful thing that they shared?

Brian was waiting for him to say something. "Wow." It sounded flat and weak. Much like Darius felt. "That's—wow."

"Yeah, she's good all right. Special." Brian was watching Darius out of the corner of his eye. "I found that out right away." He chuckled as if he had inside knowledge of Addisyn that Darius couldn't share. "In fact, you could say I was a bit more than a coach, if you know what I mean."

Darius's stomach was one hard, revolving knot. He swallowed desperately, trying to moisten his throat enough to speak. More than a coach? He eyed his passenger with new horror. Could—could he have been Addisyn's—boyfriend?

"You mean—" he had to swallow again. "You two were an—an item—or something?"

Brian chuckled heartily. "Or something is right, man." He rubbed his hands together. "We've been together for years." He squinted his eyes into knowing slits. "And by together, I mean—living together." He smirked. "We're gonna get married, sometime soon. I'm thinking a nice romantic ceremony in Vegas then a laid-back honeymoon in Aruba."

Darius gripped the wheel tightly to keep his hands from shaking with anger. Partly at this man who was so obviously egging him on. Partly at Addisyn. She'd been with Brian for years? Years? Living with him? Basking in his embrace?

Looking at Brian with the same eyes of love she'd gazed at Darius with on the mountain?

Darius swiped his palm hard against his mouth, as if he might somehow erase the memory of her kiss. What a traitor she'd been. Sitting there in the rain, smiling and lying.

His skin was hot, prickly. All this time he'd worshipped her…and she thought he was just a toy.

"You're awful quiet, buddy." The words were jocular, the tone light, but when Darius looked at Brian, he saw pure hatred in his eyes. Hatred with an overtone of sadistic satisfaction.

And he also saw—jealousy. Aha! So the man was sweating a little. Darius stared right back at him. He'd dealt with bullies before. "Just surprised." The anger was boiling in his stomach, making it hard to breathe. His chest burned and tingled in an odd way. "She never mentioned it."

Brian smiled. "Well, she probably wouldn't to you. There would have been no need. It might"—the man's eyes narrowed further—"have messed things up between you."

"What are you saying?" Darius's tone was mild, level even. He braked for a second to let the light change to green and then moved on. His thoughts were moving faster than his windshield wipers and not nearly as predictably, but he could put up a poker face as well as anybody.

"Well—" Brian leered. "Girls are pretty sly, aren't they?"

The line echoed Darius's sentiments exactly at the time, but he wasn't going to hear something so crass. Before he could retort, though, Brian jabbed him again. "Maybe you wouldn't know. You don't look to have had much experience. But—you know, don't take it too hard."

"Take what?" Darius wanted to scream. But he wouldn't. He wouldn't give this bully the satisfaction. He couldn't control the fact that his face was beet red, but he could keep from grabbing Brian by his throat.

"Not knowing sooner. She probably just wanted to have some fun. You know, a little something-something on the side. But, whatever you two have been doing, it needs to stop." Brian's tone hardened. "I'm her man, and now I'm back, so I get dibs, okay?"

"Dibs?" Darius's pulse was racing. What was this guy accusing him of?

"No more fun with my chick." Brian chuckled as if this were the funniest thing ever.

Professional or not, he couldn't take it. Darius slammed on his brakes so suddenly that Brian's head jerked forward like a marionette's and the car behind blared its horn. Darius ignored it. Let him be rear-ended! He didn't care at this point. He unsnapped his seatbelt and leaned across the console. "Let's get one thing very clear." His hands were shaking so badly now that he clenched them into sweaty fists. "I have viewed Addisyn as a very good friend and a wonderful woman." He took a deep breath. Well, more like a gasp. "I have never treated her with anything but honor and respect. I'm not that kind of guy."

He gestured to the door. "The hotel is two blocks down that street. Maybe you would prefer to walk the rest of the way."

Brian glared at him a minute. Darius focused his gaze and leaned a little closer. "Sure. Okay." Brian held up his hands as if in mock surrender, then opened the door and hopped out into the rain, retrieving his luggage from the back seat.

Before he closed the door, he leaned back in and threw one last dart. "Just remember to keep your honor and respect and friendship to yourself. I won't have your hands on my girl." He slammed the door and marched off down the sidewalk.

Darius slowly reentered the line of traffic and began driving again. All that revolved in his mind was the horrible truth: Addisyn loved another man. A man who was the antithesis of him.

And she was a successful almost-Olympian. A brilliant, talented young woman who'd found relief from small-town boredom by flirting with a naïve Canadian hick.

He gritted his teeth. His chest was throbbing with a horrible pain. With as much speed as he could build up in the narrow streets, he drove as fast as he could to a wooded stretch of road. Then, he pulled off onto the shoulder, leaped out, and threw up.

CHAPTER 15

Who am I?

It was the question that had led Addisyn across a continent, the problem that drove her from New York City to remote Whistler. Well, now she had her answer.

She was a failure. A complete and utter failure.

Lying back on her bed, she stared at that stain on her ceiling—the same one she'd gazed at the night of her arrival. She was right back where she'd started.

Except worse, because her heart had rebelled for the sake of a dark-haired, gentle-eyed man named Darius. A man who didn't want her, didn't love her, and would hate her if he knew the truth about her past.

Addisyn took a deep breath and forced thoughts of Darius from her mind. Aside from finding some way to mend her broken heart, she needed a real, feasible plan. One that preferably didn't involve staying in Whistler much longer.

Rain sloshed against the windows of her hotel. Addisyn was sick of today's weather. It had been as dreary and nasty as possible. By the time she left work at three o'clock, cars were already using their headlights, and street lamps were flickering on. She hadn't dared call an Uber—what if Darius answered!—and had been forced to ride the bus home, although she hated the crowding hassle of public transport on wet days.

Addisyn pressed the heels of her hands against her eyes and sat up. *Approach this methodically,* she lectured herself. She pulled a pen and notepad from the drawer of the bedside table and sat cross-legged on the comforter.

Uncapping the pen, she tried to think.

Go to the Athletes' Center and try to hire a new coach.

The idea was as ludicrous as it was audacious. Just march up to the Center? That was off-limits to ex-stars. She'd found that out the hard way. And her chance was over. Whom could she hope to hire? Did she even want to try again? Her spirits seemed to have no emotional energy to keep them buoyant.

Additionally, she couldn't forget that she was in a foreign country. If she wanted to compete for Team USA, she'd have to return to the States. She could try to be accepted to Team Canada, which had a strong skating presence internationally, but she was far from ready to commit to the residency requirements.

Make a permanent home in Whistler and save enough money to go back to college. Then find a good job.

This time she rolled her eyes at her own stupidity. Sure, pay her way through school on a coffee-shop salary? And she didn't have any other skills. Skating was all she knew—the only job she'd had except a brief summer stint working at a pet shop when she was in high school. She wasn't the shining star employers were searching for. No degree, no permanent residence, no skill set. And certainly no references.

Addisyn felt the tremble of tears on her lip. Angrily she swiped at her eyes and scribbled one more word on the corner of the paper. Then circled it several times.

Anyway, staying in Whistler would put her in uncomfortable proximity to Darius. She couldn't handle that. Not until she managed to get a grip on her mutilated heart and remind it why this could never happen again.

The truth was clear: she had no options. The fact gave her a panicky feeling. What was she going to do?

Again she thought about Avery. Her sister's voice floated into her head. "Skating isn't everything, Ads. Make some room in your life for learning and growing as a person. And for El Shaddai."

El Shaddai. The name was a mystery to Addisyn. Goodness, she wasn't even sure how to spell it. But she knew who her sister meant. God.

Addisyn blew out a long breath. Avery had been so earnest, so sincere in her faith. She'd tried to teach Addisyn, but it just didn't—connect, somehow. Back then, Addisyn had had skating and Avery. Who needed some man in the clouds?

Now she thought back to the years Avery had raised her. How often had she seen her sister on her knees in front of the wooden bench in the corner of their apartment? Carrying all her burdens to God. She'd always rise with new strength, new resolve.

What if she prayed? Like, right now? It couldn't hurt, right? The possibility floated in her mind like a shiny balloon until it popped on the sharp edges of reality. Who was she kidding? Avery was disappointed in her, angry. The last time she'd seen her sister, she'd been scowling, crying, distraught. Telling Addisyn that this was sin and God would not honor her decision and stuff like that.

At the time, Avery's warnings had seemed like legalistic rules. Moving in with Brian had felt right somehow. Natural, logical, beautiful even. But how ugly and twisted it had become.

If God ever had noticed Addisyn Miles, He was probably just as angry as Avery. Addisyn knew enough of the Bible to realize she'd broken quite a few of His commands.

Still, what other option did she have?

She bent her head but kept her eyes open. "Dear God." Her voice stalled. *This feels weird.* She tried again. "Dear God, I am sure You are angry with me. I know I shouldn't have done a lot of that stuff." Was she crazy? "I need help." She could hear the flat resignation in her voice. "I don't have a plan."

She paused, but she didn't see the thunderbolt of judgment that zapped the less-than-perfect folks in cartoons. Instead, a crazy realization flashed into her mind. One that shocked her almost as much as the lightning bolt would have. One she would never have expected.

She suddenly realized that she would have kept any rule, endured any tongue-lashing, and borne any repercussions in the world for just one thing—to see her sister walk through the door of her hotel room.

If only she could rewind time, go back to that moment when she was stepping into Brian's swanky BMW to drive away, leaving Avery sobbing on the iron steps of the apartment building. She'd leap out of the shiny black ride, drop her luggage. She'd run back into the embrace of the sister who'd loved her more than life and beg for forgiveness for even considering something so stupid.

But she couldn't go back, and she couldn't change things. Sobs began rising from a place deep inside, a sensitive, pure place that had been dormant for far too long. A place that was shouting the most horrendous truth at her.

She had traded her sister for Brian.

△△　△△　△△

BRIAN COULDN'T RESTRAIN his gleeful smile. He stepped out of the elevator like a man who'd just won the lottery. Because he had.

At the end of this long hallway was Addisyn.

He marched purposefully down the hall. Room 308…309…310…Brian rounded a corner. 311…312.

Her room.

His fingers were trembling slightly as he made a fist and knocked on her door. Four knocks, then—

"Hello?" A muffled voice from inside the room.

A grin soared across Brian's face. It was her voice! He tried to deepen his own, disguise it somehow. It would make an even better surprise for Addisyn. Deep in his mind was the thought he wouldn't face—that Addisyn might not open the door if she knew who it was.

"Special delivery," he mumbled.

There was a pause inside the room, then a shuffling sound. "One second." Addisyn's voice sounded choked, somehow. Had she been crying? *Baby, you'll have no reason to cry now that I'm here.*

There was the sound of a drawer closing, soft footsteps on the carpeted floor, and a sniff. Then the door began to open.

△△   △△   △△

ADDISYN OPENED THE door fully expecting to find a hotel employee standing there. At any other time, she might have been a bit more cautious. She might have checked the peephole or demanded further explanation.

But—well, it sounded crazy, but part of her wondered if God had sent someone to help her. Like a supernatural answer to her prayer—already. If you asked Avery, things like that were possible—although Addisyn figured they didn't happen for her.

But still, what if?

So she pulled the door open with no reservations—and Brian Felding stepped into the room.

Her gasp was the only assurance that her lungs could still work. Like a physical blow, the astonishment pushed her back a couple of steps. The shock seemed to entwine around her throat, threatening to suffocate her. She could feel her face flushing as her knees began to tremble.

Meanwhile, Brian just coolly closed the door behind him and leaned against it with a triumphant leer. He was clearly willing to wait for her to quit disbelieving her senses.

The shock rapidly faded before the wake of an impending rage, a rage that swept every other emotion before it like an out-of-control wildfire. Fear, confusion, regret, uncertainty—all were driven before it like leaves on the wind. Addisyn clenched her fists, empowered by the anger.

"Brian, what the *devil* are you doing here?"

"Addisyn." He opened his arms wide. As though she might just dash into his embrace. Addisyn glowered at him even more fiercely. Yeah, she'd just as soon run into the mouth of a tiger. Seeing no reaction, his brow darkened, and he awkwardly lowered his arms. "I've searched the entire United States for you."

Figured. Addisyn wondered if Brian was this obsessive about

everything in his life. Still, she felt the need to point out the obvious. "You're not in the United States now."

"True." Brian chuckled. Probably from nerves, Addisyn guessed. He wasn't used to meeting any reluctance from her whatsoever. "That's because I couldn't find you anywhere. So I broadened my search field."

"What did you need to see me for?" Addisyn crossed her arms over her chest. Partly to hide the uncontrollable shaking of her hands, partly to send a message to him that she was not open to—anything.

"Aww, Addisyn…" He gave her the polished smile that had once melted her heart. "That's no way to welcome your man."

"You are not my man." There was no need to raise her voice. Addisyn could handle this in a ladylike manner. If not—well, if she screamed, surely somebody would hear. "And I prefer for you to state your reasons for barging in on me and then take your leave." He started to say something, but she interrupted. "Nicely."

He stared at her for a moment, apparently sizing up the seriousness of her opposition to him. What he saw must have alarmed him. His brow furrowed, and for just a moment, Addisyn saw what Avery had seen all along. Hardness.

Appearing to change tactics, he slowly ambled to the edge of the bed and sat down, as if he planned to be there a long time. Addisyn swiveled to face him, eyeing him warily. She didn't trust him for a moment.

"Well," he began. He seemed to be taking a long time to settle himself. "I have come to you, Addisyn, with the answer to all your dreams." He paused, then clarified with special emphasis, "Your *Olympic* dreams."

Addisyn's heart lurched within her chest. Then it began thudding with an unnaturally heavy rhythm. She swallowed painfully. Her Olympic dreams? Oh, was it possible that—? She checked herself. *Of course not. Don't trust him.* Probably it was just a pick-up line he'd concocted during his flight. She refused to relax her poker face one iota. Whatever he meant, he wouldn't have the satisfaction of knowing that he now held every ounce of her attention.

Brian was evidently waiting for her reply, so trying to steady her voice, she merely ordered coldly, "Speak your piece."

No, she did not trust Brian. A half-formed idea floated through her mind of walking to the door and ordering him out, threatening to call the police if he didn't comply. But the word *Olympic* seemed to have hypnotized the rational part of her brain.

What harm could there be in hearing him out?

BRIAN TRIED AGAIN to gauge her reaction. Boy, she was being very difficult. Irritation growled inside his mind. He'd never seen her so hard to get along with. Sure, he knew she'd be mad, but sheesh, not this bad. Standing there with that haughty look and those folded arms, face as immovable as if carved from steel, she reminded him more of Avery than of his compliant little girl.

Still, he had every confidence in his plan. It was foolproof. And was it his imagination, or was she weakening slightly? *Yeah, I knew the word "Olympic" might do the trick.*

Now to seize his opportunity. He took a deep breath. "You understand that by failing to place in Sectionals and advance to Nationals, you lost your opportunity to be considered for the U.S. Olympic Team. Also, for someone who has been training for the short amount of time that you have been, your chances of being selected any other way are very slim. Thus, it would appear that your Olympic dreams are over."

He could almost see the ice forming on the edges of her soul. She drew her small frame up stiffly. "I am well aware of my unfortunate situation, but thank you for coming all the way to Canada to reiterate the point." A dagger seemed to fly from her every word.

Brian allowed himself a sheepish grin. "Okay, okay. I get it. You're unhappy with me." She opened her mouth, probably to assure him that "unhappy" was putting it mildly, but he held up his hands in surrender. "And I know. You have every right to be. I was—I was a jerk. And I apologize for my—uh—unbecoming behavior."

Now there was no mistaking it. The girl was slowly warming up. She shifted her shoulders slightly and inspected him suspiciously. Probably shocked that an apology came out of Brian Felding's mouth. Well, an opportunity like this was worth eating a little crow for.

She still preserved her stony silence, however, so Brian continued. "I feel like, after—" he gestured uncomfortably—"what happened, I owe you one. Or more." He grinned, and Addisyn actually gave a small half-smile for the first time. "So…I called a guy. Name's Ed Bourns. He's an agent with Team Unlimited." He leaned forward and looked her straight in the eye. "Addisyn, they want you."

△△   △△   △△

ADDISYN'S MOUTH FELT fuzzy. She tried to swallow twice before she could do it. Her head spun faster than her body did when she performed a perfect layback spin.

"T-Team Unlimited?" She couldn't stop the stutter.

"Yes." Brian's eyes locked onto hers. For once, he looked completely and totally sincere. He stood up, took a step toward her. "Addisyn…baby…do you realize what this means? Team Unlimited is huge. It's international! Sponsorship, so you don't have to worry about the money—big advertising bonuses—support from experts—this is the greatest deal to ever fall into the lap of a figure skater."

His eyes were glowing. Addisyn narrowed her own at him. As usual, he was being melodramatic. But still…she had to admit, the deal was almost as great as he said it was.

"But I didn't even medal in Sectionals." Her voice sounded breathy to her ears. As though she'd just had a long session at the gym and couldn't quite get enough air.

"But he doesn't care!" Brian waved his hands wildly. He was getting more and more excited. "This dude—Ed—he doesn't care a hoot. He saw you perform at Sectionals. He knows you're brilliant. But he wants to meet you in person before he makes his final decision. He wants to see one more skate from you too."

A handshake and a smile? A simple routine on the ice? Could that really be the only roadblock between Addisyn and her dream? For the first time she realized her palms were slippery with sweat. She wiped them hard against her jeans. From deep inside her, she heard the words come out. "What kind of routine?"

196

"Easy." Brian waved his hand and leaned forward as if to impart a secret. "There aren't even any choreography requirements! You can show off your talent as much as you like.

"There is one requirement, though."

Unpleasantness dashed Addisyn like a bucket of cold water. She gritted her teeth. Hadn't she learned to expect strings attached with Brian?

"The guy wants to see you in Chicago in nine days."

Addisyn's jaw dropped. "Brian, you honestly expect me to learn a routine—for a Team Unlimited agent—in a little over a week?"

"Listen. You can definitely do this." Brian was talking in that sharp, fast tone that Addisyn hated. It made him sound like a used-car salesman. "We'll take a flight tomorrow for Chicago, okay? Get you back in the gym on some workouts, although—" his eyes lingered as they traveled up her body—"you clearly haven't lost any conditioning. You look great, baby. Then, we start learning the routine. It will be super simple but super impressive at the same time. I already have part of it figured out. I've got a nice K-pop piece. You'll love it, lots of movement to it. You open with a Salchow and then a—"

"Wait." Addisyn held up her hands as if to stem the tide. A horrible thought had occurred to her. "Brian Felding, are you lying to me about this?"

"No, I swear!" He held up his hand as though taking an oath. "Upon my honor."

Right. She looked at him pointedly. "Your honor?"

Brian flushed. For just a second his face contorted into a nasty look, but then his features quickly straightened. "Okay. I get it." He dug his iPhone from his back pocket and quickly swiped a few options. "Here. Check it out for yourself."

An email was displayed on the screen. Addisyn could see the date was two days ago. Snatches of phrases seemed to leap from the screen. *Ed: I received your email and am happy for the chance to work with you…Miss Miles is top-notch…one of the best figure skaters in all of…looking forward to your assistance. One line in particular snagged her eye. Miss Miles will be performing for you in Chicago, at the Rayard Arena, on the afternoon of the 1st, as per our earlier discussion.*

She scowled and looked up at Brian. "You already signed me up?

Without my permission?"

"But of course you're going to do it! It's Team Unlimited!"

With every second she witnessed Brian's excitement, her own seemed to cool. Yeah, Team Unlimited, but at what cost? She'd do well to be wary. She took a step back and turned to inspect a scratch on the wall. "I don't know."

"You—you don't know?" Brian seemed to be incredulous. No, that was too mild a word. He was downright shell-shocked. "I come all the way to Whistler—"

"Which no one asked you to do—" Addisyn interjected coolly.

"Baby, you can't miss this chance!"

Addisyn took a deep breath. Everything was so badly scrambled inside her she couldn't even diagnose her emotions. But wasn't this what she had always longed for? What was wrong with her?

One thing she knew for sure. Until she could take a closer look at what was happening inside her heart, she couldn't make any sweeping decisions. "I need to think about it, Brian." Her voice was steady, even if her spirit wasn't. "This has been very—unexpected. Also, I have a job at the local coffee shop here now." She took a deep breath. "I will let you know tomorrow."

"Addisyn—baby—this is—" Brian seemed at a complete loss for words. "We have limited time—the flight leaves at five thirty tomorrow afternoon, and there's still the bus ride back to Vancouver before we could even—"

Addisyn strode resolutely to the door and held it open. "Come by here tomorrow afternoon at one o'clock. I'll give you my decision then."

Addisyn could see the frustration bubbling up in Brian's mind, but he seemed to swallow his irritation as he left the room. On the threshold he turned. "Fine. Tomorrow. But—" His eyes bored into hers. "This is your future!"

And he was gone.

Addisyn closed the door and locked it. Then she walked slowly to the bed and plopped down on it.

Her insides were a cauldron of emotions. Shock—confusion—anxiety—uncertainty. But as she tried to grasp what was going on, as she held her emotions up to the light, one by one, to examine them, she suddenly realized one was missing. The one Brian had expected to evoke. The one that she herself would have expected more than any other.

In the swirling storm of her heart—where was excitement?

△△　△△　△△

IT TOOK ALL his willpower not to slam Addisyn's door shut behind him. Brian squeezed his eyes shut and raked his fingers through his hair. Seriously, what was wrong with that girl?

He waited for a moment outside her door. Half expecting that she'd come running out, frantic to catch him. She'd look up at him with those melting eyes and tell him she'd lost her mind temporarily, tell him that passing up a chance like this would be nothing short of insane.

She'd thank him for getting her the deal and pull her dreams out of whatever storage box in her heart she'd crammed them into. He'd wrap his arms around her, feel her heartbeat against his once more. Next thing you knew, he'd be sipping pinot noir on a first-class flight to Chicago, with his sweet little baby perched next to him. Maybe resting her head on his shoulder or holding his hand.

He gritted his teeth and glared back at the door. It remained firmly shut. Seeing her had nearly driven him crazy. She was even more beautiful than he remembered. Perfect for the ice rink, where skaters were chosen— Brian was sure of it—on appearance and personality as much as talent or ability.

He tiptoed to the door and tried to listen. Only complete stillness. Clearly she wasn't feverishly packing bags or even pacing the room in concern.

Anger pulsed hard and strong through Brian's body. For a moment, he was a heartbeat away from kicking her door in and pitching a king-sized fit. Just in time, he stopped himself. *If you lose it now, you blow it! Keep cool, man.* He swung away from the door and strode back down the hall toward the elevator. What could she be thinking? She wasn't, that was all. She couldn't be. No athlete in her right mind would pass up a chance at Team Unlimited. Team Unlimited! The outlandishness of it felt like a physical blow.

He stabbed the elevator button and stood with folded arms as it began its descent. At the lobby, he took a deep breath and smoothed his hair before exiting.

When he came out of the elevator, he wasn't the same man who'd entered it with a heart full of rage. No. He couldn't afford that. Instead, he was now the picture of cool precision. With elaborate care, he pulled down his shirt sleeves, twisting his arms to find the best fit, and straightened his collar.

He made his way to the lobby area and sank into one of the overstuffed red armchairs. The pattern was blurred where so many had rested their elbows on the armrests. He couldn't avoid a sneer of disgust. Addisyn hadn't invested a lot of money into getting a nice place, that was for sure. The carpet looked like it hadn't been vacuumed in a month.

He leaned back and crossed his legs. Okay. Time to do some deep thinking.

I have a job at the coffee shop. Addisyn's words drifted through his mind. He tried to put himself in her shoes—admittedly, a challenge he'd always found difficult. So, when she got here, maybe she was bored, or maybe she needed a little extra pocket money. Okay, so she got a job at a coffee shop. Fair enough, so far—but she wanted to keep it now? He frowned and shook his head. Seriously, that made zero sense. With a chance at Team Unlimited on the horizon, she should have been turning her apron in immediately. Nobody would choose being a barista over being an Olympian! Yet she'd cited this stupid blue-collar job as her excuse for staying in Whistler.

No matter how he examined the facts, they didn't fit. There had to be something else at play here.

Was it that guy? Suddenly he felt cold all over. The long-haired Uber-driver dude? No. No, surely not. Addisyn couldn't have fallen in—

Could she?

His heartbeat skipped and slurred. Boiling anger made it feel as if his hair was standing on end. He clenched his jaw and fisted his hands.

Calm down. It wasn't possible. Addisyn wouldn't fall for a guy like that—even if he was, Brian had to grudgingly admit, rather nice-looking in a rough way. Brian pictured the man again, his lean frame, his wavy hair, his stocking cap and plaid shirt. Typical millennial hippie. No, Addisyn wouldn't look twice at a loser like that.

Would she?

Recovering from the numbness of epiphany, Brian's brain began to gradually accept the idea as possible. Maybe even—plausible? He willed his heartrate to slow as he mentally ticked off the reasons it was more than a crazy paranoid idea. She'd come to Whistler alone and lonely. The guy wasn't ugly, even if he was quite obviously not somebody with his act all together. He drove for Uber—an inglorious job, but then her height of ambition was apparently working at a coffee shop. And wouldn't an Uber driver drink plenty of coffee? Most telling of all, the guy had a picture of Addisyn taped to his dash. And not just Addisyn—Addisyn and him. Together. Didn't there have to be—well, something there?

Hot blood pumped through Brian's veins. What had this jerk been doing? Some nerve, helping himself to Brian's girl. Sure, Addisyn should have told him she was taken, but that in no way excused this punk. Pictures of them eating together, laughing together, maybe even cuddling together flashed through Brian's mind.

For an instant the anger seemed to strangle him. He thought about hunting the lowlife down, giving him the ultimatum, letting him know if he so much as thought about Addisyn again, he'd get all his teeth knocked out.

Could this have happened? Addisyn felt impossibly distant suddenly—as if she'd slipped out of his grasp and hung, tantalizingly beautiful and desirable, just above his reach. After all this—cajoling Ed, braving Avery, flying all over North America—that was it? The end of her Olympic career? And her exit from Brian's life? For some low-life drifter with that irritating West Coast dip to his voice?

Brian forced himself to take a deep breath. No! She hadn't seen the last of him yet. Oh, he'd be there tomorrow, all right. And in less than twenty-four hours from now, she'd be on a plane with him, heading back to Chicago. That Uber driver wasn't an impediment. Not in the least.

No, he was just one more reason for Brian to get his baby out of Whistler—asap.

Chapter **16**

Addisyn breathed a sigh of relief when she finally heard Brian's indignant footfalls stomping down the hall toward the elevator. Creeper, loitering outside her hotel door. She permitted herself a wry smile. She was familiar enough with Brian's character that she hadn't expected anything less.

Now it was time to try to collect her scattered thoughts, gathering them like bouquets tossed onto the ice rink by admiring fans.

She nibbled on a hangnail as she forced herself to face the encounter with total honesty. She had to admit, she'd been impressed by the offer. More than impressed—astounded. And, despite her best efforts to remain wary, she was forced to acknowledge that she'd been touched by Brian's dedication to find her. Add to that the fact that he'd gone to all the trouble of securing this amazing Team Unlimited business for her. Plus, he'd been fairly well-behaved during their exchange, even though Addisyn's refusal had to have driven him insane. Okay, so maybe he'd gotten a little excited once or twice, but that was just the intensity of his enthusiasm over Team Unlimited, right?

She shook her head hard, confused and more than a little annoyed with herself. What was her problem? This was a Disney-style moment. Her Prince Charming had returned to whisk her away in a pumpkin coach— okay, a passenger jet—to the life of her dreams.

Hadn't she dreamed of this? During lonely nights in Whistler, hadn't she fantasized of what would happen if Brian came to his senses, begged her forgiveness, and ushered her back into the skating scene? And now…here it was, within reach. And she wasn't making a move to grab it.

Addisyn slowly wandered toward the bed, deep in her thoughts. She perched herself in the exact spot where Brian had sat. She hadn't forgotten how handsome he was, but seeing him in real life reminded her of all the reasons she'd once found him dazzling. He was sophisticated, successful, charming, and had the heart-stopping looks of a movie star. Maybe he'd learned his lesson, after that Valentine's party.

But thinking of that night brought back the image of Brian, standing there screaming, shaking her in his vice-like grip. Backstabbing her with Marty Moorehouse and then smearing her most precious dream in the mud.

No. She sat up and folded her arms. No matter how nice Brian seemed now, she just couldn't trust him.

But the thought felt uncomfortable, as though it didn't quite fit, and her mind swung, pendulumlike, in his favor again. After all, was it fair to send him away without a chance to earn her respect again? If he was truly sorry…and the Team Unlimited offer, wow! It seemed rather ungrateful to slam the door of her soul in the face of a man who'd done so much for her—especially when she'd once called that man the love of her life.

Addisyn nibbled more frantically than ever on the hangnail as her thoughts gathered speed. She had loved him—hadn't she? She'd been over the moon when he first started lavishing his attention on her, singling her out from among all the other girls. Just the sight of him had sent chills up her spine. She knew the other skaters thought she was born under a lucky star, with such a perfect knight in shining armor ready to sweep her off her feet.

Addisyn swallowed hard. Yeah, she'd thought enough of him that she'd done more than simply accept his affections.

She'd traded her sister for him.

But now…now the nights spent together in his townhouse just made her feel used and dirty. She recoiled from the thought of how his eyes had scanned her body just now. It made her feel cheap, somehow. *"Baby, you're gorgeous."* Was it a compliment? Or an innuendo?

Desire and fear, repulsion and attraction, were all swirled together in her mind. The thin walls of the hotel room felt as though they were caving in on her soul. She glanced out the window, where the rain was still falling, then at the clock. 8:03 p.m. Less than twenty-four hours before she was supposed to give Brian her final decision. Less than a single day to make a choice that would change her whole life. Forever.

She couldn't think anymore in the room. She donned a thick sweater—the rain had made the air cool—and then slunk down the back stairway of the hotel. Brian was somewhere in Whistler, and who knew where. Knowing his persistence, he could even be in the hotel lobby. He was probably waiting for her to come running to find him, slobbering over his Team Unlimited offer.

Addisyn took a deep breath as she pushed open the door. The cool, fresh air seemed to sharpen her senses but calm her soul at the same time. Maybe if her feet were moving, her brain would start doing the same, instead of freezing up into a logjam.

She shook her head, wondering again why she couldn't have said yes. Why she hadn't squealed and screamed with joy and jumped on the chance to go to the Olympics, after thinking her dream was dead. What was holding her in Whistler? What part of her had urged her to wait?

The humidity was incredible tonight. Addisyn blinked hard—tiny particles of mist were settling on her eyelashes. She could see her breath, a poufy cloud around her mouth.

That same cloud seemed to be hovering in her mind. Why couldn't she get a grip on her thoughts?

Without warning, Avery's face appeared once more in her mind—tender, loving, with the strength of a woman who had fought with wild beasts of the soul and come out victorious. Addisyn lowered her head. She'd often complained about Avery's advice-giving, but now she wished she could have access to some of her sister's wisdom again. Avery would know exactly what to do in a situation like this. Between her salt-of-the-earth good sense and her uncanny intuition, Avery was never at a loss in any situation—at least, Addisyn had never seen her wandering in bewilderment.

Not to mention her strong faith in God.

Addisyn passed a restaurant that was still open. She glanced through the window briefly, watching the couples tucked confidentially around tables with a soft ambient light.

God. Hmm. She thought about her own prayer. Had God answered that by sending Brian? Somehow, Brian and God just didn't fit together in her mind. Was God trying to force her into a decision? Was He testing her and sitting back to watch her performance? Shame turned Addisyn's stomach. If God had been laying tests before Addisyn Miles, she'd probably failed every single one.

She realized that this afternoon was the first time in years she'd asked God for anything. She didn't even know if they were still on speaking terms. But on this dark night, suddenly she didn't want to just do what she thought would make her happy. She wanted to do the right thing. God's thing. The thing that Avery would tell her to do—and not just because Avery was making her do it.

With a magnetism she couldn't stifle, her soul swung to Darius. She needed him more than ever. Needed his strong support, his upright soul. She needed to sit somewhere and look into his gentle eyes and tell him everything. The skating—the failures—even Brian. She needed his advice, his understanding.

Slowly, like the sun peeking over the rim of the mountains, she began to see the truth forming. There was no one else who could hold her whole heart in his hands. Who could see into the depths of her soul and stir the deep parts of her spirit.

There was no one else with his blue-green eyes, filled with light, or his quirky lopsided grin. There was no one else that she—

Addisyn could feel her heart pounding. Wasn't it time for her to face the truth about her feelings, quit playing games in her mind?

"Okay." She whispered the word into the darkness, watching the night swallow her voice and keep her secret. "I—I love Darius Payne."

Her voice shook. She could feel her face flushing like a shy schoolgirl. But at the same time, everything seemed to be making sense.

That answered her question, didn't it? That gave her the words to tell Brian that she wasn't following his rules. She wasn't going to the Olympics, wasn't joining Team Unlimited.

She thought back with amazement to how she had once compared Darius to Brian. It was true they were nothing alike—and now, she couldn't be more thankful for it.

True, Darius didn't sparkle like Brian. He didn't wear a Rolex and four-hundred-dollar shoes. But he was solid, authentic, humble. Brian—well, once you got past that Rolex, there wasn't much gold in him.

For the first time since she had left Avery, Addisyn started to feel light. A smile teased the corners of her mouth until she had to give in and let it tip her lips up. Suddenly, the humidity and mistiness, the darkness and the long walk, seemed to fade into obscurity. What did she care for any of it?

She'd come to Whistler to figure things out, to find what she wanted. Well, she'd finally done it. Here, alone, in the dark, silent night.

Her heart felt so light, she was sure it could have soared above the streetlamps, above the buildings, above the mountains—right up into the stars. A shiver of relief tingled through her, as if she'd finally reached a safe place in her spirit.

She didn't know what was going on with Darius. She didn't know if the two of them had any future together at all. But she wasn't leaving Whistler. She wasn't chasing the spotlight anymore. And most of all, she was not going to go with Brian.

Instead of going to Chicago tomorrow, she was going to tell Darius that she loved him.

△△　△△　△△

WHEN ADDISYN AWOKE the next morning, the rain had taken itself away, and only bright sunshine streamed through her window, onto the ragged carpet of a hotel room that had become a home.

Addisyn's enthusiasm of the night before held true. She could feel a nervous fluttering in the pit of her stomach, but it was more excitement than anxiety. She glanced at the clock and grinned. In about five hours, Brian would get some news that would turn his world upside down.

She was so excited with what was about to unfold that she couldn't concentrate on anything. If it had still been raining, she'd planned to try Darius's house, but on a gorgeous day like this, he was undoubtedly taking people up Whistler.

She carefully brushed her hair and put on a knee-length summery dress over capri leggings. For some reason, she felt the need to look extra nice today—as if she were stepping into a whole new world.

A whole new world! It would be indeed, with Brian out of the way and her free to pursue her own life. The only question mark was Darius.

She was going to put her heart on the line this morning—unload all her baggage and ask for his help in sorting it. The thought was completely terrifying. Because once she let down the armor around her heart, it would be very vulnerable.

And who knew what was going on with Darius? Addisyn had never claimed to have her sister's intuitive abilities, but she felt as though something was haunting him beyond the simple facts he'd conveyed. Whatever it was, it had torn them apart on the mountain. And she had to face the fact that it could strike again.

Darius could tell her he didn't want to see her. He could listen to that voice of darkness instead of to her words. He could put his hands in his pockets and walk out of her life. If that happened…

She stopped herself. Darius couldn't want to write her off entirely; he'd come by the coffee shop looking for her, after all. Somehow, on this morning, everything seemed possible—even a relationship with Darius. Nothing was too hard.

Addisyn didn't feel much like breakfast, but she'd eaten a light meal, called Chelsea to let her know she was taking a personal day, and even done a good deal of pacing around her room by ten o'clock. She had decided that the time to look for Darius would be at noon at the climbing center. He'd be in between tours and ideally have some time to talk to her.

If she was catching the bus to the center, she needed to leave at eleven thirty, so that gave her an uninterrupted hour and a half to do nothing except alternately sit on her bed and wear ruts in the floor with her pacing. She was too afraid to go downtown; what if she ran into Brian? The last thing she needed was to bump into him right now. For starters, she wasn't ready to face him yet, not with her future still so tenuous. Even more importantly, though, he didn't need to know about Darius. She grimaced at the thought of how he would react. She knew full well just how jealous he was. He'd once pushed a janitor into the wall at one of the rinks where Addisyn had been competing, just because he thought the guy was looking at Addisyn too much. The janitor had never reported the incident, of course. Brian was much too important.

"God, help me today." She whispered the prayer almost without thinking about it. Strange, she'd not thought about God in years, and now she'd offered two prayers in twenty-four hours. Maybe that was because she was becoming more and more convinced that God was listening. And she was also convinced that somehow, all of this hung on His reaction to her.

And Darius's.

By eleven o'clock, her morning optimism had drained out of her. She wasn't sure if it was the nearing time or her unoccupied mind, but somehow her mood was dampening. Seriously, what was she thinking? Okay, so Darius kissed her once. What did that mean? Nothing—especially given what happened immediately thereafter. And the coffee shop thing. Maybe he just wanted to apologize and ask to be her friend. Or ask her to stay out of his life altogether. For crying out loud, maybe he was just there to order a coffee—although he hadn't.

And what was she going to do, exactly? Go up to him and beg him to love her? Beg him to put his arms around her and tell her not to go to Chicago?

By the time Addisyn was standing on the bus, holding to a swinging ceiling strap as the overcrowded vehicle lumbered downtown, clouds were beginning to roll over the sun. And one truth had risen to the surface of her swirling mind.

For whatever reason, what Darius said to her in their upcoming meeting would change her life. Her next move hung in the balance—able to be tipped either way by his response.

△△ △△ △△

HE WAS THERE, just as she'd known he'd be. A friendly middle-aged guy working behind the counter directed her to a back storeroom.

Addisyn paused right inside the doorway. Darius was unloading boxes of something, probably T-shirts or souvenirs, throwing them around a bit recklessly, she thought. She cleared her throat. "Darius?" Her voice sounded weaker than she would have liked. There was so much riding on this moment.

At the sound of her voice, he jerked, dropping the box he held to the floor. He spun to face her, the look on his face a mixture of shock and pain—and—no, was it anger?

"I'm sorry to bother you at work." Addisyn could hear the hesitancy in her words. Darius just shifted his weight, shoved his hands in his pockets, and stared at her with the greatest unconcern she'd ever seen on his face.

"Yeah, I'm pretty busy." His comment was matter-of-fact, abrupt even, with no hint of welcome in his tone. He jerked his chin toward the stack of boxes behind him.

"I figured you might be on lunch, and I—well, I needed to talk with you for a minute." Addisyn bit the inside of her lip. This wasn't going well. She could tell. But why? What was this tension she felt? Darius seemed like a smoldering powder keg. What had she done?

Apart from kiss him on a rocky mountainside.

She'd thought he'd at least offer to talk, tell her to wait just a minute while he finished, and then he could take his lunch. Instead a short bark of a laugh slipped from his lips. "Talk to me?" Anger flared hard and bright in his eyes. He took a step toward her. "Addisyn Miles, I don't have anything to say to you."

Addisyn felt as if some iron fist was squeezing her heart into a funnel-shaped fragment of what it had been. "What?" He didn't respond, so she tried again. "Darius, I don't understand. What's going on?"

Was all of this over that stupid kiss?

"You used me." Darius's jaw jutted forward. He crossed his arms over his chest. "You let me think you actually cared about me, actually wanted to be with me me—for crying out loud, maybe even loved me!" His voice had climbed a staircase with each word, but he lowered it for his last jab, spacing his words. "And it was all a fake."

His last three words drove into Addisyn's soul like so many spikes. "Darius—" She wiped her trembling palms on her dress. "If this is about that kiss—" Her face was turning scarlet just saying the word.

"That kiss?" Darius snorted. "Of course not, Addisyn. This is about the fact that you—" His voice rose again. He jabbed a finger at her—

accusing, convicting, and sentencing. All in one. "You are not some sweet little innocent girl from America on a nice road trip. You are Addisyn Miles, famous figure skater, future Olympian." Darius choked a bit over the last word. He swallowed hard and seemed to be waiting for her reaction.

Like steam from humid ground, waves of shame rose over Addisyn's spirit. Coupled with amazement. How in the world had Darius found out? He had to have been looking at some skating website or something.

"Well?" Darius's voice reverberated in the cramped space.

Addisyn tried to gather her thoughts. She'd always meant to tell him eventually—but not like this. She tried to speak twice before words would come to her command. "Yeah." She muttered the word, looking at the cement floor like a little girl caught in a fib. "It's true. But—" she raised her eyes to his defiantly—"that doesn't change things between you and—"

"Oh yes it does!" Darius rode over the top of her before she could even think about finishing her statement. "It changes everything. It means you lied to me about—"

"Darius, I did not lie to you!" Her breath was wheezing in her lungs, but she wouldn't give an inch of ground. "I told you that I was from the United States and I wanted to see Whistler. All of that is true." She paused, considering reminding him that he hadn't exactly been upfront with her either at first. No, better not mention that. Yet. "You knew there were things I hadn't told you. You were okay with that." She searched his eyes, looking for any hint of the man she knew. "What changed?"

His spine was as rigid as a steel rod. "What changed is finding out who you really are!" His voice was rising again. "You're not some girl from nowheresville off to see the world, you're a very talented and successful figure skater." Again, he said it as if it were an accusation. Almost as if he were mad at her for being that.

If only she could get inside his mind for just sixty seconds and see what was really happening in there. Something bizarre to make him act this strangely. "So what?" Frustration boiled over in her soul. "Okay, so I'm a figure skater. What's wrong with that?" She shook her head. "You're a skater too."

"Not anymore."

Was that it? His injury made him resent her? She cocked her head, trying to read the situation. "Darius…if that bothers you, maybe you should be back on the ice. You could—"

"Never." For a moment, aching pain rose in his eyes. "Remember? I can't compete anymore."

Addisyn took a deep breath. She'd been doing some hard thinking, and she'd come to a realization. Maybe it was time to tell him. "I don't believe you."

The room was quiet for a few seconds before he spoke. "What?"

"I don't believe that you can't compete."

Suddenly, just like that, he was listening to her again. For the moment his anger seemed to have fled. "What are you saying?"

Here goes. "You told me that you couldn't skate because you had back injuries and had to be really careful. But I've been thinking. You carried me on Whistler Mountain—on your back. And you climb Whistler Mountain every day. And"—she gestured to the storage shelves. "If you're truly hurt, why are you loading heavy boxes like it's no big deal?"

She stopped to inspect him. His lip was trembling. All the color was gone from his face. He looked suddenly so small and fragile that she said her next words in a much softer tone. "You weren't honest with me either. I think—" she tried to look deep into his soul. Like Avery would. To the part he wasn't listening to today. "I think you're scared of the ice. Afraid to get back out there."

Like lightning Darius's countenance changed. His eyes flashed back to life. "I am not afraid." He took a deep breath. "I do have back injuries." He shoved his hands into his pockets. "You need to leave."

"What?" Was he serious? "Darius, we need to finish this conversation. I—"

"No, we don't." The molten anger had drained from his voice, leaving it dull with pain. "There's nothing left to talk about. We were friends and it was fun, and now it's over." Grief flickered behind the hardness in his face. "I was just your little side fling until your real man got out here."

"I have no idea what you're talking about!"

"I met your boyfriend yesterday!" Darius's voice rose again. "Mr. Preppy little GQ model with his fancy haircut and nice gold watch. You've just been using me to play with!"

Addisyn reeled. *No.* Never had she thought about the possibility of Brian and Darius finding out about each other. What in the world had happened? "How did you—"

"Never mind how I found out." Darius's eyes were like stone. "Interestingly, I learned that you two are a serious item—and have been for years. Even live together, as I understand."

Like a raw cowhide whip, his words sliced into Addisyn's soul. She felt as if she might crash onto the cement floor. Now the tears sprang to the surface.

Of all the things she'd ever done, giving in to Brian was her worst regret, her most egregious mistake. Looking back, she couldn't imagine why she'd ever done it. Now, to hear the dirty details spilling from the mouth of the man she truly loved was too much.

Suddenly all she wanted was to get out of this conversation. Get out and leave, crawl away like a wounded animal hiding from daylight. If only she could run out the door of the climbing center and keep on running until she ceased to exist.

There was no point in staying there. No wonder Darius was so furious. No wonder he wouldn't listen to her. What could she say? Certainly Brian had probably talked their relationship up to heaven without once mentioning that she had broken up with him. The filthy creep.

But she had to try, had to say something to fill the void. "Darius, I am not that person any—"

"Oh, so you've changed?" Darius widened his stance. "Then why is your boyfriend here in town? Cause he's ready to sweep you away to Chicago so all your dreams can come true." His tone dripped with sarcasm. "Yeah, I heard all about it. He gave me all the details. Guess he was jealous of me or something." He gave that sharp bark of a laugh again. "Imagine that."

"Please, Darius, just talk to me!" Addisyn took a step toward him, but he turned and shook his head.

"Like I said, there's nothing to say." He took a deep breath and ran his hands over his face. When he met her eyes again, his own were wet. "Look, Addisyn. When I met Brian, I was pretty mad." He sucked in a breath. "But—you don't owe me any explanations. I thought—I thought we had something, maybe, but—" His voice broke off. "I'm glad you're going to the Olympics." He had put up his armor. She could tell, could almost hear the gates of his soul thudding closed. His tone was as flat and expressionless as if he'd been talking to a stranger. "Go to Chicago with Brian and skate your heart out. You deserve somebody better than me anyway."

"Darius, please listen to me!" Addisyn was sobbing now, the pain too brutal to withstand. She reached out to Darius, willing him to listen. To just listen. "Yes, I have made some bad mistakes." She tried to get control of her voice and failed. "But Brian is no longer my boyfriend and I am not who—"

Darius turned away, cutting off her words. He grabbed another box off the floor and heaved it onto a high shelf effortlessly. Clearly the conversation was over. "Not who I thought you were? Clearly." He reached for another box. "You're a fake. And you had me fooled, Addisyn Miles. Big time."

Addisyn went numb all over. His words reverberated in her mind.

There was nothing else to say. Nothing to do. Because he was right. She turned as if on autopilot and stumbled out of the center. Made her way automatically to the bus stop. Boarded the first bus that came.

She felt as if her soul had been gouged out of her and left bleeding for all the world to see. She spent much of the bus ride with her head lowered, her mind whirling around the horrible thing that was true. The reason she could never face Avery—and now Darius.

She was a fake.

It wasn't until they'd gone fifteen minutes down the road that her mind started working again, enough to realize that she'd boarded the bus going out of town by mistake. She got off at the next station and caught the one heading toward the Whistler Village. It was twelve forty-five. She needed to be back to the hotel in time to see Brian.

Because she was going with him. What else could a fake do?

ADDISYN CRANED HER neck to see out of the small porthole in the side of the plane. There it was—Whistler, spread out below her like a beautiful painting framed on a wall.

It felt weird, seeing it from this high up. The peaks that had seemed so insulating when she first arrived looked like molehills now. And in the end, they hadn't been able to protect her anyway.

Well, that was it. Her last glimpse of Whistler. She resolutely dragged her eyes from the window and stared straight ahead.

Her heart felt as leaden and unresponsive as a chunk of stone. As if everything in her had been frozen. She couldn't feel, couldn't think, couldn't even be afraid. She was far too numb for any emotion.

That was the only reason she'd been able to come with Brian at all. If she hadn't been shell-shocked, she would have told him to get on the next plane to NYC—alone.

After she'd gotten off the bus, she'd gone quietly and determinedly back to her hotel room and met Brian at the appointed hour. She'd told him calmly and briefly that she would go with him. He'd been unsurprised, she could tell, from his smirks and lifted eyebrows. He'd been expecting her submission. At any other time, that alone would have been enough to get her fighting spirit up.

But now she felt only a wearied frustration that was beyond any resistance. She couldn't find an ounce of fight left in her. Really, what was the use?

She'd already failed Avery, Darius, God, and herself. Who was left?

"Ahh, thank you." Reclining next to her, Brian regally accepted a tray from the flight attendant. On it were two glasses of red wine. He smiled winningly at her. "Care for a drink?"

She took the wine glass, held it daintily by the stem the way Brian had taught her to. "To your new life." He smiled and clinked his glass to hers. "Cheers."

"Cheers," Addisyn mumbled. The word was bitterly ironic. She took a tiny sip of the wine, her mouth crinkling from the spicy-fruity taste. She swallowed quickly and tried to keep a straight face. She'd forgotten how weird wine tasted when you weren't used to it.

Brian, in contrast, was sipping his drink calmly. He swirled the liquid with the air of aristocracy and peered into the bowl. "I don't like that wood-smoke flavor." He frowned. "I've noticed it comes when they use hickory for the barrels. Then, during the maturation process, the wine—"

Addisyn's attention quietly pulled up stakes and moved away. Her younger self would have hung enraptured on every word out of Brian's mouth and then forsworn wine aged in hickory barrels forevermore. Now she was just disgusted with it all.

Fake. The word kept rolling in her brain. Every time she heard it, she felt a little bit sicker.

Fake.

Fake.

Fake.

That couldn't be who she was, could it? Couldn't be her only identity.

You are a child of God!

The phrase darted into Addisyn's mind with startling suddenness. Weird. Avery used to say that all the time. She was always telling Addisyn not to do this or that—because she was a child of God and should act like it. Or at the end of a bad day, she'd give Addisyn a big hug and say, "Remember, you are a child of God."

A child of God.

Addisyn rubbed her thumb absentmindedly over the bowl of her glass. Certainly Avery would never say so now. What child of God would be caught dead with a man who'd seduced her, going voluntarily back into his clutches, and drinking wine while she did it?

"—don't you think?" The interrogatory tone of Brian's voice made Addisyn jump. He was looking expectantly at her for a reply.

"I'm—I'm sorry. What?"

Brian looked a little annoyed. "Addisyn, I've been talking to you. Have you heard anything I've said?"

She evaded his eyes. "Not everything." She made an attempt to drink a little more wine.

He sighed. A heavy blanket of silence descended over them both.

He's darkness, Addisyn. Her sister's words were coming back in full force. Addisyn set her wine glass back on the tray. She couldn't drink anymore. *He's darkness... He'll make you like him...*

She flinched at the touch of Brian's hand on hers. "Baby, look, I know you're a little nervous."

Nervous? She turned and stared at him.

"About performing, I mean." He smiled—doubtless it was meant to be reassuring. "But I promise you, you'll do just fine. And I'll handle all the legal matters for you, the contract and everything," he was quick to add. "You just focus on skating. And that beautiful face." He tipped her chin up with a crooked finger and kissed her lightly on the lips before she could push him back.

"I'll always be with you, baby." He squeezed her hand before releasing it. "Always."

He leaned back into his seat and closed his eyes, evidently not waiting for a response. Addisyn looked out the window again. Brian's words both infuriated and terrified her.

Nervous? About skating? Oh, she could have laughed if it weren't so pathetic. She'd never been less nervous about a performance in her life. What did it matter? If she did well, she was stuck with Brian. If she did badly, well…she was still stuck with Brian.

Because he would always be with her.

There was no escape. Addisyn gazed down below the plane. A thick blanket of clouds had rolled in. She couldn't see the ground anymore. When had she lost sight of her footing the first time?

Probably whenever she allowed herself to be pulled off course. To be swayed by the man next to her right now.

She folded her arms over her stomach. The wine was disagreeing with her. Or maybe it was just her conscience.

No, she hadn't gone with Brian because she wanted a gold medal anymore. She hadn't gone with him because he'd been persistent. She hadn't even gone because she felt anything for him besides repulsion.

She'd gone because she had burned so many bridges with the people who loved her that Brian was all she had left.

CHAPTER 17

Axel. Spiral. Crossover. Somehow everything hard and horrible about what her life had become was able to be exorcised while she skated. The intensity, both physical and emotional, shredded Addisyn's breath. She flew into a combination spin straight from her Salchow landing. The rhythm of the music merged with her heartbeat.

She ripped the pain out of her soul, threw it to the wind. Glide, twizzle, turn. At times like this, she was flying, she was escaping from all—

"No!" Brian's shout abruptly shattered her reverie. He switched the music off and began waving wildly at her, signaling her to come to the side of the rink.

Addisyn bent and gripped her knees, gasping for breath. Her dreams of perfection seemed to vanish like her cloudy breath in the cold room. Once again, she remembered where she was—in an ice rink in Chicago, practicing the routine that she would perform for Ed Bourns in five days.

"Stop singling your double Axel!" Brian's face was scarlet. Impatience grated on the edges of his voice. "Remember, that forward lunge has to be there; that's a much more impressive entry. And don't cheat that last bit of rotation! Ed is going to notice that." He waved his hand in disgust. "Try that section again. Starting at the Lutz."

Addisyn wearily glided back to the middle of the arena. The rink was cold, so cold that Brian was wearing a white cardigan, but she could feel sweat running down her back. She positioned herself and waited for the music to start.

How long had she been in Chicago? She rotated her head, trying to ease the stiffness in her shoulder blades. Let's see. Their flight had come in late Tuesday night…and now it was Friday morning.

It seemed both unreal and obvious that she would be there. Part of her still believed that this felt natural, that yes, she had skated her whole life, and she'd never really left the rink.

But part of her—a bigger part—was still back in Whistler. Watching the cream swirl in a cup of perfect coffee, waiting for Darius to walk through the door and toss his lopsided grin at her with all the glow of morning light in his blue-green eyes.

Addisyn didn't cry anymore when she thought about Darius. Not because she wasn't upset about the situation, but because she couldn't cry. Her heart had become a granite rock from which no tears could come.

Every day in Whistler had been an adventure. Every day in Chicago was about the same. Get up, eat breakfast with Brian, hit the gym. Lunch, then practice all afternoon. In the evenings Brian usually took her out to eat at some ritzy place.

"Hang on!" Brian's voice was brassy with exasperation. He was fumbling with the wires attached to the portable sound system they used. "It's not working. Gimme two seconds."

"All right." Funny, the relationship they had. She was disgusted with him. He was often impatient with her. They talked about skating, Ed's discerning eye, whether Addisyn should wear her hair in a bun or a ponytail for the competition. They'd never looked down the road of their own relationship. Probably because neither of them wanted to know.

She glanced over at him, feverishly jiggling tangled electrical wires. He still called most of the shots. Just as he always had. But not all.

A tiny smile tugged at the corners of Addisyn's mouth as she remembered. Their first night in Chicago, Brian had walked her confidently upstairs to a luxurious master suite.

"Here, baby." He pushed the door open to reveal the epitome of opulence. "Got us the best room in the house."

Addisyn hadn't thought through her reaction. Her decision wasn't predetermined. But suddenly resolve swelled her soul. Her feet didn't cross the threshold. "Brian, if it's okay with you…I would like my own room this time."

Brian had stared. Then laughed—a half-laugh, incredulous and outraged. "Your own room?"

It was her chance to retract the statement, to give in and shrug it off. But not this time. Addisyn had bitten her lip and nodded.

"You want a room by yourself?" Brian had turned red all the way to the roots of his hair.

She shrugged. "I'd like that very much. If you don't mind."

She couldn't meet his gaze, but she could sense his fury, feel his eyes burning right through her. Then, just when she'd thought he might explode, he had seemed to come to terms with the situation. "Right. Okay." He still looked a little disoriented—like the bird that had hit the window of their apartment in New York City once. "I'll reserve another room."

Immense relief had washed over Addisyn—along with an incredibly satisfying feeling, the feeling of having, for once, done the right thing. She'd half-expected Brian to harass her later about it, or give her the cold shoulder for a while, but he'd never mentioned it again. Maybe he was trying to be more of a gentleman himself.

"Addisyn!" Brian was calling her. Addisyn pushed the toe of her skate into the ice and effortlessly glided to the wall, turning sharply to brake. Brian's face was tired and haggard. "It's not working." He sighed. For the first time he looked like just a normal guy instead of a millionaire in the making. "I'm gonna go see if I can find the maintenance man to help me check some circuits, stuff like that."

"Okay." Addisyn nodded. "What do you want me to do?"

Weird, she was repelled by this man, yet she could talk to him with some degree of civility, even obey his orders. It was as if they were partners, in a strange way—fellow travelers on the road to the Olympics, forced to share their journey with each other.

"Just..." Brian looked vaguely around the arena, then met her gaze again. "Just take five and sit on the bleachers. Maybe stretch a little. Listen to the music on your phone." He took her hand. "You've earned a break, baby. Look, I know I'm a little edgy, but you really are doing good, okay? I'm just worried about Ed. I want this to go perfect for you."

His grip on her hand had tightened. Addisyn gently released her fingers. "Yes. Okay." Her mind and heart were too tired to come up with anything else to say. Like, why was he so worried about her success that he had to scream at her all day for her to achieve it?

"Be right back, then." Brian turned and plodded out of the arena. Maybe he was as weary as Addisyn was.

She snapped her blue skate guards onto the bottoms of her blades and made her way to the first row of bleachers. Slumping down, she gazed across the ice. Mentally she ran through her to-do list for the rest of the day.

She would practice for about an hour and a half more, then take a thirty-minute break. After that, Brian wanted her back in the gym studio to practice the jumps on mats to make sure her rotation was sufficient. After that she had a stretching session at…

Thoughts of the day and days ahead slowly drifted from Addisyn's mind, swallowed by the hollowness in her soul. When had the ice stopped exciting her?

She narrowed her eyes and tried to envision herself skating on that rink, gliding with freedom and joy over the ice. The people crowding the stands would cheer and toss bouquets in her direction. She'd receive a personal letter from the International Olympic Committee requesting her attendance as part of Team USA for the next Olympics, and she'd get the rings tattooed on her forearm.

Wasn't that exactly what she'd always wanted?

Yes. Addisyn took a deep breath and leaned back against the bleacher behind her. But somehow, she would trade it all for one more hug from Avery, one more kiss from Darius. One chance to know they forgave her, that they still loved her and were behind her. Believing in her the way they once did. Before she blew it.

What was she doing, thinking this way? She should be excited, pumping herself up for the big skate for Ed. Psychological prep was just as important as technical practice. Especially when she knew Brian was counting on her to project an upbeat, youthful vibe.

She pulled her iPhone from her pocket and pulled up the music she was performing to—an instrumental version of BTS's "Fake Love." The driving beat and metallic sounds seemed to fit nicely with her mood, helping her ease the pain.

Forget everything and skate. It was all she could do. She stood and made her way back to the ice. She could practice some while Brian was getting the sound system fixed.

Addisyn Miles might not ever be the best in the world. But she could still be great. At skating—if not at life.

△△　△△　△△

IT WAS A particularly busy day at the climbing center—one of those days when Terry had to wear a lot of hats. Being the owner and general manager didn't exempt him from more mundane duties. In fact, he felt very strongly about the importance of humility.

"A servant's heart means you are prepared to lend a hand in any place, at any time, for any reason," he'd always drilled into his workers. Being the man at the top of the hierarchy, to him, just meant increased responsibility—the ability to perform not only his own job but every other job underneath his, from booking appointments to cleaning equipment, right down to taking out the trash.

So today, when a receptionist was out with the flu, customers were crawling all over the mountain, a glitch was found in the safety checks, and a shipment of new equipment arrived ahead of schedule, Terry had been feeling pretty overwhelmed. By the time four thirty rolled around and the last climbing group of the day was descending the mountain with Dexter, one of his most experienced guides, Terry was ready to hop in his Acura and head home to his wife. Maybe take her out to dinner tonight.

"Glad it's over," he muttered to himself, throwing a few last-minute papers in his briefcase. His stomach growled. The low-cal sandwich wrap he'd had for lunch seemed a long time ago.

He ducked into the hall—and nearly collided with Darius.

"Sorry!" Darius thrust out his hands to try to dissipate his momentum.

"The fault is mine." Terry glanced at the young man, studying his eyes. "I wasn't watching where I was going."

Darius's face was still shaded, sad even. He couldn't have appeared more burdened if he'd had a gorilla on his back. Terry hesitated. The last thing he needed was another problem. But he knew his convenience was a flimsy excuse for not trying to help someone in need. "You know, I actually wanted to talk to you, Darius. Could you step into my office for a moment?"

Darius looked apprehensive, but nodded. "Uh…sure."

Terry led the way back into the room and flipped the light switch. "Have a seat." He tried to ignore his growling stomach. This was more important. Settling into his swivel chair, he hesitated a moment before speaking. "Darius, you haven't seemed like yourself lately."

Darius was studying him as if he were speaking in riddles. "In what way?" His tone was even, guarded.

"Well…" Terry took his time. "You seem—very distant. Withdrawn." He searched his mental thesaurus for the precise words he needed. "Depressed about something."

The closed-off look in Darius's eyes didn't ease, but Terry noticed him twisting his hands together nervously. He leaned forward. He didn't want to intimidate the young man or force him into a confession. "Whatever is going on in your personal life, it's none of my business. I understand that. But I can't have you taking people up the mountain if you're going to be distracted enough to potentially make a mistake." He paused. "I'm sure you understand that."

"So you're saying I'm not doing a good job?" Darius's tone sharpened. Terry could see his jaw muscles ripple underneath his beard.

"Not at all." Terry was determined to keep this calm. De-escalate the situation, as his latest management seminar had taught him. "In fact, you're one of my most dependable and reliable employees. I just get the feeling that something is troubling you. And after you missed that day of work, I—"

"I told you I'm sorry for that. It won't happen again." Darius's nervousness filled the space between them as he shifted in the chair.

"I'm not here to fire you, man." Terry chuckled softly, but Darius's face remained rigid. "I'm not here to beat you up either." He made a calming motion with his hands. "Relax."

Darius's eyes didn't leave Terry's face, but some of the tautness seemed to fade from his expression. "So…what are you saying?"

Terry didn't flinch. "I'm saying that I am here for you, Darius." He stared deep into the younger man's eyes, willing him to hear the sincerity in Terry's voice. "I want to help you in any way I can. Whether it's work, or life, or God. Or anything."

For a moment Darius must have thought about opening up. Terry could see it, could see the secret that was killing him bubbling to the surface, waiting to overflow. *Lord, please help him—show him I'm his friend—*

But before the words could escape, Darius pressed his lips together and broke his gaze. "Thanks. I appreciate that. I've just been—busy lately." He stood, clearly ready to end the conversation. "Thanks for talking with me today."

"No problem." Terry's soul ached. The kid wasn't being honest. And as long as he lied—to Terry, to himself, to God—he'd keep dying. He kept his tone light but made no attempt to hide his sincerity. "If you need me, I'm here, okay?"

"Okay. Thank you." Darius slipped out the doorway. "Have a nice weekend."

"You too." Terry's earlier impatience to get home had melted. He slumped in his chair, defeated.

What was troubling Darius? Not an overloaded schedule, of that he was sure. What was it that had almost—*almost*—risen to the surface of his soul?

Terry swallowed his disappointment. He had hoped Darius would accept his help, grasp the hand he'd extended him. The kid was wallowing in some slimy pit of the soul. He wouldn't be able to escape on his own.

Had Terry approached the conversation the wrong way? He let out a sad sigh and bowed his head. *Father, what did I do wrong? I'm sorry—he wouldn't talk to me.*

My son, even the wrath of man shall praise Me.

Terry felt comfort, deep and warm, soaking into his soul from the familiar Bible verse. Gradually his feelings of failure dulled. If God used even the twisted efforts of ungodly people for His glory, then surely He could also redeem Terry's inadequacies. And maybe this hadn't been all for nothing.

Terry stood. It was time to get home to his wife. But before he left the quiet room, he bowed his head and prayed.

That God would use his feeble efforts to break through Darius's wall of pain—and that in the midst of all, God would lead the young man home. To Himself.

CHAPTER 18

The situation was getting more desperate.

Avery could tell by the sense of urgency that constantly dogged her, the vivid dreams that floated through her sleep. She hated the fear she felt—for her sister.

Even now, on the way to work, she could barely breathe around the anxiety. She took a slow breath and flexed her fingers. She'd been gripping the steering wheel too hard, as she often did lately. When she paused at a red light, she took the opportunity to stretch her arms over her head and exhale slowly.

El Shaddai… Every time she felt this way, she simply prayed. Prayed that somehow, some way, Addisyn would escape from the downward swirl she was in. That she would cut all ties with Brian and break away from his evil influence. Most importantly, that she would come to know how much El Shaddai loved her.

And, on a selfish note, that Avery would see her again.

She'd never forget how much she'd cried the day that Brian had taken Addisyn away. She'd stood on the iron steps outside to watch them drive away, but once they were out of sight, she'd collapsed full-length on the cold tile in their apartment and sobbed until she started throwing up.

She could remember feeling so defeated. Defeated? The word seemed too weak. She'd saved Addisyn from their father, smuggled her to New York, prioritized her schooling, managed to keep her grounded, somehow, even in the middle of their insane life. She'd been two parents in one, juggling a medley of jobs, clipping coupons for cheap groceries, and still finding time to help Addisyn with her algebra homework when she entered tenth grade.

And then she found out, one horrible day, that all of that was for nothing—that in everything she'd done, she'd somehow missed the most important thing of all, the one thing that truly mattered. She hadn't been able to teach Addisyn to love El Shaddai.

What had she done wrong? It wasn't like she'd been blindsided. She'd seen trouble coming, glimpsed the darkness looming over Addisyn's soul. She'd watched the light in her sister's eyes gradually become submerged in pools of darkness.

The dreams had begun, vivid nightmares, warning Avery about impending danger. She'd talked with Addisyn. Poured gallons of prayer on her. And when she'd met Brian, she'd beseeched her sister to stay away from him—at all costs.

"He's darkness, Addisyn." She could vividly remember saying those words. She'd been ironing shirts one morning, Addisyn helping fold the rest of the laundry.

"Oh, Avery." Addisyn had frowned and rolled her eyes. "Don't you think you're overreacting a little? Just because you don't want me to grow up?"

Avery had turned and peered hard into her sister's soul. That shadowy something was there, and fear contorted her insides. "Addisyn, this isn't about that," she'd said slowly. "I just—I just don't feel right. It feels bad to me."

Addisyn had huffed and slapped another folded garment on the stack. "You and your feelings and your dreams and your whatnot." She must have seen the hurt look on her big sister's face, because her voice softened. "Look, I know that you get lonely when I'm at these tournaments or practicing, and I'm sorry. But still—"

"Addisyn, this isn't about me!" Thinking back, Avery winced, remembering how frustration had sharpened her tone. "This is about you and the choices you are making! You and your relationship with El Shaddai!"

"No, this is about you and your weirdness!" Addisyn had thrown down the next garment, marched toward Avery, shaking a finger. "You think you have all the answers. My wonderful big sister, dropped down from Heaven, knows everything in this life and the next." Avery had never heard Addisyn give a sarcastic laugh like that before. "Well, this time you're dead wrong. You don't know what it's like to be—to be—" her voice had blurred—"in love."

"Addisyn, Brian is not—"

"Brian is a good guy!" Addisyn had sworn with all the passion of eighteen. "Don't you dare say anything bad about Brian!"

"Ads—"

But Addisyn had turned and swept out of the room. "I'm not talking about this with you anymore!" she'd yelled. "And don't ever call me Ads again!"

It was one of the last conversations they'd ever had.

Bleep! The car behind honked. Avery snapped back to life and realized the light had turned green. Apologetically she pulled through the intersection and stayed in the righthand lane as the impatient driver whizzed past.

As we lovingly speak the truth, we will grow up completely in our relationship to Christ, who is the head. When Avery had read Ephesians 4 the night before, those words seemed to leap from the page. Was that the problem? She had spoken the truth, certainly. But had she done so without enough grace, enough love, to season it?

Oh, if she could just see Addisyn one more time, tell her how sorry she was. Assure her that the love had always been there—but sometimes it had been lost in translation.

As if that would ever happen. Ads probably still hated her—deservedly so. Anyway, she was off chasing her dreams and never giving her childhood a second thought.

Right?

The question mark hung limply in Avery's soul. What *was* Addisyn doing these days?

Almost without thinking, she pulled over in the parking lot of a little restaurant on Elkhorn Avenue. She glanced at the clock on her dashboard. She still had time before work. Traffic was light today—odd for a Monday morning.

She could take a minute for some detective work.

Avery brushed her hair behind her ear and picked up her cell phone. Before she could talk herself out of it, she pulled up her browser and typed "Addisyn Miles figure skater."

Instantly a plethora of results leaped to her screen. Her eyes widened as she began to read the titles. The interior of the truck seemed to slant at a crazy angle. What was this?

All the titles were nearly the same: "Miss by a Mile(s)"... "Addisyn Miles Falls Short" ... "Harbor Takes Bronze, Miles Devastated" ... "No Olympics for Miles."

No Olympics for Miles? Avery shook her head in disbelief. What had happened?

Feverishly she jabbed the first article. It opened to show a YouTube video. She held the phone a bit closer and watched as a sports reporter came on the screen.

"After a star-studded career, it looks as if Addisyn Miles won't get the one thing she wants." Footage began to roll of Addisyn skating, gliding over the ice in perfect time.

"Despite her relatively late training start, analysts predicted that Miles would secure an easily earned and well-deserved position on the U.S. Olympic Team, with numerous victories under her belt. Having begun by making a strong showing in the U.S. Junior Championships, Miles advanced to..."

When had Addisyn become such an accomplished skater? So beautiful and powerful. Despite the reporter's ominous words, Avery couldn't help but smile. *Addisyn, I hope you knew how proud I was of you. How proud I'll always be. No matter what happens.*

"Miles and coach Brian Felding became a power duo set to take the world of U.S. Figure Skating by storm. A medal of any color at this year's Sectionals would have been enough to secure a place for Miles in the upcoming round of competition. Unfortunately, Miles failed to reach the medal stand by only three hundredths of a point, losing the pewter medal to Sheila Harbor in an emotional moment. Harbor, a native of..."

Avery did not care where Sheila Harbor was from. She was riveted on the screen. Three hundredths of a point? A willowy blonde girl—

apparently Sheila—grinned at supporters, catching flowers that fell on the ice.

The scene abruptly changed to a shot of Addisyn herself. Glitzy outfit. Sparkling makeup.

And sobbing.

"Addisyn Miles, we know that failing to medal here could have disastrous effects on your career. How are you feeling right now?" The reporter shoved his mic into her face.

Addisyn's eyes looked glazed, as if she'd been slammed on the head and hadn't yet registered how badly injured she was. Her words were so distorted by sobs that Avery could just barely make them out.

"I left everything I have on the ice. There's nothing left." She began crying harder than before, then wheeled and darted away from the nosy reporter.

Avery didn't realize tears were running down her own cheeks until she looked up from the video. She laid her phone down gently and buried her face in her hands. A dozen emotions swirled through her mind. Amazement—sadness—empathy. But most importantly, anger. At herself.

How could she have used the mountains as an excuse? Hidden from the one person who needed her—who had always needed her?

She gazed with distracted eyes at the busy street. Cars were darting here and there. Pedestrians scurried in swarms down the sidewalks. A plane rumbled overhead, a tiny triangle of silver, on its way to Denver International Airport.

Somewhere in that crazy insane world was her sister—wandering, lost and broken. Somewhere she was hiding, just like Avery was, nursing her wounds and trying to find something to hang onto.

Avery pressed the heels of her hands hard into her eyes and started the car's ignition. She pulled out into the stream of traffic and began driving again. The research had taken longer than anticipated. She was probably going to be late for work. That was okay.

But in the midst of the confusion in her mind, something was becoming clearer:

She'd now let Addisyn down not once, but twice. And she could stand still no longer. She had to act, and act fast.

Before her sister's soul was gone for good.

△△   △△   △△

"MORNING, MIZ AVERY."

Avery quickly summoned a smile. "Morning, Laz. I'm sorry I'm a little late." Her detective venture by the side of the road had put her ten minutes behind her normal schedule. "How are you today?" She peeled off her jacket and brushed her hair back.

"Purty darn good." Laz nodded reflectively. "And you?"

"Oh…" Avery smiled feebly. "I'm okay. Good," she amended quickly, since Laz was not the kind to politely refrain from asking, *Why just okay?*

"Hm." Avery could feel Laz's eyes on her as she made her way to the back room to hang up her jacket and grab her name tag. She tried to appear just as happy as normal, but when she entered the storage area, it was a relief to not have to assume that perky façade—at least for the few minutes she'd be in there.

Skating is my heaven, Avery. Addisyn's sweet voice floated through Avery's mind. She remembered the day Addisyn had told her that while they were taking a Sunday afternoon walk through Central Park. "If I didn't have skating—" Addisyn's face had suddenly assumed an uncharacteristically melancholy expression—"I don't know if I'd make it. Sometimes."

Avery knew her sister was right. Skating had been a release for her, a way to untangle the knotty emotions her unconventional childhood evoked. So how was Addisyn possibly coping without her passion? If the date on that news report was to be believed, it had now been about eight months that Addisyn had been off-ice. What was she doing—and where was she doing it?

Questions Brian had asked her—now his visit made sense. Questions Avery would be able to answer, if she'd been the sister she should have been.

Avery didn't regret warning her sister about Brian. She had never trusted him, not one smidgen. She'd watched him exert a great deal of suavity to try to win her approval of his relationship with Addisyn—and become sullen and angry when that failed. The man Addisyn had loved was as imaginary as a department-store mannequin. The real Brian Felding was cruel, greedy, and hateful. Avery would have been downright negligent not to warn her sister—like watching her step in front of a moving car without saying a word.

But what would have happened if she had refused to let Addisyn's drifting become the focal point of their relationship? If she had continued to show her how much she loved her? What if she had expressed her concerns, doused her words to Addisyn in love, and not allowed her terror and hurt to tangle her meaning—and then showed her sister that she trusted her enough to give her room to make her own choices? She had to admit that things might be radically different if she had. It might have saved her relationship with Addisyn.

It might have saved Addisyn herself.

El Shaddai, be with my sister. Help her find her way. It had been Avery's constant prayer since that day at The Loch. But praying didn't seem like quite enough, somehow—especially since she now knew the full truth about how disastrous Addisyn's life was. She wanted to be boots-on-the-ground, doing something.

"Avery?" Laz was peering around the corner. "You okay?"

She'd been supposedly hanging up her coat for ten minutes. "Yes!" Avery snapped out of her reverie and tried to look alert. She followed Laz into the front part of the store. *Focus, Avery. You're at work.* Spiritual warfare would have to wait until after hours. "Is there a shipment coming in today of anything?"

Laz squinted and scratched his beard thoughtfully. "Don't reckon so, unless I overlooked something in the books."

"Which is highly possible." The "books" were literal spiral-bound notebooks, crabbed and crowded with Laz's unruly and—in Avery's opinion—entirely illegible handwriting. His insistence on using this unreliable method of tracking business had always driven her crazy. She had tried to persuade him to embrace technology, but he'd clung to the old ways with his usual stubbornness.

Laz just shrugged. It wasn't a war he wanted to fight again, apparently. "We do have some boxes of magazines to unpack, if you want to do that."

Five minutes later Avery had located the cartons in the equally unruly storeroom and had carried them out to the magazine rack—with Laz's help. He couldn't stand to see her, or any other woman, carrying something heavy. She sliced the top open with a boxcutter and examined the contents. Laz sold issues of *National Geographic Traveler, Outside, Backpacker, Trek & Mountain, Field and Stream,* and *Guns & Ammo,* among others. Avery liked to take home an issue of *Outdoor Life* herself every now and then.

Good thing they had come over the weekend. The white wire rack was almost empty, probably because Laz's store was as much a destination to glean outdoor tips and tricks and the latest trail info as it was a place to shop.

Mindlessly she began cramming the slick magazines onto the rack. The front of a *National Geographic Traveler* caught her eye—a giant color photograph of New York City.

"Life in the Capital of the World," the white block font read. Avery stared at the words. She didn't need to read the featured story to know about life in the city. She had lived it. And so had Addisyn.

Recklessly she thrust another stack of magazines onto the rack. Maybe growing up in NYC had contributed to Addisyn's problems, given her temptations that Avery hadn't prepared her to resist. Maybe the glitz and glamor had been too much of a pull. Addisyn had always been less grounded, more impressionable than Avery—especially in her teens. Maybe Avery should have never taken her to such a crazy place.

But the alternative was staying with their father, which was no choice at all. Avery shuddered at the mere thought. She couldn't let that man get his hands on Addisyn. She'd had to leave, and an enormous, frenetic city like New York was much more protective than a small country town, where they could have been easily found.

In New York, work was plentiful and food was cheap and questions weren't asked. Even two young girls living alone attracted no more attention than the humble pigeons that fluttered on the street corners.

For a moment, Avery wondered if Addisyn might possibly have gone back to the city. The idea sank deeply into her mind for a few minutes, but then her shoulders slumped in defeat. Of course Ads wouldn't be in the Big Apple. Brian's visit told her that much. Surely he'd combed the city before trying anywhere else—and he must have been truly desperate to seek out Avery, knowing exactly how she felt about him.

The thought made Avery even more discouraged. What if she never saw Addisyn again? The idea was like a knife in her soul, but she had to consider the possibility. If Brian, with all his money and connections and persistence—or obsession—couldn't find Addisyn, who could?

Oh, if only she could just know Addisyn was okay! *Just one word or sign would be enough. And then—if she never wants to see me again—I'll accept that. But I need to know she's all right. Need to tell her how sorry I—*

"Miz Avery?"

Avery started in surprise. The stack of magazines she'd been holding cascaded in a sleek wave to the floor, crumpling the covers and creasing the pages. "Oh, Laz!" The incident was the tipping point of a landslide in her soul, and all her pain avalanched onto her heart. Avery felt her eyes begin stinging. "I'm so sorry."

"Now don't you worry." Laz spoke in the same soothing tone he used for injured animals. "Seems to me, though, that you're mighty skittish today. Somethin' troublin' you?"

"No, I'm—uh—" Lying was foreign to Avery. About as foreign as hiding her emotions. "It's nothing."

"Hm." Laz cut a glance at her that clearly showed he wasn't buying her fib. "I see. And is there any particular reason why you saw fit to put them there magazines on the rack with their tails in the air?"

Avery spun around to see with horror that her fifteen minutes' work putting the magazines on the rack had resulted in a neatly arranged display—with all the magazines upside down! Her hands flew to her cheeks. "Oh! I can't believe I did that." Heat crept up her neck. "I was just—just thinking. I'll fix them." She reached toward the display.

"Hold on a minute." Laz's calm yet authoritative voice stopped Avery in her tracks. "Let's talk for a minute about whatever is rippin' yer mind to pieces."

"I said. It's nothing." Avery held her arms rigidly at her sides.

In the course of her life, she'd learned to trust no one—not her father, not her mother, not Brian. And not even her own sister, in the end. As much as she liked Laz, she wasn't opening up to him about personal details.

"This nothin' got somethin' to do with that city slicker fella that got you all worked up that day?"

The mere mention of Brian was enough to make Avery break out in sweat. "Maybe." She cleared her throat and stooped to begin gathering the dropped magazines.

"Hmph." Laz gave a disgusted huff. More like a snort. "Wal-l-l…if ya don't wanna tell me, you don't hafta. But you got the air of a gal who's—" Laz searched for the right word—"who's lookin' for somethin.'"

Lookin' for somethin.' How could he have read her that well? Suddenly Avery stood up. The words didn't have time to be censored by her mind before they came out. "Laz, why did you come to the mountains?"

His brows knit together. "That's my story, not yours, girl."

"I know." Avery's breath caught in her throat. "I know, Laz. But—" she hesitated. How could she explain this? "I came to the mountains because I wanted away from the world."

"Know that feeling right well." It was after eight o'clock, yet he hadn't made a move to turn the OPEN/CLOSED sign on the door. He leaned an elbow on the top of the rack and gave her his full attention.

"The world is a bad and ugly place, and I wanted away. I wanted to be somewhere safe where—where I could forget things." Why was she telling him all this? Maybe because she saw her soul in his eyes.

"This is a good place for forgetting." He stared into space for a moment. Then looked back at her. "A darn good place. The mountains swallow up the bad you've had."

Yes. He was speaking her language now. "Laz, there were some— some people I wanted to forget. One of them I loved so much that it hurt too badly to remember." She bit her lip, but the tears came anyway. She willed her voice to steady. "I left those people on the other side of the High Peaks. I came here to be—to not be hurt anymore."

Laz's eyes glistened with a compassion she could trust. "We've all done it." He shrugged. "Only so much pain a body can take. This ole life, it don't seem to know when you've reached that limit. Or care. And when you get to the wall, sometimes—" he looked out the window at the mountains, the early morning light glancing off his eyes—"sometimes you gotta go up."

"I did." Avery's voice quivered with the intensity of the statement. "El Shaddai—God—I fell in love with Him here, Laz. I knew Him before I came, but here He is so much more—"

"Real." Laz smiled, a gentle smile she'd never seen before.

"Yes." Avery took a deep breath. "But the people I left—they're real too. And I ran away from them."

"Avery." Laz was looking at her as a father might gaze at a well-loved daughter. "Ain't no shame in running away. Folks do it all the time, you know." He looked down at the floor. "Thing is, most run into and inside themselves. They don't run away on the outside, like you did."

"I think I did both." Avery stopped, tried to think what to say. Laz was quiet, watching her. Giving her the space to listen to her thoughts.

"I have a sister." The sentence came out with force.

Laz lifted his eyebrows. Said nothing.

"She needs me." Avery folded her trembling arms across her torso.

"She tell you that?"

Avery avoided his gaze. "We don't talk. Haven't in years. I found out—another way."

He nodded slowly.

"She needs me." The repetition came from her urgency. She bit her lip desperately. "I don't know what to do."

Laz rubbed his nose contemplatively. "Seems easy to me."

He must have seen Avery's perplexed look, because he sighed. "S'pose that Mercy was lost—what would you do?"

"Look for her. All over creation if I had to." There was no hesitancy in Avery's reply.

"Then don't you do as much for your sister?"

Avery felt the impact of his words. She lowered her head. "It's not that easy, Laz. I'm here, and—"

"—And you have to go outside the hiding place to find her." Laz's voice was quiet, steady. He took hold of her shoulders gently. His hands were rough but warm. Like his heart.

"Avery, girl, listen to an old mountain goat that's made purty near ever' mistake a man can make in his life." His voice had smoothed from its usual hearty tones into a quiet huskiness, unmistakable in its sincerity. "We come to these mountains for beautiful reasons. We come for ourselves, our spirits, and we come for God, too. Even the people that just say they come cause it's purty and makes 'em feel special, they're feeling the Spirit of God, and they don't even know it. But—" he sighed. "God ain't just the God of the mountains. He's the God of it all. And sometimes—sometimes He takes you out of the mountains. Into the valleys."

"I can't go." Avery didn't know if her whisper was directed at Laz or El Shaddai.

"Avery, listen." Laz gave her shoulders a gentle squeeze. "This is important. 'K? Yes, the mountains are safe. Yes, the mountains are wonderful. But—"

He paused. Were those tears in his eyes? Avery had never seen, or even imagined, Laz crying.

"But now, you're gonna hafta leave the mountains. For a little while," he added quickly. "You gotta go back out into that nasty world and get your sister. You're gonna hafta be real brave. It's darn scary, but you're strong."

He was right. And now the tears wouldn't wait any longer. Avery could feel the fingerprints of El Shaddai all over the conversation. And from Laz, of all people. The crazy old mountain man. But he had just delivered the truth that set her free.

"You've got to go, Avery girl." He looked at her with understanding mingled with pain. Pain for her or him or both? "You've got to go, because you can't hide from God." He gave a rumpled grin. "Guy named Jonah done tried that trick."

Avery laughed. And kept laughing. Maybe because she didn't want to cry anymore. Maybe because she felt something wonderful.

A sense of direction—the call and prodding of El Shaddai—even from a scary place.

And following Him, wherever He went, was very wonderful indeed.

She was going after her sister. The way she should have a long time ago.

FOUR THIRTY, AND time to be off work for the day. "Miz Avery? You leavin' now?" Laz was counting the money in the cash register drawer.

"Almost. Just have to finish this sweeping." Avery made it a point to sweep the shop each day just before closing.

Laz groaned and shook his head. "Girl, once a week is good."

"Once a week is lazy and you know it." This was an ongoing battle. Similar to their divergent perspectives on the old-fashioned notebook system. Avery was of the belief that a clean, pristine store attracted customers and bolstered their faith in the quality of the merchandise. Laz found daily cleaning unnecessary—unmanly, even—and maintained that an outdoors store was expected to have a little of the outdoors in it. As far as Avery could tell, that meant dirt and dead bugs in the corners.

"Well." Laz was not going to argue this time. He'd been unaccustomedly gentle that day, after his advice to Avery in the morning. "I'm just wantin' you to get home afore it starts stormin'."

"Are the weather reports calling for storms?" Avery batted at a cobweb in the corner behind the kayaks. Seriously, how did spiders spin such elaborate creations in twenty-four hours?

"Weather reports, your grandma." Laz snorted in contempt. "You think I listen to a city slicker in a three-piece suit tell me what it's gonna do in my mountains?"

Avery glanced over at Laz. His brawny six-foot, four-inch frame was offset by the bear head on the wall behind him—Laz had shot the bear himself years ago. She hid a smile. "No. I guess not."

"Take a look out yonder and tell me you don't think it's gonna storm." Laz jerked his chin toward the front door of the shop.

Avery gathered up the dustpan and opened the front door to toss the contents off to the side, in the dirt and grass. She caught her breath. Boiling purple clouds obscured the very tops of the mountains above the tree line. The daylight was dim, and a wind was blowing strongly—a cool wind, rushing down the slopes of the High Peaks. She hastily ducked back inside and turned to hang the dustpan up. "Will it be a bad storm?"

Laz shrugged. "Dunno. Probably not. Just another summertime baby.

Purty common in the afternoons around here."

Avery nodded. "Guess I better go."

She was halfway out the door when Laz said, "Oh, Avery?"

"Uh-huh?"

"You gonna need some time off work?" He crossed the room, his boots thumping on the floorboards, and stood beside her. The odd light from the approaching storm made him look almost otherworldly.

"Time off?"

"For your trip back into the world." His gaze met hers full-on.

Funny, how Avery dreaded leaving the mountains more than anything, yet she still felt such an upwelling of purpose at the thought of finding Addisyn. A feeling of purpose so deep that it brought her a joy she couldn't explain—even in the face of a fear that threatened to consume her. She cleared her throat. "Possibly…"

"Take the rest of this week off. With pay." Laz held up his hand to stop her from saying anything. "It's my gift, girl. Just don't stay gone too long." He gave a sad smile.

Tears tickled the corners of Avery's eyes. "I won't. I swear I won't." She grabbed the older man in a quick hug. "Thank you, Laz. For everything."

"Aww…it's nothin.'"

Avery waved and ran across the parking lot to her truck. As she put the truck in gear, she noticed Laz still standing in the doorway. She rolled down her window and yelled, "Thank you!"

Laz smiled and cupped his hands to his mouth. "Go find yer sister!"

Avery grinned and waved once more. She turned onto Marys Lake Road and settled back into the cracked leather seat. Time to follow El Shaddai—and find her sister.

A storm was definitely coming, but she wasn't afraid.

CHAPTER 19

Darius heaved the axe into another piece of kindling. It struck the wood squarely with a satisfying *thunk!* He straightened for a moment. Easing the kinks out of his back, he wiped his forehead and gazed off at the mountains.

His only oasis.

Over the last few days, he'd spent a lot of hours driving in the mountains, as he'd done after his parents died. Marking time, trying to ease the pain—a pain that shattered his bones. Sometimes he didn't want to come home from those drives. Other times he would rather crawl in a corner and never leave his parents' house at all. And sometimes he just wanted to hop in his car and drive north. Until he reached the world's end.

Tears were coming. He'd always cried easily. Angrily he swiped at his eyes. Emotions only got a guy in trouble. Hadn't he learned that by now? He took a deep breath and grabbed another chunk of wood. In July, the house didn't necessarily need firewood, but he needed something to whack. And a way to fill his day off work.

As he pounded, snatches of memories whipped through his mind. The time he and his dad had argued over his training schedule for Nationals. The orange windsuit of the skater in front of him the day he fell. The way the light had left Addisyn's face with the suddenness of a summer storm cloud blotting out the sun when he turned on her.

Forget it, man. Another piece of wood flew off to the side. Another piece of his life falling apart. *It's over. You're over.*

He needed more, needed something else to hit. He grabbed another log. He wouldn't stop till the pain was at least bearable.

This reminded him of the way things had been right after his parents died. The agony had dogged his steps. He couldn't stop running or it would catch him.

Keep chopping.

Why had he fallen in love with Addisyn? Why had he ever allowed her to reawaken his soul at all? He had never deserved her.

Keep chopping.

Where was she now? With that preppy guy?

Keep chopping.

Finally he couldn't keep chopping any longer. In a final blaze of disgust, he flung the axe across the yard. Sweat was streaming down his face, rolling down his spine, dripping off the ends of his hair. He opened the door and went into the house.

And saw the portrait of his grandfather.

There was nothing strange about that. The picture had hung there since his grandfather lost his battle with cancer—the year after Darius's Olympic gold. He'd passed it a dozen times every day since then. But today, it seemed to reach out to him. As though Grampy were calling his name.

Darius stopped and stared at the photo. The old man's face was beaming with a simple, homely joy. He was standing on the steps of the little church he'd pastored in Whistler, a Bible under his arm.

For by grace are ye saved through faith; and that not of yourselves: it is the gift of God.

The words flashed into Darius's mind with such suddenness that he stared around the room. Hadn't he always heard Grampy say that to him? Tell him that in moments of decision? Preach it from the pulpit and live it with his life?

"Grampy?" The whisper barely brushed his lips.

A Presence seemed to stir in the room around Darius. He held his breath, waiting. Was his grandpa with him?

Or was it Someone else?

"God?"

No answer. Of course not. The Lord he'd failed had left him long ago.

And with that, Darius braced his palms on either side of the photo, leaned into the wall, and wept. Not just tears that rolled tamely down his cheeks, but heart-ripping, gut-wrenching sobs. The kind of tears that a man cried. The kind he should have cried a long time ago.

"Grampy!" The sobs were shaking his soul, dredging up all his past pain. "Oh, Grampy!" How disappointed and angry the man would be to see him now. How heartbroken that his only grandson had strayed so far.

"I've failed!"

He had. He had drifted a million miles from the eager young boy who sat on a pew in his grandpa's church and led a youth group. He was no longer the kid who loved God and strived to lead a clean-cut life. No, he was ruined, a broken vessel no longer fit for anything but garbage.

All because of the mistake that had ruined his life.

He knew full well why he'd lashed out so terribly at Addisyn. Because she'd been right. He did have a secret.

And because of that secret, he'd hidden from God. Crashed his Olympic career. Lived a purposeless life. And now, he had lost the woman of his dreams.

The pain struck him with an intensity that took his breath away. He stuffed a fist in his mouth to stifle the sobs. What was he doing, falling apart like this?

Everything was coming down, the walls he'd so elaborately constructed crashing down in his soul. He was done with the lying and hiding and pretending. He didn't care anymore. If he could only talk to his grandpa. He'd tell him everything.

He stared at the picture again. Suddenly another face came to mind—Terry Williams.

At first he dismissed the idea. Absurd. But slowly it gained force.

Terry had offered to talk with him. Terry was a man of strong faith and unspotted character. Terry was compassionate and kind.

Terry was the closest person to Grampy.

With the force of light breaking over the predawn earth, Darius realized what had to happen. No matter what it cost, he had to break free.

Not giving himself time to think about it, he grabbed his cell phone and shot Terry a text. Is your offer still good?

In less than thirty seconds a reply swooped onto the screen. My offer???

Darius typed back simply, **To talk.** Then waited.

Yes!!! Where u at, man?

Are u at the center? Darius was shaking with the sudden urgency, the need to tell someone the thing he had never wanted to tell anyone.

Yes, want to come here?

Yes. Darius looked at the simple reply a moment before sending it. He was committed now. No turning back. After today, he wouldn't be able to pretend anymore.

Maybe he was crazy. Maybe that loose something in his brain had finally snapped all the way. But as he grabbed his car keys and sprinted out of his house as if something was chasing him, he had the strangest feeling. It took him all the way into the car and out of his driveway to diagnose it. Because he hadn't had it in so long.

Hope.

He swerved into the stream of traffic and drove steadily, his gaze fixed straight ahead. He was about to do the craziest and most wonderful thing he'd ever done.

He was going to find God. Because if redemption was still possible for Darius Payne, he wanted it more than he wanted his next breath.

△△ △△ △△

THE CLIMBING CENTER was humming on a Tuesday afternoon, but when Darius stepped inside Terry's office, the soundproof walls made it seem as if they were the only two people in the world. Terry was waiting behind his desk. "Hey there." His smile was completely warm and open. No indication that he resented being interrupted in the middle of a busy workday. "I'm glad you texted me." He indicated a chair. "Please, sit down."

How he managed to awkwardly perch on the edge of the chair, Darius didn't know. Now that he was here, what was he going to say? His heart hammered so hard it hurt.

"Um…let me just say…I'm scared to death." Darius tried to laugh, but his chest was too tight.

Understanding washed over Terry's face. He leaned forward, giving Darius his full attention. "Look, whatever you want to tell me, it's okay. Like I told you—" his voice reverberated with a compassion that couldn't be artificial—"I've got your back."

Darius hadn't been going to cry. But something in Terry's tone reminded him so much of his grandpa. His eyes burned, and he pressed the palms of his hands against his face, totally embarrassed. "Thanks." He cleared his throat. "I—I—" The words sounded dumb, but he said them anyway. "I need to get free."

Terry smiled. "Free is good. And—" he looked Darius straight in the eye. "Free is scary. Am I right?"

"Yes, sir." Darius gathered all his courage and burst forth. "I used to go to church. I led a youth group."

Terry's eyebrows raised, but he displayed no other visible sign of surprise. "Didn't know that."

"Most people don't." Darius knew he was traveling the long way around to get to the real issue. "My grandpa was the pastor."

"That's neat." If Terry was wondering where Darius was heading with all this biographical data, he didn't show it. He seemed completely accepting and infinitely patient. "Which church was it?"

"Somerset Christian. The little one out on Turquoise Lane." Darius didn't have to close his eyes to picture that church.

"Oh yeah." Terry rubbed the bridge of his nose. "I know right where that is. Out by the Pacific Coast Highway, right?"

"Yes, sir. That's the one."

"Guess you spent a lot of time there, huh?" Still Terry's voice was gentle, soothing even.

"Yes. Yes, I did." Darius took a bracing breath. If he waited any longer, he'd lose the guts to walk this road altogether. "Terry, I'm going to cut right to the chase. I'm here today because—" Darius closed his eyes, but the tears came anyway—"because I have let everyone down. But most importantly, I have let God down, and He's—He's not with me anymore."

"Darius." Terry's words radiated with compassion. "Son, you haven't let anyone down. You're a fantastic athlete and a wonderful young man.

So many people are rooting for you!'

Darius gritted his teeth. Just what he'd always heard—the applause of a crowd mesmerized by a falsity. It was time to put an end to the lies. Once and for all. "No!" His voice was a cry for help. "No, I have let everyone down. They just don't know it." He was trembling now, shaking in every limb. His very insides felt like a quivering mass of jelly. "Do you—do you know that I fell? In Sochi?"

"Yes, I heard about that." Terry released a slow breath. "That was just an accident. It could have happened to anyone. There's no need to—"

This was the moment. Do or die. No turning back now. Darius took a deep breath—and spoke the truth he had never breathed a word of. "It wasn't just an accident."

For the first time Terry looked taken aback. "I—what?"

"It was my fault." With every word, Darius felt as if white-hot claws were ripping the hard splinters from his heart. But it was going to be worth it. No matter what Terry thought of him when the truth was exposed, he had to finish his confession.

"I was totally to blame. Because the night before, I had made the biggest mistake of my life."

From an early age, Darius had been taught by his father that there were two beverages that hampered athletic ability. One was coffee.

The other was alcohol.

The Olympic committees were somewhat ambivalent about alcohol in general. It wasn't sold inside the Olympic Village, but athletes could go out to drink or bring their own booze. To counteract this leniency, some countries restricted alcohol use or banned it entirely.

Canada was not one of those countries. However, that didn't mean all the Canadian athletes drank. In fact, most of the ones Darius knew wouldn't touch the stuff. They claimed it hurt their performance.

"Always dehydrates me," one of Darius's teammates in Vancouver had sworn. He'd shrugged. "I'm not a tee-totaller type, so yeah, I might have a beer or two with dinner back home. But here, I stay a mile away from anything strong."

"Yeah," another guy had chimed in. "I've worked way too hard to mess it up now."

"It's not just about that," an older man in their group had huffed. He was a veteran athlete at his fourth, and probably last, Olympics. "It's not the Olympic thing to do." His chest had puffed out as he added, "Remember, gentlemen, we are the world's role models right now!"

Darius had taken all they said to heart. Besides, he was a good Christian kid. He didn't drink.

But in Sochi, things were different than they had been in Vancouver. He was no longer the young golden boy, the idol of his nation, flanked by the support and love of his parents. And it was probably his grief—and the pressure he'd faced—that made everything start rolling downhill.

△△　△△　△△

"EVERYBODY EXPECTED ME to take gold in the thousand meters." Darius could remember how uncertain he'd felt, how scared he'd been. "I barely got bronze. Third place." He spread his palms. "The media ate it up. 'What's wrong with Payne? Will he recover?' And…I had no one in my corner. All my friends were figure skaters, not short-track guys. My grandpa was gone, and my parents too."

"I know that had to have been hard." Pure understanding, that was Terry.

"It was plenty hard." Darius remembered walking the sidewalks through the Olympic Village the day before the five hundred meters, feeling as if his soul might crack under the load of expectations. The five hundred meters was his specialty. He was determined to medal. He had had only one chance left to bring home gold—for his parents. And for himself. One chance to finally be a man—a great man.

The pressure had bowed his soul and warped all his priorities. By that time, he was no longer the naïve little fellow at the Vancouver games. He'd been around the block and knew a thing or two more. Plus, God had— well, sort of drifted, stuffed away with the memories of his parents and the pain of their deaths. Or maybe it was Darius who had drifted.

He'd felt horrible that night. Neither his heart nor his body was cooperating. Shaky and sweaty, he'd wandered around the city of Sochi long past dark, returning to the Village right before curfew. The whole time, the tension pounded him like a hailstorm.

Just inside the gate, he'd run into a fellow athlete. The guy was also a short-track skater, from Germany. Darius had met him briefly during the opening ceremonies and even skated against him in the thousand meters, but he hadn't gotten a chance to talk to him much. The Germans were lodged in a building far from the Canadians, but Darius had heard that on most nights, loud party music and raucous cheers came from the Germans' part of the Village, their country having no policy restricting alcohol use for athletes.

"Hallo, friend!" The wiry little guy grinned at Darius. He spoke English with a heavy accent that was sometimes hard to decipher. "How you doing?"

"Nervous." The invisible bands on Darius's chest kept him from taking the deep breaths he needed. "I've only got one race more. Tomorrow."

"Relax!" The kid clapped him on the back, grinning at him. "You have trained hard. Nothing to worry about, ja?"

Darius had rolled his eyes at the skater's careless attitude. "I wish. I'm so scared I can't stand it."

"You are too nervous, my friend!" Even now, Darius could remember how bright the man's grin had flashed in the darkness. "Come! I show you to have fun!"

Despite Darius's hesitations and questions, the energetic young man had dragged him to the German camp. All the guys were so nice. Sitting with them, Darius found himself feeling better. Even laughing a little at their crazy jokes. And when they clapped a can of German beer into his hands, there didn't seem to be a good reason to say no.

The effect of the alcohol was instantaneous and miraculous. The anxiety and pain were gone, and instead he felt stronger, smarter, happier. Even the tightness in his muscles eased, leaving a comfortable warmth instead. All the pain inside his soul, the wounds that had ached for so many weary months, seemed to melt under the hypnotizing influence of the beer.

He needed a second can. He got one.

And more after that.

"I WOKE UP wishing I could erase everything that happened that night." Darius rubbed the sides of his head. Even now, he could remember the pain of that morning—his first and only hangover. "I threw up three times within fifteen minutes."

He sneaked a look at Terry. Still the man didn't seem repulsed or withdrawn. If anything, his eyes shone with more compassion than before.

"The race wasn't until six o'clock that evening, so I had all day to recoup. By race time, I felt—okay. But definitely not normal."

His head was no longer throbbing, but his skull still felt too small for his brain. And although the incessant vertigo had ceased, the earth continued to wobble and tilt every now and then. A feeling Darius hated, like he'd lost his footing.

Maybe he had.

But as his physical torpor subsided, his mental and spiritual discomfort was just kicking in. Had he really stayed up half the night drinking alcohol and singing ribald songs with a gang of foreign frat guys? His cheeks burned red every time he thought about how he'd tarnished his character.

No matter, he told himself. *No big deal. I'll go out here tonight and score a medal. And I'll never touch alcohol again.*

When he lined up in the starting lane, pre-race alertness had overshadowed most of his symptoms. He was taut, focused, ready to redeem himself—even if his head was still pounding and the stadium lights seemed painfully bright.

He'd skated hard—harder than he'd thought possible. His whole life seemed to have been concentrated in those few minutes. In a field of five, he'd soared ahead of three skaters and positioned himself in second place with relative ease.

But the guy in first was a Dutch skater, and the Dutch were masters of short-track. Darius made his turns as tightly as possible, took longer strides than normal. All of it was no use. The bright orange Dutch windsuit remained in position—ahead of him, but maddeningly close.

The sharp note of the bell had filled him with panic. Only one more lap—and silver wasn't good enough.

After what he'd done, he had to get gold. It was the only way to wipe out his guilt. The desperation had made him a little careless.

"I thought there was a small gap to pass the guy in front of me." Darius swallowed hard. "I tried to hug the inside and come up next to him. It was a crazy thing to do. And, of course, he tried to move over and block me. It was a mess for about half a second, and then somehow my blade caught his."

The moment still dogged his worst nightmares. He'd felt a jerk on his leg, and he wasn't able to stride forward. He'd grabbed for his balance and found only the air. In a split second, he was crashing into the ice with the Dutchman on top of him and the rest of the field falling over them. The impact had been enough to sling the confused jumble of competitors into the barriers.

"Next thing I knew, I was howling in pain with paramedics around me. I don't know which hurt more—my back, my wrist, or my leg." Darius rubbed the scar on his knee, where the skate blade had ripped him just above his Kevlar shin guard. "And the impact was horrific. The barriers are inflatable, but it felt like hitting a concrete wall. I guess when you're skating at thirty miles an hour, any collision is going to hurt. I got banged up pretty bad, and so did some others. But—" he took a deep breath. "The athlete behind me crushed his ankle and suffered a serious concussion." He could still remember watching the EMTs lug the skater's crumpled frame out of the arena. "He never skated again."

Terry leaned forward, his brow furrowed. "Darius, short-track is a dangerous sport. The guys who do it know the risks and accept them. You can't possibly hold yourself accountable for the whole thing. It was just a mistake."

"That's what the judges said." Darius shrugged. "Of course, they did an investigation, complete with extra blood-testing on all of us. They found the alcohol in my bloodstream, but they ruled it wasn't enough to affect my performance."

Terry stared at Darius. "So how do you get that this is your fault?"

"Because the judges can say what they want. I know my body. I know the alcohol was still affecting my performance. I didn't feel right." He swallowed hard. "I betrayed my parents and grandpa. I did something I knew was wrong—something I should have never done. After I got drunk, the responsible thing to do would have been to just bow out of the competition. Instead, I shattered everything for four other great athletes who'd worked just as hard as I had. And...I killed myself."

"Darius." Terry leaned forward in his chair, arms stretched out, hands folded.

Darius felt utterly drained. He'd told the secret. The huge shameful thing that had derailed his whole career, his whole self-image, his whole life was out in the open. And the exorcism had wrenched him to the core of his being. His body ached worse than it did after he finished a grueling workout.

He couldn't bear to look at Terry. Would the man give him a lecture about consequences? Order him out of his office? Maybe fire him on the spot?

"Darius, look at me."

It was the last thing he wanted to do, but slowly, Darius raised his head. The older man's eyes shone with an intensity, a burning light Darius had never seen. Terry's voice almost trembled with the passion of his words. "Darius Payne, I want you to know one thing right now. You are forgiven."

Forgiven? Darius squinted in confusion. Hadn't Terry heard what he'd said? "Terry, I can't. That's the horrible part." He gestured vaguely, trying to convey a sense of the hopelessness of his situation. "I can't expect God to overlook a horrible choice that was all my own fault. That hurt a lot of people."

"Overlook? Certainly not." Terry stared intently at Darius. "I'm talking about forgive." Seeing the baffled stare on Darius's face, Terry rephrased his statement. "To overlook a sin is to sweep it under the rug and allow it to fester in darkness. To forgive is to call it out, acknowledge it—and then heal it."

This still wasn't making sense. Darius shook his head. "I don't understand, Terry."

"Surely with all your years in church you've heard the gospel, son."

Darius was beginning to feel impatient. "Sure, I heard the gospel a time or two...thousand."

"Tell it to me." Terry leaned back in his chair.

Darius fumbled with his words. Disappointment was wriggling through him. He'd been Mr. Brave, coming in here to tell Terry his darkest secret, and the man couldn't help him. He was about to give him some canned—

"Tell me the gospel, son."

Darius sighed. "Okay. People do wrong things that separate them from God, so God sent His Son, Jesus, to earth. Jesus died on a cross, taking on Himself the punishment we deserve, so that we can ask Him for forgiveness and live with Him in Heaven forever." He felt like a trite Sunday-school boy as he said the words. That time was over for him.

Terry smiled knowingly. "You left out the most important part."

Darius leaned forward. "What?"

Terry's words were simple but profound. "Love." His voice was almost a whisper. "You left out the love. God sent Jesus to rescue us because He loves us."

Like a daybreak cracking open a grey sky, Darius could feel his soul stirring. Love? God's love? Had he really missed that all along?

"Darius, let me tell you something."

Gone was Darius's impatience. He was hanging on Terry's every word now.

"I think all your life you've seen God as a judge and your life as a performance. You've compared your relationship with God to going on that ice and skating. You've focused hard on getting your routine right, not missing any steps, and watching your timing carefully. Because you knew that God was watching, scowling, ready to crack down on you over any little mistake. You thought God wanted perfection.

"But Darius, that's not true. God never asked you to give Him perfection. He asked you to give Him Darius Payne. Heart and soul. Even with all the flaws."

So many foreign emotions were stirring in Darius's heart. Hope— grief that he'd never realized this—amazement—gratitude—and—was it—freedom?

Terry opened the drawer of his desk and pulled out a battered Bible, stroking the worn leather cover reverently. "Darius, God doesn't sit on the mountaintop and wait for us to climb up to Him. He knows nobody can do that. There's not a perfect person on this planet." A smile gently spread across Terry's face. "That's why the gospel is *good* news, son. God isn't using your good deeds and your bad ones to try to figure some composite score. Instead, He sent Jesus. And now all He wants is for you to love Him and trust Him."

Terry turned his head and gazed out the window. "The Bible says His mercies are new every morning. Every day when I get here to the center and see the light breaking over Whistler, I remember that. Son, there are as many fresh chances in the love of God as there are days in your life—and then some. God knows you can't be perfect." He paused, and his eyes focused onto Darius's face. "He loves you anyway."

"Oh, Terry." The tears were coming. "I can't believe this."

Darius bent his head and cried. Not just a quiet trickle of tears, but the kind of sobs from a man who has been lost in a desert his whole life and sees an oasis before him. Terry left his chair and knelt beside Darius, wrapping an arm around his shoulders.

After a few minutes, Darius swiped the back of his hand across his face. "Terry." His voice was still cracking. "Thank you for this."

"Don't thank me. Thank God." Terry's eyes were damp too. "He did the work for you, son. We were never designed to carry the weight of our sins on our own shoulders." Terry squeezed Darius's shoulder. "It's not a competition. God isn't angry if you don't win the medal. He just wants your love."

"I realize that now." Darius still felt as if he might cry at any moment. "I need to talk to Him."

Terry smiled. "I would agree. He's been waiting for a while."

"Yes." Darius sniffed and nodded. "A long while."

The two men exchanged a hug. "I'll be praying for you." Terry squeezed Darius's shoulder with the affection of a father.

"Thanks." Together they slowly made their way out of the climbing center.

They were in the parking lot when Terry suddenly smiled. "I've been meaning to ask. How're things with that girl?"

Darius felt his face turning bright red. "Well—not good." He looked at Terry apologetically. "Turns out she had another boyfriend."

"Really?" Terry cocked his head.

"Yeah." Even after his newfound hope, the thought of Addisyn still stung the tender places of his soul. Briefly he told Terry about meeting Brian. "She came to see me at work the next day, but by then I knew everything." He shrugged sadly. "It just wasn't meant to be."

"Hmm." Terry rubbed his chin. "So what did she come to the center to tell you?"

Darius opened his mouth, then closed it again. "I—" For the first time, it struck him. What had Addisyn come to tell him?

He'd never given her a chance to say. He'd had his mind made up, been determined he knew all the facts. She'd come to tell him something, and she'd run into his walls.

He hung his head. "I don't know." The admission seemed so incredible now. "I never asked."

The knowledge stung like salt in a wound. He'd been so consumed in his own pain, he'd lashed out—ushering her out of his life before she could come any closer to his dark secrets.

Terry nodded. "I guess when you live within a wall of shame, nobody can get too close, can they?"

"No." Darius shook his head. A short laugh of disbelief slipped out as he looked at Terry. "I've—I've been an idiot."

"Not an idiot. Just a learner. Like us all. But after you talk to the Lord, I think you have some other unfinished business to take care of." Terry clapped Darius on the back. "Brother, I'm so proud of you for talking to me today. Thank you."

"No, thank you." Darius wiped his eyes and waved again as Terry headed back inside the center. Then he slowly opened his car door and sank into the seat.

It was time to finally talk to the One he'd been avoiding for all these years. The God Who had never, ever stopped loving him.

And right after that, he had a journey to take. A wry half smile tugged his lips at the echo of Brian's boastful swagger.

Chicago…Wednesday…Rayard Arena.

Darius turned the key, and the Traverse roared to life. He needed to find the girl who'd come too close. He needed to hear what she had to tell him. And he needed to share what was on his heart.

Because now he knew—love was stronger than secrets.

CHAPTER 20

Avery was beginning to think Addisyn had simply disappeared.

There was no other explanation. Slumped at her desk, Avery dropped her head into her hands. The rough fist of failure slammed into her soul.

As soon as she'd arrived home from work on Monday evening, she'd assumed her best James Bond persona. Snuggled in the comfy chair in her cabin while Laz's predicted storm rolled through and thunder cracked the sky, she'd begun an Internet search for her little sister.

First she'd Googled Addisyn's name, hoping to find her Facebook page. She couldn't go to Facebook directly—she'd never had an account—but she'd hoped Addisyn's page would appear in the search results.

However, nothing had risen to the surface besides news articles and videos—some recent, some older. As the storm growled away beyond the horizon, Avery had read each post, studied each photograph, watched each video.

She hadn't unearthed any clues that would help her now, but she had filled in the blanks in her sister's career—how she'd secured sponsorship, climbed the ranks faster than anyone could have guessed, and then watched her dream unravel.

The search had broken Avery's heart all over again. Every photo she saw, every video she watched, every news article she read only made her more aware of how much she ached to have Addisyn back. Memories she'd shoved beneath the surface had tapped gently on the door of her heart the whole evening—the joy of feeding the ducks together in Central Park, Addisyn's delight with the pair of suede boots Avery had once given her for a Christmas present, the times they went window-shopping on Fifth Avenue pretending they were going to buy all the prettiest dresses.

Avery rubbed her eyes. She was tired—exhausted from an evening fraught with the tidal tug of the past, exhausted from the sleepless night that followed, exhausted from remembering how her sister once was.

Before Brian came.

Brian. There was a thought. Avery lifted her laptop screen again and Googled Brian's name, coupled with "figure skating coach." This time, one of the first results was his Facebook page.

Between her lack of an account and his privacy settings, she wouldn't be able to see most of his information, but it was worth a glance anyway. She scrolled past photos of him and Addisyn together—none more recent than some Valentine's Day party, over five months ago. However, his bio details clearly proclaimed he was "in a relationship" with Addisyn Miles.

Nothing more there. Avery clicked back to the search results and tried the next link. And the next. And the next. An hour later, she rested her head on her desk and closed her eyes. Tuesday afternoon, and she had no ideas—not even any clues. And somewhere out there, her sister was dying.

She fought to swallow the panicky urgency. Didn't she know that El Shaddai held all the threads of time in His hands? Wasn't she willing to trust that when the way was clear, she'd be shown what to do?

But the urge to go, do, act squeezed her soul in a grip that grew more relentless each hour. If only she could find her sister. The lectures and warnings were over. Now she would simply wrap Addisyn in her arms and beg to be allowed into her life once more.

Oh, El Shaddai. I have sinned. I did not reflect Your love, Your grace. And now it's too late. A crushing load of guilt settled onto Avery's soul. She who had tried so hard to toe the line and mind her p's and q's. When had she forgotten the power of grace? Why had she tried to make Addisyn believe that perfection was mandatory?

But if she could just find Addisyn, she'd change all of that. It wouldn't matter what Addisyn had done or how far she'd lost her way. She only wanted her back—flaws and scars and all.

El Shaddai, please give me the chance to correct my mistake. Give me the chance to show Ads Your love. Give me one more opportunity. Please, Lord.

My mercies are new every morning.

The gentle words stilled Avery's spirit and calmed her soul. Yes, El Shaddai was merciful. He was as full of power and compassion as the mountains were full of snow. She breathed in deeply, soaking in His presence. He would show her grace. She knew it.

Now if only she could show that grace to Addisyn—before it was too late.

Avery opened her eyes and gazed at her laptop with renewed determination. She wasn't giving up. There had to be another way, another option, another—

Suddenly a moment of pure inspiration flashed inside her mind. Brian!

Brian was tenacious. Brian was rich. Brian had friends—or at least what he referred to as such—all over the country.

And Brian was looking for Addisyn.

Avery grinned with the sheer brilliance of her plan. Of course! Why not take a good opportunity when she saw one?

She chuckled wryly. So Brian was looking for Addisyn? Perfect. She'd piggyback on his efforts. Maybe his Facebook page hadn't yielded any hints, but that didn't mean he couldn't still be useful.

A plan was taking shape in her mind. She lay back in the big chair and let it come—watched it softly materialize, growing in power and feasibility. So it was crazy, yes. Radical? Certainly. Expensive and difficult? Who cared! This was about finding Addisyn. No matter how thorny the road there.

Avery was suddenly aware of a dim thumping noise. She sat up to see Mercy walking by the big chair, slapping it with her wagging tail as she looked hopefully at her owner. Avery laughed and sat up. "Whatcha doing, Mercy? Would you mind staying with Laz for a few days?" Still sweet-talking the dog, she rose and headed for her bedroom.

She had a bag to pack and a flight to catch.

△△　△△　△△

THE WINDY CITY was certainly well-named. Addisyn's hair whipped around her face in the rough gale coming off Monroe Harbor. She brushed it out of her eyes and continued strolling along the path. A little wind was a small price to pay for finally having some alone time.

Especially when the opportunity might not come again for a long time. *Wednesday, August 1.*

The date rumbled ominously in Addisyn's mind. Ed would be arriving around six o'clock that evening—which meant that in a little over eight and a half hours, her life would change forever. One way or another. So yes, she'd take all the alone time she could get right now.

Brian had been busy with paperwork—filling out her application for Team Unlimited, he said, although that seemed rather premature. Brian had wanted her to hit the gym for one final workout this morning, but at the last minute he'd changed his mind, told her she could have some free time.

Even in the midst of what was the greatest opportunity of her life— to quote Brian's catchphrase—Addisyn couldn't help but resent the fact that she had to wait for Brian's approval in order to have even a couple of hours to herself. Coaches were supposed to help you, yes. They were supposed to give you nutrition advice and exercise help and force you to stick to training regimens. They might point out flaws in your performance and monitor the mineral content of your meals and occasionally give you a kick in the tail when you needed motivation.

What they weren't supposed to do was take over your whole life. Good grief, Addisyn had specific rules to follow—things she could only do with Brian, places she had to wait for his permission to visit.

Like last night. Addisyn's cheeks burned just remembering it. Brian had taken her out to eat at the Carlton Supper Club. It was an elegant and expensive bar and restaurant, with a romantic ambiance, great cuisine, and friendly staff—there was no denying he planned wonderful dates.

They'd been ordering their food, and Addisyn had been skimming the menu. She'd been starving—her workouts had been crazy yesterday.

The waiter was standing attentively with his pad and pen. Brian scanned the pages perfunctorily. "Wedge salad for me with seasonal soup." He gestured to Addisyn expectantly.

"Smoked trout Caesar salad with asparagus." Addisyn reached for an appetizer.

Brian frowned. "You don't mean that. Don't you know Caesar salads can cause food poisoning?" His voice wasn't quiet enough. "Baby, you can't run that risk."

"Brian, I'm serious. That's what I—"

"A French onion gratinee salad for my girl." Brian cut her off abruptly. "And two lemon margaritas."

The waiter merely bowed slightly. "Thank you, sir."

After he left, Addisyn realized she was shaking from anger. "Brian…why did you do that?" She felt tears in the corners of her eyes. "You just embarrassed me in front of everyone."

Brian stared at her, seemingly shocked she was even upset at all. "What? You're worried what that punk waiter thought about you?" A frown congealed on his face. "Look, it's not that big of a deal."

Thinking back to it now, Addisyn shook her head. Brian was right. The waiter's opinion didn't matter at all. And changing a salad order wasn't exactly earth-shattering—even if Brian had done it in a less-than-tactful way. She couldn't put her finger, exactly, on why it had upset her so much. But for some reason, Brian's actions had caused a volcano in her soul.

Relax, baby. His words from the night before. *C'mon, you know it's true. Caesar salads use raw eggs. We can't run the risk of you getting sick right now.*

When Addisyn's demeanor still didn't lift, he'd leaned in and kissed her on the lips. She'd been too confused by all that had happened to pull away, but she hadn't returned the kiss either. When he drew back, there was something in his eyes that Addisyn didn't like. A hardness there—a hunger that had nothing to do with a salad.

I just want the best for you, baby. Just trying to protect you and make sure things are good for you. You know that by now.

The breeze was still blowing. She turned her face into its blustery good nature. The sun and wind felt wonderful after so many days spent inside a smelly gym or stuffy ice rink. And the gentle walking helped ease the soreness from her muscles, pushed to exhaustion every day.

Addisyn had never been to Chicago before, but she'd heard Brian rave about it as one of his favorite cities in America. Now she could see why. It was like him—restless, prosperous, dirty.

She'd needed a break badly. So today she'd walked down East Ida B. Wells Drive and headed to Grant Park—"Chicago's backyard," touted the guidebook. So far, it reminded her of Central Park, one of her favorite places in her former hometown. Baseball diamonds were scattered throughout, most occupied by yelling, laughing kids chasing flyballs. Addisyn had seen some people flying kites, others picnicking. A group of teenagers was just ahead of her, playing with a Frisbee.

She felt a little guilty. Brian would be furious if he knew where she was. She was fully aware that by telling her she could "have some free time," he didn't mean go downtown alone. He claimed his constant hovering was for her safety. Like not eating Caesar salads.

Addisyn glanced around the park. So far she felt absolutely safe. It was around nine thirty in the morning, she'd seen multiple traffic policemen, and she was only a quarter of a mile from the hotel, for crying out loud. More importantly, though, she felt peaceful. She could hear the tumult of the city—roar of traffic, honk of horns, a jet rumbling to Chicago-O'Hare. But within Grant Park, she seemed secluded, protected, as if she were in the eye of a hurricane. It was a good place for thinking things over—including Brian's disturbing control tendencies. Really, who changed an order for another person? A sudden, spasmodic rebellion flamed high in Addisyn's soul. For a second, she wanted food poisoning— or at least the freedom to get it.

Somehow, she'd become absorbed into Brian's world—just a small cog in the giant machine of his schemes and plans. The longer she was with him, the less like herself she felt. And the less control she seemed to have over any part of her life. The feeling twisted a tight cord of anxiety around her neck.

A tugboat churned into Monroe Harbor. Addisyn paused for a moment to watch it, fascinated with the way the water slapped its shiny hull. Lake Michigan was right in her lap, separated from the park by only one road.

Slowly Addisyn wandered to the center of the park, until she reached the brick plaza. It was hedged by perfectly trimmed square bushes and the white tents of snack vendors. In the very middle was the magnificent sight of Buckingham Fountain, its jets of water gushing high into the air. Set against the backdrop of the city, the fountain seemed like an eternal epicenter of joy.

With a sigh, Addisyn perched on the stone edge, pulling her knees to her chest. Looking into the pool, she noticed some goldfish sliding through the clearness as well as pennies and dimes twinkling on the bottom of the fountain.

She stared at the loose change. If she had a penny and a magic fountain, what would she wish for?

At one time, without hesitation, she would have wished for—well, exactly what she had now. A romantic boyfriend. A lavish lifestyle. A shot at the Olympics. But now…now her priorities had shifted.

A jet growled overhead, searing the sky. Addisyn squinted up against the blue, watching the white steam stretch behind in a perfect contrail.

So what was keeping her here? Here, in Chicago and with Brian?

She had some money in her purse. She had her purse with her. That afternoon she could be on a jet just like that, roaring through the skies, escaping from Brian for good. She could get on a public transit bus, drive to O'Hare, catch a flight to—

Her brainwave sputtered and died. Addisyn sighed. What nonsense. She couldn't leave.

She couldn't miss an opportunity like this, for one thing. Sure, Brian was overplaying it some, but it was still the moment she'd hoped for her whole career. A chance for the Olympics.

For another, who else was there who hadn't written her off, tossed her aside? Nobody, besides Brian.

She forced herself to face her thoughts with gut honesty. If Darius loved her, she would be on a flight to Whistler within the next half hour. And if she had any hope, no matter how small, that Avery might ever forgive her, she'd get to New York as fast as she could, grovel at her sister's knee if she had to. Plead for another chance.

In a fairytale, both of those would be possibilities. But reality was harsher than that. Darius had flung sharp words at her that still quivered in her soul like daggers. And if Addisyn was disgusted with herself, she could only imagine how much blacker her faults would appear to Avery—

she who was so good and pure and served a God Who demanded holiness. She'd be repulsed by the very sight of her younger sister.

Vrrrt! Vrrrt! Addisyn's phone vibrated urgently in her pocket. She pulled it out and sighed at the name. Brian. Of course. He'd probably combed the whole hotel for her and was now going ballistic.

She'd have to talk to him sooner or later. Addisyn stood and started walking toward the exit of the park. Might as well be able to tell him she was on her way back to the hotel. "Hello?"

"Addisyn, what in the world?" Brian sounded nothing short of frantic. "Where the heck are you?"

"I'm in Grant Park, taking a nice morning walk." Addisyn knew her tone was unnecessarily loud, but Brian was seriously annoying her.

"What? You went that far by yourself?" Brian gave an exasperated groan. "Addisyn, this isn't Hicksville, Canada, anymore. You're in a big city where anything could—"

"—And I am perfectly capable of taking care of myself." A sweet-looking lady walking a Jack Russell Terrier in a striped sweater passed Addisyn, entering the park. She rolled her eyes. Danger, indeed. "Look, Brian, I know you mean well, but I grew up in New York City. I'm used to—"

"You didn't even tell me where you were going? How do you think that makes me feel, Addisyn? Don't you have any consideration for my feelings? I start looking for you and can't—"

"Brian, you don't have to know where I'm at all the time." Addisyn bit her lip to keep the frustration from spilling out. "I just went for a walk to relax and enjoy the park. Okay? I didn't get captured by a drug ring or run over by a taxi, and the whole time I've been in the city, I haven't seen one single psychopath." *Except maybe you.*

Brian wasn't going to lighten up any. "How did you get there?"

"I walked." Addisyn was surprised at the victory in her voice.

"Walked?"

"It's three tenths of a mile. There was a sign in the courtyard outside the hotel. Straight shot down Ida B. Wells Drive with a well-maintained sidewalk. See, very safe." Hopefully her voice didn't sound as smug as she felt.

Brian exhaled. "Okay. We'll talk about that later. Right now——" his voice pitch rose again—"you've got to get back right away."

"I'm walking back." Addisyn intentionally slowed her pace by a fraction. Really, who did Brian think he was?

"It's important, Addisyn! Look, Ed is here."

Ed? Addisyn stopped. The skyscrapers seemed to tilt and warp around her. "What? He wasn't supposed to be here until——"

"This evening. Right." Brian sounded as unprepared as she felt. "That's what I thought. Next thing I know I get a call that he's just left O'Hare, got here early." He paused. "He wants to see you skate at noon."

"Noon? Like, skate for real? The trial skate?" Addisyn's thoughts jumped about like grasshoppers.

"Yes."

"He can't do that!" Addisyn saw a couple staring at her as they walked past. She lowered her voice, but the panic remained. "Brian, you said I had till this evening to prepare, to get my mind where——"

"That's what I thought, but he's early."

"Then he should still give me till this evening."

"I don't disagree. But—Addisyn, he's with Team Unlimited. This is the way it works. They're the big guys. They can call the shots. And right now, he wants to see you early. Something about having to be in Memphis, something came up or whatever."

Addisyn took a deep breath. Suddenly the urge struck to turn and run back to Buckingham Fountain as fast as she could go. "Brian, I——"

"You're ready. You're so ready for this." Brian was talking fast again, that used-car-salesman tone Addisyn hated. "Baby, you've worked hard. You've done great. This is your chance!"

"Brian——"

"Your last routine looked so good. Don't think about him coming early. Just think about how ready you are."

"Yes. Okay."

"Great." Brian sounded relieved. He'd probably worried she'd abandon the plan at the last minute. "Where are you?"

She started walking again. "Almost to the courtyard."

"Perfect. Just meet me in the lobby as soon as you get here, okay? I'm calling a taxi to take us to the rink right now."

"Okay." Addisyn hung up.

So Ed was there. She could skate for him at noon. Today, she could cement her place on Team Unlimited. By the end of the day, she'd practically have her ticket punched for the next Olympics.

Addisyn squeezed her eyes shut. Suddenly she didn't want to skate for Ed at all. She wanted to go back to Whistler.

But what else could she do?

She took a deep breath. Sure, she'd skate. She'd do her best, as always. She'd maybe even get selected, join Team Unlimited, go to the next Olympics. She might spend her life chained to Brian—right now she didn't see any way to escape him.

But one thing she would never do was enjoy any of it.

And as she jogged up the marble steps of the hotel, already feeling her nerves tense, she suddenly realized what she would wish for if she had a magic fountain.

No Olympics. No fanfare. No opportunity to be the greatest.

Just a chance to rewind the tape, a way to be Addisyn Miles again, a girl without shame who could face Avery and Darius—and a chance to see the love and acceptance in their eyes.

△△　△△　△△

IT WAS THE kind of atmosphere Avery hated. Everything about it brought back all the bad from her whole life—her life before the mountains.

She was perched gingerly on a metal chair in an airport terminal. A businessman ran by her, dragging a set of spinner luggage. He glanced frantically at his watch and cursed loudly, causing Avery's ears to burn. The wail of a toddler made her jump, and when the airport transit bus pulled up outside and the diesel engine roared, she flinched.

Things felt skewed somehow, tilted on their sides. The inside of the terminal was spinning. Or was she spinning?

The floor seemed to roll and plunge. Millions of people, all open eyes and open mouths, all swirling around her.

Avery closed her eyes and clapped her hands to her ears—anything to block out the roar and hum of so much humanity. Images reeled through her consciousness—images of big, dirty New York. This was the same anxiety that had gnawed at her soul after she and Addisyn ran from their father.

Her chest felt too tight to take a deep breath. Her heart was fluttering wildly. This was too much. She couldn't do it. The world was too strong for her.

Peace I leave with you; My peace I give to you.

The storm in Avery's soul quieted for a moment. She tentatively opened her eyes. *Is that You, Lord?*

Not as the world gives, give I unto you. Peace be with you.

Peace. Avery found her muscles relaxing. She took a deep, shaky breath. The roar of civilization was still assaulting her senses, but she wouldn't drown in its waves. Not when El Shaddai was with her.

For the next few minutes, she concentrated on simply breathing deeply, inhaling and exhaling purposefully, trying to help her overloaded mind calm. After a few minutes, she opened her eyes and discovered she was able to look around without the terror she'd experienced earlier.

Maybe she needed some water. Something cool to drink would help her recover from her near-panic attack. She rose unsteadily and walked across the terminal on legs that felt as weak and wobbly as if she'd been hiking at high elevation for too long. She found a vending machine and punched the number for bottled water.

BLEEP!!! The sharp tone made Avery jump as the machine flashed a warning on its screen. **INSERT EXACT CHANGE.**

She shook her head to clear her foggy mind. Duh, of course. Money first, then drink selection. Her hands shook as she fed a five-dollar bill into the slot. Hadn't she learned that like the back of her hand in NYC? Good grief, was she so overwrought she'd forgotten how to work a simple vending machine?

"El Shaddai, please help me." Avery looked up at the high-domed terminal roof and whispered the words. "I can't do this alone. It brings back—too much." Quarters rattled into the change slot as a misty bottle of water plummeted through the machine and clunked into the drawer. Avery pulled it out and opened it—as best as she could with her hands still trembling. A few sips of the cold liquid seemed to wake her mind back up.

Focus, Avery. She leaned against the machine. It was positioned in a quieter alcove, where the terminal noise wasn't so intense. *Focus on why you're here.*

She didn't need to close her eyes to picture the face that was motivating her to make this trip. A laughing girl's happy countenance—eyes bright with hope and promise, silky brown hair tossing in the breeze, features like Avery's, only a shade softer, more delicate. Addisyn's dear face.

Avery sighed. Nothing less than pure, shining love for her sister could have induced her to make this trip—to run pell-mell into the very chaos and confusion she'd fought so hard to escape.

That was why she was here in Chicago—in one of America's busiest cities. She, the girl who hated cities of any description. She checked her watch. Nine fifty-one on Wednesday morning. She wondered what Addisyn was doing right then. Did she ever miss Avery? Ever think about her at all?

The thought reminded her again of how much distance truly yawned between them. What could she say when—if—she caught up with Addisyn? How could she bridge the gap? There were no words that could erase the pile of misunderstanding between them.

"FLIGHT 2673—CHICAGO TO NEW YORK CITY—BOARDING—BOARDING."

That was it. Avery resolutely shouldered her backpack—no fancy rolling luggage for her. She pulled her favorite baseball cap on her head—the one with the embroidered mountains—and felt the back pocket of her cargo pants for the tiny New Testament therein. Face straight ahead, eyes wide and fearless, she joined the throng of people hustling toward the sky gate.

She didn't panic anymore—not going through security, not boarding, not when the plane shot skyward with a force she wasn't prepared for. Not even when she realized that in about two hours, she would be back in New York City—that place where she had once lived—and died.

She'd never wanted to see the horrible town again, the sprawling overgrown city like a hideous beast with claws and teeth. But her reasoning was sound. She was sure of it. It was the last place she knew of where

Addisyn had been. It was the city where they'd both lived. It was a good place to hide in. And of course—Avery made a slight grimace—Brian lived there. It was highly possible they were back together by now.

No, there was no question in her mind. She had to go to New York City.

The jet made a slow circle over the City of the Big Shoulders. Avery pressed her face to the glass. She could see a beautiful park below her, a stain of bright green on the shoulder of Lake Michigan. A tug—it looked like a toy from here—had just entered the harbor. Just a short distance away, an elaborate ivory-colored hotel boasted another courtyard area. Skyscrapers in abundance danced below her eyes.

The plane banked gradually. Chicago was soon behind them. Avery faced forward in her seat and pulled out her pocket Bible.

She needed all the encouragement she could get. She was going back into New York City—into Hell itself.

But she would find her sister there. She just knew it.

CHAPTER 21

Addisyn quite honestly wasn't sure how she would skate at all. Not with the giant rock in her chest.

She used to have a heart where that rock was. Now, there was only a cold, hard deadness.

Funny, two hours before, she'd been in Grant Park, on the brink of walking out on the whole deal. Then Ed had announced his early arrival, and now she was getting ready to go on the ice and fight with all her soul for something she no longer wanted.

Addisyn shifted slightly in the large black chair. She was getting restless. There was no excitement or anticipation—just a weary desire to get the whole thing over and done with.

"Hold still, dear. Almost ready." Ms. Arkins smoothed something over Addisyn's cheeks. She was the makeup specialist—in charge of making Addisyn as flawless as possible.

On the outside, anyway.

"Yes, ma'am." Addisyn had always wished she could just go out on the ice and skate the way she really was. All the fripperies of makeup and hair arrangements had been her least favorite part of the process. Today, with her life in tatters, they seemed even more obnoxious.

"Close your eyes, dear." Obediently Addisyn complied. She could feel Ms. Arkins fluttering a soft brush over her eyelids. Probably that sparkly pink stuff.

"Guess you're excited, huh?"

"Yes, ma'am." Truthfully, Addisyn was feeling those pre-performance jitters—more from habit than anything else—but excited? Not exactly.

"Well, I know you're going to do just great."

"Thank you."

"You're going to look really nice too." Ms. Arkins was an intrusive sort of person who'd hovered over Addisyn since she'd arrived at the rink an hour and a half ago. She expertly flicked eye liner up at the outer corners of Addisyn's eyes. "We're getting you all fixed up pretty, dear." She giggled coyly. "My, I expect Mr. Bourns will usher you into the team on the spot."

Somehow this annoyed Addisyn. "It's my skating he's judging, Ms. Arkins." She felt bad immediately. Why take her frustration out on this lady? "I mean, he's looking at my skill, not my…"

"Your body." Ms. Arkins finished coolly. "Let me tell you, honey, he is."

What? Discomfort snaked up Addisyn's back, but she tried to shrug it off. "Well, maybe he'll look at costume design. I think they count for that."

"Sure he will." Ms. Arkins's voice dripped with innuendo. "Your costume…and everything else." She turned for a brush and began vigorously brushing Addisyn's hair. "Hon, I've been in this business for a long time. It's the pretty girls that get ahead. Eye candy, you know." Her fingers deftly began braiding Addisyn's hair. "I mean, just look at you and Brian Felding."

"What about me and Brian?" The room was feeling far too small.

"Well…" Ms. Arkins gave a laugh that didn't strike Addisyn as appealing. "Let's just say you're one lucky girl. I've known Brian a long time. He's had some pretty girls on his arm before, but he's never looked at one the way he looks at you." She laughed again. "Don't tell me he doesn't have eyes, honey. He's not just interested in you as a great skater."

Before Addisyn could question or protest or even think how to respond to such information, Ms. Arkins spun her chair around dramatically. "There! What do you think?"

It took Addisyn a second to realize she was looking in a mirror. There stood Ms. Arkins, smiling with a smile that could only be described as oily. And there was Addisyn herself.

"Thank you." Addisyn knew her words sounded flat, but she couldn't mask the sinking she felt in the pit of her stomach. Controlling her nausea left her no mental energy to expend on false enthusiasm.

"No problem." Ms. Arkins apparently didn't notice anything wrong with Addisyn's tone. "It's my job, sweetheart. Making people beautiful." She winked. "Now I'll go so you can get your outfit on."

Ms. Arkins scurried out, closing the door behind her. Addisyn continued staring at her reflection with a cold, muddy feeling in her stomach.

Was that her? The woman in the mirror with more makeup than a streetwalker in Vegas? The woman who looked worldly and tawdry and years older than Addisyn herself?

Eye candy, honey. Ms. Arkins's words reverberated in her mind. Her soul had that dirty feeling again. Involuntarily she folded her arms over her chest. Eye candy, really?

Her heart had ceased to argue with her mind. The truth of the words stared her in the eye. *Brian… He doesn't see you as just a great skater.* Addisyn swallowed the sour taste in her mouth. No, he certainly didn't. And what about the "other pretty girls"?

The question marks were cluttering her soul. So unlike when she had first started skating. Then, pure joy had flooded her veins when she was out on the ice. It had made her feel fully alive and fully free.

Now she was burdened, trapped, enslaved. So much weight had been loaded onto her spirit that its wings had been crippled, and it had forgotten how to fly. She leaned in closer to examine her reflection. In spite of all the glitzy makeup, her eyes looked hollow and lifeless. Shadowed, somehow. Was that the darkness Avery had claimed to see in her? Way back then?

Eye candy. Ms. Arkins's words weren't new information—rather a concise way of explaining what she'd been feeling for some time. That was it, wasn't it? Hadn't that always been what she was to Brian? A pretty ornament to dangle from his arm. A cute trophy to show off. A prize to be exhibited…and profited from.

Addisyn wanted to cry, but she couldn't. If she did, she'd smudge the makeup of the woman who was getting ready to perform for Brian and Ed—the woman who was an ornament, a trophy, a prize, but who was no longer Addisyn Miles.

△△ △△ △△

THIS WAS IT. The big one. Everything hinged on now. Brian took a deep breath and smoothed his hair as he strode down the hall toward the elevator. He glanced at his Apple watch.

11:19. Perfect. Ed had told him he would be arriving at the hotel by eleven thirty. Brian planned to take him to the bar for a tall glass of something to loosen him up. Hopefully he would be nice and relaxed, charmed by Brian's hospitality and ready to be generous, by the time he saw Addisyn skate at noon.

Come on! Brian cursed under his breath. Why was the elevator taking so long? Finally the light blinked, and the metal door slid smoothly open. He darted inside and punched the button for the ground floor.

On his way down, he glanced around. Nice elevator. Wood paneling on the inside, real tile floor. Brian maintained that you could always tell the quality of a place by the interior of the elevators. And the Rayard Arena had the classiest setup in Chicago. Nothing but the best for him and his girl.

Addisyn was upstairs getting ready, or so he'd heard. They'd picked out her outfit day before yesterday—a stunning black velvet backless leotard with an A-line mini skirt and a plunging neckline. His heart beat faster at the thought. He couldn't wait to see her in it. His girl—all dressed up and beautiful.

He breathed in deeply. He felt a little apprehensive. No, *apprehensive* was the wrong word. He just wanted everything to go well. He arrived in the lobby, took a seat on one of the overstuffed chairs, and watched the doors.

A man swinging a briefcase marched briskly through the entrance, pushing his sunglasses on top of his head. Brian was just jumping up when he realized the man was a fellow about his own age with a thick black beard. Ed was forty-five, bald, and clean-shaven. Brian sat back down.

Some nice classical music was playing in the background. Brian forced himself to focus on the melody, to try to relax. There was absolutely no reason to suppose everything wouldn't go just fine. Even after more than half a year out of training, Addisyn was skating gorgeously—like an ice angel. She had a delicate, graceful style of motion—with the power to support even the most difficult jumps. Plus, she was strikingly beautiful.

But despite her talent, Addisyn herself was one of Brian's top worries. He'd been evading the issue in his mind, but no question about it—she'd been undoubtedly different since she came back from Whistler.

For one thing, she was just quieter. She didn't talk and giggle as much. Brian had tried to reason that maybe she was just growing up, leaving that teenage exuberance behind. But it seemed more as if she were quiet because she was thinking. Thinking—and remembering.

But it wasn't just quietness. It was—Brian searched through the archives of his mind and finally found the perfect phrase. It was a loss of passion.

Addisyn skated like a dream. She worked with a relentless determination. She continued to pour just as much of her time and energy into skating as she had before Whistler. But the sparkle was gone. The passion was missing.

Passion for skating—and passion for him. Brian clenched his fists. She almost seemed as if she weren't in love with him any longer. He could remember the time when she'd hung on every word he said. Now she was indifferent to him at best. She almost seemed as if he didn't matter to her anymore one way or the other.

She'd insisted on her own room, for crying out loud. That thought still infuriated Brian. Her own room? Really? As though she were some holy model of purity. He snickered. They'd shared enough nights together that it shouldn't matter anymore to her.

Just you wait, baby. Brian blew out a slow breath, trying to calm himself, and worked the muscles in his jaw. Okay, so he'd gone along with her ridiculous thing about needing her own room—hadn't even complained— even though it doubled the hotel expense for him and deprived him of some real fun. And you would have thought that after all he'd done for her, he was entitled to some—compensation.

He'd given in with a good grace just to keep her happy through the performance. Deep within his soul was the unspoken certainty—a thought he refused to even glance at—that she had the power to completely train-wreck everything. She could refuse to skate for Ed—refuse to skate anymore, period. She could pack her bags and catch a plane for somewhere else, anywhere else—and there wasn't a thing he could do.

But after today's deal—one way or another—that was going to end. Brian had never been thwarted by a female before, and he wasn't about to start now. He'd had to keep Addisyn calm until her skate was over, but tonight, she'd be his girl again, body and soul—or else.

△△△ △△△ △△△

EYE CANDY. EYE candy. Eye candy. The words jerked rhythmically in Addisyn's mind in time with her steps. She paced the length of the tiny dressing room, turned around, paced back. Over and over.

The tight turns in the small space were making her dizzy. She plopped down in a small metal chair and looked with distaste around the room.

Like every other little dressing room she'd used before, it had slightly worn and dirty carpet, stark furnishings, a mess of cosmetics and clothes, and a wall of mirrors.

It was the mirrors that Addisyn hated now. Because every time she glanced in them, a streetwalker looked out.

A moan fled from the scarred chambers of her heart. "I can't do this!" The frantic whisper sizzled in the air. She rose and started pacing again.

Her thoughts whirled about like confetti. What had happened to her? How had she gotten to this point?

Who was she?

Sickness curled around the edges of her torso. She folded her arms over her stomach.

A knock on the door made her jump. "Yes, who is it?" Her voice cracked slightly. She hoped the person didn't notice.

"Baby, it's me. Everything good?"

The sick feeling intensified with the sound of Brian's voice. Addisyn swallowed hard. "Just fine. I'm getting dressed." Well, technically she was getting ready to get dressed.

"Great." Brian's voice was nervous but confident at the same time.

272

"Ed just got here. I'm gonna take him to the bar, calm him down a little before your performance. Remember to be on the rink no later than eleven fifty. That leaves time for you to warm up. And I want you to stretch first, okay?"

"Right. Okay."

"Are you sure you're all right?" Brian sounded worried.

It wasn't her he cared about. It was what she could do. The sudden realization sliced through her heart like a knife. Brian had never seen her soul the way Darius had. He'd never sought to explore the hallways of her spirit. That had never mattered to Brian—only her performance. And her body.

"I'm fine." It was probably the biggest lie she'd ever uttered.

"Great, then." Brian paused, and at first she thought he'd left, until he added, "Good luck, baby. See you at noon." His quick footsteps tapped down the stairs.

Good luck. Avery had always insisted there was no such thing as luck—that God arranged everything. Addisyn thought about that for a moment. What would Avery say about her current situation? Would Avery say that God had brought Addisyn to this place, where she stood in a provocative outfit getting ready to chase a selfish dream under the tutelage of a man who'd used her every way he could?

"God?" The word was a tentative whisper. The next second Addisyn shook her head. How crazy. If Avery had been angry, Avery's God was certainly infuriated with her. If Addisyn was nauseated by her own actions, she could only imagine how deeply she'd offended God. What nerve, asking God for anything at this point.

But who else would hear her last cry for help? Her final SOS before her soul was gone forever?

Always before she'd wanted God on her terms. Wanted Him to overlook her behavior. Wanted Him to leave her alone. Wanted Him to keep His distance so that she could do what she wanted. Well, He had. And maybe now it was too late.

But in case it wasn't, Addisyn looked up at the dingy ceiling, peppered with dim electric lights, and asked one simple question—the first of its kind she'd ever asked God. Only four words—yet words that she somehow knew held the power to change everything.

"What should I do?"

△△ △△ △△

ADDISYN FIGURED HER smile looked fake.

She couldn't help it. Inwardly, her stomach was tossing and pitching so hard that she worried she might just vomit where she stood. She forced herself to concentrate.

"—placed fifth in Sectionals." Brian gestured to her with a look of pride, like a man showing off his flashy car or his new suit. "Mr. Bourns, meet Miss Addisyn Miles."

Ed Bourns was a thin, angular man with a lined face and olive-colored skin. The arena lights glinted off his bald head as he bent forward and offered Addisyn his hand. "My pleasure, Miss Miles."

Addisyn grasped his hand. "Likewise, Mr. Bourns. I'm so grateful you could come see me skate today." She remembered to smile prettily, to grip his hand firmly, to keep her tone light and feminine—all those things Brian had rehearsed with her. Yet somehow the whole exchange was dulled, numbed, as if Addisyn stood on the bleachers and watched herself meeting Ed Bourns.

"I am very excited." Ed's smile was a bit stiff, but nice. "You have an excellent track record. I hope you can join our athletes for Team Unlimited."

"Yes sir, I definitely hope so as well." Perfect, so far. Perfect, except for the pain in her soul that felt as if it were squeezing her very lungs. Fragments of disconnected thoughts whirled through her mind—eye candy—Caesar salads—Avery.

"I understand you began training late, relatively speaking. In your teens." Addisyn nodded, and Ed continued. "That impresses me even more…that you've come so far in such a short time." He stroked his chin solemnly. "I must confess, I'm so excited to see you skate that I'll dispense with the usual interview until after I see you in action."

"Mr. Bourns?" Brian was practically oozing charm and charisma. "May I suggest we go out to dinner after you watch Miss Miles perform, and you could speak with her then, get to know her a little better? My treat, of course."

"That sounds perfect." Ed smiled approvingly. "Well, Miss Miles, this is your moment. I know you realize what rides on the next few minutes, so I won't increase your anxiety by unnecessary reminders. Just go out there and—" Ed waved his hand toward the ice—"chase that dream."

"Here, sir, we can watch from those seats over there. The view is best from that end." Brian motioned Ed in front of him, waiting until the man had turned away, then grabbed Addisyn's upper arm. "Listen, baby, go out there and do your best. 'K? Don't blow this for us." His gaze was almost angry in its intensity. Roughly he kissed her on the mouth, his hand gripping the back of her neck. When he pulled back, she shuddered at his eyes. "Love you, baby." Then he was gone, jogging after Ed.

Addisyn didn't dare wipe the back of her hand across her mouth. She might smudge all that nasty makeup. But his kiss repulsed her. It had been too hard, too—too greedy. *Eye candy.*

Woodenly she made her way to the ice. Positioned herself. Waited for the music to begin. Her pulse was pounding, yet oddly enough, she wasn't even thinking about the upcoming performance. A slight ache told exactly where Brian had grabbed her arm. Did he have to be that rough?

And what had been that look in his eyes when he gazed at her?

Addisyn was honestly afraid she might just faint before Brian could turn the music on. She was acutely aware of every external sensation, everything from the slight unsteadiness of balancing on the ice, to the cold air stinging her eyes, to the soft *whoosh* of the air conditioner kicking on. Even the hissed whispers of Brian and Ed sounded ridiculously loud. Suppose Brian couldn't get the sound system to work again!

"Okay, Addisyn." Brian's words carried clearly over the ice. "Three…two…one."

And with that, the music started, the driving, pained beat of "Fake Love." Addisyn began skating, and as her body moved, she seemed to pierce the fog of despair and uncertainty that had enveloped her. Her stomach settled. Her head felt clear and light again.

Double loop, camel spin. Her skate blade sang as she glided across the unscarred smoothness. It was frictionless. Perfect ice.

The movements came fluidly, easily. The haunting strains of the music were entwined around her spirit, lifting her. The cries of the violin were deeper than a mere melody—they were the sobs of her own soul.

The percussive beat was strengthening. Addisyn listened for the cue in the music and launched a double Axel, almost holding her breath in the air as she plunged forward. The impact of a perfect landing traveled up her leg. She sneaked one glance at Ed and noticed he was nodding approvingly.

The passion that had seemed dry and dead was back, crackling in Addisyn's soul. Her whole spirit was alive again, and she was skating with all that was in her. With every time she'd raged or cried or prayed or wanted to throw up in the last few days. All the pain was being turned into power. And even as she carried out the routine, she knew, deep in her soul, that she had never performed like this. Ever. She would meet Ed's requirements. She would make the Olympic team.

And she wasn't the least bit excited about it.

As the music intensified, so did the depth of her feelings—the speed at which her mind was reeling. She flung her pain skyward, watched it soar away. But more pain remained, more uncertainty. Why?

Darius's face leaped to her mind. He had skated on ice like this. He had missed his chance somehow. He was a failure, he said.

Yet Darius had been kind and gentle.

Layback spin, turn, twizzle. Addisyn flew forward out of that one with a leap that made her own breath catch. She heard Ed murmur something that sounded impressed.

And Darius had never looked at her the way Brian did.

And suddenly the realization flew out of the air and hit Addisyn, hit her so badly she almost missed her next step and had to recover quickly. That was it. The look in Brian's eyes.

Hunger.

Hunger for her—or who he thought she was and tried to make her be. Hunger for her success—the success that would stoke his own. Hunger for her beauty—the need to have her as a trophy on his arm.

We can't afford for you to get sick.

We?

Don't blow this for us.

For *us*. Always it had been *us*. But really—it had been him. All along.

He's darkness, Addisyn…he'll make you like him… Avery's voice rang as clearly in her ears as if Avery were standing right there, once again begging Addisyn not to make the mistake of a lifetime.

And look at what Brian had brought to her life. A phony façade and a pressure-packed life. She'd traded the sister who'd loved her, the man who'd amazed her, and the freedom to make her own choices for expensive cocktails, glitzy lifestyles, forbidden kisses, and a man who was nothing more than hungry for her.

Double toe. Lutz.

The music continued, swirling around Addisyn. Fake Love. So true. Brian had never known the meaning of the word.

He'll make you like him… He had. No wonder she'd seen such darkness in her eyes. She could only pray it wasn't too late to go back, to become Addisyn Miles again.

God, what do you want me to do? Addisyn's own desperate prayer in the dressing room flashed back into her mind. Well, now she knew. And she'd never been more certain of anything in her life.

The song built to its moment of crescendo. She flew through a jump combination, landing her Salchow with perfection.

And stopped.

"Addisyn!" She vaguely heard Brian's gasp of amazement. She was also dimly aware that her muscles were screaming and her breath was hard and hurting in her chest—the result of the spiritual struggle as much as the physical intensity.

But none of that mattered. Standing there on the ice, lungs heaving, the driving beat of "Fake Love" still grating insistently on her consciousness, Addisyn was fully, forcefully aware of one thing and one thing only. She was not, ever again, going to give in to the darkness. She had broken its power.

A hand snapped like a vise around her forearm. Brian's whisper seared the air. "What the heck do you think you're *doing*?"

Addisyn turned and saw him for the first time. Saw not the charming, suave professional with unmistakable poise and undisputed success, but the scheming, lustful bully. She looked at him without terror, without guilt, even without disgust. The hold he had maintained over her soul cracked and blew away like an empty husk in the wind. She saw him as Avery had always seen him—as she should have seen him long ago.

"Get your hands off me!" she snapped, yanking away. He slipped from the sudden motion, almost losing his balance on the slick ice.

Regally Addisyn pushed off and glided to the edge of the rink. She glanced around her one more time as she skated. This was the last time she would ever skate in an arena of this size, but somehow, that didn't matter.

She calmly stepped off the ice and snapped her skate guards on. Methodically. Left and then right. Then she stepped to where Ed Bourns stood.

"Miss Miles, what's this all about?" He was obviously ruffled. "I have come a long way to—"

"Mr. Bourns." She did not have time for his lecture. "I am sorry to have inconvenienced you and I am sorry to have wasted your time, but I am not interested in your offer anymore." She paused. "Thank you, sir."

With that, she grabbed her nylon shell from the back of a bleacher and almost ran out of the arena. She made it as far as the locker room area before her legs gave out. She sat limply on a plain metal folding chair, slumped over, and cried. Her face in her hands. Yet somehow, these were purging, cleansing tears. She cried not because her chance was gone.

But because she had finally had the wisdom to let it go.

It was oddly enough one of the most wonderful moments she had ever experienced.

△△   △△   △△

A FEW MINUTES passed before Addisyn suddenly became aware of someone else in the small room. When she looked up, there was Brian, leaning against the wall, arms folded. Not saying anything, just glaring at her with stony hate.

Addisyn sighed. She wasn't truly free yet. Not until she finished her business with this man. She looked at his dashing frame, his perfect features, and felt not the slightest bit of attraction. How could she have ever thought he was her Prince Charming? He was a user. Nothing more. She had been not his soulmate, but his commodity. Something to be manipulated, exploited, and ultimately discarded.

"Fine exhibition you made of yourself in there." Brian's voice dripped acid.

What could she tell him? Nothing. She lifted her hands and then let them fall to her sides. "You wouldn't understand why I did it."

"You're right. I don't understand. I don't understand at all." Brian's voice was becoming more agitated. He pushed off from the wall and took two steps toward her, his eyes blazing with suppressed fury. "Addisyn—" He looked at the ceiling and gave a sharp bark of a laugh. "We had the world at our fingertips! You were gonna go to the Olympics, you realize that, right? Ed—he was crazy about you. And you were skating like—like I've never seen you skate. Better than Sectionals, better than—" Brian broke off and shook his head wordlessly. "We had it all!" He held out his hand and pointed to his palm. "Right there. We had it all right there."

We. We. We. Addisyn wondered how she had never noticed that before. Anger sizzled through her veins. "Yes, we did." She stood slowly and stared up at the face of the man she had once thought had her best interest at heart. What a laugh and a half. "Actually, isn't it you you're thinking of?"

"What are you talking about?" Brian snarled. Addisyn braced herself. His ugly side was getting ready to show.

"I'm talking about the fact that you are the most selfish person I have ever met. You have never cared about me in the least."

Brian's facial expression would have been amusing at any other time. "Baby, that's crazy! Haven't I always helped you with your skating?"

Addisyn didn't let her gaze waver. "When it was good for you."

"What's that supposed to mean?"

The truth had to be said. "You've always gotten what you wanted, Brian." Addisyn locked her eyes onto his. "I've been your ticket to a lot of good stuff. Top-notch endorsements, envy from your colleagues, really good PR for your agency. And of course—you had me. Body and soul, I was yours. Because I truly believed you loved me."

Brian snorted. "What nonsense. Of course I love you. You're the most beautiful—"

"That isn't me." She couldn't tolerate one more tacky compliment. "The person I really am is in here." She laid one hand over her heart. "You never saw that person. You never wanted to see that person." Her voice was even, firm, but not loud. "And don't call me *baby* anymore." She paused, trying to slow her breathing. "We're done, Brian."

"Done?" Brian's face drained to a chalky white. His lips parted, and his next words were breathy, as if he couldn't get enough air. "What do you mean, done?"

"I mean that I don't love you. And you don't love me." This was hard work, but it had to be done. "You have probably never loved anyone. You don't know what love is."

Brian's face flushed to a mottled red. "Addisyn, you can't do this to me!" A fierce, hard look burned on his face with an intensity that made Addisyn shudder. "Who has taken care of you all this time? Who got you to this point? Look, if you're gonna try to get to the Olympics without—"

"I am not going to the Olympics!" Addisyn shouted for the first time. She stopped and took a deep breath. She didn't want this to get nastier than it had to. "I am not going to the Olympics," she repeated in a calmer voice. "I am going to find something better."

"Something better?" Brian almost choked. "The Olympics are the top of the world. What are you thinking?"

"I am going to find my sister. And God." Again a surge of joy washed over Addisyn. She almost laughed at the irony. She was standing in a bleak locker room, breaking up with her boyfriend, and turning her back on her lifelong dream. And she felt amazingly joyful. Maybe she was just numb.

"God?" Brian rolled his eyes. "Come on, Addisyn. Don't tell me you're turning into a religious freak like your stupid sister."

"Don't you ever call my sister stupid!" The fight that had been suppressed for so long was rising up in Addisyn. The fight to be free.

"And don't you yell at me!" Brian took another step toward her. He was too close. She flinched.

"Brian, stop!"

Instead he grabbed her shoulders, his furious face only a few inches away. She could hear his rattling breath. Pain cracked through her torso as he shoved her into the wooden wall.

She squirmed for some way out. The back of her head rolled against the boards. "You filthy—!" Brian screamed curses at her. His fingers dug into her shoulders and arms like vises. She tried to reach up, tried to push him away, but the pain was too much.

He'll kill me. Terror flickered through Addisyn's mind. How could she have loved this man? Ever? She closed her eyes, tried to turn her head. Brian gave her body a hard shake that made her neck feel as if it were snapping.

Suddenly, a voice cut through the maelstrom of Brian's violence and her own mental turmoil.

"Good work, Addisyn. Now let me finish."

A familiar tenor voice with that West Coast accent.

And then—the paralyzing grip on her shoulders was gone, so abruptly that Addisyn fell to the floor.

She scrambled up in a second, ready to run, ready to fight. Then she saw she wouldn't need to. Brian had backed away and now stood, breathless and defensive, facing another man. A man who stood with arms folded, strong and solid.

Darius Payne.

Addisyn gasped. "Darius!" She blinked rapidly. How hard had Brian thrown her into the wall? Was she hallucinating? *How could Darius be here, in—*

Brian wasn't one to be cowed. He straightened himself to his full height—still not that of Darius, Addisyn noted. "Well, well, well. If it isn't the glorious Uber driver, here to save the lady in distress." His sneering tone was like an abrasion.

Darius locked his gaze. "That's right." His tone was calm but firm. "I am the Uber driver who picked you up at the bus stop that afternoon."

"You're the man who was messing around with my girl." Brian's eyes were mere slits.

"I'm the man who had a photo of Addisyn Miles on my dashboard, yes."

Addisyn felt her heart flutter. Darius had kept a photo of her on his dashboard?

"Mr. Felding, I think you need to leave." There was no bucking Darius's tone.

"Leave?" Brian gave a sarcastic laugh. "Actually, I was having a private discussion with my fiancée when you—"

"A discussion that involved pushing her into a wall. I saw."

Brian's eyes smoldered with rage—and maybe fear. "If you are insinuating—"

Darius sighed and even gave a small smile. "Mr. Felding, if I am insinuating, I apologize. I meant to be perfectly clear. Let me state this simply. You need to leave."

"You have no right to be here." Brian's mocking tone made Addisyn think of Satan, circling a lost soul. "You're an Uber driver, not a skating professional."

"I am an Uber driver." Darius nodded slowly. Then took a deep breath. "And I am also Darius Andrew Payne."

For a moment Brian stared at him. Then his mouth dropped slightly. "Andrew Payne—from Vancouver?" He swallowed. "You won gold in the—"

"Olympics. Yes." Darius stared at him. "I have many friends in this industry. Should I choose to report this incident, I'm sure enough of them will believe the word of an Olympian that you may find a career change necessary."

Brian was scared now. Addisyn could see the beads of sweat on his brow. He tried a smile, offered his hand. "Look, I just didn't realize who you were. I didn't—"

"Leave. Now." Darius's tone had increased slightly in pitch.

Brian scowled at him and shot one more hateful glance at Addisyn. "Fine." His eyes seared Addisyn. "You stupid girl. You weren't worth the time I wasted on you."

His parting words, and with that, he was gone. Addisyn felt her whole body go limp. For the first time she realized she was shaking rigorously. Not surprising. She'd been through a cornucopia of emotions in the last half hour. And judging from the fact that Darius's presence seemed to pull the breath out of her body, she was about to experience some more.

Questions whirled rapidly through her mind. Darius—in Chicago?

What was he doing here? And how could he have appeared right then—just when she needed him most? Seeing him when she had been thinking about him so much was surreal, as if he were a figment of her overwrought imagination.

"Are you okay? Did he hurt you?" Darius's voice was low, his tone even. He turned and looked straight at her for the first time. She couldn't read anything in his eyes.

"I'm fine. He didn't have the chance to do much." The back of Addisyn's head hurt, and she was sure her upper arms would be bruised for a week, but she had no major injuries.

Shame inflated her soul, hot and brassy. She hung her head, unwilling for Darius to see her in this kind of costume, in so much makeup. The man who once accused her of being fake must surely believe it now, seeing her like this. Self-consciously she tugged on the hem of her miniskirt, trying unsuccessfully to lengthen it.

"Thank you for—for being here." The words sounded weak, inadequate. There were so many questions she couldn't ask. One she dared. "How—are you here?"

Darius quirked his mouth to the side. "I had a—a tip you were here. I caught a flight from Vancouver. Got in about four hours ago and came straight here."

That still didn't make sense. "No, I mean—I guess I mean why are you here?"

Darius paused. Addisyn dared to look up for the first time. She saw emotion in his eyes.

He started to speak, stopped. Swallowed hard, started again. "Because you, Addisyn Miles, are not a fake."

Heat raced in a flaming wave over her face. What did he mean?

"I—I don't understand." There was so much she didn't understand.

Instead of answering, Darius just smiled. Without warning, he reached out and caught her hands in his. "First of all, I want to say I'm sorry." His head hung slightly. "You came to see me at the center, and I was a complete jerk. It wasn't until later that I realized I didn't even let you tell me anything. I was so scared of being hurt that I had my mind all made up. I thought I understood everything." His eyes were damp. "I should have never let Brian change my mind about who I knew you were."

Tears filled Addisyn's eyes. She would have given everything in her soul to be able to stand before him and tell him that Brian had lied, that she'd never been that girl or done those things. The weight of the past felt like an iron chain around her neck. "Darius, everything Brian told you is true." Oh, she would give anything to make it not so. "I am a skater, and I did live with him. After I broke up with him, I came to Whistler to try to figure things out. Find answers." She couldn't meet his eyes. "I've ruined everything so badly." Tears made dark drips on the velvet dress. "I've failed so many times in my life, and I wish I could undo it all." She had to wait for a sob to jerk loose before she could continue. "I don't even know who I am anymore."

"Hmm." There was no hint of anger or condemnation in Darius's tone. "Lucky for you, I do."

"You do—what?" She sniffled and dared to meet his gaze for the first time.

His eyes were like the ocean in summer—calm, gentle, and full of sunshine. "I do know who you are." His tone was as soothing as the waves on the beach. "You are Addisyn Miles. You're a beautiful figure skater who performs with her whole heart on the ice. You're a courageous person who climbs mountains and chases dreams and pushes for answers. And best of all, you're a survivor." His thumbs gently rubbed the backs of her hands. "You're a woman who's gone forward when everyone told her she couldn't. Sure, you've fallen some, but you've gotten up every single time. You're a warrior, Addisyn." Intensity rang clearly in his voice.

If only she were all of those things. Addisyn shook her head. "Darius, I've made so many mistakes."

"I left out one part." Darius leaned closer. "You're a woman with a second chance."

"How do you know?" This all sounded wonderful, but none of it made sense.

"Because I just got one." A smile like she'd never seen on him before irradiated his face. "Addisyn, I've been trying to measure up. Trying to meet my own bar of perfection. I forgot about something." He sighed. "God's grace."

God's grace? "Darius, I'm so far away from God now." She shook her head. "I can't find my way back."

"That's the great thing about God. He comes to you."

He comes to you.

The words comforted like a warm spring breeze. Addisyn felt her insides settling. "Like you did."

Darius just shrugged. "When you love someone—" his eyes held hers—"you go to them." His grip tightened on her hands. "I've been waiting in the back of the arena all morning to see you skate. It was amazing. But that wasn't the most amazing thing I saw today."

"What was that?" Her voice was almost a whisper.

The passion in Darius's voice told her he meant every word. "I saw you stand within a stone's throw of gold and give it all up. I saw you run off that ice because you were done with being fake. And then I followed you back here and saw you break chains that you'd willingly worn for years." Addisyn didn't even try to stop the tears as Darius continued. "I saw you make a big decision today—the decision to live in the light. God's light. Now I just want you to believe it's possible." He smiled. "Don't do what I did. Don't try to be perfect. There's a new beginning waiting for you. It's a gift, so don't try to repay it." He leaned forward and briefly touched his forehead to hers. "Just accept it."

Addisyn took a deep breath. Her soul felt strangely fragile. All the emotions of the past few days had wreaked havoc with her heart. Yet at the same time, the shadows were rising from her spirit and floating away on that fresh, sweet breeze of hope.

Darius was right. She still wasn't sure about God—what He expected from her, what He wanted for her. But this she knew: the love He offered her was real, as real as if it were a tangible rope she could use to pull herself out of the pit she'd been trapped in for so long.

She was done with fake love—and not just the song. In fact, she was done with all things fake. She was ready to be Addisyn Miles—whoever God had meant for Addisyn Miles to be. It might take her a lifetime to figure that out, but finally, she was willing to try.

Chapter 22

There wasn't much to say. Addisyn sat on a hard metal bench inside the terminal at Chicago-O'Hare. She checked the clock on the wall. Her flight would probably be called in the next ten minutes.

She sneaked a glance at Darius, sitting beside her. His mouth was a straight line. The sadness in his expression spilled over into her heart. She reached over and touched his hand.

He turned and mustered a smile. When he met her gaze, she could see that the sadness she'd sensed was mingled with hope. He took her hand and squeezed it tightly. "I'll miss you." The words were soft, so soft they sounded loud against the backdrop of the terminal hubbub.

"I know." Addisyn held his hand tighter, gazed deeper into his eyes. He had such a sterling soul.

"I wish I could come back to Whistler with you." She looked out across the mobs of people swarming in the dome. She was not going to cry. "But—I can't."

"Hey." Darius's voice was soft, kind. Gently he placed two fingers on her chin and turned her face back toward him. "It's okay." He gave her one of his lopsided smiles. "I understand. This is something you have to do."

"Yes." Addisyn nodded. With everything in her, she knew that to be true. This next step in her journey was not optional.

She and Darius had talked for hours. He'd told her his story, and she'd shared more of hers. She'd also talked to God—and she was starting to believe He was truly listening, the way Darius insisted He was.

And finally, she'd decided that to fully embrace the light, to completely deaden the darkness, she needed to return to where she'd made her first mistake, where she'd initially veered the few degrees off course that had ultimately placed her on such a lost and lonely trajectory.

She had to make amends with Avery.

"Call me every now and then. 'K?" Darius's eyes looked watery. Addisyn blinked. If he started crying, she surely would.

"Right." She couldn't drag her eyes from his face. She wanted to soak in enough of his presence to saturate her mind with him, to last her through the long days ahead without him. "You too."

A voice echoed over the loudspeaker. Flight 2037 to New York City. Addisyn stood up reluctantly. "Well." She gave a shaky laugh, not sure what to do with her hands. "Guess that's my flight."

"Yeah." Darius stood too. Awkwardly they faced each other for a moment.

"You know I'll be praying for you."

Tears did fill her eyes then. "I know."

"Don't forget about grace. God's grace." Darius's lips quivered. He reached out and rested his hands on her shoulders. "Don't forget about second chances. And mercy. And love."

Addisyn ducked her head. Tears were rolling down her cheeks, but they were healing, purifying tears. "I won't."

Darius pulled her to him in a strong embrace. Addisyn buried her face in his chest and wrapped her arms around his neck. How on earth could she leave this man? She'd miss him with every heartbeat. She needed him, needed his gentle strength, his quiet love. She needed him to help her remember how to love—not only others, but also God…and herself.

She needed him to help her heal.

"Darius." She whispered his name into his shirt front. "It's not too late…I can change my flight…go back to Whistler with you." She raised her tear-streaked face to his, searching for safety in his eyes.

"Shh." He gently traced her cheek with his fingers as if trying to memorize her soul. "You have to go."

Her spirit could protest, but she knew he was right. "Yes."

This time she took the lead. Stretching onto her tiptoes, she raised her face to his. Now when their lips met, there was none of the doubt and fear that had ripped them apart before. There was no darkness anymore, no shadows lurking in the wings.

Nothing except light, and two people who were learning to walk in it after believing lies of darkness for so long.

Finally Darius pulled back. "Be safe, Addisyn."

"You too."

Gently he released her from his arms. "God go with you."

"And with you." She wiped her eyes and smiled at him—a simple, brave smile. She didn't want him remembering her tears.

With that, she picked up her bag and marched purposefully through the terminal to the security. Once she was in line, creeping along in the moving conveyor belt of people, she glanced back over her shoulder. Darius was still standing there. As he waved, his smile flashed through the crowds of people like a laser through darkness.

Addisyn returned the smile and wave. Then she resolutely squared her shoulders and looked straight ahead. This was no time for tears and fearfulness.

She was going to her sister. And somehow, she knew she had not seen the last of Darius Payne.

A story like theirs couldn't be over.

△△ △△ △△

THERE SHE WENT, his incredible girl. Darius blinked his tears back and watched her thread her way through security. Shy yet sparkling— frightened yet brave.

Oh, how he'd miss her. Miss the way his heart sang every morning when he sauntered into the coffee shop and saw her behind the counter. Miss her laugh—her sweet, marvelous laugh, like bells in his soul.

For a moment, he toyed with the idea of going with her. He'd gladly forget his job, his house, his whole life in Whistler. He'd be happy to hop a flight now to New York City and never leave her side. But he knew he couldn't. Not at this point.

For one thing, he had to go back to Whistler. He had some healing and growing to do. He needed to practice walking God's way alone before he could try it with someone else.

And the same was true for Addisyn. This was a journey she had to take solo—returning to the place of her greatest pain to face the person she needed most at this moment. He couldn't make the leap for her.

He closed his eyes for a moment. *God, please protect her. Give her safe travels and help her find restoration with her sister.* His prayers were just that direct these days, just that simple and straightforward. He'd hidden from God for a long time. From now on, he wanted their relationship to be as clear and open as the sunlight on the mountains.

As a boy in youth group, he'd prayed eloquent, scripted prayers, as if his feeble humanity could possibly wow the Creator. Now as a man, he knew he couldn't impress God. But—he smiled—he also knew he didn't have to.

Thank You for sending her to me. A wave of gratitude submerged his soul. He snagged a quick breath, fighting for composure. *Thank You.*

Addisyn claimed he'd been a part of her healing. Well, he didn't know about that, but he did know she'd been a huge part of his. Wasn't it just like God to send him not only a second chance but also an amazing girl?

As he walked back into the concourse to watch her flight take off, he realized he didn't feel any of the sadness he'd thought he might experience. He missed her, sure, but there was no sense of loss, of grief of any kind. No, all he could feel was gratitude, thankfulness that they had both escaped from the darkness…and that their relationship had been salvaged.

He was a blessed man, that was for sure. Even standing alone in a Chicago airport, watching the woman of his dreams leave. He'd come light years since Addisyn had first arrived in Whistler. If only he'd turned back to God sooner.

He sighed. For a moment he was tempted to curse the years he'd wasted wallowing in shame. But then he stopped himself.

He remembered the Bible verse Terry had shared with him. *Forgetting those things which are behind, I press toward the mark for the prize of the high calling of God in Christ Jesus.*

That's what he'd do, all right. He'd press forward toward the mark, the prize. God was with him. That was all that mattered.

He gathered his bags and headed for security. He had his own flight to catch. But on the way, he whispered one last prayer.

That someday, when God saw fit, Addisyn and he would be together again.

△△　△△　△△

AVERY FELT MORE like an outcast than ever.

She had never fit in well in New York City. She'd never embraced the hectic pace or felt any sort of solidarity with the craziness. But as she glanced at the narrow streets, thronging with swerving cars, she realized that her aversion to the city had only increased in the year she'd been away.

How had she lived—existed—here for so long? Over six years. She craned her neck to look out the window of the mustard-yellow cab in which she rode. On each side of her, perpendicular blocks of buildings sheared off the clouds—drab, ugly giants, in lackluster monotones. The only sky she could see was a narrow strip between the skyscrapers, and even it was a sad, milky pallor, as unlike the vivid blue of Colorado afternoons as could be imagined.

The cab veered sharply, jerking Avery in the seat. She glanced over at her driver. He was coolly maneuvering through the maze of traffic, apparently unruffled. Avery winced as a flashy little Fiat shot by them, scraping within twelve inches of their front bumper. She let out a breath and realized her palms were sweating. She'd remembered New York traffic as being dicey, but she'd forgotten just how bad it was.

"Ma'am, the New York Figure Skaters' Agency, yes?" Avery's driver was an older man with an New York accent thicker than the stream of traffic. A dilapidated Homburg hat was perched precariously on his salt-and-pepper hair.

"Yes. Thank you." Avery studied the man as they drove. Reading him. He was busy—fairly impersonal—something on his mind, something that flicked at his edges. Something worrisome but not enormous. She caught herself and looked away. *Save your soul-reading for Brian.*

They turned a corner, and the needlelike Empire State Building pierced the clouds before them, a thin, elegant spire. Avery stared at it until her eyes blurred, remembering the day she took Addisyn up top. They'd yelled and waved from the observation deck like crazy celebrities until they finally burst into giggles. The memory made a bittersweet smile creep to Avery's face.

Now they were on Thirty-seventh Street. There was Brian's agency— a sleek modern tower of black marble. Avery fumbled in her pocket and pulled out the fare—along with a nice tip. "Thank you, sir. Have a blessed day."

He looked up quickly and smiled an instant too late. As though her courtesy was completely unexpected. "Yes. Youse too."

Avery stepped out of the cab onto the sidewalk and swung her backpack onto her shoulders again. Horns blared incessantly. She'd forgotten the rudeness of New York too, forgotten how just standing on the sidewalk felt like getting a million slaps from all directions. A woman talking on her cell phone shouldered past roughly. A sandwich man hawked his wares at the other end of the sidewalk. Avery dodged a gaggle of tourists and pushed open the door to the tower.

The lobby, Avery had always thought, was just like Brian himself. Brilliantly sophisticated and incredibly fake. An artificial waterfall gushed down a lighted panel on the wall, cascading into a pool filled with smooth pebbles. Potted palms graced the corners. Soft music tinkled in the background.

"May I help you?" A middle-aged woman with dyed blonde hair removed her glasses and looked condescendingly at Avery. The receptionist desk was built of the same white marble as the floor.

"Yes, ma'am." Avery had learned over the years that her respectful speech was not an asset in this cutthroat environment, but she'd never been able to train herself out of the habit. "I'm looking for Mr. Brian Felding, please."

The woman gave her a long look, her mouth pinched into a straight line. "Are you one of his clients?"

"No, ma'am." Why hadn't she thought of this? What if she had to have credentials to enter? "I—my sister is." *But won't be much longer, God help me.*

The woman still eyed her warily but seemed to have no further excuse for stalling. "Very well. His office is on the fourteenth floor. Elevator that way." She pointed over her shoulder. "He may be out of town, though. He travels a lot. I don't keep up with his schedule." She put her eyeglasses back on and stared at her computer screen. Clearly the conversation was over.

"Thanks," Avery mumbled, but the woman pretended not to hear. Once she was safely inside the elevator, she let out her breath in frustration. What was wrong with people here, anyway? Of course, they lived in New York City. No wonder they were grouchy.

Fourteenth floor. Avery disembarked from the elevator and began wandering what seemed like miles of corridors. She smiled shyly at a few people who passed, but most seemed to be in a hurry and ignored her. A mezzanine she came to had a soft bench and floor-to-ceiling windows.

Avery didn't have time for the bench, but she couldn't resist big windows. She paused, staring out through the glass. Cars screeched by while skyscrapers stood guard. A big, messy place. And somewhere out there, Addisyn was in the city. Avery was sure of it. Fresh sweat made her palms slick as she realized Addisyn might even be in this very building.

It was time—long past time—to start thinking of what she might say, frame the well-chosen words that would persuade her sister to love her again. The most important conversation she might ever have, but her mind stayed as blank as a clean whiteboard.

BRIAN FELDING. The gold words on the door snagged her eye. She gulped. Tried to breathe deeply. This was it. His office.

Slowly she pushed the glass door open. She was in a small outer area, with one bored-looking secretary. On the back wall was a brown mahogany door, closed. Apparently that was Brian's office proper.

The girl looked up dully without saying anything, so Avery smiled and began. "Hello. I'm looking for Mr. Felding."

"He's out of town."

Avery felt disappointment crinkle all over her. "Oh."

The girl nodded. "Sorry."

"Yeah. Okay." Avery had come across the country for this moment. She couldn't leave without more information. "Um—do you know when he'll be back?"

"No clue." The girl shook her head. "He's been traveling all over the country here lately."

Something sparked to life with that sentence. "Really?" This girl seemed more communicative than most New Yorkers—and Avery needed to keep her talking.

"Mm-hm. He's been going to different Olympic training centers." She sighed. "It's a hassle making all the reservations, but that's what comes of being a secretary."

Avery nodded slowly. "I know he was in Colorado. He came by to see me while he was in town."

The girl looked up, surprised. "You know him personally?"

Avery smiled. Hopefully it looked real. "Well, my sister is one of his clients."

"Cool." The girl nodded. "Well, I'm sorry you missed him. He's out of town this week with a client. Seems like she didn't do so well this season, and then she didn't get a good enough score at Sectionals to advance, so he was going to take her to some other event or something in Chicago. Some kind of an audition, I think."

Chicago. Avery's heart began to pound. She had come right through Chicago on her way here. She forced her voice to remain matter-of-fact. "That's neat. What was the girl's name?"

The girl shrugged. "I don't know. Why?"

"Oh...I just wondered if it was someone my sister or I knew." It wasn't a lie.

"Yeah, I'm not sure." She looked at Avery sympathetically. "Again, I'm sorry he's not here."

"Me too. But I'll catch him later." Avery had the information she needed, and now there was no time to waste. She was already backing out of the office. She waved at the girl. "Take care."

Out in the hall, she forced herself to walk calmly. Inwardly she wanted to run, sprint out of this crazy fake building as fast as her feet would carry her. Brian and Addisyn were in Chicago. He was trying to get her back into competition. If that happened, she'd be tied to him for good.

Avery gripped her backpack straps and forced the panic down. She needed the next flight to Chicago.

ADDISYN REMEMBERED THE place exactly. She set her face with determination and marched through the streets.

The constant blare of traffic horns was shredding her nerves. She fought the urge to clap her hands over her ears. Again she felt a wave of compassion for Avery. This turmoil had been even worse for her shy, sensitive sister. Yet she'd stayed—for Addisyn.

If only she could have the chance to thank Avery for what she'd done.

Her insides churned wildly when she considered that in just a few minutes, she'd be standing face-to-face with Avery again. Her sister would probably blast her with a lecture, a tirade about sin and judgment. Or maybe she'd refuse to see her—slam the door in her face and turn away.

Just as Addisyn had done three years earlier.

Addisyn swallowed hard. There was no denying that she would deserve all of that and then some. But as gut-wrenching as it would undoubtedly be, Avery's reaction wasn't important. Addisyn was in New York City because there were some things she had to say. She wanted five minutes, that was all. Just five minutes to tell Avery what was in her heart.

And then her sister could kick her to the curb if she wanted to.

Odd, she hadn't thought about these directions in years, but somehow her feet still knew the way to the apartment the sisters had shared for so long. This part of town looked grungy to her now. Had it always been this dilapidated?

There was that same old sign, although the paint was chipping now. HUDSON APARTMENTS. The building was still as pompously square as ever. Addisyn's chest pulled tight. Oh, what would Avery say? For that matter, what would *she* say? How could she ever apologize enough?

She opened the door to the ground floor. The ugly green carpet hadn't changed, and the desk still had that peeling Formica countertop. But the faces were entirely different.

Addisyn looked around for the kind older woman who had helped Avery and her so much when they first arrived in the city. "Uh—is Maggie here?"

Two men sat behind the desk. One of them was talking on the phone in a low tone. The other, a wiry guy with glasses, shook his head. "No, she retired six weeks ago." He held out his hand. "I'm her son, Jake."

Addisyn shook his hand automatically. "Addisyn Miles. I'm here to visit my sister. It's apartment three sixteen."

"Three sixteen…let's see here." The man studied a book on his desk. Then he looked up, frowning. "I'm sorry. I don't have anyone down in that room right now."

Addisyn felt as if a whip had been flicked across her face. "What?"

"There's no one living in three sixteen."

"My sister lives there." Addisyn grasped desperately to the only reality she knew.

The man must have sensed the agony in her soul. "Well—" he turned and pulled out a fat file folder. "What's the name?"

"Avery Miles." Addisyn was not going to be sick. Not in here.

"Miles—" the man muttered. His finger traced down a spreadsheet, then jerked to a stop. "Yup. Here it is."

Addisyn began breathing again. The man was going to tell her he'd made a cruel mistake, that Avery was still there, on the third floor, that Addisyn hadn't lost the last hope she had of ever connecting with her sister.

"She lived in three sixteen for six years. But she left."

"She—she left?"

The man's mouth quirked to one side compassionately. "I'm sorry. This shows she left in late July of last year. So, a year ago."

A year. Avery could have gone anywhere in a year. Addisyn clutched the counter to steady herself. "You don't know where she went?"

"No, I'm sorry."

"She didn't leave a forwarding address? A phone number?"

The man shrugged helplessly. "No. But like I said, I'm new. I started working after Mom left."

"And you said your mom retired how long ago?" This was way too much information to process at once.

"Six weeks." The man glanced at the wall calendar, which still read July. He frowned and flipped it to August. "She had a big retirement party mid-June, that's how I remember. Then off she went."

Addisyn swallowed hard. "Did—did she ever say anything to you about us? My sister and me?"

He shook his head regretfully. "Sorry, no."

Addisyn turned and walked blindly toward the door, feeling unsteady. Avery wasn't living there anymore. Avery was gone, lost somehow in the trackless maze of the world. It was too late to fix things.

She could feel the panic fluttering its wings in her chest, but she beat it down. No, it couldn't be too late. Surely she would yet have a chance to make good her mistake.

She turned back to the young man, who was watching her sympathetically. "Is your mom still in the city?"

He sighed. "No. She moved to Florida. Cocoa Beach area. My aunt has cancer, and she wanted to be nearby to help her out."

Maggie had to know what had happened to Avery. She had to. Addisyn couldn't bear to think otherwise. "Could I have your mom's number? Avery and I knew her well. Avery may have said something to her about where she went."

"Certainly." The man pulled a notepad to him and scribbled down the number. "Here you go. Sorry I couldn't be of more help to you."

"Thanks." Addisyn took the paper from him with trembling fingertips. She needed to leave. "Bye."

"Hope you find your sister!" he called after her.

Addisyn merely waved in response. Once out in the open air, she leaned against the side of the building, out of sight of the people inside. Her body was shaking so hard that it felt as if her very insides were vibrating. She slid down the side of the building and sank into a huddled heap on the sidewalk. Stared dully at the street, the skyscrapers, the exhaust in the air.

She felt suddenly very lost and small and alone. She could feel sweat trickling cold and relentless down her spine. She glanced back over her shoulder at the exterior of the building. She was grateful, at least, that the man had been nice enough to not ask what he was surely thinking: *If she's your sister, why don't you know where she is?*

Addisyn leaned her head back against the wall. *Because I was an idiot, that's why.*

Avery was gone. Really and truly gone. Disappeared, like somebody in a mystery novel. Addisyn chastised herself for not considering the possibility. Knowing how much Avery loathed New York, had she really expected Avery to still be there, living in a cut-rate apartment? And doing what? Treading water, working menial jobs, and waiting on her prodigal younger sister to return?

It had been stupid of her, but somehow she'd always thought of Avery in New York. She'd had no hesitations at all about that. The idea that her big sister might have moved somewhere else had simply never crossed her mind.

Addisyn tried to view the situation through Avery's eyes. She had always feared and hated New York. She'd existed in it like a frightened animal in a trap. After Addisyn left, what was there to hold her in the city? She'd probably seen it as an excellent opportunity to start over fresh somewhere else.

And maybe she'd seen it as a chance to get as far away from Addisyn as possible. Maybe she'd even planned this…so that Addisyn would never find her.

The thought turned Addisyn's stomach. But what did it matter? Regardless, Avery was gone. Tears brimmed over and flowed down Addisyn's cheeks. The reality was beginning to sink its slow weight into her soul. The pain in her spirit made her feel weak, nauseated.

She took a slow, deep breath. Maggie. She clutched at the strip of paper the man had given her like a drowning person grabbing at a twig. Yes. Maggie would know. She would call Maggie. It would all be okay.

Her fingers were shaking so badly she could barely dial the number. While it rang, she tried to calm herself. There was no need to sound utterly insane when Maggie answered. An image floated to her mind of the kind older woman, who used to give Addisyn a Tootsie Roll every day when she passed through the lobby on her way home from school.

She'd know where Avery was. Addisyn had learned early in her stay at the apartments that what Maggie didn't know wasn't worth knowing.

On the third ring, someone answered. "Hello?"

The voice didn't sound like Maggie's. Addisyn cleared her throat. "Uh—I'm looking for Maggie, please."

"Oh, I'm sorry, dear." The voice was that of an older woman.

"Maggie is out of town this week on a cruise with a few friends. I'm her sister Dorothy."

"Oh." The bottom did sink out then. Addisyn closed her eyes but immediately opened them again. This was New York City. Young ladies did not sit on sidewalks with their eyes closed in New York City. "When will she be back?" She knew she wasn't being very polite, but the words felt as if they were being wrenched from her soul.

"She just left yesterday. She won't be back for another ten days." The woman had a gentle, soft voice, very much like Maggie's. "I'm terribly sorry."

"That's okay." Each word was an effort now. "I'll call back in a couple of weeks. I knew her when she lived in New York City."

"Oh, yes!" Dorothy's tone brightened. "Would you like me to let her know you called?" She gave an exasperated sigh. "If you knew Maggie, you know she is hopelessly old-fashioned. She swears she won't get a cell phone. But I do miss her while she's gone, so her friend has agreed to let me call her phone."

"That would be wonderful." A tiny bit of hope trickled through Addisyn's soul. "Please tell her Addisyn Miles called." She paused to spell out her first name for the woman. "Tell her—" She hesitated, but all pride was gone. "Tell her I'm looking for Avery."

The woman promised to relay the message. Addisyn hung up after thanking Dorothy and leaving her cell number with her. Then she sat rigidly against the building.

It was 3:47 in the afternoon. She only had a few hours before dark. She took a deep breath and tried to collect her scattered thoughts. Slowly she stood, leaning on the building for support. *Okay. It's going to be okay. I will find her. Maggie will know. Maggie will call me. All I have to do is wait.*

She looked up at the smoggy New York City sky—or the narrow stripe that passed for sky. *God, please give me another chance.* The tears spilled over, dripping off the edges of her face. *Just one. I know I've blown it, but I need to see Avery. Please.*

I remember your sins no more.

Addisyn took her first deep breath. The soothing comfort of the words seeped into her soul, saturating the dry and thirsty ground there. God promised second chances, right? Wasn't that what He was all about? Then surely He would give her one this time.

She was as weak and shaky as if she'd just finished a skating competition. She marched out onto the sidewalk and held up her arm to flag a taxi.

Clearly Avery wasn't in New York, and the city that had captivated Addisyn in her teen years felt like a tsunami now. So she'd return to the airport and get the next flight back to Vancouver. She'd wait in Whistler to hear from Maggie—in a familiar place with a job, beautiful mountains, and—Darius.

And if Maggie didn't know where Avery was…

Addisyn straightened her shoulders and brushed her wayward tears away. *If Maggie doesn't know, I will still beat all the bushes to find Avery. I'll visit every town in America if I have to. No, in the whole world.*

And most of all, she would keep praying.

That the God of second chances would lead her steps to the sister she needed more than she had ever realized.

CHAPTER 23

Avery glanced at her watch as she headed through the gates of LaGuardia. 2:05? She frowned in confusion, then realized she'd never changed it from Estes Park time. It was actually 4:05 in New York.

2:05 at home. She'd be working at Laz's store, selling fishing poles and snowshoes and everything in between. Later she'd probably head to the mountains with Mercy, walking and talking with El Shaddai. This evening she'd be snug in her cabin—curled up in her favorite chair, safe and content, maybe watching a thunderstorm crackle through the High Peaks.

Her whole soul cried out for Estes Park. She missed the mountains with her every breath. She missed the peace, the wholeness, the beauty. She missed the way life seemed to matter there, how every moment was significant and important—unlike in New York City, where life shrank to the size of a dusty rut. She missed the Avery Miles who lived in the mountains, the girl who was much stronger and braver and happier than the one who cringed now in the concourse of LaGuardia, desperately waiting for a flight.

But most of all, she missed El Shaddai, missed His breath on her, missed the glory of His Presence and the knowledge that He was as close as the snow on the mountains.

Missing El Shaddai? Avery took a deep breath. What was she saying? Laz's words trickled back to her. *He's not just the God of the mountains…He's the God of it all.*

If He was God of all, then He was even the God of LaGuardia, of the swirling storm that was around and inside Avery at this moment, and she could talk to Him just as she could when she sat on the shores of The Loch. *El Shaddai, help me...* Avery paused, then finished her prayer with the simplest yet most important request on her mind.

Help me get out of New York City.

That summed it up, didn't it? If she could only get out of New York City, everything would right itself. Urgency wriggled through her soul. It was selfish, maybe, but escaping from the city just might save her own sanity. She wasn't sure how she'd lived there for six years. Now she couldn't even spend six hours in the Big Apple without having twice that many panic attacks.

More importantly, though, somewhere in Chicago—maybe at this very minute—Brian was ensnaring her sister. The very thought made Avery clench her fists in terror until her knuckles whitened. Mentally she berated herself—for the thousandth time since talking with Brian's secretary. *I came right through Chicago on my way here. Right through the middle of town. I even had a layover.*

No use blaming herself. The only thing to do now was get out of this horrid place as quickly as possible and backtrack to Chicago. Avery stepped up to the first kiosk. "I need a flight to Chicago." She swallowed the urgency that made her breath catch. "The soonest one, please."

"Today?" The man behind the counter raised his eyebrows.

"Yes." Definitely today.

"I'm sorry, ma'am. All flights to Chicago are booked."

Avery's mind raced frantically. All flights booked? Really? "Okay...could I take a flight to another city and connect somewhere?" She knew she sounded as if she didn't know what she was doing. She didn't.

"Hmm...no, I'm sorry." The man studied some charts on his computer screen. "The best option I can offer you is a five thirty flight to our hub in Boston. Then you can catch the nine p.m. to O'Hare."

"Umm...thanks. I'll—I'll have to think about it." Avery stepped away from the kiosk, her heart pounding in her ears. Nine p.m.? That would never work. She needed to be in Chicago with the speed of thought, not still stuck on the East Coast five hours from now. Every second was precious.

Surely she could do better with one of the other airlines. But half an hour and seven airlines later, she learned she couldn't. All the direct flights to Chicago that left any time in the next twelve hours were already booked.

"That's why you should plan ahead and buy your ticket online," one of the employees had told her, an edge to his voice. "This time of day, everything's sold."

"I know. This was an emergency." Avery didn't bother to elaborate her explanation, not when her mind was reeling and her very soul was weary with noise and turmoil and failure.

There was nothing to do now except go back to the first airline and book the flight to Boston. She tried not to think of the minutes slipping by—each one putting more and more distance between her and her sister.

El Shaddai…why haven't You gotten me out of the city?

△△ △△ △△

IT WAS ALMOST five o'clock when Addisyn scurried into the airport. She shuddered as she entered the terminal. The fog outside gave everything a weird yellow light. Maybe a storm was coming. She could be in LaGuardia for a while.

Not that it would really matter if she were stranded. Her schedule stretched ahead of her, blank and barren. She checked her bags and headed for the first airline kiosk she saw. "What's the next flight to Vancouver?"

The man behind the counter consulted a computer screen. "I'm sorry. There's not another flight to Vancouver International Airport until tomorrow morning."

Addisyn groaned. Seriously? What else could go wrong?

Five different airlines later, she'd had no better success. Finally, at the last kiosk, a woman must have taken pity on her. "We have a hub in Detroit. You could take a flight there and connect with another flight to Vancouver."

Addisyn ran one hand through her hair. Vaguely she realized she hadn't eaten since—when? This morning? Or last night? "Umm…okay. When is the next flight to Detroit?"

The woman squinted at the screen. "Next flight will be at 8:05 p.m."

She gave Addisyn a sympathetic smile. "Sorry. I know it isn't what you wanted to hear."

Nothing I've heard today has been what I wanted to hear, Addisyn wanted to scream. Instead she sighed. The woman's option wasn't the greatest, but it was better than anything the other airlines could offer. "Okay. I'll do it."

Ten minutes later, she had a boarding pass downloaded to her iPhone and was sitting on a bench in the terminal, swinging her legs in boredom.

LaGuardia was a massive place. Addisyn had been there before on flights with Brian, but she'd never realized how overwhelming it was when you were alone. She glanced at the gates leading to security and the concourse. Should she go on through security and into the concourse now? She sighed. Well, what was her rush? It was only five fifteen. She had at least two hours before she would need to be ready for her flight to leave.

A Starbucks across the aisle caught her eye. She grinned and hopped off her bench. No need to go to the concourse yet. She'd get a sandwich, maybe some chips.

And coffee. A Cuban, of course.

△△ △△ △△

ONE HOUR AND thirty-six minutes…plus a few seconds. That was how long Avery had been at LaGuardia. Every instant seemed like an eternity. She'd taken to pacing up and down the concourse. At least the feverish motion kept her from going stark raving mad. She'd memorized the number of her flight—4706. It was 5:41, and her 5:30 flight hadn't even started boarding yet.

She couldn't bear it any longer. She marched to the kiosk. "Excuse me."

A harassed-looking woman turned wearily. "Yes, may I help you?"

"I have Flight 4706, a five thirty flight from New York to Boston. Why—" Avery made it no further before the woman interjected.

"That flight has been postponed due to inclement weather conditions. However, we are hoping to depart by seven thirty. We apologize for the inconvenience."

"Inclement weather conditions?" There hadn't been a drop of rain.

"The fog. It reduces visibility for our pilots and air traffic controllers."

Avery stared out the window in shock. Sure enough, a thick grey blanket was rolling over the airport. *El Shaddai…why?* "Seven thirty?" She took a deep breath. "Ma'am, it is crucial that I be in Boston as soon as possible. I need to get to Chicago tonight. It's an emergency."

"We understand that our passengers are impatient. But it's FAA policy." The woman leaned over the counter and locked eyes with Avery. "Until the fog lifts, this plane will *not* be leaving the terminal."

Numbly Avery turned away. Tears filled her eyes as she gazed out the window. How could El Shaddai let this happen? Her sister needed her!

The city felt like a strangling boa constrictor, wrapping around her soul and squeezing the life out of her. *El Shaddai!* Avery took a deep, shuddering breath to keep from dissolving. *You have to get me out of New York City!*

5:52. The clock was relentless, and the fog was equally persistent. Avery settled down on a bench to wait.

△△   △△   △△

SEVEN FIFTEEN, AND a flight was being called. Fully recumbent on a hard metal bench, Addisyn raised her head briefly from her carry-on bag, then let it sink down again as she realized this was for a different airline. Flight 4706, to Boston.

She sighed. Every part of her felt tired and achy and sore. She really wanted nothing more at this point than a hot bath, a quiet room, and a soft bed. Her eardrums throbbed from the incessant buzz of the terminal— even though the concourse, where she'd now relocated, was at least quieter than the main hub.

The air was beginning to lighten, the fog rolling away toward the horizon. Addisyn squinted her eyes to block the diluted sunshine stretching through the oversized windows. Like every other part of her body and soul, her eyes needed a rest. Addisyn wasn't sure, not having a mirror, but she figured her eyes were swollen. They tended to do that when she was really upset or really tired—or both.

She adjusted her position, shoving her bag more firmly under her head. She'd had more comfortable beds than a rigid metal bench, but right now, any horizontal surface was good enough for her. She closed her eyes and considered once again how she could go about finding Avery.

The need to locate her sister had gripped her mind every second of the time she'd been sitting idle in LaGuardia. And yet she still had not a single shred of an idea. The best she could do, so far, was just to hope that Maggie knew something…and that she called her back soon.

And pray. Addisyn realized that she'd done more praying in the last forty-eight hours than she'd done in three years. She breathed in deeply and once more begged God for the same blessing she'd been requesting all day. *God, please, please, help me find Avery. I don't deserve another chance.* She squeezed her eyes tightly to keep the tears inside. *But please, God, give me just a few minutes with her—just to tell her how wrong I was.*

Suddenly a peace, warm and comforting as a blanket, settled over her. Without really knowing why, she left her bench and strolled toward the big plate-glass window. Leaning on the pane, she idly watched the passengers milling through the jet bridge for that Boston flight—the fortunate people who were escaping from the spider's web of LaGuardia. With the lingering remnants of the fog, in the odd interplay of sunshine and shadows, the lights on the runway looked almost—beautiful. Sparkling, even.

Some of the worry that had enveloped her for the last few hours seemed to spread dark wings and swoop away. God knew where her sister was. He had known all along. And somehow, she was suddenly quite sure that He had the situation under control.

She would see Avery again.

△△ △△ △△

WHEN AVERY HAD glimpsed a golden shaft of sun penetrating the thick fog blanket, she'd shot to her feet as though someone had stabbed her with a hot poker. Sure enough, within five minutes, the flight had been called.

Now it was finally happening. 7:26, and Avery was boarding her flight to Boston. She breathed a prayer of gratitude as she walked through the jet bridge with the other passengers.

Once inside the plane, she chose a window seat, as she had on the previous flights. Shrugging off her backpack, she relaxed into the cushioned seat and stretched her legs out, crossing them at the ankles. The hop to Boston wouldn't take long, and then she could catch the flight to Chicago and be there by—

Stop!

Out of nowhere, uneasiness slammed into her stomach. She jerked upright in her chair, alarm ringing in her soul.

No!

The urgency of the message crackled in her spirit like chain lightning. Her heart pounded, galloping wildly over the fields of confusion. What was wrong? This was all good. Her flight was leaving. She was on her way to Addisyn. Why the warning?

Avery realized she was gripping the arms of her chair, the cold metal slippery in her sweaty hands. She took a deep breath. Surely she had misunderstood the message. Everything was okay. Right?

But instead of easing, the tension in her soul tripled.

This is not the way!

Not the way? Really? Avery had fought with crazy recklessness to get to Addisyn. She'd maneuvered the obstacle course of Brian's office, LaGuardia, rude people, big cities, connecting flights, bad weather. And only by getting to Chicago as soon as possible could she ever hope to see Addisyn again. A brief sizzle of irritation flared inside her mind. Of course this was the way!

No! This is not the way!

With everything in her, Avery wanted to ignore the warning. Yet she'd learned that the messages were not something to be taken lightly. They were the words of the God she served.

Okay, El Shaddai…then show me what I am to do…

Looking for clues, Avery glanced around the plane. Other passengers were boarding and choosing seats as if nothing were out of the ordinary. She turned her focus to the runway. Under the blanket of violet clouds and fitful bursts of sun, all was clear. The air traffic controllers were conversing on the runway, waiting to usher them into the sky. She saw no disturbances, no signs that anything was amiss.

There was only one more place to check. Avery peered out the window toward the airport. Again, all was fine. A transport bus had just pulled away with a roar and a cough of exhaust. Some people were coming out of the big front doors, while others were standing in the windows, looking out at the—

With the impact of a high-speed train, Avery's world crashed into a crystal wall of disbelief. There, framed perfectly in the big plate-glass window of LaGuardia, stood a girl, staring out into the evening. A girl with big, expressive eyes and chocolate-colored hair. A girl whose face was as familiar to Avery as her own.

Avery grabbed a single gasping breath. *Addisyn?* No, that couldn't be. Addisyn was in Chicago with Brian. She pressed her face to the glass, straining her eyes. Was she so frantic to see her sister that she had started imagining things? Surely she was wrong!

The girl in the window was seemingly staring right at the very window where Avery was sitting. She flicked her hand restlessly through her long hair.

With one bound, Avery was on her feet, heaving her backpack desperately onto her shoulders. That was Addisyn. The mannerisms, the hair, the expression—she couldn't be mistaken, especially in the bright lights from the airport. She didn't know how or why, but her sister was here.

Disbelief was still throbbing insistently in her mind, but the questions would wait. Now all that mattered was getting to Addisyn. Avery scrambled out of her aisle, nearly losing her balance as she caught her foot on the metal leg of one of the seats. Before she could think, she was running, pushing past the last few passengers to board, ducking by the flight attendant who stood ready to close the door.

A handful of tardy people were still making their way up the jet bridge. Avery was dodging them, shoving them out of the way. Her breath ripped at her lungs. What if Addisyn went somewhere else? What if she vanished again?

She was into the concourse. Now she was running as fast as she could, feet pounding, heart racing, backpack bouncing on her shoulders. Her eyes flew wildly around the huge area. Which window had it been? Things looked different than they had from the plane. Disoriented, she slowed slightly.

Oh, suppose it had been her crazy imagination after all?

There! The girl was still huddled by the window. As if she were just waiting for Avery to find her.

Running wasn't fast enough. Avery kept her eyes riveted on the petite figure. "Addisyn!" The girl didn't even look up. Avery tried again, screaming her sister's name this time, loud enough to be heard over all the noise of LaGuardia. *"Addisyn!"*

Her sister wheeled at the sound of her name. Confusion rippled her expression as she scanned the mobs of people. Then she met Avery's eyes.

As if hope were shining directly on her soul, her whole face lit up in a joyful glow. "Avery!" And she was running toward her sister as fast as she could.

The tears weren't long in coming. Avery could feel them pouring down her cheeks as she closed the final gap between herself and Addisyn. Her doubts and fears and anxieties had vanished. As she caught her sister in her arms, all she could think about were the miracles.

The miracle that Addisyn was here, in her arms. That when she had seen Avery, she had run toward her, not away from her. That she was apparently willing to give Avery another chance.

The miracle that the timing had been so carefully choreographed that somehow, in the crazy mayhem of connecting flights and out of the over two hundred thousand people that passed through LaGuardia on any given afternoon, the two of them had found each other—just in the nick of time.

And the miracle that in this place, this place above all others that Avery had hated and wanted to escape, she had found the one treasure above all others that mattered more to her than anything else on earth.

Her sister.

△△ △△ △△

ADDISYN COULDN'T BELIEVE she was truly in her sister's arms again. One moment she'd been praying by the window, longing for one more chance.

And the next she'd heard her name slice through the tumult of the concourse, and her memory had throbbed to life at the sound of the voice who called her.

And she'd turned to see the person she'd come to New York to find. The person she'd never realized how much she loved. The person she'd thought was lost forever, slipped between the cracks of the crazy insane world.

Avery, crying her name, running toward her with a joy on her face that outshone every neon light in New York City.

Running. Not lecturing, not scolding, not slamming doors or building fences. Just dashing wildly toward her. As if she couldn't be happier to see her. And as Avery pulled her close, Addisyn felt the tears coming—tears that cleansed the last shred of darkness from her soul, tears of release that told her she was finally, finally warm and loved, after being cold and lonely for so long.

Doubts still crackled beneath the surface of her mind. Had Avery forgotten the animosity that had existed between them, the way they'd been at war for so long? Part of Addisyn whispered that this was just a lovely dream, too good to last. Any moment now, Avery would push her back, turn away again.

But as she buried her face in Avery's shoulder, basking in the security of her sister's arms about her once again, Addisyn decided that for now, those worries could wait. She would enjoy her sister's presence while she could.

"Addisyn!" Love broke Avery's voice. Addisyn could feel her sister's hand trembling on her hair. "Oh, Addisyn."

"Avery—" Addisyn pulled back just enough to look up into her sister's face. Avery looked much as she always had, but there was a dream behind her eyes, a peace on her features that had never been there when she'd had to live in New York City and wake every morning to an anxiety that ate her alive. The joy Addisyn felt seemed to swallow her words. "You look wonderful—so happy—"

"I am." Avery's eyes swam with tears. Her laugh slipped over a sob. "Now that I've found you."

Now that I've found you? The words made no sense. Unless—

Realization tingled over Addisyn's being. The idea was unbelievable, even absurd. But while Addisyn had been desperately searching for Avery, was it possible Avery had been looking for her too?

If so, then she deserved to know the truth. She deserved to know exactly how low Addisyn had fallen, how unworthy she was of this moment. As Avery reached to embrace her again, Addisyn forced herself to pull back. "Wait." She stood stiffly, as if facing a firing squad. "I need to tell you something." She took a deep breath. "I've been a horrible person, and I've made a mess of—"

"Oh, Addisyn." Avery reached out and gripped her sister's forearms. As if she couldn't bear to break the contact between them. "I don't care about any of that. All I care about is having you back."

Addisyn's heart shattered a little more. Her sister still didn't get it, wasn't hearing the true story. Otherwise, she'd be gone, leaving Addisyn alone. The way she deserved to be. "But—but you were right. All along." Addisyn steeled her soul to the breaking point. This was what she'd come to New York to say, and she had to tell it, even if it ruined everything. "I have—I have sinned." The shame burned her throat. "I—I didn't listen to you. I went with Brian—I—I made so many awful, awful choices."

She paused, struggling for breath. She couldn't look at Avery now, couldn't bear to watch the love in her eyes freeze to ice, so she examined the pattern of the tile floor. "And I—I forgot all about God." Avery would never love her again after this moment. "I've disappointed you. I've disappointed everyone. I asked God to give me one more chance to tell you how sorry I am for—"

"Addisyn." Her sister's voice was quiet, calm.

Addisyn continued to gaze at the tile floor. What a dreary victory. She'd done the hard thing, told her sister all of her scrapes and scars. She didn't deserve Avery's love, and she'd been right to tell her so. Now, if Avery truly had been searching for her, she'd know her quest was over. She could turn around and walk out the doors of LaGuardia with a clear conscience and never have to think of her failed younger sister again.

"Addisyn, please look at me." Avery's hands were gentle on her shoulders.

What else was there to say? But slowly, Addisyn raised her head and looked into her sister's face. And a jolt of amazement electrified her soul.

She'd pictured a dozen possible expressions on Avery's face. Anger, disgust, aversion, maybe even sadness. But not one of those emotions swirled in Avery's eyes.

Instead, her face reflected the kind of intensity that only came from the deep wells of the heart—the same protective resolve that Addisyn remembered seeing the night Avery had told her they were leaving their father. And there was no distance growing in her eyes, no sign that she was stepping back or checking out. No hint that she might turn on her heel and leave Addisyn drowning in grief in the mess she'd made.

Only love and concern shone from her face.

Softly, Avery laid one hand alongside Addisyn's face. "I know, Addisyn. It's okay."

"No. It's not okay." Addisyn shook her head firmly. "I hurt you, and all along you were right. And you are so—so—devout. Such a good person." If ever a person had loved God, it was Avery. "You deserve better than—"

"Oh, Addisyn." The pain in her sister's voice withered her words where they stood. "Addisyn. You still don't understand, do you?"

Understand what?

Her sister's smile was as gentle and genuine as a spring sunrise. "Addisyn, I love you. No matter what you've done, no matter what you ever did, I would always love you." For the first time in their conversation, sorrow floated over her face. "I was wrong, Addisyn. What I told you was right, but the way I told it to you was wrong. It did nothing except drive a wedge between us." She sighed, seeming to sink under some spiritual weight. "I've asked El Shaddai over and over for a chance to tell you how sorry I am."

Shock burrowed through Addisyn's soul. What was going on? "You don't need to apologize to me! You've done nothing compared to—"

"That's right. I've done nothing." Her sister's eyes held a regret she couldn't fathom. "I let you go…and until now, I've done nothing to get you back."

"Until now?" Addisyn couldn't breathe, couldn't blink, or the moment might end.

"Well—I moved to Colorado after you left. I've lived there almost a year now. And I came back here—" Avery's gesture encompassed the whole concourse—"to New York City. The place I hate." Her eyes bored into Addisyn's soul, the way they'd always been able to do. "Because I was looking for you."

"Avery—" Addisyn couldn't stand back any longer. She wrapped her arms around her sister's neck. There was so much she wanted to say, but the tears had stolen her words.

"Neither one of us was perfect," Addisyn heard Avery whisper near her ear. "Maybe that's what El Shaddai was always trying to teach us. Neither one of us has to be."

Addisyn looked up at her sister's face. "Perfect? I wasn't even close." Her voice broke. "I did everything wrong—and I didn't become a great figure skater either."

Avery's smile was the rarest kind of beauty. "Addisyn, I never cared if you were a great figure skater. You're something much better." Her voice seemed to carry healing with it, washing over the stains and creases on Addisyn's soul. "You're my sister. Forever."

As if a two-ton rock had rolled off Addisyn's soul, relief—hope—joy flooded her. She let Avery gather her in her arms again, rocking her softly, holding her close. She felt like a small child once more—letting Avery take care of her, drinking in her sister's strength, breathing in her faith. The way she always had.

God had answered her prayer—and then some. She had not only had the chance to apologize to her sister—she'd had the chance to see that her apology was unnecessary. Avery had come clear across the country—had she said she lived in Colorado?—to find her. Even though she had been so awful.

And as Avery held her in her arms, and as they stood in the middle of LaGuardia and wept, a place deep within Addisyn's soul was trembling to life. Slowly, Faith unfolded its wings and quivered with promise.

Because if Avery could forgive Addisyn…then for the first time, it truly seemed real that Avery's God would too.

⟁ ⟁ ⟁

"YOU STILL LOVE ketchup as much as I remember?" Addisyn's eyes gleamed with fun as she tossed Avery a packet of condiment.

Avery deftly swiped it out of the air. "You better believe it." She glanced at the label on the packet. "'Spicy Hot Ketchup with Jalapeños.'" She laughed out loud. "This might be too much even for me!"

Addisyn laughed also—her wonderful laugh, like glistening bells. Avery had missed that music so much. She tore open the packet and smiled lovingly at her younger sister as she dumped it onto her sandwich.

Sitting across from each other on a metal airport bench eating Jimmy John's sandwiches from the concourse might not have been the reunion dinner Avery would have planned. But now, everything about the moment felt completely perfect. Really, she would have been willing to sit on a hot stove and eat dirt as long as she had Addisyn back.

She couldn't stop looking at her beautiful sister. Cross-legged on the bench, tearing into the sandwich as though she were starving, Addisyn still had the perfect features and glittery brown hair. But Avery saw something different in her eyes, and it made her heart sing. That slowly-clouding darkness was gone.

She still didn't know where Addisyn had been for the last six months, but it didn't matter. Wherever she'd gone, she'd found healing.

Was it too much to hope that she'd found El Shaddai too?

"I like your hair shorter. It looks really pretty." Addisyn smiled.

"Thanks." Avery felt the warmth of the compliment. "I had it cut right before I moved."

"About that." Addisyn blotted the corner of her mouth with a napkin and looked expectantly at her sister. "You said you lived in—Colorado?"

"Yes!" Avery flipped her hand under her hair and grinned. "In the most beautiful place in the world. I have a log cabin in Estes Park, Colorado. Well, not in Estes Park proper. It's outside the city, up in the mountains. There are forests all around and lots of animals." She knew she was rambling, but her excitement refused to slow down.

"Awesome!" Addisyn leaned forward, as if drinking it all in and eager to hear more.

"Yes. It is awesome." Avery grinned, relishing the thought of her home. "And you're coming back with me." A moment of uncertainty poked at her. Wasn't that what she'd always done? Direct Addisyn's life? She took a quick breath and reframed her statement. "Only if you would like to, of course."

"I wouldn't dream of doing anything else!"

Avery felt peace spreading through her, slow and steady. If only she'd looked for her sister sooner. Better yet, if only she hadn't pushed her so far away to begin with. She sighed and studied her sandwich. "Addisyn, I'm sorry. I told you all about God's justice—and I forgot to tell you about His grace."

She looked up when Addisyn took her hand. "Avery, you did tell me about His grace." Addisyn's face was serious, every word seeming to come from deep inside her soul. "You showed me the love of God when you left everything behind and sacrificed some of the best years of your life to take care of me and get me away from our father. You loved me and watched out for me and tried to make sure I did the right thing and had a good life." She blinked hard and paused for a moment. "And you told me about God's love another time."

"When?"

Addisyn looked her straight in the eye. "Well, Avery, I—I—" She fumbled awkwardly, as if unsure of her words. "I think—I know God now."

Hope, powerful and pounding, surged through Avery. "Are you serious?"

Addisyn's smile was shy, but her words were firm. "Yes. I believe I do."

"Oh, Addisyn!" Avery gasped and squeezed her sister's hand. "It's what I always prayed for!"

The heart-joy in Addisyn's eyes was unmistakable. "It's all because of you."

Because of her? She, who'd been full of lectures and lessons, who'd let her terror conquer her love? Addisyn wasn't making sense. Avery shook her head. "I—how?"

"Because." Addisyn's voice rang with a depth that told Avery she meant every word. "I thought I was too broken, too messed up for God to forgive. I thought I had lost every chance of redemption." She pressed a hand to her mouth for a moment and glanced down, as if roaming shadowy corridors in her mind. When she looked up again, tears stood in her eyes. "It's—it's been dark, Avery."

Her poor sister. Alone in the darkness, struggling with fears too big for her. Avery couldn't let her worry another minute. "Addisyn, forgiveness is always—"

Addisyn held up her hand and continued. "I know that now. You showed it to me."

"I wasn't even with you! What do you mean?"

"I started to have hope God would forgive me. I met a—a friend who told me about Him." Addisyn tipped her head to one side. "But I still felt unworthy—until today." Joy beamed forth dazzlingly from her face. "Today, I saw God love me."

"How?" Avery didn't even dare breathe. This was a sacred moment.

Addisyn gripped her sister's hand tighter as a few tears traced her cheeks. "I saw you running across LaGuardia toward me. No questions, no comments, no lectures. Nothing except pure, real, unconditional love. For me. Not for what I could do or what I could be." Addisyn leaned forward and spoke straight to Avery's soul. "So, Avery, if you can forgive me—" She suddenly smiled, like a sunbeam piercing a raincloud. "I truly believe the God you always told me about can too. Because He sent you to me."

Like a flower bursting into bloom under a glowing sky, the full impact of the miracle finally unfolded in Avery's mind. What a divine appointment this had been! Addisyn had truly been found—in more ways than one. *Thank You, Lord!* She bowed her head for a moment, then smiled at Addisyn. "He's the God of restoration. And redemption."

"Yes. He restored us!"

Avery nodded. "I didn't even want to still be here! My flight was supposed to leave at five thirty."

"Really?" Addisyn grinned. "See, God couldn't let you leave then. I didn't even get to the airport until five o'clock."

"So He sent the fog." Avery's mind was whirling with the goodness of El Shaddai, Who had so meticulously orchestrated this event.

"Right."

"I saw you out the window of my plane."

"Really?"

Avery nodded. "Yup. I was already on a flight to Boston. I was heading to Chicago because that's where I thought you were." Even now, thinking about how close she'd come to missing her sister made her shudder. If she had left on that plane, she might never have found Addisyn. "I'm sure people thought I was crazy when I came barreling out of the plane and started clawing my way down the jet bridge! It was like a salmon swimming upstream!"

Addisyn giggled. "I *was* in Chicago…but I left. Did you know I came to New York just for the purpose of finding you?"

"What?"

"I wanted to apologize." Addisyn looked pensive, sad for a moment. "I wanted you to know I had changed."

"Oh, Addisyn…"

"And I couldn't find you!" Addisyn groaned and leaned back. "I just expected you would be at our old apartment. When you weren't, I had no idea where to look." Her eyes showed that the panic of that moment was still fresh.

Something didn't add up. Avery frowned. "Wait, did you talk to Maggie?"

"I couldn't. She retired—just six weeks ago!" Addisyn looked at Avery seriously. "I almost lost you entirely."

Peace spread through Avery again—the peace of serving a God Who held every coordinate of time and place in His hands. "No, that wouldn't have happened. El Shaddai knew we needed to be together. And He made it possible."

The light had never glowed more strongly in Addisyn's eyes. "You're right. And now neither one of us can ever be lost again."

△△   △△   △△

"WELL, THAT'S OUR flight, Ads." Avery hopped off the bench and held out her hand to Addisyn. "Ready to go home?"

Ads. The old, comforting nickname made Addisyn feel completely safe and completely happy. And completely loved. Happiness crashed through her like a wave. She was going home, indeed.

She stood and grabbed her sister's hand. Smiled into Avery's familiar kind face. "Completely ready."

As they headed to the gate, Addisyn was sure her feet weren't even touching the ground. The tumult of LaGuardia couldn't shake the peace inside her heart. The whole world was a fresh beginning, waiting for her, and she was wrapped in a cocoon of love. Love from Darius—from her sister—from God, Whose light had thawed all the frozen corners of her soul.

She smiled at Avery. How had she gone so long without her best friend? "Tell me more about your cabin."

"Absolutely." Avery's face shone with a holy joy that couldn't be denied. "Don't worry." She laughed. "You'll have a five-hour flight to listen to me chatter!"

Addisyn tipped her head back and joined her sister's laughter. What a wonder it was to be able to laugh again—fearless and free.

Her cell phone bleeped in her pocket. A text from Darius.

How are you doing?

She smiled. Darius would always be a part of her life. She knew that now. Whether she lived in New York or Colorado, Chicago or Vancouver, the bond between them would never—could never—be broken.

She typed just three words back to him.

I am fantastic!!!

She was with Avery. She was in the arms of God. And Darius held her in his heart.

The gates opened. The people surged through, Addisyn keeping a firm grip on Avery's hand to make sure they weren't separated in the throng. To make sure they were never separated again.

All was well.

Keep Reading!

I have more exclusive content for you—a special prologue scene that takes place seven years before *When the Ice Melts*!

When Addisyn learns that Avery is taking her to New York City to escape their abusive father, she has hope for the first time. Avery, however, struggles with the decision and questions her ability to protect her sister. Together, they must escape the shadows of their past and find light where their future dawns.

It was so much fun to go "back in time" and explore this scene, and I can't wait to share it with you! Just scan the QR code below or visit www.wordsfromthewilderness.com/keep-reading to download your free copy today!

Thank You!

Dear Reader,

When I was inspired to write this book, I wanted to explore a single question: when we lose something on which we've based our identity, how do we ever remember who we are?

It's a question that I believe many of us are asking, especially in today's world. To be worthy, we're told, we must look this way, hold this title, achieve this goal, perfect this image. As a result, we're left with shrinking souls, scrambling for something—a degree, a relationship, an accomplishment, an occupation—on which we can build our identities.

By contrast, the truth is, as always, both freeing and frightening. You cannot manufacture your own worth—but you also do not need to. When the Son of God stood in your place, when He spilled His priceless light to forever shield you from the powers of darkness, the question of your value was settled forever. No feat can add to His sacrifice; no failure can subtract from it.

And that is the beauty and the blessing for us. No matter what we do or where we hide or how we fall or why we run, the love of God pursues us, still as beautiful and tender and magnificent as a Rocky Mountain sunrise. All it takes is a single choice to once more open ourselves to the light.

Thank you, dear reader, for joining me on this journey! May you always remember that sometimes, losing our dreams means finding ourselves. May you see the hand of grace reaching to rewrite even your most desperate decisions. And most of all, may you always cling to the Love that never lets go.

– Ashlyn McKayla Ohm
June 2022

CLIMBING HIGHER

Don't miss the other two installments of the Climbing Higher series!

Where the Wings Rise **(Climbing Higher #2)**
The flight of freedom starts with letting go.
In Colorado's Rocky Mountains, Addisyn struggles to find common ground with Avery, the sister she once betrayed. But an encounter with an injured hawk forces her to confront the fears that have left her just as wounded—or to allow her darkest enemy to sabotage her future.

Why the Mountains Stand **(Climbing Higher #3)**
Her darkest story might just be her greatest strength.
When a legend resurfaces in the Canadian mountains, Addisyn forms a reluctant alliance with Kenzie, a girl with a troubling link to Addisyn's own past. Now, they must move past the secrets that haunt them…and discover the purpose to their shared pain.

Find out more about the Climbing Higher series and read the first four chapters of each book for free by scanning the code below or visiting **ashlynmckaylaohm.com/my-writing/** today!

About the Author

A worshiper of the Creator and a wanderer of creation, Ashlyn McKayla Ohm is most at home where the streetlights die and the pavement ends. She is passionate about shaping stories that weave together unfailing truths, vivid characters, and dramatic natural settings—bringing readers face to face with not only the mountains but also the God Who still moves them. If she's not daydreaming about her next book, you'll find her hiking, birdwatching, or otherwise getting lost in the woods.

Follow Ashlyn's writing at the links below!

Website: www.wordsfromthewilderness.com
Instagram: www.instagram.com/wildernessashlyn
Facebook: www.facebook.com/WordsfromtheWilderness

ACKNOWLEDGMENTS

A story may start as an idea tucked away within the author, but it takes so many hearts and hands to bring it to the light. It is with humility and immense gratitude that I acknowledge all who have helped me along the way.

For my friends who prayed for me, believed in me, and never laughed when I told them I was going to be a writer. If I began to list names, I could fill this entire book, but please know you are all so dear to me.

For my fabulous cover designer, Hannah Linder. Thank you for taking my sketchy vision and translating it to a cover that captures the spirit of the story.

For my dedicated figure skating experts—Erin Mifflin, Kristin Wallin, and Marie Wallin. Thank you for fact-checking me at every turn and providing such excellent feedback.

For my extraordinary beta readers: Sonya Chittum, Lydia Vidanage, Alan Robinette, and Eric Capaci. Thank you for the patient reading, the stellar suggestions, and the love for the story that bolstered my own.

For my amazing parents, Ralph and Derri Ohm. I would never be able to fly if you hadn't been my wings. You have given me strength in weakness, light in darkness, courage in the face of fear, and always, always, a love beyond measure. If I could count the stars or weigh the wind, I might be able to tell you how much I love you.

For my Savior, Jesus Christ. No words I could command would come close to describing the glory of Your infinite gift. Thank You for spinning this story in me and for guiding me through Your grace. On every night of *not-enough* or day of *don't-know*, Your love has never let me go. May You continue writing Your story on the pages of my life, and may Your fire fall on this altar where I offer it back to You.